DARK
HARVEST

Books by Anitra Lynn McLeod

WICKED HARVEST

DARK HARVEST

SEXY BEAST VII
(with Kate Douglas and Shelli Stevens)

Published by Kensington Publishing Corporation

DARK HARVEST

ANITRA LYNN MCLEOD

APHRODISIA

KENSINGTON PUBLISHING CORP.
http://www.kensingtonbooks.com

APHRODISIA BOOKS are published by

Kensington Publishing Corp.
119 West 40th Street
New York, NY 10018
ISBN-13: 978-0-7582-3534-3
ISBN-10: 0-7582-3534-8

First Trade Paperback Printing: May 2010

10 9 8 7 6 5 4 3 2 1

Printed in the United States of America

This one is for Patricia
and the Princess.

Nothing says I love you
like a book dedication.
Well, perhaps a Ferrari
but I couldn't afford that.

This should square us for several birthdays
and at least two holiday seasons.
Just kidding!

I wouldn't be here today
without each of you!

1

How long did it take to be harvested?

Kasmiri glared at the fresco-laden ceiling. At least there was something for her to look at while she lay flat on her back. Unfortunately, the artist's technique was abysmal. Religious artwork tended to the wispy, but this rendered everyone insubstantial, as if in dire need of a good meal. The painted Harvester didn't come close to the magnificence of Chur Zenge. If any man embodied masculinity, the current Harvester was it. And soon, very soon, he would select her as his bondmate.

If Kasmiri worried over ethical dilemmas, she might feel a twinge of shame at how she had manipulated Chur in order to force him to choose her. However, Kasmiri was of the mind that she deserved to get what she wanted. There were those who called her ruthless, but only behind her back. Kasmiri considered herself ambitious. Chur would be the perfect consort, and nothing would change her mind. Morals and ethics were best left to the acolytes.

As the daughter of the empress, Kasmiri didn't think it was proper for her to wait with all of these nobodies, but the Harvest wasn't about social status. Every woman of age must undergo the ritual. Kasmiri wasn't supposed to be any different from the hundreds of women waiting, but that was preposterous. She was different because she was royalty.

Kasmiri wriggled against the padded surface of the table in an effort to scratch her back. All this while keeping her head still on the pillow so as not to muss her elaborately styled hair. Three servants had spent hours meticulously arranging her rich black tresses in a cascade over the gem-encrusted pillow. They then studded strands with glimmering diamonds and touches of red paint.

Her diamond-studded crimson *astle* robe clung to her body, showing off her full, ebony curves. When the Harvester parted her thighs, the fabric would slide open perfectly, exposing her decorated sex. Kasmiri had ordered a servant to fetch a mirror so that she could inspect her pubic hair. Tiny diamonds studded the tight curls, but she had refused any paint.

"Red paint *there*? The thought alone is nauseating."

She had worried the tiny gems might irritate Chur when he penetrated her, but the servant assured her the *estal* oil deadened all sensations.

"You are anointed and so is the Harvester."

She should have known that from the preparations, but she hadn't been listening to Undanna. As her teacher and protocol liaison, Undanna had a tendency to pontificate at length about everything. Kasmiri wished the rasping old woman would learn the art of brevity. As disappointed as she was to realize she would not feel Chur's possession, Kasmiri decided it didn't matter. Forever afterward, she'd be able to feel him whenever she wished.

A delicious erotic shiver surged from her sex to her nipples. During the Festival of Temptation and again at her own pre-Harvest celebration, Kasmiri had felt Chur's erection nudging her belly while they danced. Large and hot, she couldn't wait to see him unveiled today.

Frowning, she remembered something Undanna had said, that his arousal had nothing to do with Kasmiri's allure but a drink. By ritual, a *paratanist* aroused the Harvester; then he consumed *umer*, a drink that kept him hard but unable to achieve orgasm. He would be under the influence of *umer* for the Harvest today as well.

While she waited for the ritual to begin, she wondered what it would be like to be stimulated, then denied satisfaction. Torturous. Perhaps his amazing self-denial was what made the Harvester so appealing. All his lust contained. Another shiver puckered her flesh when she thought of unleashing his pent-up desire in a cataclysm of passion. Kasmiri vowed that Chur would not suffer one more day of torment, not as her consort.

Of all Undanna's lessons, those on sex were the only ones Kasmiri paid attention to. The instructions became more clear when Kasmiri had witnessed the elite in moments of passion. She found it odd they spoke of virtue and fidelity, then scampered off to the first empty room to fondle another's bondmate.

Kasmiri swore she would not be of that ilk. She would be faithful to Chur and he to her, for she would tolerate no less than utter devotion. Moreover, they would not need others when they found one another so endlessly fascinating.

Booming steps alerted her that Chur had finally entered the Harvest room. With a sigh, she settled back, but the smell of too many women in the overheated room spun her head. Dozens of perfumes, some laced with pheromones, tormented her body. If this was even a modicum of what Chur suffered, he had her undying sympathy.

"*Paratanist!*" Chur bellowed.

His voice broke the silence and Kasmiri wasn't the only sacrifice to flinch. His *paratanist* was his servant, the one who ministered to all his needs during the ritual. Kasmiri hoped there wouldn't be a further delay as her body felt in knots from lying still for so long.

A commotion at the north end of the table caused her to twist her head as far as she could without disturbing her hair. She couldn't see beyond the woman next to her.

"What's happening?" Kasmiri asked in a whisper.

"I don't know." The woman tried to look but met with the same problem. All of them waited on their backs, side by side, down the length of the massive sacrifice table. No one but the woman closest to the Harvester would know what was going on, unless one of the virgins dared to lift her head. As the daughter of the empress, Kasmiri thought she could probably get away with such a breach in protocol, but with the gods glaring down and watching her every move, she didn't dare deviate from the rigid code of the ritual.

A chain of whispers moved toward the north, then an excited rumble of murmurs rolled back to Kasmiri's ears.

"The Harvester has chosen his bondmate!"

Her heart skipped a beat, then pounded a flush across her skin. Chur had chosen another over her? There must be some mistake. Wasn't her mother's threat clear enough? Either he picked Kasmiri or Clathia would destroy his chosen. There wasn't another person on planet Diola who wielded greater power than Empress Clathia. Going against her mother's wishes would only lead to sorrow. For Chur to defy Clathia could only mean that his chosen was worth his very life.

Hot, angry tears streamed down Kasmiri's face, ruining her makeup, but she didn't care. Everything she had done from stealing his ceremonial sword to engaging in a mock relationship with Arianda Rostvaika was for naught. Kasmiri had debased herself with another woman to prompt concern on her mother's part, and that scheme had worked beautifully. Her mother had demanded Chur select her, but something had gone wrong. The mighty, magnificent Harvester preferred another woman to her.

Once a Harvester picked his bondmate, the decision could not be undone. Whoever she was, she could not refuse him, nor could Clathia order him to Kasmiri's side. All of her dreams with Chur as her one and only consort dissolved into bitter betrayal.

As she lay there waiting for the next Harvester, she vowed she would find the responsible person and destroy him or her. One way or another, she would have Chur Zenge for her lover. Even if she had to kill his bondmate with her bare hands, Kasmiri would know the taste of his stern mouth, the feel of his scar-riddled chest, and the thrust of his heavy penis. As the future empress, Kasmiri would one day wield the power of her mother, but until then, she would be ruthless in her pursuit.

She swore to refuse any suitors her mother brought forth. Kasmiri would wait for her chance with Chur. Perhaps she would not have to wait long and might not have to dirty her hands herself. When her mother found out Chur defied her order, she might kill the woman, thus making Chur free to bond to Kasmiri. A Harvester's choice of bondmate was eternal, but if the woman were dead . . .

Kasmiri settled back and fixed her makeup with rock-steady hands. Having a plan strengthened her. All she had to do was make it through the Harvest ritual. She wasn't a full-fledged citizen until the Harvester received the gift of her virginity. Afterward, she could bond with a mate, have children, and enter into contracts. One thrust of his penis elevated her from child to woman. Then she could focus all her ambitions on obtaining Chur Zenge.

Kasmiri woke to calloused hands on her knees. She startled, then glanced up into brown eyes flecked with golden shards. His eyelashes were impossibly long, giving his glance shocking erotic power. It was as if he could see right into her soul. His shaved head was perfectly sculpted, as if he were born to be bald. Only two small scars marred his chest. This Harvester wasn't as stunning as Chur, but he wasn't hideous either.

When he smiled, white teeth flashed in a sensuous smirk that tingled her toes. He seemed terribly self-assured, as if he had known she would be here waiting for him. The thought gave her pause. She waited for Chur, not this stand-in, but she did remember him from the Festival of Temptation. Many of the recruits had attended in order to see if they might find a woman worth issuing a challenge to the current Harvester.

Her eyes popped wide and her mouth made an O as she remembered this man boldly asking her for a dance. She'd promptly turned him down with a roll of her eyes and a toss of her head. The daughter of the empress didn't dance with a lowly recruit; she danced only with the current Harvester. Of course, now he was the Harvester, and apparently, he remembered her snub.

As he continued to part her knees, the robe slid against her thighs with a teasing stroke that warmed her sex right before cool air rushed in. She shivered with the contrast of sensations. And, too, something about the power in his hands sizzled her nerves. She could not refuse him. Kasmiri found the sensation of force exhilarating. Never had any man been in such a position of power over her. As strong as she considered herself, being vulnerable was strangely appealing. Not being able to say no caused her body to blush with excitement. Defiantly, she blamed the pheromone-laced air. About the only thing she knew for sure was that this man was not responsible for her response.

His gaze darted down to her sex and one eyebrow drew up. He caught her gaze and smirked. His face was playfully surprised, as if he couldn't believe she'd gone to all this trouble for him.

She wanted to upbraid him and tell him she had suffered hours of preparation for his predecessor, but she could only speak her sacred words after he spoke his. All her tingling pleasure at being vulnerable vanished. It infuriated her to be at his mercy, especially when he seemed to enjoy his power so thoroughly. He should be on his knees begging her to accommodate him!

For the thousandth time, Kasmiri cursed the rituals. Her entire life had been one obligation after another. When she was empress, she swore she would never again have to suffer through any ritual not of her choosing. So what if the magistrate predicted doom and social upheaval? She failed to see how any of the rituals did any good. If she couldn't see a benefit, a real true benefit, and not some silly mystical benefit, then she would refuse. None would be powerful enough to force her compliance. If they tried, she'd have them executed. That would keep her advisors in line. She smiled at the power she would one day wield.

When she looked up, the Harvester smiled too, as if he'd read her mind. A frown instantly darkened her face. *I wasn't smiling at you,* she wanted to say but determinedly held her tongue. Soon this ritual would be over and she could move on to her plans for capturing the delicious Chur Zenge.

Once the Harvester parted her thighs, he placed her left foot on the hilt of his sword and the right he lifted toward his shoulder until her leg was almost straight against his chest. Hot, oiled flesh pressed against her smooth calf, causing another surge of pleasure. The drug-laced air must be responsible for all her sensations because this man was nothing compared to Chur. He wasn't as tall, as broad, as battle-scarred, but there was something engaging about him. She just couldn't put her finger on what it was exactly.

As he slid her forward, her head slipped off the pillow, causing her to have to hold her head up to meet his gaze. Why did he seem pleased to cause her discomfort? When this was over, she would hunt this man down and find some way to pay him back. She wasn't sure what she could do to a Harvester, but she would certainly find out.

Now that she was in position, he spoke in the ancient tongue, "By might of the blade I claim that which belongs to me." Before she could get her words out and get this over with, he finished, "I claim you as my bondmate."

Her shock must have shown in every line of her body. This was not supposed to happen. Chur was supposed to speak those beautiful words to her, not this second-rate stand-in! She and Undanna had spent hours practicing the exact inflection and tone of the ancient words. Kasmiri had spent her nights visualizing the moment when Chur forever bonded himself to her. It was romantic, sensual, powerful—and apparently just a fantasy.

Trapped by the ritual, Kasmiri had no choice but to respond, "I freely give myself to you as my bondmate." Her gaze held steady with his, but where his glowed with satisfaction, hers blazed with a thousand future punishments. She would make this nothing of a man regret his reckless claim.

He slid his elaborate codpiece aside and plunged into her so forcefully she lost her breath. She felt no pain; just a curious fullness that stripped her of her innocence, yet clothed her with tremendous power: She was now a full-fledged citizen, a woman, and not a child.

His eyes lowered as he thrust. He grunted satisfaction, then opened his eyes wide, capturing her gaze with feral intensity. She thought he couldn't feel anything either, but by the rapture on his face and the sparkle in his gaze, he certainly felt something.

According to the ritual, he should have plunged once fully, then withdrawn, but he didn't. He held close, pressing himself firmly against her, parting her thighs wider to gain greater depth.

When he leaned over her to kiss her, she let him get very close, and then whispered, "Enjoy this now, for it will be the one and only time."

He pouted mockingly, then whispered, "You say that with such conviction I almost believe you."

He bit off her retort by taking possession of her mouth. His kiss was not tender and sweet, but brutal and demanding. She had no choice but to suffer it for she couldn't push him off. The ritual was not yet complete. Knowing this, he continued his invasion by plunging his tongue to her mouth, forcing her tongue to duel with his. Again, she experienced a quivering thrill at being forced, then berated herself for allowing him to persist.

When she tried to bite him, he pulled back and whispered to her lips, "I knew you would be a biter, but that's not where I want you to bite me."

"How dare you speak to me this way?! Do you even know who I am?"

A broad smile caused a dimple to appear on the right side of his mouth. "I know precisely who you are. You are the wickedly beautiful and dangerously headstrong daughter of the empress." He paused for a moment, tilting his head as if deep in thought. "I think your name is something like Kasmi."

Before she could blast him with fury, he laughed and teased his fingertips to her lips.

"I was only teasing, Kasmiri. Stop scowling like that or you'll etch deep lines into your face."

Her mother often admonished her the same way, which didn't endear him to her at all. "You are my consort, not I yours. You belong to me, not the other way around. Not in a thousand seasons would I have chosen you, but since I had no alternative, the deal is done. However, you will take your orders from me, not the other way around. Do you understand?"

He waited patiently during her entire speech, then said, "I am now and forever your faithful servant."

"That would be more believable if you weren't grinning." If she could have put her hands on her hips, she would have.

He strove to put on a sober face, but the effort fell flat. He had a face made for laughter, lips made for smiling, and eyes that sparkled with mirth.

She despised him.

She was stuck with him.

And she didn't even know his name.

2

Sterlave had no desire to end his total possession of Kasmiri. He knew it would be a long time before he found himself between her tawny thighs again. As much as he anticipated the challenge, he more anticipated the conquering. She would not be easy to persuade, but he would have fun trying. Deep down he knew she would be worth the effort. Not only was she gorgeous, but also something in her called to him. A part of her that not only needed to be tamed but wanted to be tamed. A strong hand to provide for her strong needs. He had survived the challenge with Chur for a reason, and he believed Kasmiri was his destiny. He had known it from the moment he saw her at the Festival of Temptation.

Each season before the actual Harvest, all the sacrifices, the current Harvester, and the recruits gathered to celebrate the Harvest ritual. The sacrifices showed off their glory, hoping their beauty would inveigle the Harvester to select them during the Harvest. The recruits could see if there was a virgin worth challenging the Harvester for, and since it was a fight to the death, a woman had to be worth the ultimate sacrifice.

Amid the many beautiful young women, Sterlave's attention fell onto a burnished-skinned woman dressed in crimson. Her garment clung to her curves as if painted on. Black tresses had been styled into an elaborate cone atop her head. The style achieved the desired effect of making her appear taller, but she was still much shorter than he was. She had plastered a look of cool serenity on her face, but he knew it was a mask. Her face belied the anxiety expressed in her jerky movements and darting gaze.

Sterlave had watched her watching the others. Her eyes remained cold until Chur Zenge, the current Harvester, had entered the room. Striding in, dressed in a uniform of pure black with a slash in the chest that exposed his most fearsome scar, Chur ate up the room with his presence. Kasmiri's eyes had blazed with a determination that would have terrified Chur had he seen it. Kasmiri wanted him and she would do anything to get him. Sterlave's heart sank. Clearly, she had eyes only for Chur. Sterlave watched her flirt with him, but Chur remained indifferent—polite, but indifferent.

Sterlave couldn't believe Chur didn't want her for himself. Not another woman in the room came close to the exquisite intensity of Kasmiri. Then he thought Chur played the mating game with much more skill than she, for Kasmiri would never want something that came to her so easily. She seemed to thrive on challenges, and Chur certainly offered her that.

Sterlave watched them dance and noticed how Chur only barely touched his hand to the small of her back and the way he only tilted his head politely to hear her words. Chur wasn't interested in Kasmiri at all. Then something quite strange occurred—Kasmiri deftly removed Chur's ceremonial sword, hid it in the folds of her dress, and then swiftly darted away. She'd forced Chur to follow her out of the great room. Sterlave watched, but when Chur emerged he did not have his sword by his side. What was Kasmiri up to? Clearly, she was infatuated with him, but stealing his sword would get her nowhere. Once she'd returned with a bitter cast to her face, Sterlave surmised she had tried to get Chur to perform some type of favor to retrieve his sword. Clearly, Chur had turned her down.

After that, Kasmiri floated around the recruits like an exotic bird, flirting, laughing, but still her gaze always drifted back to Chur. Taking advantage of her effort to make him jealous, Sterlave had angled himself near. Her face was even more stunning close up. Her full crimson lips nipped at the top into a bow that made him think of kissing. A slight overbite of her white teeth made him think of her mouth wrapped around his straining cock. He imagined her golden brown eyes would be closed as she focused to her task, but with a touch of his finger to her cheek, she would open them. He almost laughed when her eyes were dark, angry pools of resentment. Even in his daydreams, Kasmiri rejected him.

Her face was a study in angles and curves—prominent cheekbones but a soft chin, delicate ears but a sharp nose. Separate each part and there would be nothing of interest, but put them all together and the effect was mesmerizing. He thought she had a face that he would never tire of looking at. Even in old age, he would find beauty there.

Gathering his courage, Sterlave had asked her to dance. She'd rolled her eyes and tossed her head as she walked away. Apparently flirting wasn't working, and she would not lower herself to dance with a recruit just to inflame Chur's jealousy. Her dismissal plunged Sterlave back to his tribe. Resentment and shame surged fury along his skin, tightening his muscles until he stood as rigid as one of the statues lining the great hall.

Immediately, he decided to challenge Chur for the right of Harvester. If he won, he would claim Kasmiri as his own. She would not be able to refuse him, and once he had her, he would compel her submission, whether she wanted to submit or not. However, he thought that was exactly what she wanted. A

ATTENTION ATTENTION ATTENTION
TELL YOUR CSM/CDS ABOUT THIS RECEIPT

REGISTER PACKAGE

AN UPDATE WILL APPLY TO YOUR REGISTERS
AT 4:00 AM. THIS WILL CAUSE YOUR
REGISTERS TO RELOAD.

REGISTER RELOAD MAY TAKE 10-15 MIN

CALL FIELD SUPPORT IF YOUR REGISTERS
ARE NOT FULLY FUNCTIONAL BY 5:00 AM.

$35/mo
for first line

UNLIMITED
TALK, TEXT & WEB

Includes up to 2.5 GB of 3G data

Powered by T-Mobile. Limited time offer. Taxes & fees add'l. See associate for details.

www.whatsahead.com/tm001

Walmart ※
FamilyMobile

strong man who wouldn't take no for an answer and wouldn't fall for her manipulative games. Not that he could truly force her. Having been on the receiving end of such brutality, he had no desire to inflict it on another, yet something in her needed what he offered. If he were her bondmate, she would have no choice.

At the challenge, Chur had bested him. Sterlave had chosen to fight barehanded, and they were evenly matched until some power filled Chur with unbeatable strength. Chur wrapped his arm around Sterlave's neck and squeezed the life out of him. As darkness descended, Sterlave watched all his dreams fade away. He would never be able to revenge the wrongs done to him by his tribe or anyone else. Sterlave woke hours later lying next to the other recruits who challenged Chur and lost. They remained dead; however, the gods granted Sterlave a second chance. Another recruit, Loban Daraspe, had claimed he was the next Harvester once Chur selected his mate, but since Loban had not the courage to challenge, the magistrate reluctantly denied his claim.

Loban's black eyes burned with resentment as he watched Sterlave walk out of the training rooms. In the back of his mind, Sterlave knew that, for Loban, the fight wasn't over. Loban wanted to settle the score between them, for a variety of reasons, but Loban would just have to wait.

Sterlave underwent a hasty indoctrination and preparation ceremony. In the temple, he signed documents, received the sacred ceremonial gear, and then the magistrate assigned him a *paratanist,* who shaved his entire body except for his eyebrows and lashes. Sterlave found it odd to go from the training rooms where he must do everything for himself to the care of an individual who did everything for him.

His *paratanist* even hardened his cock with a deft hand, anointed him with *estal* oil, and then offered him a cup of *umer.* His servant answered any questions he had with a droning voice that did not reveal his or her sex. A beige robe proclaimed him or her a servant, but the robe had an enormous hood that more than covered the face. When he asked, his *paratanist* simply said, "I am female."

Having a woman attend to him in such an intimate way astonished him, but such was the nature of the ritual. She dressed him in a pair of black *mondi* leggings, attached the elaborate codpiece, placed a pair of booming boots on his feet, and then clipped the ceremonial sword to his belt. He felt rushed through the entire thing, but he didn't mind. Sterlave knew exactly what he wanted as the Harvester. He only hoped Chur had not selected Kasmiri.

When Sterlave entered the Harvest room, he saw the sacrifice table lined with hundreds of virgins. Hard as Onic steel, his cock stood ready to take them all, but then he spied a flash of brilliant crimson. The object of his affections was twelve sacrifices south of the head of the table.

A moment of annoyance cast a pall on his joy for he realized the tales were lies. The Harvest was not about luscious women waiting for his rigid shaft. The truth was they waited for him to perform a ritual so they could become full-fledged citizens. He felt nothing because of the *umer* and *estal* oil. As cheated as he was, he didn't really care. With his goal in sight, he approached the first sacrifice. Sterlave paused, for he didn't see an empty slot on the table and he wondered whom Chur had selected.

Pushing aside his curiosity, Sterlave stood in front of his first sacrifice. Bright orange fabric clashed with her enormous blue eyes and her kinky red hair. Her trembling lips broke his heart. When Sterlave placed his hand on her knee, she flinched. He tried to soothe her by projecting every bit of concern he could muster into his gaze.

He wasn't allowed to speak to the sacrifices unless he uttered the sacred words, but her terror compelled him to whisper, "Relax, *tanata*, I will not hurt you."

She forced a smile at his endearment and relaxed slightly. She tensed again when he parted her thighs and put her feet into position. He spoke the words, she mumbled hers; then he slid slowly into her. All he felt was slight pressure around his shaft. Her eyes widened with surprise that his thrust didn't hurt. She offered him a relieved smile. He withdrew. He helped her from the table and she scampered out of the room.

His *paratanist* cleaned and anointed him for the next sacrifice. Golden blond with sun-kissed skin, her eyes sparkled with ethereal joy. She was tall, heavy, her body thick with curves. Her robe was washed-out blue with two slits that exposed pale pink nipples. Fraying bits surrounding the edges told him this robe was old, probably handed down for generations. He performed the ritual and helped her from the table.

The variety of the women, clothing, and decorations amazed him. In his region of Gant, all the women were tall, thin, with brown hair and eyes. These women came from all regions and all strata of society. The sheer diversity astonished him, but he always kept his goal in sight. Sacrifice by sacrifice, he drew closer to Kasmiri, and once he had her, he took his time.

Her clutching heat still surrounded him, and even though the *estal* oil blocked the full sensation, he found himself quickly addicted to the plush, wet pleasure of her snug sex. One plunge was too many and a thousand wouldn't be enough.

"You are supposed to penetrate, then withdraw," Kasmiri reminded him with a sharp murmur that managed to convey her disdain. Even her whisper sounded haughty and privileged.

"Who is here to stop me?" He pulled back, then plunged forward with a grunt of satisfaction. "Your innocence is too sweet to be plucked quickly. No, you are to be savored, Kasmiri. Always with you the pleasure should be sipped not gulped."

Her glare could have stripped the paint off the ceiling. When he refused to move on, she apparently decided not to bother even looking at him. Determined to get her attention, he continued to pull slightly back, then push forward again. Fury turned her sharp cheeks red. Even the tops of her ears turned crimson. Sterlave spared a glance to the woman on the other side of them, but she turned away, affording them as much privacy as she could. A secretive smile told him she would never tell, and she didn't seem to mind having to wait for another Harvester.

He did not want to step away from Kasmiri, but it would take hours for the *estal* oil to wear off and the *umer*. Neither one of them would be able to achieve orgasm for a while, so this would only torment his body further.

Reluctantly, he withdrew.

Kasmiri flung herself up and didn't even take his offered hand to help her from the table. She dropped to the ground with an ungainly plop, then grasped his arm to steady herself. After all that time on her back, her feet must have gone numb. Once she steadied herself, she tossed her head, flinging some of the gems off, and strode to the door.

He grasped her arm to stop her. "By protocol you will exit at my side."

"I will do no such thing!"

He tightened his grip, not enough to hurt her, but just enough to warn her that he would not tolerate her headstrong antics. "Kasmiri, you may be the future empress, but I'm your bond-mate, now and forever."

Kasmiri whirled on him as if to strike, but when she realized they had an audience of sacrifices, she gritted her teeth and looped her arm through his.

He whispered, "You might try smiling as we leave."

"I see no reason to pretend I am happy when I am not."

Sterlave chuckled. "As you please. If you wish to have the people snicker at how a Harvester forced you to submit to his unwelcome touch . . ."

The mere thought of mockery caused Kasmiri to plaster a smile to her face. If nothing else, she understood the importance of appearances. It simply wouldn't do to have the populace speculate that she was anything less than happy. Well, in public, anyway. He doubted her facade would extend to their private time. At least if he ever needed her to be calm he could simply drag her into a public place.

"Be sure to understand—"

"That this is just for the sake of appearances. I understand completely, my mate."

"Do not address me in such a derogatory way. You may call me Kasmiri."

He did not think mate was disparaging, but he simply said, "As you please."

She frowned, but a smile sprang up when he pushed open the double hung doors of the Harvest room. On the other side of the doorway stood four palace guards, who moved aside. Several members of the elite flashed hopeful looks that dashed when they didn't see their daughter on his arm. The same eyes went wide with shock that he'd selected the daughter of the empress. Tongues instantly started wagging. Kasmiri brightened her smile. Still, the joy never touched her eyes.

Sterlave had expected Clathia to be among those who waited, but she was not there. Kasmiri clutched his arm and he thought he understood that her mother must have realized Chur had selected another. If mother were like daughter, Clathia would have left in a pique.

Whispering so that the others couldn't hear, Sterlave said, "Fear not. I will send a guard to fetch her."

He'd misjudged Kasmiri's panic because she pinched his arm. Through her smile, she whispered, "You will do nothing of the sort. Fetch my mother like a commoner?" With a hiss of breath, she rolled her eyes. "We will go to her."

3

_____

Kasmiri practically yanked him down the hallway to get him away from the prying eyes of the elite. At least he was smart enough to realize the importance of keeping face. However, that didn't mean she trusted him to maintain the illusion for long. The faster she got him away from the gossiping hordes, the better. Once she got him into her rooms, she planned on a lengthy diatribe about every fault she'd noticed so far, and a few she hadn't. Then she realized she could place him in his own rooms. She could put him in a suite as far from hers as she could get it, perhaps at the other end of the massive palace.

As they moved down the hall, her bare feet picked up every bit of grime on the floor, which irritated her to no end. She despised being dirty. His boots boomed so loudly she almost asked him to take them off, but then changed her mind. It would be best not to delay the inevitable.

Trying desperately to contain her fury, she moved forward with purpose, hardly noticing the gilded walls and artwork that lined the hall.

He chuckled with a low rumble that reminded her of her mother's Golden Bird warming for flight.

"What do you find so amusing?"

"Your impatience to complete the bonding ceremony."

She darted a glance up and down the hallway. There were palace guards within earshot, so rather than berate him, as she wanted to, she snarled, "I wish to get this over with. Once the ceremony is complete, I plan to leave you to your rooms as I return to mine. I will only suffer your company when I must."

He stopped in his tracks while she continued forward. Their looped arms practically yanked her off her feet.

"I will not sleep in a separate room."

She pulled her arm free of his. "You will do as I say!" Her voice echoed off the Onic tile floor, so she lowered it. "You are my consort and you will follow my orders."

He stood as if a statue. "When I swore to be your humble servant, I did so in jest. I am not your servant but your bondmate and consort, and in this, I will not give. We will share the same rooms."

"No, we won't." Kasmiri grabbed his arm and tried to pull him down the hallway, but he wouldn't budge. "Move, you *cratifan!*"

His jaw clenched and his hand closed over hers with stern reprimand.

Suddenly, she realized the folly of trying to push or pull him around physically. If he wished, he could crush her bones within his grip. He was so much bigger than she was. He was not as big as Chur, but still, his muscles were thick, bulging, riddled with blue veins. This commoner had spent his life training with weapons. He probably knew a multitude of ways to kill a person, with or without weapons. Despite her prominence, if she truly enraged him, she may not be able to run from a burst of maniacal fury. He would not have the refined control of the elite. Even if they executed him right after, she would still be dead. She hated the truth, but she would have to watch her tongue.

Forcing the words through tight lips, he said, "Never again will you call me a worthless son of *yondie*. My mother was not a whore."

Rather than apologize, which she thought beneath her, she simply nodded, then snaked her arm through his. Calling him a *cratifan* certainly touched a nerve, one she'd rather not poke again. She took one step, but he didn't move. Reigning in her annoyance, she politely asked, "What now?"

"We have not settled the issue of where I will sleep."

Guards had now turned their attention to them. She didn't wish any gossip to reach her mother's ears, so she reluctantly gave in. "I will allow you to sleep in my rooms, but not in my bed."

He still wouldn't budge. She didn't want to, but she had to admire his spirit. "You may sleep in my bed." When he began to move down the hall, she smiled to herself. She would let him sleep in her bed, for she would sleep elsewhere. He couldn't be angry later that she had backed out on her promise, for she would keep her word.

He placed his head close to hers, so close she felt the heat of his breath when he said, "Do not even think it, Kasmiri, for you will sleep there with me."

It wasn't exactly a command, but the way he said it caused the hair at the nape of her neck to stiffen. His powerful voice and the intent behind his words flushed pleasure along her exhausted body. What was it about him? Never had she found domineering men appealing. If fact, she took great pleasure in cutting them down to size, but this man would not be humbled before her. She had a terrible and unshakable premonition she would bow to him. Worse, the image excited her.

She dismissed the thought as merely the culmination of a day devoted to erotic ritual. Tomorrow, her mind and body would be back to normal, and she would be able to best him verbally. Not physically, for that was not where her strength lay, but with her mind and her words, she would master him.

Hallway after hallway, each more lavish than the last, led them to the Empress Hall. As soon as Kasmiri entered, tears blurred her vision. White and crimson flowers filled the room with a heady perfume. In the center stood a raised dais covered with white *astle*, the perfect stage for her bonding ceremony. The most momentous occasion of her life should have been with Chur.

Even now, she envisioned him standing there, nude, his body primed and waiting as the magistrate spoke the invocation to bind their souls for all eternity. Now, she must perform the ritual with a man she didn't desire. How had her plans backfired so greatly? Had her willful disregard for the gods caused them to punish her in this most ironic fashion? For no matter what she said, she would have to spend at least one night in her bed with her consort in order to provide an heir. Once she did, she would be free to take other lovers, but until then, she could not.

As she entered the room, she thought it might be for the best to hurry things along and fornicate with this man until a girl child came of it. Then she could move on to her plans for Chur. For even with this, Kasmiri had not changed her mind. She would fulfill her obligations, then satisfy her own desires. During that time she would seek Chur out to tease and torment him, so that when she was free, he would want her more than she wanted him.

Sterlave could practically read her thoughts as they entered the room. All this finery was for Chur, not him. Kasmiri and her mother must have been planning for days because this elaborate display was not a coincidence. Something this magnificent would have taken time to execute. White and crimson flowers covered almost everything in the room. The sweet perfume was almost overpowering. Petals decorated the walkway, and padded benches surrounded the dais in the center. The seats were empty but probably not for long. The elite would come to witness the moment of the future empress bonding to her consort.

Plush drapes lined the walls, covering up the artwork that normally hung there. Sterlave had been in this room once when the empress needed extra guards as a show of force for a visiting dignitary. Clathia had posted guards in every room of the tour to impress upon the man that Diola was a mighty power. Only the common people lived in huts and thatched roofed hovels.

"Wisely," Clathia said, "we have kept technology out of the hands of those too intellectually inferior to handle it."

Sterlave had never forgotten that moment, or how Clathia tilted her face high, as if the gods themselves blessed her for her selfishness. Technology could have saved his mother from her injuries. But the empress withheld vital services to keep the bulk of the populace ignorant and, therefore, pliable. Often a simple wound led to a painful death.

Sterlave had struggled long and hard to win his place as a recruit only to stumble when brought to the palace. So many men fought for the right to become the Harvester. Sterlave wasn't the weakest, but he was far away from being the strongest. Three seasons he sweated and strained to get to where he was today. He had challenged the most powerful Harvester ever known. He had lost, but the gods had chosen to let him live.

At the back of the room, *serbreds* pulled aside plush drapes. Just the sight of the deliberately bred humans shivered his spine, for they were further proof of the elite's entitlement. For thousands of seasons they had bred humans to provide themselves with intellectually limited servants. *Serbreds* were like domesticated animals. They would be lost without guidance. All of them looked the same with brown hair, brown eyes, and bland beige robes. A snarl darted across his face for he believed the original mating pairs had come from his region of Gant: the members of his tribe had the same coloring.

The diminutive servants had to reach well over their heads

to hold the fabric open for Empress Clathia. A body-hugging red dress encased her voluptuous form, but a terrible sadness lurked in her eyes. Clathia was a beautiful woman, but she possessed a cold beauty, like a glittering gem. A jewel was stunning but still just a rock that offered no comfort.

Clearly, she had not expected anyone to be standing there for she startled back. Shock widened her eyes, then a smile graced her face. Apparently, Clathia didn't care that Chur had not chosen her daughter. She seemed pleased Kasmiri had been selected at all.

Clathia hardly spared him a glance as she rushed toward Kasmiri. "My daughter, how wonderful!" Clathia embraced Kasmiri, who winced at the hug as if a blow. "Take a moment to refresh yourselves, and I will call the guests."

Whatever fight Kasmiri had left fled in the face of her mother's joy. She didn't respond to her mother, she simply moved off to the split in the drapes as if pulled by unrelenting strings.

Sterlave followed.

In a smaller room, they found food and drink. While they ate, a horde of servants filled two tubs with steaming water. These were not of the *serbred* class, but they were still dressed in the same beige robes all servants wore.

As soon as they finished eating, the servants stripped them and motioned them into the tubs. Sterlave tried to get a glimpse of Kasmiri, but the female servants blocked his view as they soaped her from head to toe. At that moment, he wished he *were* her faithful servant so that his hands could cleanse and anoint her body. He laughed. He would end up delaying the ceremony for hours with his need to be thorough.

Sterlave allowed three male servants to do the same to him, but he found their intimate touches uncomfortable. Especially when the one who looked like Chur with black hair and light blue eyes caressed his cock and balls with a bit too much enthusiasm. Since his *paratanist* had shaved him for the Harvest, his body was extremely sensitive. Even the lightest stroke sent his senses reeling.

Traces of the *umer* that kept him hard but unable to orgasm lingered, because despite his arousal, he wouldn't be able to orgasm for quite some time. However, the servant's strokes were pleasing, especially the way he tightened his fist as he went down the length. Whoever had trained this man had trained him well in the erotic arts. But, too, he could be removing the *estal* oil, for the more he stroked, the more Sterlave could actually feel. When the servant lowered his face but kept his gaze riveted to Sterlave's, he knew the goal was both: to clean and to pleasure. Sudden shame made him want to shove the man aside, but just as he moved to do so, the servant moved on to washing his legs and feet.

Sterlave relaxed into the water and closed his eyes. Not once since he was a child had he known a touch that was not brutal. When he closed his eyes, he could imagine the hands as Kasmiri's, which only made his arousal worse. Desperately, he turned his mind to the battles he had fought in the training rooms and the bitter revenge lurking in Loban's gaze.

Finally, they deemed him clean enough and compelled him to rise from the water so they could dry him. After rubbing him briskly, they anointed his body with fragrant oils. Not *estal*, but something that instead of deadening sensation, increased it. Now when the blue-eyed servant stroked his cock, Sterlave felt his balls swell with a need for climax. Only the *umer* held his orgasm at bay. In addition, he didn't think that was the intent. The point seemed to be to arouse him, not release him. All this must be part of the bonding ceremony. Or so he hoped. He wasn't sure what bothered him so much—the servant's obvious enjoyment, or his own.

When they finished slathering him, they covered him in a hooded white robe trimmed in crimson, then led him to the dais. A drape now enclosed the raised platform and separated the two halves of the circle. Once enshrouded, they removed the robe and bowed their way out of the enclosure. Beyond the drapes, he heard the shuffling and murmurings of a small crowd of people. They must be the guests Clathia had spoken of, but he hadn't seen them because the robe covered his head. Sterlave knew nothing of the elite's ritual bonding ceremony, but he grew bored waiting. Knowing Kasmiri as little as he did, he still knew the delay was of her making. She probably fussed and berated the servants to put her hair just so. She was a vain creature, but then again, her vanity was justified on this her bonding day.

A rustle of fabric across from him and the dead silence from the witnesses made him aware the ceremony was about to commence.

With a whoosh, the fabric around the dais and the fabric that separated him from Kasmiri dropped. He didn't have a moment to worry that he was utterly bare and painfully aroused in a room full of people because the vision of Kasmiri consumed his attention. Despite her nudity, she stood with her shoulders back, her head held high, and a look of determined bliss on her face. Determined, because her smile didn't touch her eyes. She put on her soon-to-be-empress face for the attendees.

Her shoulders were wide, her clavicle bones only slightly prominent. Her breasts were heavy with dark nipples the color of fresh *gara* fruit. Her waist tapered sharply from her ribcage, compelling him to wrap his hands about the indentations to pull her close. Her tummy curved around her belly button, perfect for nuzzling. A few gemstones still glittered in her pubic hair, entrancing, drawing his gaze to seek the other treasures hidden there. Her thighs were strong but sleek, curving down to dimpled knees, slender ankles, and surprisingly small feet. He couldn't have designed a more perfect body. Much like her face, if he separated the elements they would be nothing of note, but together they were impossibly intriguing. She had a body he would never tire of exploring.

Kasmiri didn't move her gaze from his face. He frowned slightly, wondering why she wasn't even remotely curious about his body. Then he wondered if he had broken some type of protocol. Perhaps he wasn't supposed to look. Which was silly since why else would they be naked? So everyone else could get a good look?

Sterlave wished someone would have told him what to expect, for in his tribe, a bonding ceremony was very, very different. The two intended would walk from different ends of the main road to the center of the village. Once there, they would clasp hands, proclaim their vow of eternal companionship, embrace, then receive a blessing from the most elder member of the tribe. After that, the entire village celebrated with food, drink, and dancing until the wee hours of the morning. And everyone kept his or her clothes on.

Out of the drapes along the side of the room, Ambo Votny emerged wearing a white robe and a ridiculously large fur hat. The rotund man could barely move his head or the towering monstrosity would fall off. Sterlave gritted his teeth to stifle his laughter. He'd rather be naked than dressed like a fool.

Ambo approached the dais to Sterlave's left and began to recite an invocation in the ancient tongue. All Sterlave knew was his words for the Harvest ritual, so he had no idea what Ambo said. Kasmiri seemed to understand, which made sense since she would be educated more thoroughly because of her station. A niggling doubt invaded his calm. Kasmiri would always know more than he would. He worried she might lord her superior education over him.

Ambo stopped speaking and pointed to a spot in front of Sterlave.

Sterlave glanced at Kasmiri and shrugged his shoulders slightly as he had no idea what to do.

"Kneel," Kasmiri whispered. "You must show your obedience to me as the future empress."

He hesitated for a moment, but then fell to his knees. He looked up. A glow of power lit Kasmiri's face as she took a step toward him. She placed her hands upon his head and maneuvered his face to her sex. Despite her recent bath, her sex smelled musky with excitement. Apparently, his mate enjoyed being on display. "Kiss me."

His eyebrows shot up. What kind of a ceremony was this? He discovered he did not take pleasure in putting on a show, but her scent invited him to comply. As he placed a reverent kiss upon her mound, he darted his tongue out for a quick taste. Nothing in the world had ever tasted as good as her slick sex. Her shocked pleasure caused his cock to twitch as he smiled up at her. She flashed him a look that could only be a caution for him to behave.

Kasmiri compelled him to rise with a hand to his chin. Once he again stood facing her, Ambo droned another speech. When he stopped, he handed Kasmiri a small green vial festooned with gems. She removed the stopper, poured a glittering clear liquid into her hand, and then handed the bottle back. Working her hands together caused the substance to sparkle. Kasmiri uttered a short speech, then cupped her hands around his cock.

Vibrations and heat exploded sensations along his shaft, then deep into his flesh. His head spun as he lost his breath. His penis felt huge, bigger than the entire room. So demanding was the pulsing flesh, it consumed all his thoughts with a desire for climax. He took a deep breath to hold steady, but the taste of Kasmiri on his lips only increased his hallucination. He was no longer a man but a rampaging cock. If he did not possess her, he would die.

Kasmiri turned, presenting him with her back; then she bent at the waist, offering herself to him. He didn't need any instructions. He grasped her hips and plunged into her with startling accuracy. Kasmiri gasped at the invasion. Unlike the Harvest where they couldn't feel anything, here, they felt everything. Even the most minute texture within her luscious sex stroked along his sensitized shaft. As she circled her hips, trying to pull him deeper, he thought the liquid was now tormenting her as well. She moaned low in her throat as if she could never get enough.

Time slowed to a dreamlike consistency. His large hands contrasted the tawny darkness of her hips. He gripped her so firmly he knew he would leave fingertip bruises. Cascades of rich black tresses flowed down her back like an exotic waterfall. When she looked at him over her shoulder, her eyes were fever-bright, her crimson lips parted against her panting breath.

Drawing her up, he pressed his chest to her back as his hands cupped her breasts. Firm but yielding, they felt too big for his hands with a thousand distinct textures he greedily explored. When he teased her rigid nipples, she growled and angled her hips to afford him greater depth. Her bottom plushed invitingly around his groin and rippled with each plunge of his hips. Wrapping his arms around her to hold her, he thrust so determinedly he lifted her off her feet.

Her sex tightened with a fierce orgasm that almost crushed his cock. Every muscle in his body tensed as he poured his climax into her. Wave after wave jetted from his body until he felt utterly drained.

Carefully, he lowered her to her feet, placing a gentle kiss to her neck. He had wanted their first time to be slow and tender, but the magical liquid ruined his plans. Still, he would never forget this moment with Kasmiri. This one moment with her rendered all his sacrifices insignificant.

A burst of applause startled him, causing his penis to slip from her. The loss was so profound his heart clutched painfully in his chest. He had entirely forgotten about their audience. As he glanced around, he realized these people were not guests but witnesses: Sterlave had to kneel to her power, but Kasmiri had to bow to his possession. Moreover, there would be no question that they had consummated their relationship.

4

Kasmiri drifted back to reality when her feet touched the dais. Powerful arms encircled her, and she never wanted him to let go. If he did, she feared she would simply float away. As she caught her breath, she could smell his fresh sweat and thought it the most intriguing scent she had ever known. She wanted to turn and lick his chest, to taste the salt of his exertions; then she would stand on tiptoe to plunder his mouth. Only his flavor would soothe her needs.

Throughout the ceremony, she tried to imagine he was Chur, but his presence was too intense to ignore. In those sacred moments, she had been with him, and only him. She frowned when she realized she still didn't know his name.

Clapping hands rumbled like thunder, shocking her, for the elite surrounding her had ceased to exist. For a brief, shining moment, her entire world was nothing but mutual bliss between her and her consort. He too startled at the noise, withdrawing his softening cock from her aching sex. Tears caused her vision to double, then treble. She felt bereft, as if she would never again know such sweet completion. Was the *jaras* gel responsible for her sudden and profound attachment to him? Only those of the empress line could use the liquid during the bonding ceremony. Did *jaras* gel possess magical properties as Undanna's tales intimated?

Before she could ponder the question, Undanna's protocol lessons kicked in. Kasmiri blinked back her tears, turned, and faced her eternal bondmate. She could have many consorts, but she would have only one bondmate.

A blush turned his entire body softly pink below his lightly bronzed skin. Being on display embarrassed him. His eyes widened as he considered the people around them as if he, too, had utterly forgotten them.

Kasmiri spared them a glance but looked away when she noticed bulging trousers and nipple-tented blouses. How could such a sight not arouse them? Only an empress or a future empress underwent such an elaborate and public bonding ceremony. She wondered how many of these men would mount their mates while thinking of her and how many of the women would think of—

"What is your name?" Kasmiri asked in a breathless whisper.

Shamefaced, he grinned as he whispered, "Sterlave."

She thought the name suited him. Sterlave was a strong name indicative of the Gant region. Judging by the expressions on the women's faces, they would think of Sterlave as their mates worked between their slick thighs this night. Such a thought didn't disturb her, it excited her, for they could fantasize all they wanted, but they would never know his actual touch. She would make sure of that. For now and forever, Sterlave belonged exclusively to her.

Kasmiri still wanted Chur, but now she also wanted to keep Sterlave. Since she was the future empress, she felt she had every right to be greedy. Who would dare to advise her otherwise? Tales of her great grandmother indicated she had a collection of consorts and often sampled them three at a time. Clathia denied the stories, but Kasmiri didn't believe her; too many others had recalled them in exact detail. Her mother held firmly to the idea of one man, one woman as the only natural relationship.

Ambo gave a closing speech about how they were now eternally bonded and even death could not separate them. He spoke in the ancient tongue and she realized Sterlave did not understand any of it. For a moment, she despaired that he would not be her intellectual equal but consoled herself with the thought that one didn't have to converse much in bed. She had no doubts he could satisfy her there, and she would find other ways to occupy her mind.

When Ambo waddled off clutching his oversized hat, two servants approached and helped her and Sterlave slip on their robes. Constructed of the finest *astle,* the robe still felt harsh against her sensitized skin. Even the air itself seemed too heavy and thick to breathe. She longed for her rooms. Without a window to the outside world, she still knew the twin suns, *Tandalsul,* had set behind the Onic Mountains. This day had gone on almost endlessly, and all she longed for was the comfort of her bed.

Her agreement, that he would share her bed, drifted back, but she thought they were both too tired to make an issue of it tonight.

Sterlave wrapped the robe around his enormous frame. Both his eyebrows lifted in question when he glanced at her.

In that moment, she could be cruel. She could leave him standing there without any idea of what to do. However, she didn't want to. Unwittingly, he destroyed her dream, but she still wanted him to follow her to her private rooms. Shocking, hot possession during the ceremony was part of it, but she had witnessed how the blue-eyed Rown aroused him. Kasmiri wanted to explore her own desires and his, no matter what they may be. He now belonged to her. As her consort, she could do as she pleased with him. A thrill charged her body for she realized she could do absolutely anything with Sterlave. Deadly and dangerous, he was now her consort, and he could not deny her needs. A thousand erotic scenarios flashed through her mind. Perhaps he could be a tool, a way for her to learn all the techniques of the lusty arts. By the time she did have Chur in her bed, she would be able to satisfy him beyond his wildest dreams.

"Follow me." She turned sharply on her heel and exited the room via a door hidden behind the drapes.

Sterlave followed, his bare footsteps now as quiet as hers. She noticed he stepped lightly, using the front pad of his feet, not like most men with the heel. Such gave him a soundless stride. She thought he must be a hunter, for while stalking prey one must be quiet. The Harvester boots must have been designed to create a booming noise.

"You again rush impatient, my mate. Do you long for privacy as do I?"

His voice molded around her, causing her nipples to thrust and her sex to wet. She blamed the *jaras* gel but flashed him a smile over her shoulder despite the fact he had not addressed her in the way she demanded.

"I never rush, Sterlave." A quiver ran through her at using his given name for the first time. "I move swiftly, for I have never been one to linger over things that concern me not."

Her comment chaffed his pride, for the ceremony meant everything to him. He felt truly and irrevocably bonded to her. To discover that, to her, the bonding was just another ritual broke something inside. Not his heart, for he was not in love with her, but a piece of hope shattered. Would they actually make their relationship work, or was this just the beginning of Kasmiri's cruel indifference?

Never one to shy away from a challenge, Sterlave redoubled

his determination to prove to her that they belonged together. He knew from the moment he saw her. He just had to find a way to show her the same attraction was there within her. Today was a good start. There was no way she had faked her arousal during the bonding, and that would be his way into her heart.

Sterlave was familiar with the layout of the palace since he had often filled in as a palace guard, but he wasn't sure exactly where Kasmiri's rooms were. They walked for a long time. The deeper they went into the palace, the more elaborate the decorations became. He knew they had arrived because simply everything glittered in a garish display of wealth. All of it clashed with his humble cell in the training rooms.

Two guards snapped to attention when they saw Kasmiri. Without a word, they pulled open two massive Onic wood doors. Sterlave didn't recognize either man and thought they might be members of her private guard. Once he and Kasmiri passed through, they closed the doors behind them with a soundless whoosh of air.

Luxurious furs covered the floor, silky fabrics hung in decorative hanks along the walls, and the ceiling . . . there was no ceiling. The towering walls opened right into the night sky. Stars sparkled in darkness, reminding him of the gems glittering in Kasmiri's hair. Yet still, the room was bright. That's when he noticed the walls glowed with embedded lighting crystals.

Kasmiri passed her hand over a spot on the wall and the lights dimmed.

Everything from the tile to the furniture was of various shades of crimson with smaller touches of white and black. It was beautiful, but a cold kind of beauty, especially with the open ceiling.

"A glass dome covers during harsh weather," she said, following his gaze. Dismissively, she turned away.

Clearly all these riches bored her. Why wouldn't they? She

had lived her entire life surrounded by decadence. He drew his gaze off the open ceiling and tried not to appear slack-jawed over everything.

"This room is all for you?" He almost kicked himself. "I mean, this room suits you."

Kasmiri glanced around, frowned. "It's not as nice as my mother's suite."

He found her attitude unbelievably ungrateful. "It's a far cry from the cell I've been living in for the last three seasons." Of course, his cell was a step up from where he slept back in his village.

She bristled at his harsh tone. "You could always return there if you wish."

Three long-legged strides brought him near. "I'm sleeping here." He towered over her, getting so close she had to lean back to maintain eye contact.

Surprise parted her lips. When he looked down, her nipples tented the silken fabric of the robe. A musky scent, part her, part him, stiffened his cock, causing it to slip between the folds of the robe.

He placed her hand on his shaft, and asked, "Do you want me to leave?"

Short, sharp puffs of her breath warmed the fabric against his chest. "I want you to stay." Glittering satisfaction filled her gaze when he pulsed beneath her caress. "You are going to help me learn all about pleasuring a man."

His heart leaped, but then he realized she had no interest in satisfying him. "So you can use your skills to seduce Chur?"

She shrugged while lifting her sleek brows. "What does it matter to you? When I am empress, you will be but one of my many consorts."

There was no point in arguing with her. Besides, if she thought their encounters were only about him instructing her, she would be far more pliable and indulge his darkest desires.

For if Kasmiri thought he had no firsthand knowledge about the lusty arts, she was in for a big surprise.

"The first thing you must learn is to touch more firmly." He wrapped his hand around hers, tightening her grip. "Don't tickle when you wish to arouse a man."

Once he showed her how much pressure to apply, he removed his hand so he could slip off his robe.

Kasmiri kept her grip tight, then moved her hand in a similar way to the blue-eyed servant.

When he startled and caught her gaze, she flashed him a wicked smile. "I saw how he affected you."

"Any skilled hand on my cock would arouse me. Male or female." He tried not to sound defensive but did anyway.

"I think you enjoyed it more than you are willing to admit." One speculative eyebrow rose up as she tilted her head.

"Second lesson: don't speak of others when with a man. It's not as arousing as you think."

"No?" She grasped him with both hands, tightening her grip on the down stroke. "Close your eyes and picture him doing this to you."

"Why would I do that when I can actually watch you?" Her hands were dark against his flesh, arousing him both visually and physically. However, for a brief moment, he did picture the servant stroking him and then falling to his knees to take his thick cock between trembling lips. Rather than analyze his strange attraction, Sterlave grasped Kasmiri's hands to stop her.

"Do you wish for me to send for him?" she asked, her breathy voice inviting and mocking all at once.

Arousal glittered in her eyes. Did she too notice the servant's resemblance to Chur? Did she wish to witness such an encounter as a way to bring Chur down in her estimation? Since she could do nothing directly against him, this would give her a viable substitute. In all honesty, he had to admit there was a bit of that in his own attraction. Picturing the servant as Chur was profoundly erotic. To have Kasmiri witness such an incident only increased his lust.

"Not on this our first night."

Her pout was masterful, truly a thing of beauty and well rehearsed. One touch of his fingertip to her swelling breast parted her lips, turning her pout into the pursed lips of pleasure.

"Be honest, Kasmiri, you don't wish to share me tonight, do you?"

"No." Her eyes drifted closed.

He continued to touch her breasts, using the fabric to soften his calloused hands. Arching her back, she pushed them out, begging him to continue without a word. He lowered his mouth and took one turgid peak between his lips. Flicking his tongue, he moistened the fabric, then bit her gently. Her sharp sigh inflamed his nerves. Capturing Kasmiri may not be as difficult as he thought. By nature, she was lustful and unashamed of her desires. If he helped her obtain the peak of ecstasy time and again, such might bind her to him, for he was already bound to her.

Deftly, he removed the tie and then slid the robe off her shoulders. Before she realized his intent, he bound her wrists together.

"What do you think—"

"Hush, or I'll find something to bind your mouth. Remember, you wanted to learn how to please a man."

Her eyes narrowed, but she kept her mouth tightly closed.

"You must be very careful not to struggle, Kasmiri. Doing so will tighten the restraints and possibly hurt you."

Curiosity replaced her fury. "What do you intend to do with me?"

"Whatever I want."

Her pupils dilated and her breath caught. Just the thought of being at his mercy excited her. What a complex creature. In less than a day, he discovered she enjoyed exhibition, voyeurism, and submission. He idly wondered what he would discover to-morrow.

"Think of it, Kasmiri." He pressed his mouth to her ear. "I can make you come and come until your body collapses." When he bit her earlobe, she gasped but held steady. Thrusting his hand between her legs, he found her wet and swollen with need. "But I won't stop." Her clit was tight, nestled between slick lips. When he pinched it between his fingertips, she jumped.

"Hold still," he admonished. He wouldn't berate her too much as this was her first time. "I don't want to have to cut you free. I'm assuming you don't have a knife in your rooms."

"No." She peered down at her wrists as if she just now realized how dangerous this game could be.

"Then I would have to go and get one. That could be most embarrassing."

She nodded.

Using the tie as a leash, he led her to her bed. Large and square, her bed sat upon a raised platform, several steps up from the floor. Layers of silky bedclothes covered the surface. He frowned when he realized there was nothing to tie her to. Drawing on his creativity, he found a perfect solution and a way to test her resolve.

"Kneel."

"Before you?"

His eyebrow rose automatically. "As much as I like that idea, I want you to kneel before the bed. Bend over, placing your upper body on the bed, with your hands up over your head."

She did as he instructed.

"Since there is nothing to tie you to, you will act as if your hands are bound."

She nodded, and asked, "Men take pleasure in binding a woman?"

He didn't know about all men, but he certainly enjoyed taking command of her. His cock jutted out from his body as if seeking her heat. "Most men enjoy being in charge and many women enjoy the sensation of helplessness." He stroked his finger lightly along the crevasse of her bottom. "Do you like being at my mercy?"

"I . . . I don't know yet." She gulped. "You're not going to hurt me, are you?"

"Pain isn't a part of bondage unless that's what you want." He really hoped she didn't, because he'd never found that particular part stimulating.

"I don't find pain arousing." The covers muffled her voice.

"Then I promise to give you only pleasure."

She relaxed into the bed, which was the perfect height to display her plush bottom. Her skin glistened a lovely tawny color, contrasted by the white tie and the crimson bedcover.

Kneeling behind her, he traced his hands along her back, her hips, and then the cup of her bottom. His hands were pale against her burnished flesh; the sight alone was tremendously exciting. He wondered how many servants had worked rare potions into her skin to create such perfection. His rough hands seemed a sacrilege against such softness. Kasmiri clearly enjoyed his ministrations for she uttered low, keening noises.

When his hand slipped between her legs, she attempted to part them.

"No, Kasmiri, you are not allowed to move unless I tell you to."

"But I want—"

"Don't make me punish you for disobeying." The words were harsh, but his voice was not.

"No wonder men enjoy this," she mumbled into the bed, her voice petulant. Clearly, she did not often hear the word no.

"I could always stop," he threatened.

Silence.

"Very good." He continued to tease his hand between her

legs, but since she couldn't part them, he could only manage the barest brush against her clit. She writhed under his delicious torture and again tried to part her legs. He realized she would never stay still, not voluntarily.

He stood with a sharp, disappointed sigh. Glancing around the room, he didn't find anything that would work to bind her to, not with *astle* ties that could tighten dangerously if she struggled. As Kasmiri wriggled her torso around the bed, a solution came to him.

"Stand up." When she did, he removed the tie, which had already constricted. "This isn't going to work." Her crestfallen look pleased him to no end. "I do have another idea." He yanked one of the blankets off the bed, had her place her hands at her sides, and then wrapped the fabric around her upper body and part of her hips. Carefully, he placed her on her back.

"Perfect."

Kasmiri tested his solution and found it very limiting. All she could do was wriggle slightly side to side. She could lift her legs but not part them. When she glanced up at him, she seemed to suddenly realize she was now completely at his mercy. Panic caused her eyes to blink rapidly.

"Relax," he soothed, climbing onto the bed beside her. "I can unbind you in two seconds." The last thing he wanted was for her to be afraid.

She swallowed hard and took a deep breath. "I have to trust you."

"Yes." He traced his fingertips over her face, smoothing away the worry lines that furrowed her brow. "Bondage is all about trust. I know that trust is difficult for you, but think of it this way: Why would I have gone through all I did to have you only to hurt you?" His gentle reminder helped her to go limp.

"Besides, if you dared to hurt me, my mother would castrate then kill you."

"Sounds unpleasant." He smiled. Even bound, Kasmiri retained her sense of entitlement. Not quite the subservient, quivering woman he strove for, but it would do for now. Her trusting him restored that broken part of his heart. Perhaps there was hope for them after all.

Sliding down the bed, he traced his fingers along her legs. Kasmiri had a ripe figure, cushioned and curvy, but still powerful with sleek but strong muscles. A few gems sparkled in her pubic hair, encouraging him to comb his fingers through to dislodge them. Moving down her body, he kissed the dimples in her knees, then continued down to her feet.

When he realized they were filthy, he retrieved a small towel from her bathing unit and cleaned them thoroughly. Her red nails fascinated him, for he had never seen more pampered toes. Her feet were silky soft and lighter on the bottom than the top, like the palms of her hands. When he lifted her foot and kissed the instep, she gasped.

"Beautiful, sexy feet," he murmured, taking her big toe into his mouth and sucking hard. Toe by toe, he worked his way across her foot, then performed the same ministrations to the other. Feet had always fascinated him, and hers were the most lovely he'd yet seen. As he kissed and suckled her toes, he massaged the instep and her ankles. Clearly, she enjoyed having her feet played with. Such a fascination probably started with her servants pampering them. His interest sprang from his childhood. In order to avoid his father's blows, he had hidden under furniture. In that position, all he could see were feet.

"I have never thought of my feet as . . . sensual," Kasmiri said, melting under his touch. Clearly, his unique focus eased her mind that he would do something untoward against her.

"Have I changed your thoughts?" Pointing his tongue, he stabbed it between two toes, wriggling it suggestively.

"Most definitely."

After giving each toe a thorough tease, he clasped her ankles and lifted her legs, nibbling and biting his way along as he angled her legs up. He was careful not to push too far, but Kasmiri was flexible, and he could comfortably bring her legs up over her torso, thus exposing her sex to his gaze. Luscious pink against her darker skin, her dewy lips called him close without a word. A few sparkles remained from the gel they'd used during the ceremony. Engorged from arousal and pungent with musk, he lowered his mouth and breathed a moist sigh that caused her to groan. Teasing, he blew slow, hot puffs to torment her before he finally lowered his mouth to suck at her pink sex.

Her taste was more sublime than any treat he'd ever known, better than sugar-drenched *nicla*. During the bonding ceremony, he'd swiped a quick taste, but now he could take her full essence into his mouth.

Kasmiri tried to part her legs, but he'd wrapped her far too well. She struggled, growling her frustration, which only excited him more. Her clit pulsed, thrusting beyond the tiny hood, begging him to soothe the ache. He plunged his tongue everywhere but there, causing her to thrash in her cocoon.

"Suck on my clit," Kasmiri ordered.

He angled around her legs to see her flushed face. "You're not in charge." With a grin, he lowered his face back to her sex. "Now you understand why I wanted to bind you." Holding her legs up with one hand, he traced a fingertip around her nether lips, up and over the hood, then around and around her slick passage.

"You said you would make me climax until I collapsed!"

"Be careful what you wish for." Slowly, he worked his finger into her, rolling an expanding circle into her depths. "Now, tell me, Kasmiri, why did you want to see me with the blue-eyed servant?"

For a moment, he didn't think she would answer, but she finally said, "Because you wanted to."

"That explains my motives; I'm asking about yours." He stroked his finger perilously close to her clit. Her guttural moans of pleasure twitched his cock, but denial was not new to him. All the recruits in the training rooms were taught to suppress their sexual urges in order to exploit their physical power. She would surrender long before he would. "Answer me."

"He looks like someone I know."

"Who?" Sterlave already knew, but he wanted to hear her confess the truth.

"If I answer, will you at least touch my clit?" She had dropped the demanding tone.

"Perhaps." He reveled in his power over her. "However, if you don't answer, I guarantee I won't."

Growling plaintively, she said, "He reminds me of Chur. I wanted to see you with him because I can't see you with Chur."

Pressing two fingers together, he stroked upward until he trapped her clit between them. If she could have arched her back, she would have lifted herself off the bed. Since the blanket impeded her movements, she wriggled helplessly.

"You want to watch Chur suck my cock?" Sterlave withdrew his fingers waiting for her answer. It wasn't a horrible thought, actually. Chur embodied power and masculinity. Having him kneel down to pleasure him was a heady thought. Not that it would ever happen. Chur had waited three seasons to find his bondmate; she had to be worth such a great sacrifice. Besides, after three seasons in the training rooms together, Chur didn't strike Sterlave as a man interested in other men. Sterlave had never thought he was either, but he wasn't opposed to exploring his desires, whatever they may be.

"I want to see you two together and then have both of you pleasure me."

Multiple-partner fantasies were another thing to add to the growing list of her wildest dreams. As much as he would enjoy bringing that one to life, they would have to settle for a substitute. Perhaps the blue-eyed servant would be amenable to such a situation. As he considered, he suddenly realized he was willing to go to great lengths to please Kasmiri. Lowering his mouth, he sucked her clit between his lips. Kasmiri exhaled a relieved sigh and rocked her hips in a desperate bid to get more of her sex into his mouth.

Rolling his words over her sensitive flesh, he asked, "Do you think your servant would be agreeable?" After the look on his face during the bathing, Sterlave thought the question moot.

"He will do what I say or suffer the lash."

A shiver of revulsion slammed down his spine, deflating the tightness of his erection. He lowered her legs and started to unwind the blanket.

"What's wrong?"

"I won't rape him."

Kasmiri uttered an annoyed sigh. "He is *ungati.* They are trained to provide pleasure."

"I don't care." Once he freed her, he turned and sat on the edge of the bed. He thought he could do anything to please Kasmiri, but rape was a line he wouldn't cross.

5

Kasmiri's body throbbed painfully. Being bound had been frightening but also invigorating. For the first time, she was free of all her responsibilities. She found comfort in the confining blanket, almost as if the thin fabric shielded her from all the demands placed upon her. Despite her frustration, she'd enjoyed his teasing. Her clit felt enlarged, so thick with need it was almost a living thing, separate from the rest of her body. He'd made her want him desperately, then he withdrew. She wanted to rail at him, to demand he place himself between her legs and work his magic tongue upon her until she climaxed. However, one glance of his proud back warned her that commanding him would backfire spectacularly.

Sterlave sat on the edge of the bed with his shoulders straight and his body rigid. At his side, he clenched his fist repeatedly, turning his flesh white. In the subdued light, she saw the first shadow of hair regrowing on his head. As he turned to the side, she noticed he gritted his jaw much like his fist.

She knew he wasn't upset about her confession that she

wanted to see him with Chur. A shiver caused her flesh to pucker. Just the thought of the two powerful men, sweaty and straining to find pleasure together, quivered her entire body. Her mother's diatribes made same-sex scenarios profoundly erotic. All her mother's ranting had accomplished was to make the forbidden desirable. Her servant, Rown, would be a pale substitute for the mighty Chur, but compelling nonetheless.

Sterlave had withdrawn when she said Rown would perform his duties no matter what his personal preferences. However, judging by the sparkle in Rown's eyes when he caressed Sterlave, she knew he would be more than willing. What infuriated Sterlave was when she said Rown would perform, or else.

"Sterlave?" Kasmiri moved across the bed and touched his lower back. "I wouldn't hurt Rown. He's been my servant since we were both children." Even then, it was clear Rown preferred men to women. Kasmiri had cautioned him, for her mother might have punished him for what she called *unnatural lust*.

Sterlave caught her gaze over his shoulder. "Then why did you say he would suffer the lash?"

Because I spoke without thinking, she thought, but she said, "I'm used to getting my way. When I don't, I can be . . . harsh." At times, she had been so driven she behaved foolishly without any regard for the consequences of her actions. "I wouldn't force him to do something he did not wish to do." Manipulate him yes, but she wouldn't force him, not sweet, shy Rown, who would do anything to please her.

Sterlave turned away. "Then the rumors about you are unfounded."

"What rumors?" Here she was trying to comfort him when she didn't have to. He was her consort. He should be grateful she even bothered to put his fears to rest!

"They say you don't care who you hurt. They say when you want something, or someone, you crush everyone who dares to stand in your way." He sighed, causing his muscles to bunch below her hand. "I don't want to be chewed up and spit out on your way to obtaining Chur Zenge."

His tone was gentle, but the words were sharp enough to wound her pride. "I didn't ask you to select me during the Harvest. You knew from the Festival of Temptation that I desired him, but now, rather than blaming yourself, you place the fault on me for your own idiocy."

Rising from the bed, she took one step away before Sterlave stood and grasped her upper arms, yanking her back into his embrace. Crushing her against his chest, he glared down at her with such intensity his eyes glowed.

"You wanted me a moment ago." He forced his hand between her legs, sliding his fingers between slick lips. "Admit it, you want me now. Thoughts of Chur don't make you wet, I do."

Her breath caught as she rapidly went from fury to lust. How did this man cause such primal reactions with his mere touch? She wanted to deny him. She wanted to push his probing fingers away, laugh in his face, and tell him she would never desire him as much as she longed for Chur. When she opened her mouth, all that came out was a breathless sigh.

He covered her mouth with his, slipping his tongue against hers with the same rhythm as his talented hand. Involuntarily, she rocked her hips, working herself into a frenzy of need.

Sterlave picked her up and tossed her down on the bed. He leapt upon her, forcing her legs apart with his knees. His possessive intensity sent her senses reeling.

"I'll make you forget him. I'll make you climax until you're blind, deaf, and dumb. And then I'll do it again. And again."

Roughly, he shoved his fingers into her sex, pumping so strongly she bit her lip in an effort to accept each wicked thrust without growling. Every vein in his arm stood out with his effort. Sweat beaded his brow. His body exuded musk that only heightened her longing. In his passionate rage, he became a magnificent wild beast. All she could think of was how fully his thick cock would fill the empty inside.

"You like that, don't you?" he demanded. "You don't want tender and sweet, you want hard and nasty. And I'm just the man to give you what you crave. A lowly peasant pleasuring the soon-to-be empress."

Before she could argue, he rubbed his thumb across her clit, causing an orgasm to tighten her around his fingers.

"That's it, you lusty *yondie*, come for me, prove to me what I already know."

Him calling her a paid courtesan should have infuriated her, but it didn't. His derogatory term only excited her, prolonging her climax until she truly lost her breath. He didn't stop. He continued to rub her and pump her until another orgasm raced through her body. When she tried to draw her legs together, he held them apart with his knees.

"Oh, no, my lusty mistress, you said you wanted to come and come." His face lowered so he could watch his hand, his eyes luminous within his flushed skin. "Beg for my prick. Tell me how badly you want me to fuck you."

She refused with a toss of her head. She would not beg any man for what they should beg her for permission to do; however, the longer she refused, the more he tormented her. Wave after wave of climaxes left her breathless and weak. In the end, she submitted.

"Please, Sterlave, I want you to fuck me." Oh gods, she honestly did want him to cover her body with his and thrust into her as a man possessed. Never in her life had she wanted a man more than she wanted him. At this moment, she wanted him more than she wanted Chur.

"Look at me. I want you to look right at me so there is no question in your mind who is filling your greedy, grasping slit."

Kasmiri did as he bid. His eyes drilled into hers with frightening intensity. No thoughts of Chur could enter her mind, not when Sterlave became her entire world. All she could think of was how much she needed him. All that mattered was she gave him what he wanted—her willing submission to him and no other.

When he pushed her legs wide and nudged his penis against her dripping core, she cried out. Slowly, inexorably, Sterlave pressed into her, stretching her around him, forcing her to accommodate his thickness. Nothing had ever felt so good, so perfect. He belonged inside her, and she belonged wrapped around him.

A grunt of satisfaction escaped him as he sank fully into her. His lips peeled back in an animalistic snarl of raw hunger that caused her to shiver. As he leaned over her, balancing his weight on his arms, he lowered his face to her neck. His bite prompted another sharp burst of gratification. He marked her, claiming her as his very own, but such only thrilled her.

"Say my name."

"Sterlave, Sterlave," she chanted.

He punctuated each breathless word with a mighty thrust.

"Say my name again."

"Sterlave." She wrapped her arms and legs around him, welcoming his frenzied motions. Each plunge pushed her into the bed, trapping her almost as thoroughly as the blanket had.

He climaxed with a roar that caused a final series of convulsions in her sex. He collapsed on top of her for a brief moment, then angled back on his elbows so he could peer down at her face.

A flash of vulnerability caused her to lower her gaze. In a moment of passion, she bared her soul, then feared his triumph. The encounter had been so intense that conflicting emotions overwhelmed her.

"Ashamed?" He rolled off her. "Can't believe you begged a lowly commoner?" He laughed as he fluffed pillows below his head. "You do understand that Chur is from Ampir, which is far less prosperous than Gant."

His ridicule obliterated the intimacy between them. How could he be so cruel? She hadn't felt ashamed at all, but simply inundated with so many diverse emotions she hadn't been able to meet his piercing gaze. Not once had she thought about Chur. Not until his mocking had she felt humiliated.

Summoning her pride, she slid off the bed and moved to the bathing unit. She wanted to wash away his scent and the evidence of her lust. Never in her life had she felt so dirty.

She didn't even bother to glance back at him when she said, "Why should I be mortified that you acted like an animal? I expected no less from a *cratifan*." She expected him to launch himself from the bed, but he didn't, so she continued, "At least Chur has demonstrated the ability to control himself." When she glanced back, she discovered he'd rolled over.

Let him sleep, she thought, because only in his dreams would he ever touch her again.

A mélange of food scents woke Sterlave. Kasmiri, resplendent in a crimson robe, stood beside a long table tucked to the side of the room, picking among twenty different warming platters. She filled her plate, then sat at the head of the table. With a touch of her finger, glowing blue text floated in front of her face.

As she read, she would occasionally tap a button to verbally relay her instructions and then go back to reading. For a moment, he simply observed her. She had gathered her hair at the base of her neck, which gave her a sleek profile, like one of the goddess statues in the temple. Full, plush lips pursed with concentration while her brows lowered with intent. In-between dealing with her schedule, she would take delicate bites of her selections. Every movement she made was graceful, deliberate. He could lie in bed all day and simply watch her.

After what happened last night, he was safer in bed than anywhere near her while she had sharp implements within reach.

Of course, she had only herself to blame. He needed to master her, needed to know that he was the only man in her mind at that moment, and he thought he'd succeeded. His orgasm had been so profound, so complete, that he swore he touched the mythical land of *Jarasine*. When he looked down into Kasmiri's face, he had expected to see anything other than shame. Her eyes darted away from his so fast his joy evaporated. What he thought would bind them together only pushed her away. After the fact, she seemed horrified that she'd begged a commoner to fuck her elevated self.

He'd laughed and rolled away to conceal his humiliation. She resembled every woman in his village. They took their pleasure, then couldn't get away fast enough. Everything was fine between the covers, but once the pleasure faded, the ugly reality of what he was set in. Everyone shunned him in the light of *Tandalsul,* but in the dark, the women couldn't get enough of him. They said he was like a wild animal, forbidden and exotic. He indulged them because, for a fleeting moment, he was superior. He made them beg, he made them perform lewd acts they would never do with their mates. He ate their food, slept in their barns, and then walked away with a smirk of contempt.

Afterward, the satisfaction dissolved into disappointment. He wanted a woman to want him, not some sexy beast, not some forbidden fruit, but him. Puffed pride couldn't overcome a deep-seated self-loathing. What hurt him most of all was that they shunned him through no act of his own. They shunned him because of his brutal, vicious, drunken father.

Kasmiri's rejection destroyed all the pride he'd carefully built in the training rooms. She had begged him to give her everything he had, but when it was over, she couldn't even look at him. All the dismissals he'd ever suffered paled beside hers because this time, he actually believed that she wanted him for who he really was. Kasmiri could not have heard the rumors from his village, she would have no idea how they loathed him there.

He couldn't blame her denunciation on his father. Kasmiri discarded him because there was something inherently wrong with him. All his life he blamed his father, but he couldn't blame him now.

When she rushed to wash away the evidence of their passion, his soul shattered with the knowledge he was unworthy of any woman's true devotion. At the height of passion, she beseeched him, surrendered to him, her ardor had been genuine . . . it was only afterward she realized the folly of her zeal. Her downcast eyes conveyed her disgust.

Silently, he rose from the bed and moved to the bathing unit. His whole body itched. Getting all of his hair shaved off seemed like a novel idea at the time, but now, he scratched at his head, his chest, his armpits, and his genitals. When he stood at the unit, he continued scratching, but this time with perplexity. In the training rooms, the units had one knob that delivered a trickle of icy water. Kasmiri's bathing unit had six ornate knobs.

When he turned one, hot air rushed over his body and he quickly turned it off. The next two he tried didn't do anything. Another one shot a powerful stream of cold water right at his crotch. He leapt back with a howl.

Kasmiri's giggle drifted from the table.

Leaning around the edge of the unit, he said, "I don't suppose you are going to help me with this."

She shrugged and pressed a button. She said something, but he had no idea what since she spoke in a language he didn't understand.

Deciding that she was probably making fun of him, he turned back to the knobs. Before he tried another one, he stood away from the jets. Good thing, too, since hot water gushed from the crotch-level jet.

A hand on his shoulder caused him to turn. Behind him, Rown smiled shyly and stepped forward. With three deft turns, warm water poured from the top jet. Sterlave watched, but he didn't understand until Rown explained two were for temperature, one for the hot air, and the other three to activate the top or side jets.

Sterlave ducked his head under the water, then felt two hands smoothing lather down his back. Rown seemed most eager to help. Sterlave politely refused.

"I've been bathing myself for a long time."

Rown bowed and backed away with a wistful frown.

Sterlave took his time washing up since he hadn't bathed in warm water for seasons. Among a dozen bottles, he found the soap Rown used and lathered it from the top of his head to his toes. The scent was something masculine and spicy, but he couldn't identify exactly what the smell was. When he finished, he turned on the air jet and dried himself.

Stepping out, he said, "I could become used to this luxury."

Kasmiri ignored him.

He pulled his robe off the floor only to discover Kasmiri had shredded it. Dropping it, he looked around and realized he had nothing else to wear. Nudity didn't bother him so much, but he had a feeling he could make Kasmiri regret her rash decision. If she wanted him to run about naked, he'd be happy to indulge her.

Striding over to the table, he went to grab a plate but found the only one there broken. A quick glance to Kasmiri revealed a superior smirk. Since he couldn't eat like a man, he decided to eat like an animal. Plucking the covers off the warming platters, he ate directly from the dishes with his hands.

Kasmiri rolled her eyes and uttered a small mew of annoyance.

He continued to eat, but the sheer volume of food amazed him. There was so much for only two people. This feast could feed at least twenty men. All of it was perfectly prepared with just the right amount of seasonings. Warming platters kept each dish at the ideal temperature. In the training rooms, the food was often cold, unseasoned, undercooked, and he had to fight for every mouthful. Here, with so much plenty, he stuffed himself to the point of bursting.

"This is very good." He held a handful of the seared *aket* smothered in sticky fruit syrup out to Kasmiri. "Here, try some." Her upper lip curled back.

Deliberately, he dropped some on her end of the table. "Oops. Here, let me get that for you." He swiped at the spilled food, knocking her plate into her lap.

Screeching, she shot to her feet and blasted him with expletives so vile they would make a raw recruit blush.

"Such language from the future empress," he scolded.

"You *cratifan!* You've ruined my favorite robe!"

Refusing to rise to the bait of the insult, he said, "Oh, I'm sure I can clean it." Swabbing his hands around the mess on the fabric, he managed to spread the stain and feel her strong, sleek thighs at the same time.

"Stop that!" Kasmiri slapped at his hands.

He did his best to look chagrined, but he couldn't keep a smile off his face. "I guess next time you'll let me use a plate."

"Next time I'll put you in a cage and toss you a raw haunch of *aket!*" Swirling away in her ruined robe, Kasmiri stomped to the bathing unit and rinsed off. She emerged naked, holding the robe away from her as if it were coated in excrement.

Sterlave used an edge of the dripping robe to clean his hands. "There, now we're even. I have nothing to wear and neither do you."

Her glare could have stripped the hide right off him.

Another round of itching caused him to scratch at his chest. He rummaged through the bottles outside the bathing unit. When he found a pleasant-smelling one that he assumed was lotion, he poured a generous dollop in his hand.

"I wouldn't—" Kasmiri cut herself off and turned away. She went to the table and again spoke in the unknown language.

He sniffed the creamy white lotion. Was there something wrong with it? He decided it was unlikely Kasmiri would keep something dangerous in her collection of creams and potions, so he smeared it all over his body with defiant motions.

Rown entered with a clutch of crimson fabric. He tilted a curious glance to the bottle in Sterlave's hand, then helped Kasmiri on with another robe. This one wasn't as fine as the other, but still, red was definitely her color. Once covered in finery, her spine stiffened and she regained her regal posture. Oddly, she didn't lift her nose to convey disdain, Kasmiri pushed out her proud chin. She squared her jaw along with her shoulders. Solid, dangerous, not a woman to mess with, which only made him want to tangle with her more. Subduing such a conceited creature pushed all his buttons.

Rown whispered something to Kasmiri, and she responded, "I warned him, but he insisted."

Sterlave set the bottle aside. Before he could ask about the contents, his head swam and his entire body felt warm, almost gooey, as if he were melting into a puddle. As he started to sink to his knees, Rown grabbed him about the waist and helped him up to the bed. Three steps seemed massive and he barely managed to get up them before he collapsed.

Above him, the open ceiling exposed a crisp harvest sky. The blue was rich, saturated, and almost unreal. Suddenly, blue eyes appeared before his. Rown reminded him of Chur in some ways, but his eyes were unique. Rown's eyes had soft blue irises with white shards that spiraled outwards from the pupil.

"For a man, you have beautiful eyes," Sterlave said, then regretted it. He didn't want to give Rown the wrong idea. However, it didn't matter because that wasn't what came out of his mouth.

Rown said something in return, but it made no more sense than what he'd said.

Sterlave tried to respond, but his voice garbled incoherently. He decided he didn't mind. He was too sleepy to care about anything but floating on a soft bed while staring at a beautiful cloudless sky and Rown's seductive eyes. . . .

Sterlave woke in restraints. Pillows propped up his head so he had a good view of his naked body. Fur-lined animal hide manacles bound each wrist and ankle. Kasmiri and Rown sat at the foot of the bed whispering. He couldn't understand the language at all, but it sounded lyrical, as if they sang rather than spoke.

When they realized he was awake, a wicked grin flattened Kasmiri's plump lips. Rown met his gaze, then quickly looked away. Sterlave knew that look; Rown was at once ashamed but also aroused.

Sterlave tested the restraints and realized Kasmiri had solved the problem of anchoring points by strapping the line under the bed. When he pulled his right arm, he felt greater tension on the left, and the same with his legs. Utterly and totally bound, his heart pounded in his chest so hard his vision wavered with each beat.

Sterlave enjoyed binding a woman, but he had never allowed a woman to bind him. Never had he trusted a woman enough to permit her such power. Here, however, it seemed he had no choice. Plastering an indifferent cast to his face, he lifted his brows, and said, "If you wanted me naked in your bed, all you had to do was ask."

Disappointment caused Kasmiri's victorious smile to fade. For the first time, he saw the truth below her facade; she wanted him more than she would ever admit to herself, let alone admit to him.

Snidely, Kasmiri reminded him, "I'm only using you as a tool, remember? You are going to teach me all about what men enjoy."

Sterlave tested the restraints with a sharp yank that caused Rown to flinch. Realizing that resistance was futile, he sarcastically asked, "And what will I be teaching you today?"

Kasmiri motioned to Rown. With a glance to his mistress, he then cast a gaze to Sterlave, then quickly lowered his gaze to Sterlave's hips. Flaccid, his cock rested against his thigh. Rown slid up the bed, between his forcefully spread legs, and took his soft prick into skilled hands. Blood pooled in his hips, filling his sex, causing his breathing to accelerate.

"What was in that damn lotion?" Sterlave asked, trying to distract himself.

Rown lowered his face close to his stiffening member and breathed. "*Nanatul* is for headaches. You apply a small amount to your head, not your entire body. To ease your itching, I covered you with a different lotion." Skillfully, Rown sucked the tip of Sterlave's sex into his mouth.

Sterlave arched back. Gods spare him, but Rown had a mouth made for sucking cock. Deft lips surrounded the crown, slipping down, taking every bit of him into welcoming heat. Rown's cheeks drew in when he suckled gently. Twirling his tongue around his shaft, he spiraled down, then up.

Sterlave couldn't take his eyes off him. Rown's intensity was almost as arousing as his technique since he focused all his attention on giving pleasure. Rown caught Sterlave watching and drew his cock almost completely out of his mouth before plunging back down. Sterlave damned the restraints because he wanted to grab the back of Rown's head, hold him steady, and then rock his hips. Sensing this, Rown held his head still, then encouraged Sterlave to plunge by cupping his hands around his hips.

Lost in the erotic sensation, he forgot all about Kasmiri until she slid up the bed for a better view. Her heavy lids lowered over dilated pupils, her plush lips parted, and her nipples strained against her robe.

"Rather than just watching, why don't you help?" he suggested softly. Her eyes blinked rapidly as if she were just coming out of a dream. "You said you wanted to learn."

Rown motioned to Kasmiri, inviting her to try her hand and mouth at mastering this erotic art.

If he thought she would leap right in, he was disappointed. Rown began with instructions in the lyrical language. He started with basic anatomy, pointing out the most sensitive areas. Kasmiri nodded, then repeated his words, teasing her delicate fingertips over his entire cock and balls until he was practically growling with frustration.

Next, Rown performed the spiral technique, then moved back so Kasmiri could emulate him. When her plush lips wrapped around the tip and slid down with her questing tongue, he thought he'd died and gone to *Jarasine.* He couldn't help but groan and thrust.

Kasmiri flinched back, gagging and coughing.

Sterlave apologized profusely. "Kasmiri, I'm sorry, I didn't mean to, I just—"

Rown cut him off. "As I said, at times a man can move involuntarily." He flashed a cautionary frown to Sterlave. "One can only hope the man has more self-control."

Having a servant chastise him was embarrassing, but he vowed to exercise every shred of discipline to keep still. The last thing he wanted to do was frighten Kasmiri. He wanted her to learn this because he wanted her to do this to him willingly. And often.

"It won't happen again."

Rown nodded and Kasmiri tried again.

Sterlave gripped the leather straps and pulled to keep still. Her technique wasn't as perfected as Rown's, but that's what made it better. Kasmiri was raw, untried, but spectacular in her enthusiasm. When she drew away, Rown instructed her to flick the smooth back of her tongue against the point where the shaft met the head. Watching her comply almost caused him to break the restraints because she did it while looking right into his eyes.

A small drop of moisture pearled at the tip, and she flicked it away with a seductive dart of her red tongue while flashing him a masterful grin.

Much to his dismay, Rown moved her back so he could teach her something else. Sterlave's brows lowered when he watched Rown apply something slick and shiny to a slender wand with a slightly bulbous tip. He had no idea of his intent until Rown slowly inserted the device into Sterlave's ass.

A terrifying flashback to a brutal night in his cell caused him to clench and try to wriggle away. "No, wait—"

Then the most explosive pleasure radiated through his body.

Stunned, Sterlave relaxed as Rown thrust the device slowly while stroking his hand up and down Sterlave's shaft, increasing the pressure on the down stroke. Sterlave was on the brink of an explosive orgasm when Rown stopped.

A spew of expletives passed Sterlave's lips.

Kasmiri whispered something, and Rown departed with a bow and a sly grin.

Sterlave watched him leave with trepidation. He had no idea what Kasmiri's intensions were. When he turned his attention on her, she pushed her chin out, straightened her shoulders, and flashed him a wicked smirk.

6

Kasmiri knelt on the bed and removed her robe. Sterlave ran his gaze over her and she preened under his attention. Just as Rown had said, men were extremely visual creatures. Sterlave growled appreciatively when she cupped her breasts and tweaked her nipples to full attention.

"Is the lesson over?" he asked, his voice raspy with desire.

Kasmiri pouted tartly and shook her head. She'd asked Rown to stop because she recognized the signs that Sterlave would climax soon, and she didn't want him to. Not until she decreed his release. One way or another, he had to learn that she was in charge.

Having Sterlave at her mercy would be thoroughly enjoyable. After last night and his antics this morning, a little payback was certainly in order. Unlike her mother, she wouldn't tolerate an uncontrollable consort.

Grasping the end of the wand, Kasmiri worked it slowly as Rown had instructed. Sterlave arched back. His penis twitched, releasing more drops of moisture, like tears, as if his cock wept with frustration.

"When Rown first tried to insert this, why did you want him to stop?"

"Kasmiri, remember how I said conversation during sex isn't—"

"I want to know." Last night, he had refused her pleasure until she answered his questions, so Kasmiri stopped thrusting the device. His primal fear reaction so intrigued her she simply had to understand his reasons.

With gritted teeth, he glared at the open ceiling. He shook his head as if pushing a thought away. "I was raped."

Shock popped her mouth open. "In the training rooms?" No wonder he'd been adamant he wouldn't rape Rown.

"Three seasons ago, in my cell, by one of the other recruits. A man named Loban."

His cock had softened considerably and he would not meet her gaze. She now wished she hadn't asked. Her curiosity caused him a great deal of pain and ruined the moment. If she could take the question back, she would.

Cupping his chin, she turned his face to hers, then whispered, "Never again will that happen to you. Do you want me to remove it?"

Her compassion must have surprised him because his brows lifted. "I was afraid at first but not now. It feels . . . incredible. More so with you than with Rown."

"I'm sorry I forced him on you."

"No, you're not." He chuckled. "Watching him suck me excited you."

She nodded. Observing them had aroused her to the point she wanted to stoke her fingers along her dripping sex. Coyly, she pointed out, "You seemed rather excited yourself."

Sterlave laughed. "He's good at what he does. He's also an excellent teacher."

Lowering her head, she took him into her mouth as she stroked the wand. He hardened again.

"Kasmiri, straddle across my face, that way I can pleasure you at the same time."

She found it awkward to get into position, but once she did, Sterlave fastened his mouth to her sex, chewing, biting, and thrusting his tongue while she continued to tease him with her mouth and the wand.

When he gently rocked his hips, she was ready for him, and pulled back a bit so he could thrust more deeply. This also pushed her more firmly over his face. On the verge of orgasm, Sterlave pushed her over the edge when he slipped his tongue between her cheeks.

Her thighs tightened around his head as her climax washed through her. When he lifted up, growling between her legs, she worked the wand more quickly. He shot deeply into her mouth, but Rown's instructions prepared her. Swallowing while sucking more forcefully, she managed to take all his pleasure without spilling a drop.

For a moment, she lay atop him, feeling him softening in her mouth. She removed the wand, which elicited a final groan. His head fell back on the pillow and his panting tickled her slick sex.

"Gods, your whole body has the sweetest flavor, like sugar-drenched *nicla*."

The comparison to the red-orange fruit pleased her. "You taste like the Valry Sea, salty and ferocious."

He laughed and kissed her inner thighs. "So, now that you've drained me, are you going to release me?"

Kasmiri crawled off him, then lifted one brow. "Maybe I'll keep you here, where I can use you whenever I wish."

"You don't have to bind me for that." He flicked his chin as if to draw her near to tell her a secret. When she leaned close, he whispered, "All you ever have to do is ask."

She laughed, but that was something she'd always had a problem with; asking could result in refusal. She'd found she got her way far more often by manipulation. Turning her attention to the manacles, she fumbled with the little clasps, but they wouldn't budge.

"This isn't funny, Kasmiri."

"I'm not trying to be. I can't get the clasps to release." Her long nails prevented her fingertips from being able to push the tiny metal parts.

"Summon Rown, if he got me into these things, he can get me out." He sounded cool as spring rain, but his rapidly blinking eyes and straining chest revealed his rising panic. She had enjoyed binding him, but if she couldn't free him, he wouldn't want to do it again.

Kasmiri yanked on her robe while she strode to the table. She pressed the button and tried to keep her voice level, but Rown must have heard her distress because he burst into the room with wide-eyed alarm. He ran directly toward Sterlave. After examining him and finding him safe, Rown relaxed and removed the restraints.

Each popped apart almost effortlessly. Kasmiri cursed herself for not being able to work them. She took her frustration out on Rown, yelling at him until Sterlave told her to relax. Through gritted teeth, she ordered Rown to have the clasps enlarged so that in the future, she could work them despite her long nails.

Rown nodded. Silently, he gathered the leather straps together and the wand. He departed after a wistful sigh and a final glance at Sterlave.

"I have never seen him so enamored of anyone." In all honesty, she didn't think any man had ever looked at her with that level of longing.

Sterlave rubbed his wrists and ankles. "How many other men have been in your rooms?"

"None." She found his jealous tone pleasing. "Believe me, those guards are there for a reason."

He pointed to the area behind the curtains. "There is a back door."

"That only servants can use. Beyond their rooms is an access hallway with even more guards." Kasmiri sighed. "My mother isn't a fool. I've been carefully supervised my entire life." Under her breath, she mumbled, "If she could have glued my legs together, she would have."

"That didn't stop you from a private chat with Chur at the Festival of Temptation."

Jealousy turned bitter was not pleasant at all. Even though she didn't feel she had to explain, she did. "Nothing happened." In fact, Chur had rejected her so thoroughly her heart ached for endless nights. "I came to the Harvest a virgin just as my duty demanded." Her mother used the word *duty* so often that Kasmiri had nightmares where an amorphous blob called *duty* consumed her, bones and all.

Sterlave changed the subject when he asked, "Where did the restraints come from?"

"A gift from one of the guests at the bonding ceremony." Rown had giggled when he listed all the presents, most of which were designed for sexual play. Kasmiri hadn't been surprised, not after the intensity of their bonding.

"Weren't the gifts for us? Don't I get to see them?"

"Later, perhaps. We don't have time now. We must make ourselves ready."

Sterlave left the bed to clean up. When he returned, he was scratching at his chest.

"Here." She retrieved the lotion Rown had used to soothe the itch of regrowing hair.

When she handed it to him, he cocked one eye, and asked, "No tricks?"

"No." She watched him slather the lotion across his muscular chest and turned away because watching him caused her sex to wet. "The last thing I need is you scratching or incapacitated for Mother's celebration."

"What celebration?"

Kasmiri released an annoyed breath. "We are supposedly celebrating my bonding." Of course, what her mother said and what was really going on were often two different things. "Rown should have your clothing ready."

"Maybe I'll just stay here since you are clearly in no mood to celebrate getting stuck with me."

When she turned around, Sterlave stood with his hands clenched at his sides. Why was he so touchy? She hadn't meant that at all; she simply didn't care for her mother's manipulations. It seemed each time they drew together, something she said pushed him away. The sad thing was she wasn't trying to alienate him, but she refused to continue soothing his pride.

"You will attend. Remember that you chose this life by forcing me to be your bondmate." She summoned her servants and settled at her mirror.

Sterlave relaxed on the bed, watching Kasmiri's transformation. Three servants flittered around her while she sat perfectly still. They teased and smoothed her hair into an elaborate cone similar to the style she'd worn at the Festival of Temptation. He didn't care for the hairdo at all since he thought she looked stunning with her hair pulled back at the nape of her neck.

Next, they applied color to her face, enhancing her lips with glossy crimson and enlarging her eyes with dark liner. Carefully, a servant added extra eyelashes, then placed tiny red gems at the sweeping ends.

Kasmiri faced her mirror with blank eyes. As they slaved to perfect everything about her physical form, her mind was clearly elsewhere.

His anger at her harsh attitude, that he must attend since it was his fault for forcing her to bond to him, dissolved when he wondered how many times she had sat motionless while her servants poked, prodded, and perfumed her person. Like a doll with glassy eyes, Kasmiri sat in the chair with no animation at all. Sterlave found it unsettling. Would he too become bored with all the finery forced on him for the sake of appearances?

Rown entered with garments slung over his arm and motioned to Sterlave. Sliding off the bed, he moved nearer to Rown and considered the unfamiliar clothing. He had no idea where to start.

"I am here to help you," Rown said with a soothing smile. "First we start with the *echalle*."

Rown helped Sterlave slip on a scrap of silky black fabric with a complicated set of straps that nestled his cock and balls into a prominent bulge.

"If I get an erection while wearing this, it will look like I have an oversized *gara* fruit in my pants."

Rown chuckled and adjusted the *echalle*. "Yes, which is rather the point. But it won't constrict." He slipped a finger inside and pulled forward, showing that the fabric would expand if he did.

Rown then handed him a pair of black pants that seemed three sizes too small. As Sterlave slipped them on, they stretched around him, caressing him, molding to every muscle on his legs. Once he got them up to his waist, Rown fastened them together, stood back, and sighed.

Sterlave did not feel the same. How could he be clothed but feel more than naked? He was so displayed he had an overwhelming urge to cover his genitals with his hands.

He slipped on a red shirt that didn't help at all since it too clung to him like a second skin. When he moved, the fabric stroked his nipples, hardening them, which caused his cock to twitch with awareness. The entire outfit was like having a lover strapped to his body.

Rown's eyes glittered appreciatively.

"Did you select this clothing?" Sterlave asked with a bit too much force.

"I assure you, this mode of dress is customary for a consort." Rown pouted, not with as much charm as Kasmiri, but still with a practiced precision. "Are you displeased with me?"

Sterlave shrugged and instantly regretted it when the fabric shimmed all along his frame. "I am not upset with you, but this is . . . exploitive."

Rown frowned, clearly perplexed. "You are Kasmiri's consort. You will always be displayed accordingly."

"Displayed is right." Sterlave sighed and again regretted his decision to select her as his bondmate. Lead by his cock, he now had to let all in the land get a good look at it whenever he went out. Too bad he wasn't into exhibitionism because being a consort would be the perfect position if he were.

Kneeling, Rown slipped on a pair of black animal-hide boots that went about halfway up his calves. After a lingering look at his prominent bulge, Rown stood, then fastened a short black cape to several buttons on the shoulders of the shirt. Sterlave wanted to turn the cape the other way around to cover his crotch.

After stroking a pungent scent along his neck, Rown considered him prepared and left the room.

Sterlave checked on Kasmiri and discovered she was almost ready. Servants had wrapped her in crimson fabric that covered her from neck to ankles but left her arms and back exposed. Similar to his outfit, hers also clung to every curve she possessed. He tried to keep his tongue from hanging out and just barely managed. She was a goddess. Turning her gaze to him, her eyes widened as she examined his clothing. His distaste for the outfit changed considerably because of the glow in her eyes.

"You are most handsome." She seemed genuinely surprised by his transformation.

Sterlave bowed. "You are stunning." He was less surprised

because he knew how incredible Kasmiri looked without any enhancements at all.

Kasmiri tilted her face, preening under his gaze. She twirled leisurely, so that he could examine her clinging dress from all angles. Ever so slowly, his swelling erection pushed against the *echalle*, displaying his genitals in excruciating detail.

She sauntered toward him and cupped her hand against his bulge. "Obviously you like my dress."

He stroked his finger along her turgid nipple. "Just as much as you like my pants." So far, the only time they got along perfectly was in physical matters.

Her gaze oozed sex as she gave him a gentle squeeze. "I am far more interested in what lies under your pants."

Sterlave wanted to rip all their clothing off and send his regards to her mother. They would have a much better time here alone than in a room full of the elite.

They parted when Rown entered carrying something swaddled in fabric.

"What's this?" Kasmiri asked, watching as Rown placed the object on the table.

"A gift from your mother." Rown flipped open the material. Kasmiri leapt back so quickly she almost stumbled.

Sterlave grasped her waist to steady her, but she moved away from him as if burned by his touch. Confused, he approached the table. Within the fabric he discovered a belt and a gleaming sword with gems embedded into the handle and along the blade. Why would something so beautiful frighten Kasmiri?

"What is this all about?" Sterlave directed the question to Rown.

"It's a curse," Kasmiri spat.

Rown struggled to maintain his servant aplomb since he clearly thought the gift was magnificent. "Your mother meant no harm—"

"I know what she means!" Kasmiri cut him off, then launched

into a tirade about Rown being a traitor. Her voice rose in pitch and volume until Rown practically cowered into his robe.

"Stop!" Sterlave put himself between them. This was the second time he'd witnessed her verbally abusing Rown for something that wasn't his fault—first the restraints and now this. Kasmiri turned her flashing eyes on him, ready to flay him with her wrathful tongue. That's when he realized tears shimmered, threatening to fall and ruin her elaborate makeup. Whatever the meaning of this sword, it terrified her beyond comprehension. Without a word and despite her protests, he wrapped her up in his arms, murmuring soothing sounds. She struggled against him, her breath hot against his chest until she finally collapsed into his embrace. He maneuvered her into a chair and had Rown fetch her a drink.

Grateful, Rown complied, darting out the back, then returning with a bubbly liquid in a clear cup.

Kasmiri tossed it back in one mighty gulp, grimaced, and belched delicately behind her hand, which he found funny and endearing all at once. After a moment, her face softened and the fire in her eyes mellowed to embers. He would have to ask Rown to keep a supply of the drink in the room for future rages.

Sterlave removed the empty cup from her hand. "Now, can one of you calmly tell me what that sword means?"

Kasmiri dismissively waved her hand at Rown, giving him permission to speak.

Rown placed the belt aside, then used the fabric to polish the already gleaming blade. "This is the Sword of the Empress." His voice was soft with reverence. "The empress bestows it upon her consort, for he must defend the Onic Empire."

Kasmiri uttered a bitter laugh. "It also means my mother will not select a new consort. This is her way of reminding me of my duty."

Sterlave pondered for a moment because it seemed the duty

fell to him. If war came, he must lead the guards into battle, not Kasmiri.

Defeated eyes met his. "I have a duty to provide the next heir. If I do not have a girl child within two seasons, our ruling line will be vulnerable to a challenge from one of the other houses."

His brows lifted. He had no idea Kasmiri had such pressure on her shoulders. His image of her as a pampered and protected woman-child vanished. Just as he had to fight to obtain his position as the Harvester, she had to fight to retain the power of the empress. Her fight was different from his, but still, it was his fight as well, for he must father a child. If he failed, Kasmiri would turn to another, for she would have no choice.

With a nod of his chin to the back door, Sterlave dismissed Rown. Once he left, he knelt beside Kasmiri's chair and took her limp hand into his.

"This is not your duty alone, Kasmiri. I will do anything to help you achieve this obligation."

Her laugh was so cold it stiffened his spine. Rudely, she said, "As if you'd object to fucking me until I'm pregnant."

No one he'd ever met could blow hot and cold as quickly as she could. "That's not what I meant." He sought to ease her mind, but somehow he only irritated her more.

"No?" She yanked her hand from his, stood, and glided to the mirror to check her face. "What if I don't want to have a child? I don't have that luxury. Reproduce or face extinction. When another house issues a challenge, and if they succeed, they will kill all in my house, including you."

"Then we won't let that happen." He moved behind her and caught her gaze in the glass. "You are not alone anymore, Kasmiri. Whatever duty obligates you now compels me."

Dubious, she considered his reflection. "Do you want to have a child?"

He didn't even hesitate. "Yes, I do." Having a child with Kasmiri caused his chin to lift with determination; he would be the father his father never was.

"Then you're a fool." She spun away from the mirror and retrieved the sword. Hefting it up, she brandished it twice, then motioned him closer.

Sterlave warily approached.

"By might of the blade you claimed me as your bondmate. By might of this blade, I make you my protector, my defender, and the father of all my children." Kasmiri bowed deeply. She tossed him the belt, which he slung across his hips; then she affixed the blade.

A rush of obligation surged through him once the cold metal touched his left thigh. This wasn't just a sword but a tremendous responsibility. By accepting this gift, he swore himself not only to Kasmiri, but also to the entire Onic Empire. Despite the weight on his shoulders, he stood tall and faced her with pride.

Blinking rapidly, Kasmiri considered him, then turned away to hide her watering eyes.

She might think him a fool, she might still resent his claim, but something in his stance touched her heart. Turning her by gripping her shoulders, Sterlave forced her to face him, then claimed her mouth.

Crimson paint smoothed against his lips, but he didn't care. He plunged his tongue to her mouth, tilting her head back to work his way deeper. Claiming her with his kiss, he pressed her against him until she felt the threat of his engorged cock nudging her belly. She didn't struggle but opened herself to him, angling her hips to snuggle him fully.

"Tell me one truth, Kasmiri," he breathed against her lips. "Tell me if you want me to stand beside you and fight your battles with you."

Without a moment of hesitation, she whispered, "I want

you. I keep trying not to, but I do." She said it as if she confessed to the most perverse need. He worried that she wanted him in a different way than what he asked.

"Will you work with me to face all the challenges?"

"Yes." Her voice sounded more assured.

"Do you trust me?"

"Yes."

"Do you love me?"

Rather than answer, she pressed her lips to his. It wasn't the answer he needed, but for now, it was enough.

7

Kasmiri entered the Room of Ceremonies with Sterlave at her side. Every gaze swung their way and she stiffened her spine, plastering a serene smile to her face as she nodded to several people. At first, she worried over her makeup, but Sterlave had insisted on fixing her lip color before leaving her rooms. She had removed the smear from his lips, then marveled in the way he stroked crimson paint to her mouth. His focus made her think of the same attention to her sex. Everything that man did made her slick with desire.

Clasping Sterlave's massive hand gave her strength. Moving through the throng of people, she sought out the safety of the high table and took her seat. Her mother had not yet made her entrance, so the rest of the table was empty. Kasmiri settled into her padded chair with a sigh of relief.

Sterlave sat next to her and whispered, "Should we not mingle with the guests?"

Kasmiri considered the protection offered by her current situation, then realized if she did not circulate among the elite, gossipmongers would wag vicious tongues. A brief but genuine smile crossed her face when she thought of how she and Sterlave had clashed tongues. That man could kiss the robe off an acolyte. The more she fought to resist him, the more he battered down her defenses until she finally confessed that she did, indeed, want him. But more than that, she needed him. For the first time, she thought she could face her duty with him by her side. She did not love him. In fact, she feared that if she allowed him any closer to her heart, she would. That she couldn't allow. Love had ruined her mother and she would not follow in those tormented footsteps.

Drawing strength from him, she nodded, and they rose as one. Despite her reservations about his fitness as her mate, she was proud to have Sterlave as her consort. Dressed in his clinging clothing, he clearly rivaled any man in the room. Thick muscles and a prominent bulge shamed every man. Very few could wear the required consort clothing with the proud carriage of Sterlave.

As they moved to the center of the room, Chur Zenge entered with the most beautiful woman clinging to his arm. Kasmiri stopped midstride, halting Sterlave, who glanced in the same direction. His body went ridged when he too saw Chur. She felt him move his mouth close to her ear, then pull back when he considered the woman at Chur's side.

"Who is that?"

"I do not know," Kasmiri said, but she looked like a younger version of Arianda Rostvaika. Kasmiri knew Chur had selected a bondmate, but she had no idea he'd selected a woman who so resembled the woman she'd debased herself with. Was it a coincidence? Kasmiri thought Arianda didn't have any children, but this woman was clearly her child. Then again, this creature was no child but a grown woman, and far too beautiful to be ignored. Jealousy surged that she had stolen her dream. How Kasmiri had wanted Chur to select an ugly woman who would be no competition. But this woman, oh, this woman was beyond stunning. She was slender, delicate, and almost as fragile as a water nymph.

Harvest-colored hair tumbled down her back to her midcalf like a cape. Her clinging outfit of black outlined a body that was the exact opposite of Kasmiri's lush frame. This woman barely had breasts or hips, but still Chur wrapped his arm about her as if she were the most prized possession in the entire Onic Empire.

Kasmiri wanted to shave her bald, then rip her eyes out.

Chur nodded in her direction and her heart swelled with hope, but when he saw Sterlave, his face split into the most genuine smile she had ever witnessed grace his face. She had never glimpsed Chur joyful, but he was elated to see Sterlave. Another surge of jealousy stiffened her spine, and she fought the grimace that wanted to commandeer her countenance. Not once in her life had anyone ever been that happy to see her. Not even her mother had been that radiantly joyful when she embraced her prior to the bonding ceremony. Somehow, Sterlave had managed that reaction twice in one day.

"Sterlave!" Chur rushed forward and embraced her consort in an expansive hug. Wicked thoughts of her servant Rown, as a stand-in for Chur, filled her mind. Kasmiri longed to see Chur embrace Sterlave but on his knees, sucking his cock as her servant Rown had done. If she couldn't have him, she wanted to punish him, to force him to do her bidding as her servant. A thousand erotic tortures flashed through her mind of what she would do to Chur, if she only had the chance.

As she considered these wicked thoughts, she noticed that Chur wasn't the same at all. His facial scar was gone and his skin glowed with golden light. He wore the customary Harvester uniform but without a red slash to expose his most fearsome chest scar. He had transformed, not with cosmetics as she had, but something deeper, more profound. She sensed the change as soon as he drew near. Power fairly crackled from him.

Indisputably thrilled, Sterlave let go of her hand to embrace Chur. "You didn't kill me after all."

"No." Chur stepped back. "I didn't want to." With a touch to Sterlave's shoulder, Chur's smiled broadened. "I knew you would make a fine Harvester." Chur turned his intense blue gaze to Kasmiri. She had an overwhelming urge to fling herself to her knees before him. "You have selected a fine bondmate."

Kasmiri blushed and lowered her head. She found it impossible to maintain eye contact with Chur. When she looked down, her gaze fell to his crotch, where his semihard penis created an interesting bulge. A wave of longing tightened her nipples and her sex. Had the fates been kind, she would now know the taste and feel of him, but she'd been denied. She fought against rubbing her thighs together or licking her lips. When Sterlave's hand wrapped around hers, she was finally able to look up, but only at Sterlave.

"I worried that you had stolen her away from me, but I see you have chosen well yourself." Sterlave looked right at the Harvest-haired nymph with a lifted brow of interest.

Kasmiri bristled. Did he mean to say that given a choice he would have selected this other woman himself? How dare he denigrate her right before her face! Before she could respond, Chur wrapped his arm around the woman and pulled her to his side.

"My bondmate, Enovese."

Kasmiri rolled her eyes. Even the woman's name was melodious and delicate. On closer inspection, she discovered her eyes were light jade with a deep indigo starburst, and her nose tilted up at the end just like Arianda's. Desperate to find some imperfection, Kasmiri realized she scrutinized the woman like dubious marketplace goods.

"I am pleased to meet you, Kasmiri." Enovese bowed with the grace of a servant.

Kasmiri's smile was genuine this time. Enovese was dazzling, but her manners were decidedly lower class. "I believe I know your mother, Arianda Rostvaika." Kasmiri executed a modified bow with her face high; however, her snub was lost on this woman.

Pride beamed from her when she acknowledged that Arianda was, indeed, her mother.

"How is that possible?" Kasmiri asked pointedly. When they'd been playing a dangerous game with Clathia, Arianda had often bemoaned her childless state, so where had this creature come from?

Chur placed a kiss to Enovese's cheek. "That is a long story best left for another day. We are here to celebrate your bonding."

Thwarted by Chur's diplomatic charm, Kasmiri had no choice but to drop the subject. However, when Chur pulled Sterlave away to talk privately, Kasmiri found herself alone with Enovese. Once her protector was out of earshot, Kasmiri sidled close and began probing Enovese in earnest.

"I don't recall seeing you at the Festival of Temptation." Kasmiri plucked a glass of red wine from a passing tray.

"I did not attend." Enovese declined the servant's offer with a shake of her head, a pathetic lower class gesture. A woman of stature would have waved her hand in dismissal. Why would Chur, with so many elite ladies at his disposal, have chosen a woman of such low birth? Truly, the man was an enigma.

"Oh? Couldn't your mother afford to clothe you for the event?" Kasmiri arched her brows as she sipped her wine, but the snide comment had no effect.

"She did not know of my existence." If anything, Enovese seemed amused by her rancor.

How could a mother not know she had a child? Kasmiri wondered. "Surely she knew when she gave birth to you?"

"She did not give birth to me."

Furious at being treated like a fool, Kasmiri grasped Enovese's upper arm but immediately let go when a surge of power rumbled through her fingertips. Yanking her hand away, Kasmiri demanded, "What are you?"

Lifting her nose with more righteous indignation than the empress, Enovese considered her for a moment. Her eyes darkened, but the indigo starburst blazed with terrifying authority. Kasmiri felt trapped by her gaze. She wanted to grab hold of something, anything, to prevent herself from falling into the abyss. "I am someone you should not touch again." With that, Enovese released her from her gripping gaze and swirled away, her hair swinging with her steps as she moved toward Chur.

Kasmiri's hand trembled as she cupped her drink. Never in her life had anyone truly frightened her, but that woman had. She was dangerous. Like Chur, there was a strange power emanating from her, something immeasurable and unexplainable, but it was there nonetheless. Kasmiri finished her drink and grabbed another. She didn't even notice what she'd selected until she drank the cup dry. Too late, she realized she had just downed *illias,* a sparkling aphrodisiac. The elixir was meant to be sipped not tossed back in one swallow.

Within moments, her body warmed and her breathing grew unsteady. All her perverse thoughts of Chur and Sterlave swirled in her mind's eye with vivid clarity. She wanted to lift her skirt and stroke her fingers through her damp curls. She wanted every man in the room to line up while she sat upon her throne so one by one they could drop to their knees and drink from her gushing sex. Then she wanted to take Enovese and splay her upon a table so each man could find satisfaction in her tawny slit.

Kasmiri smiled when she thought of two strong men holding Enovese's arms and two stronger men parting her thighs. Somewhere in all the bonding gifts was a smooth phallus. Kasmiri imagined it wrapped around her hips so that she could be the first to fuck Chur's pretty, little mate. Kasmiri wouldn't rush; she would take her time and cause the woman to thrash in need and frustration, thus showing Chur what a *yondie* she was. When Kasmiri finished, she would insert the phallus deep into Enovese's bottom so that when each man took his turn, they would force it deeper within. After a thousand men took their fill, perhaps Chur would not want her after all. For if he'd selected her during the Harvest, no man but he had ever known her.

Clutching the glass so hard she feared it would break, Kasmiri placed it on a passing tray while her gaze desperately sought Sterlave. If she didn't have him soon, her sex would burst into flames. When she found him engrossed in conversation with Chur and Enovese, she didn't hesitate to stride forward, grasp his hand, and pull him to one of the side rooms.

"What's wrong with—"

She pressed him against the wall and plastered her mouth to his before he could finish. Breathless, she pulled back, and said, "I need you."

Sterlave considered the well-appointed basin room with a frown. "Here?"

She locked the door but didn't care if guests could hear. Let them know how much she wanted her consort. That would put any rumors that sprung up to rest. This party was to celebrate her bonding so she had a right to a more private, and fulfilling, commemoration.

Struggling to peel away Sterlave's tight pants, she met with only further frustration when the *echalle* blocked her access to his hardening cock. Just the scent of him drove her into madness.

"It won't come off unless I take my pants off."

Cursing the designer, she didn't think she could wait that long. Once Sterlave realized the frantic nature of her need, he picked her up and placed her on one of the low-slung couches.

Yanking her dress up, she couldn't get the clinging fabric much past her knees. A howl of frustration escaped her lips.

Sterlave rolled the fabric up, ripped off her panties, and exposed her to a rush of cool air. Parting her legs, he lowered his face and teased his tongue between swollen lips.

Kasmiri grasped his head, forcing him into firmer contact.

He pulled back and suspiciously asked, "What has turned you so desperate?"

She couldn't formulate an answer even though she knew he thought Chur responsible for her state. Frantic for release, she lowered her hand to vigorously rub her straining clit.

Sterlave's brows drew up as he watched her frenzied motions. His trapped penis strained against silky fabric as he riveted his gaze upon her.

She didn't care that he watched. In fact, his presence only fueled her lust.

He pushed her hands away, using his much thicker fingers to plunge into her depths as his lips sucked her clit into his mouth. As his tongue swirled around and around, Kasmiri lost her breath. Every touch felt amplified until her world spun sideways. Pleasure rose up and up until she lost all coherent thought.

Still, Sterlave plunged his fingers to her. "That's it, Kasmiri, again and again." He pulled down the bodice of her dress, exposing her breasts to his gaze and her nipples to his questing mouth. A smear of crimson paint transferred from her lips to his now stained her breasts. She didn't care.

Waves of sweet release wracked her body, yet he continued to plunge his hand and suckle her breasts. Still she needed more. Wriggling her hips up, she placed her hand over his, pointing his fingers toward her ass.

Slick with her lust, his fingers slid easily inside. No pain assaulted her, only a sweet filling bliss. Sterlave lessened his pace until she demanded more. Pushing her legs farther apart, he settled himself between so he could plunge one hand to her sex, the other to her bottom. When she looked down, his entire head was covered with sweat as his arms bunched and flexed to give her relief.

Consumed with drink-induced desire, she ordered him to remove his pants. It seemed to take forever for him to yank off his boots, the belt and sword, the clinging trousers, and then the hated *echalle*. He struggled with the straps until she rose up and helped him. Once free, she drew him to her mouth, sucking him so forcefully he bit back a groan. He tasted of light sweat, salty yet sweet, and she couldn't decide if she wanted to drink him or thrust him between her thighs.

He took the decision from her when he pulled out of her mouth and flipped her to her belly.

Placing his cock against her clenching sex, he asked, "You want me very badly right now, don't you?"

"Yes," she begged.

"Puts me at a distinct advantage."

"What do you want?" At this moment, she'd promise him anything.

"Nothing now, but remember, you owe me a favor. A big one."

When she agreed, he stroked his bulbous head along her slit, then plunged deep without warning. Her cry was a strangled gasp of shock and pleasure. Writhing below him, she begged him to thrust hard, fast, deep, but he kept to a slow pace that drove her out of her mind.

"We aren't even close to being done yet."

Sterlave slid two fingers deep into her ass, working them at the same pace as his hips. Over and over he plunged into her, wringing louder grunts of animalistic pleasure from her burning lungs. She had wanted to reduce Enovese to a caterwauling *yondie* but found she had only done so to herself.

"That's it, Kasmiri. Let everyone out there, especially your precious Chur, know what an insatiable *yondie* you are. I want him to hear you. I want him to fuck his quiet little bondmate tonight and try to wrench these same sounds from her."

Picturing Chur pounding his cock into such a slender crea-

ture while she scratched his back and growled in heat pushed
Kasmiri over the edge. Her orgasm clamped her body around
Sterlave's, capturing him, squeezing him so hard he withdrew
with a gasp of pain.

Spent, they lay in a tangle until her heartbeat returned to
normal.

"What came over you?" Sterlave rolled to his back and
propped himself up on one bent arm. She noticed his cock was
still hard and shiny with her juice. She had climaxed, he had not.

"*Illias.*"

"There's another man I have to worry about?"

Exhausted and in no mood to face a room full of people who
simply had to have heard what just happened, she yanked her
skirt down. "It's a drink, you fool. Don't you know anything
but how to fight and fuck?" Now that her needs had been met,
she sought to distance herself from him. She untangled herself
and moved to the mirror. What a disaster!

Rather than flare to anger at her comment, Sterlave flashed a
lazy, sexy grin. "You didn't seem to mind a moment ago."

"However, I'm done now." She wiped the crimson paint off
her breasts, pulled up her dress, and did her best to repair what
little makeup remained on her lips.

Beside her, Sterlave washed his hands, and said, "Maybe I'm
not."

Putting her dress to rights, she ignored him, but when she
glanced up, Sterlave stood blocking the door. "Move aside. We
have hundreds of guests and we've been away long enough."

His chuckle was low, vibrating along her nerves. "You mean
all those people who just heard you? I don't think they will
care if we spend a few more moments in here."

Exasperated, she put her hands on her hips. "What do you
want?"

He looked at the plush carpet before his feet, then touched
the edge of her mouth.

Quickly surmising his intent, she withdrew. "No."

He mimicked her pout, which caused her to giggle.

"Come on, Kasmiri, I gave you what you wanted. Can't you give me something in return?" Dark eyes considered her, gauging her reaction.

Lifting her face in contemplation, she finally smiled. "Fine, but I no longer owe you a favor."

Playfully, he scowled his face into a look of deep concentration. "Well, I hate to lose that so quickly, but if you insist."

As gracefully as she could, she lowered herself to her knees before him. When she looked up, his gaze was bright as he watched her lift his cock to her lips. Tasting herself on him revitalized the lust she thought spent. Their combined scents excited her all over again. Following Rown's careful instructions, she traced her tongue along his shaft, then pulled the swollen head into her mouth. Her gaze flew to his when he growled and cupped the back of her head.

She wanted to remind him not to mess up her hair, but what did it matter now? Everyone already knew and so what? She had heard far more outrageous tales about her grandmother. If her mother had any complaints, Kasmiri could think of a nice tight place for her to put her concerns.

Rocking his hips with easy grace, Sterlave kept his gaze pinned to hers as he worked the buttons of his shirt open. He slid the fabric off his shoulders so that he now leaned against the door nude. Sweat glistened along every muscle in his chest, beads caught in the line of stubble that fell to his belly button.

As she took him deeper into her mouth, he trailed his hands along his chest, then twisted his nipples hard when she took him all the way to the back of her throat. His growl filled the tiny room, bouncing off the basins, surging another thrill from her lips to her clit. His satisfaction aroused her more than she'd ever thought possible. Why she cared, she couldn't fathom, but his pleasure was the most intoxicating substance she had ever known.

Pulsing and thick, his cock became too much for her to take so deeply. Kasmiri used her hands to mimic the feel of her throat just as Rown had instructed.

"Do you know how many times I've imagined you on your knees sucking my cock?"

Kasmiri pulled back, nipped the tip, and then slid her lips down. She could picture him in his training room cell, under a threadbare blanket, surrounded by other recruits as he quietly masturbated while thinking of her. When she imagined all the recruits stroking their cocks while picturing her sucking them, her clit quivered, demanding attention.

She tried to get her hand under her dress but the skirt was far too tight and she couldn't maneuver while on her knees.

When she glanced up, Sterlave smiled. "Are you all sticky and hot again?"

Unable to answer with his prick in her mouth, she glared at him.

His laugh aroused and annoyed her simultaneously. One way or another, she vowed to make him pay. All the erotic gifts scrolled through her mind. Something in there would suffice for her plans. Perhaps she would use the smooth phallus on him, since she doubted she would get the chance to use it on Enovese.

"I would have you stop, but you are far too talented. With your lush, full lips and your flashing eyes, I'm not sure what's hotter—watching you or feeling you suck my cock." He leaned back on the door, cupping her chin and tracing her lips. "Such fire in your gaze. You're thinking of all the ways you can punish me, aren't you?"

She managed a nod by sliding him in and out of her mouth.

"Oh," he groaned, "do that again."

She did but added a light scrape of her teeth along the shaft, which elicited a deeper and longer "Oh" of pleasure.

A change in the pattern of his breathing alerted her that he was very close to climax. Working her mouth and hands in stronger strokes, much harder than she once thought correct thanks to Rown's training, she felt his body strain forward, rigid, waiting, needing just a bit more to reach the summit.

Cupping his balls, she stroked the sensitive flesh between them and his ass, teasing her fingertip to the tight pucker. As much as she wanted to slide her finger inside, her nails were far too long, but she could tickle the entrance without harm.

He dissolved into guttural moans and vulgar words that further titillated her. She desperately wanted to taste him, so she sucked hard while vibrating her tongue against the most sensitive spot where the shaft met the head. All of his satisfaction surged into her mouth, splashing against her throat, slaking her hunger with his powerful contentment.

Panting, Sterlave glanced down and said, "I guess now we're even."

Licking her lips, she said, "Oh, no, we're not."

8

Kasmiri rose like the future empress she was. Smoothing down her dress, she returned to the mirror while he leaned exhausted and spent against the doorway. He was grateful it opened in and not out, or he would have crashed through it during his climax. That would have been a most unforgettable sight for their guests. If any of them stood near, they would have heard his hips banging into the door as Kasmiri worked her magic.

What a talented mouth his bondmate possessed. Her technique rivaled Rown's, but perhaps it was just he found the visual of her far more appealing. Her eyes vacillated between pleasure and fury, and all the emotions in-between. Changing as quickly as the sky during spring, he never knew one moment to the next what her reaction would be. That alone excited him beyond rational thought. At any moment, she could have clamped her teeth together, emasculating him with one bite, but he knew she wouldn't, because despite her protests, she found great satisfaction with him.

At first, he worried her sudden attack of lust was directly attributable to Chur. Sterlave had never heard of *illias*, but he would ensure an adequate supply if it had this effect on Kasmiri. Under the influence, she was wild, crazed, and unable to get enough of his fingers and cock. In her need, she would have promised him anything. If only he could inspire that yearning in her without the aid of an aphrodisiac.

As he pulled on his clothing, Kasmiri struggled with her complicated hairdo. "Here, let me."

She arched a brow at his reflection. "You wish to be my humble servant?"

"For the moment, yes." He moved behind her and smoothed the wayward strands into place. Her normally soft hair was stiff from some type of styling glue. By moistening his fingertips, he managed to recreate her servant's work. "There."

He finished dressing as she turned her head this way and that. While pulling on his boots, he found her torn panties and slipped them inside. A nice souvenir he could add to his meager possessions.

Satisfied with her appearance, she caught his reflection, and said, "Thank you."

"You are very welcome, my beautiful mate."

Her brows rose and fell as she smiled. "I'm not sure how beautiful I am at the moment. My makeup is smeared, my dress is wrinkled, and my panties are—" she glanced around— "gone." She sighed. "I look—"

"Like a thoroughly satisfied woman." He stood and wrapped his arms around her, placing a kiss to her earlobe. "Look at the sparkle in your eyes, the color on your cheeks, the way you can't help but smile."

For a moment, she considered her reflection as if seeing herself for the first time. Then her gaze moved to him.

"Speaking of color, you still have some on your mouth." Kasmiri wetted a small towel, then carefully wiped her crimson paint from his face.

Capturing her hand, he tossed the towel aside and kissed her palm. "Any regrets?"

"None at all." A genuine smile tilted her lips and lifted the edges of her eyes. "Let us go and receive our guests." Kasmiri floated to the door and flung it open with her head held high and her shoulders square. A flush of admiration for her spirit touched that hopeful place in his heart. Time and time again she amazed him. She didn't seem to realize just how strong she really was.

Following behind, he felt almost every gaze turn their way, but the glances they received were not condemning or even amused, they simply acknowledged their return.

Sterlave's gaze roamed through the crowd but settled on Chur, who pressed his lips together in a barely suppressed smile, then nodded as if congratulating him. However, Chur was all the way across the room. How had he heard them? Or perhaps Chur surmised the obvious. Sterlave nodded back and then followed Kasmiri to their table on the raised dais.

Sterlave hadn't had much time to talk with Chur before Kasmiri dragged him away, but the change in him was obvious. Even from this distance, Chur glowed with golden light. His facial scar had disappeared, and his eyes, always intense, were now almost frighteningly so. When Sterlave asked after this amazing transformation, Chur said that his relationship with Enovese was responsible.

"Why do you insist on staring at that woman?" Kasmiri's voice was low but sharper than the sword on his hip.

Rather than confess he had been staring at Chur, he simply said, "I am curious. You spoke with her, what is she like?"

Kasmiri rolled her eyes dismissively. "She's deranged."

Below her snide comment, Sterlave sensed fear, but he decided not to push the issue. He made a point not to look in their direction again. Besides, he'd have plenty of time to consider Chur later.

Once Clathia took her place beside her daughter, the babble settled down and all lifted their glasses for a toast. Sterlave lost count after the fifth course and became sluggish from too much food, too much drink, and the wonderful satisfaction from Kasmiri's delightful mouth.

Throughout the meal, several guests offered personal toasts of congratulations. They often referred to people and events Sterlave had no knowledge of, but he enjoyed the lighthearted nature of the tales. Kasmiri sparkled. Where he'd only seen her putting on airs with people, tonight, her smile was genuine.

Even her mother noticed the change because she made a comment to Kasmiri that Sterlave overheard. For the first time since their bonding ceremony, he began to feel that they could become a strong couple. If Kasmiri gave a little, and so did he, they would find the common ground between them.

Dancing followed the meal, but Sterlave knew only the dances of his village. Kasmiri acquiesced even though it was clear she wanted to dance. Her eyes followed Chur, who moved with a masculine grace that surpassed any man in the room. Sterlave wanted to roll his eyes like Kasmiri—wasn't there anything the man was bad at? Why couldn't he be a bumbling oaf with no grace at all? Sterlave didn't want to feel such resentment toward his friend, especially when his friend did not encourage Kasmiri's infatuation, but it was difficult not to. Sterlave thought that since Kasmiri had met Chur's bondmate, her obsession would fade away.

"Would you teach me a dance?" Sterlave asked, leaning near.

Delight sparkled in her gaze. "We'll do a slow one with only three steps." Under the table, she showed him the steps, then they moved to the center of the room.

At first, he felt stiff and awkward since this style of dance was more rigid than his tribe's style, but Kasmiri exercised great patience. Even though he messed up and almost stepped on her feet twice, she simply laughed it off. He was self-conscious until he realized everyone else was too engrossed in his or her own partner to worry after him.

Kasmiri floated in his arms. So light on her feet, she drifted over the floor with elegance despite the confining dress. For the first time in ages, Sterlave enjoyed himself. While they danced, they exchanged lusty comments about their tryst in the basin room and what they planned to do to each other later. She had a decidedly perverse mind where sex was concerned. Her suggestions caused his *echalle* to press wickedly against his pants and he wondered just who was teaching whom.

Several men approached to dance with Kasmiri and he agreed since they could actually do the more complicated steps. He moved to the edge of the room to watch.

"She is quite graceful."

Sterlave turned and discovered Enovese by his side. "Far more graceful than I."

Enovese laughed. "I didn't know how to dance until Chur taught me. Look, together they move as if gliding on ice."

Chilled, he turned to find Chur and Kasmiri twirling about the floor as if made for each other. His erection deflated. How could he compete with him? When he glanced at Enovese, there was no jealousy in her eyes. She seemed pleased to observe her mate dancing so well with another woman.

"Kasmiri was once interested in Chur." It was a cruel thing to say and he had no idea why he did.

"This I know." Unshakable confidence emanated from her.

"Aren't you the least bit concerned?" He found her entire demeanor odd. She didn't fiddle or seek out a drink to hold or to give her hands something to do. Enovese stood statue-still but relaxed, and observed, as if she'd never been in a room full of people before. He found himself wondering who she was and where she had come from.

"I have nothing to fear from Kasmiri. You have nothing to fear from Chur." Her lyrical voice brooked no argument.

"Would you like to dance with me?"

Enovese gave him a sidelong glance. "I said I have nothing to fear from Kasmiri, not you."

"I like to play with fire."

When he offered out his hand, she accepted. Enovese kept to simple steps in deference to him, and he found himself utterly enchanted. A blissful energy flowed from her in such strong waves he felt touched by her pure essence. Her hair caught and reflected the light, so long and silky he couldn't help but touch it every chance he got. She didn't seem to mind and even laughed playfully when several strands tangled in the hilt of his sword. They stopped at the edge of the dancing area to remove them.

"How dare you touch my consort!" Kasmiri's screech rang across the room, causing all of the dancers to stop and stare.

When Sterlave looked over, he realized that from her vantage point it appeared Enovese was touching his bulge, not his blade. A flush of embarrassment slowly turned his entire face red. The attention transported him back to his village, and the time when Laarad caught him stealing bread. Laarad had pinched his ear and paraded him through the streets, bellowing to all that they had a thief in their midst. Desperate hunger had driven Sterlave to swipe the food, but he'd gone hungry afterward rather than suffer such shame again. Yet here he was. Kasmiri wasn't holding his ear, but she made sure everyone noticed him for his bad behavior.

Enovese chuckled. "You said you liked to play with fire." She deftly removed the remaining strands. By the time Kasmiri got to them, Enovese had stepped back with cool aplomb.

"I don't care who or what you are—don't you ever touch my consort again or I'll have you put to death!" Kasmiri's eyes were silted and her mouth a slash in her furious face. Her body shook with rage while her hands clenched.

Enovese tilted her nose and shrugged, as if daring Kasmiri to follow through with the threat.

Kasmiri turned her vitriol onto him. "And you! How dare you allow another woman access to what is rightfully mine, and during our bonding celebration no less? I should have you placed under the stone for your insolence."

Hot shame, similar to what he felt back in his village under the vicious tongues of the tribe, caused Sterlave to grit his teeth. He wanted to yell back in her face that she did not own him, but he couldn't open his mouth. He was too mortified to move or speak. In a flash, he wasn't a man but a very young boy. Every eye fell on him. He felt them weighing him, measuring him, laughing at him, and ultimately rejecting him. He wanted the floor to open and swallow him whole.

"I will not be ridiculed because of your actions. I knew you were too low class to become my bondmate and now I have the proof of it!" Her powerful voice flung the words at him like stones against naked flesh.

Guests drifted away, flashing him sympathetic looks that only compounded his humiliation. He couldn't even brave a glance at Chur or Enovese. He kept his attention on the far wall, waiting for the siege to end. Kasmiri's rant went on and on until she finally ran out of insults. She had done the exact same thing to Rown. No matter what happened between them, she would always look upon him as a servant. Whatever hope he had for them she just crushed under the weight of her nasty tongue.

After an interminable time, he found his voice, and asked, "Are you finished?" His stomach roiled with barely suppressed rage. Never in his life had he more wanted to run and hide himself away. Tonight their guests had seen the high and low of their relationship, and if Kasmiri worried about wagging tongues, she had only herself to blame. "Enovese's hair became entangled in the hilt of my sword. She was only trying to untangle the strands."

Kasmiri darted her gaze from his blade to Enovese's hair. Snidely, she said, "Perhaps she should cut her hair. What are you, a *paratanist* who is forbidden to cut—" Kasmiri's eyes went wide and her mouth dropped into a perfect little O. "That's what you are! That's why your hair is ridiculously long and you have no manners—you are a *paratanist!*" Revulsion caused Kasmiri to back away. "You chose a servant over me?!" Now her fury fell on Chur, who took the same implacable stance as his mate.

"I never would have selected you, Kasmiri," Chur said, his voice low but firm. "You are not for me."

She took his words as if a blow, turning her face away with a wince. "I do not wish to see either of you again. I want you gone from the palace by daybreak."

"You should speak with your mother about that." Chur nodded to Clathia at the high table, then took Enovese's hand. Arm in arm, they left the room with an easy matched stride.

Again, Sterlave envied Chur his effortless manner with his mate. Why couldn't he and Kasmiri capture that accepting comportment? He despaired that they would always be at crossroads. At this moment, he didn't want to be in the same room as Kasmiri, let alone grasp her arm and share the same personal space. Sterlave also marveled at the revelation. He'd only had a *paratanist* for a brief time, but the rules regarding them were clear: They spoke only when spoken to and were not to be touched by anyone, not even the Harvester. How had Chur braved the restrictions and lifted her hood to discover what lay below? Sterlave suddenly wondered what his *paratanist* had looked like. Not that it mattered. He was so enamored with Kasmiri he doubted any woman would have changed his mind. Even her childish behavior tonight had not lessened his attraction to her. In spite of her mature carriage, Kasmiri was still very young, impetuous, and had a thousand pressures from her duty hanging over her head. He wasn't ready to forgive her, but he thought he understood her behavior.

When Sterlave examined the room, he discovered only he,

Kasmiri, and her mother remained amid the confetti, empty glasses, and general party clutter.

Clathia sat at the high table; her countenance weary and her shoulders slumped. She had aged ten seasons in one evening. Beautiful in a severe way, Clathia had clearly bestowed her exotic exquisiteness upon Kasmiri, but now, Clathia seemed less than an exalted empress and more like an exhausted mother.

"You have not the right to dismiss them, my daughter. Come, there are things we must discuss. You may return to your rooms, Sterlave."

One final humiliation—dismissed by her mother like an annoying servant.

"Kasmiri will join you when we are finished."

Kasmiri trembled, not with fury but fear. Something in her mother's voice sucked all the fight from her. Under her breath, he heard Kasmiri mumble something about her duty, but she attended her mother with the deference of a well-trained child while he dutifully returned to their rooms.

Sterlave fell asleep waiting for Kasmiri. When she entered, she made no effort to be quiet. She stomped about, flinging off her shoes, her dress, and ripping the decorations from her hair. One hit the mirror, shattering it into a thousand shards.

A sleepy Rown entered, his black hair twisted from sleep, but she dismissed him with a wave of her hand. Before he left, Rown shot a glance toward the bed, saw the lump Sterlave made, then exited with a perplexed frown. Sterlave felt for him; he knew exactly what it was like to have Kasmiri dismiss him with such callous disregard.

Obviously the talk with her mother had not gone well. Sterlave stayed in bed and watched her destroy several items in a childish display of temper.

Burying her face in her hands, Kasmiri finally stopped her rampage. Her shoulders trembled as she fought back tears.

A part of him wanted to slip from the bed to embrace her,

but his anger still simmered unchecked. He wanted an apology. Vowing to ignore her until she asked for his forgiveness, he snuggled into bed.

Water splashed in the bathing unit for a long time and he thought she used it to mask her sobs. No matter how many times he felt the urge to go and comfort her, he resisted. Kasmiri had to learn her actions had repercussions. If he allowed her to treat him like a servant, she would continue to do so.

Eventually she slipped into bed beside him. She tossed and turned, sighing loudly, but he did not respond. Keeping carefully to his side of the bed, he feigned sleep, but her fresh, clean scent aroused him. Unfortunately, his cock didn't know how to teach someone a lesson with denial. However, he was in control, not his lust. If the training rooms taught him anything, self-denial would top the list.

A tentative touch to his shoulder twitched his penis.

Softly, Kasmiri whispered, "I want you."

"I want you too," he admitted.

She snuggled up, pressing her generous breasts against his back. Hardened nipples teased him and suddenly he wanted to relent, but he forcefully nudged her off.

Uttering an annoyed breath, she asked, "Why are you pushing me away?"

"You hurt me tonight." He almost choked on the words. Hurt didn't remotely encompass the shame and humiliation he suffered due to her jealousy.

"You were flirting with that woman." Her sultry voice swerved swiftly to condemnation, as if he'd asked for her abuse.

"Her name is Enovese, and I was not flirting with her. I only danced with her as you did with Chur." That was the heart of the matter; he was supposed to trust her with Chur, but Kasmiri refused to trust him with any woman but herself. He had to expose her double standard now or it would never end.

"I am the future empress. I will do as I please." With that

edict, she rolled over to the far side of the bed, taking most of the covers with her.

For a long moment, Sterlave considered continuing to play this childish game. He wanted her. His entire body raged for him to roll over, grab her, pin her hands to the bed, and take her as forcefully as he had in the basin room. If he tormented her long enough, denying her fulfillment, she would apologize with breathless sincerity. However, he did not trust her word in such a moment of passion. He needed her to express regret of her own free will, not because he'd beleaguered it out of her.

Ignoring his stiff prick, he burrowed into his pillow, and said, "You may be the future empress, but you still need me to fill your belly with a child. Let me know when you are ready to ask for my forgiveness."

Kasmiri sat up, yanking all the covers off him. "You expect me to exonerate you for your impertinence?"

Since the ceiling was open, cold harvest air prickled his skin. His cell in the training rooms was stark but not this cold. When he next saw Rown, he would ask him how to close the damn ceiling. Shivering, he sat up and placed the puffy pillow over his genitals.

"I expect you to apologize for the wrong you did to me." As a youth, he'd never been in a position to demand such, but he would be damned if he would let Kasmiri treat him like her servant.

Kasmiri leaned close, her breath hot against his freezing skin. "I own you. Dare you defy me and I will have you bound so I can take from you what I need." Even in the shadows, her eyes glistened with appalling determination.

Pouncing upon her, grasping her hands and forcing her to lie flat below him, Sterlave said, "You do not own me. If I have to, I will milk myself every hour until there is nothing left for your dark harvest."

Gasping, shocked by his dominant position, Kasmiri struggled, pushing at his arms with ineffectual power. His sheer size and weight afforded him control.

"You may be the future empress, but I will not allow you to force me to your ends. Do you hear me?" He wasn't a frightened boy anymore. He'd struggled and suffered, and now he demanded respect.

"Get off me!" Panic spun her voice to a harsh edge of alarm. Below him, she fought, twisting and turning her body against his.

"Struggle, Kasmiri, and you'll only excite me more." He planted his mouth to hers, forcing his tongue between her pressed lips. "Isn't this what you want?" Trapped below the covers, he thrust against her forcefully splayed thighs with sinful intent. "I'm your stud servant, am I not?"

"How dare you?!" Kasmiri fought him vigorously, but she could do little against his strong body.

"I dare because I will not succumb to your allure or allow you to force me. You will say you are sorry or we will never have sex again." He couldn't believe he'd threatened her so grandly, but he intended to keep his word, even if it drove him mad. She did not own him and she could not treat him shabbily. He refused to let her get away with her bad behavior.

He rolled off her and the bed. Shivering, he grabbed the dressing robe from the floor and several fur rugs. A long couch against the far wall would be a perfect temporary bed until Kasmiri realized he would not relent.

9

Kasmiri sat alone in her bed and considered calling the guards. She quickly dismissed the idea. Once they entered, what would she order them to do: bind Sterlave to her bed so she could have her way with him? It was bad enough her behavior tonight had embarrassed her family name for generations to come. She certainly didn't need people thinking she had to force her consort to have sex with her.

All she had to do was apologize. Once she did, Sterlave would happily share her bed again. Even though she knew he was right, that she had hurt him terribly tonight, she couldn't swallow her pride and say she was sorry. If it came down to a battle over which one could go the longest without contact, she was certain he would give in first.

"I'm not going to apologize," she called out.

"Fine. I hope you enjoy sleeping alone." Sterlave turned his back on her.

"I'll have Rown tie you down." Even as she said it, she knew it was a ridiculous idea. Sterlave could hold off Rown with one mighty arm.

Sterlave laughed. "You'll have to drug me first. If you want to have children with three eyes and horns, go ahead and pump me full of chemicals."

Kasmiri gripped the covers in a crushing fist. He was right. Drugs were not the best idea, and force would only get her so far. A sudden smile lifted her face. She didn't need force. What she needed was exactly what she had—a lush, desirable body. Curling to her side, she thought of all the ways she could tempt him. In a quarter cycle, he would be drooling at her feet.

When she put her mind to it, she could charm any man. A slight frown crossed her face. *Any man except Chur,* her mind whispered. He obviously had bizarre notions of female beauty since he chose a *paratanist* as a bondmate. What normal man would want to swear himself eternally to a servant? Absurd! She almost laughed as she pictured herself bonding to Rown.

Enovese might be beautiful but once everyone knew she was an untouchable servant of the lowest class, they would shun her and, in turn, eschew Chur. Kasmiri's mother told her she could not insist they leave, but Kasmiri would make their life in the palace so unpleasant they would gladly leave on their own.

Despite her mother's warning, Kasmiri did not need their help. An empress ruled alone. Doubt crept in because her weary mother had suddenly grown animated with fury, and bellowed, "You are going to befriend them both! You don't understand what changes their relationship brings!"

Kasmiri nodded, trying to soothe her mother, but when Clathia started spouting twaddle from the Harvest prophecy, Kasmiri turned a deaf ear. It took all her will not to roll her eyes. She did not want to hear any more of that nonsense. Time after time, her mother bent her to her will by quoting the prophecy and filling her head with doom and superstition.

Kasmiri was a bonded woman now, too old for such tales. Enovese and Chur were like any other couple. As to the re-markable transformation of Chur, Kasmiri had no idea, but she simply didn't believe the gods themselves had turned him into a demigod. She didn't accept the explanation because she didn't believe in the gods. All her life she'd performed an endless series of rituals to invoke their goodwill and nothing happened. Her mother said it was about faith, but Kasmiri had lost hers long ago. Yes, Chur had changed, but there had to be a logical explanation.

As she thought back on what ruined the evening, she realized she wasn't jealous about Sterlave and Enovese. What infuriated her was that everyone liked Sterlave with an instant ease that she had never possessed.

Tucking the pillow below her head, she tried to hold back tears but couldn't. She had no true friends in the palace. The girls her age never warmed up to her and the men only wanted something from her. No one ever liked her just for her.

Sterlave had inspired a close bond with Chur as evidenced by his warm and welcoming hug. Chur was genuinely glad to see Sterlave, but not her. Within moments, Sterlave had charmed Enovese and Rown. Rown clearly had a crush on him, but he also worried about him. Rown had looked stricken when he thought something had gone wrong with the bonds. She would never forget the terror on his face as he ran to release him.

Not once has anyone been that concerned for me. No longer could she convince herself that the women were all jealous of her riches or her station. Rown served her with implacable skills, but when she railed at him, he cringed and hung his head for days, unwilling to meet her gaze. Even her consort had easily turned away from her. As much as she wanted to place the blame outside herself, she had to face the facts. People didn't like her because of her behavior.

Tears of self-pity moistened the pillow so she turned it around to find a dry spot. How did Sterlave inspire such instant camaraderie? If she imitated him, she might be able to break free from her isolation. The thought was both exhilarating and terrifying. What if she failed? She would be exposing her heart to tremendous pain. But what if she succeeded? She would have friends with whom she could share her joys, her pains, and her regrets.

With a sigh, she realized if she wanted to change, she would have to start with Chur and Enovese. If she could befriend them, she could befriend anyone. Just the thought of being kind to that woman caused her to clench her jaw. Maybe she should start closer to home. Rather than seducing Sterlave, perhaps she could try being nice to him.

He'll laugh in your face, her mind whispered. *He doesn't want to be your friend; he wants to use you for his pleasure.*

Kasmiri shook the voice away. Sterlave was not a heartless monster. How could he be when everyone simply adored him? Even her mother remarked on his congenial regard and how attentive he was to Kasmiri during the celebration. If he could charm her mother, he could charm anyone. Even herself, because she realized she didn't want to be at odds with him.

"Sterlave?" Her voice sounded terribly loud in the darkness.

He didn't move. When she listened, she heard soft snoring. Seemed her plans would have to wait for morning. Sleep came easily once she decided tomorrow would be her first day of change.

Freezing air and pale morning light woke her. Shivering, she left her bed, pulled on her robe, and closed the ceiling. Rown entered with another platter of food for the table.

"How are you this morning?" she asked with a bright smile.

Rown glanced around, realized she was speaking to him, flashed her a dubious smile, and said, "I am fine, my mistress."

It wasn't quite the response she wanted, but people were not going to accept her new attitude overnight. When she glanced at the couch, she found a tumble of furs but no Sterlave. She didn't hear water splashing in the bathing unit or see him anywhere within her rooms.

"Where has Sterlave gone?" When Rown flinched at her demanding tone, she softened her voice. "I'm not angry, I'm just curious."

"He did not say, but he took two *niclas* with him."

"Thank you."

Rown bowed and left.

Kasmiri settled at the table to review her schedule and eat. As she scrolled down the items, she slumped. A glut of celebrations and endless meetings met her eyes. Her brief reprieve from her hectic schedule was over and demands upon her time re-emerged like a festering wound. Often she spent two or three days with little sleep, less food, and no exercise.

An emergency summons flashed. Her mother needed her now.

As much as she wanted to track Sterlave down and apologize, she didn't have time. She ate quickly, cleaned up, dressed in a simple wrap-around dress, applied minimal makeup, and secured her hair with a clip at the back of her neck.

Rushing through the maze of hallways, she entered her mother's suite and skidded to a halt.

On a couch in the main room, clad in her *galbol* climbing outfit, her mother lay motionless. No breath lifted her chest. Her eyes were open, sightlessly centered on the ceiling.

Dread held her back, but a perverse curiosity drew Kasmiri closer. She noticed a huge gash in her mother's stomach. Once she blinked back tears of horror, she noticed flakes of gray, knotty bark outlined the hole. Kasmiri knew at once that she'd fallen on one of the sharp branches of a *galbol* tree.

Had they found her dangling, so damaged they didn't bother to start emergency procedures because nothing they could do would help her? No medical equipment surrounded her, but they had removed her safety gear.

Climbing the soaring trees was her mother's favorite sport. She said obtaining the top of the trees, which often took three days or more, was like taking flight over the world.

Kasmiri often joked she could get the same effect by flying in her Golden Bird, but her mother said the sensation was not the same. Once she broke through the thickly netted tops, she could feel the wind in her hair and the sun on her face. She said slinging herself between branches to sleep, and eating only what she could carry in a small pack upon her back, made her feel more alive than anything else in the world.

Kasmiri had never told her, but she admired her mother's adventurous spirit. Only once had Kasmiri joined her on a climb. The base of the tree was enormous, as big as her rooms five times over, and spindly branches stuck out like spikes, growing larger as they went up the trunk. Kasmiri had started with grand hopes but the height terrified her, causing her breathing to accelerate, and her palms to sweat so profusely she couldn't hang on to the branches. It took three bulky guards to help her back to the ground.

Several advisors warned of the danger, but her mother dismissed them with an annoyed wave of her hand. Kasmiri hadn't climbed since she was a girl, but she knew her mother never climbed without her safety harness.

"Did you remove her gear?" Kasmiri asked the air because she couldn't take her eyes off her mother's broken form. How could someone so vital be suddenly so still?

One of the health professionals cleared her throat. "She had no harness on."

Kasmiri lifted her gaze and considered the slender woman. Glossy red hair curled around her face, highlighting clear gray eyes that were studious yet compassionate.

"My mother never climbed without taking precautions." Anger built inside, churning her belly, turning what little food rested there to stone. "Someone removed it and I want to know who."

Blank faces met her furious gaze. Finally, the woman with the kind eyes spoke. "There is some indication her fall wasn't an accident."

Kasmiri rounded on her. "Of course it was an accident! My mother would not have injured herself!" Such a suggestion was ludicrous. Her mother was strong. Clathia met every problem in life with fierce determination.

Calmly, the woman met her gaze and straightened her shoulders. "Your mother was facing an incurable disease that would have slowly ravaged her system until it reduced her to a shell of her former glorious self."

Her mother was ill? Kasmiri had no idea. Was that why her mother had been so anxious to see her bonded so that the family line was secure? All her desperate actions suddenly made perfect sense. Regret for her horrible behavior threatened to drop her to her knees and beg her lifeless mother for forgiveness. Had she known of her mother's struggle, she would have been more kind. Now it was too late.

"Perhaps now is not the time to discuss this," said a short, thin man with a sparse sprinkling of brown hair.

Kasmiri followed his gaze to the entryway.

The magistrate, Ambo Votny, waddled into the room. Huffing and puffing, he too stopped dead when he saw Clathia. "What has happened?" His already bulbous eyes bulged further as his skin washed pale against his silver uniform. He approached the body with surprisingly delicate steps. "Oh, Clathia, I told you climbing those trees was dangerous."

"My mother is dead yet you stand there and berate her on her way to *Jarasine*?" Kasmiri slapped his face. Row after row of blubbery chins shook from the blow.

Ambo clutched his cheek. His eyes narrowed to slits and his

upper lip twitched. "You round on me when you tormented her every step?"

Outraged by his accusation but more so by the truth behind it, Kasmiri launched herself at him. She'd only managed two slaps and a kick before the guards pulled her away. Still, she struggled, slapping, kicking, and screaming. Despair and rage battled within, causing tears to stream down her face, but her body would not rest. She wanted to destroy. To rail at the sky. To collapse into a heap, then hide under her mother's empress cape.

Her desire for change had come too late to include her mother. All the hateful, harmful, destructive things she'd ever said or done to her mother filled her mind in a montage of ugliness.

"Calm yourself, Kasmiri." Ambo straightened his stained and wrinkled trousers with trembling fingers. "An empress must comport herself with dignity and grace at all times."

Shock drained everything from her mind. "I am now the empress?" She had always known this day would come, but not this soon. She imagined her mother would be on the throne until her hair turned white and grandchildren played at her feet. Now, Clathia would never see even one grandchild. Oh gods, if she did not have a girl child within two seasons, the challenges from the other houses would begin in earnest.

Kasmiri wanted to run. She wanted to find Sterlave, beg his forgiveness, and then swiftly lose herself in his passionate embrace. Let the world pass her by as she wallowed in ecstasy. Duty and responsibly had always dragged her steps, but now they caught her firmly in their unrelenting grips.

"We must perform the coronation ceremony at once." Ambo issued instructions to his servant, a whey-faced young man with thick white hair and mismatched eyes. Once the boy understood, he scampered off.

"We have not even performed the rites of passage for my mother."

Ambo nodded, compassion softening his tone. "I am sorry,

Kasmiri, but your first act as empress will be to oversee that most tragic ritual."

Sterlave stepped into the training rooms. When he took a deep breath, he smelled sweat, leather, and a slight tang of blood. He smiled. The essence of the room was as familiar to him as his own skin. He'd only been gone for a few days but it seemed a lifetime. His body begged for exercise.

The elevated square platform, where he had challenged Chur for the right of Harvester and lost, was gone. A few battered mats for barehanded wrestling took up the space.

Involuntary, Sterlave shivered. If not for the gods' intervention, he would have died that night. He still didn't understand why he survived. However, questioning a gift from the gods was never wise.

A handful of recruits surrounded Chur as he divvied them up into pairs for the first round of mock battle. Chur's eyes lit up when he saw Sterlave in the doorway. He nodded, finished with the recruits, and then joined him by the mats.

"I am glad you came." Chur centered himself on one of the mats, then began the fluid moves of *kintana*.

Distracted by his power and grace, Sterlave stood still and watched. Chur executed every move with perfect precision. Thick muscles flowed around strong bones. His bronze skin glowed golden. Rapt with concentration, he still made everything look easy. Before the change, Chur had always been skilled, but now he was superior. Sterlave experienced an overwhelming urge to touch him, not in a sexual way but . . . if he touched him, some of his magical power might rub off.

"Are you going to watch me all day or actually get to work yourself?" Chur's direct gaze delved right into his mind.

Embarrassed, Sterlave set the two *niclas* aside and settled himself a distance from Chur. By comparison, he was clumsy and stiff. Rather than flowing from one move to the next, he more stumbled into them. Of course, *kintana* had never been his greatest skill, but still, he knew he could do better than this childlike display.

"Relax, it's not a competition. *Kintana* should center your mind and body for battle, not be a battle." Chur teased him without missing a move.

Sterlave laughed and took several calming breaths. Rather than worry over what Chur was doing, he kept his attention on his own exercise. Within moments, he relaxed, found his center, then let the power inherent within direct his form without.

"Now that you've relaxed, I have a proposition for you." Chur placed one arm forward and one back as he bent one knee.

"What's that?" Sterlave finished the arm sweep of his *pivsnosta,* then began the next set of motions.

"I want you here with me."

Sterlave stumbled but caught himself. Chur didn't mean what his brain interpreted. He blamed Kasmiri for putting these strange thoughts into his head in the first place. He'd never thought about Chur in that manner before she suggested it, but now he couldn't seem to stop.

"So, you want me here doing what?" Sterlave cast him a dubious glance, wondering if Chur's new powers included mind reading.

Chur lost his pose and doubled over with laughter. "I can't read your mind, but you're making your thoughts obvious by the way you're looking at me." Lowering his voice to a whisper, he added, "Even the daughters of the elite don't look at me with that much interest."

"Sorry." Sterlave kept his gaze on the far wall. "It's difficult not to. I mean, all your scars are gone and you're literally glowing. It's impossible not to stare and, well, wonder things."

"You're not the only one." Chur lifted his chin at a few recruits, who quickly looked away. He sighed and resumed his pose. "There are days where I want to shroud myself in a robe."

"Then they would only stare at you more."

"Probably." Chur laughed. "Anyway, I want you here with me because I want you to be a handler. I want you to help me train the recruits."

"What about Helton Ook?"

"I dismissed him because of his obvious conflict of interest. A handler puts the recruits first, not his own agenda."

It was a tremendous offer, but Sterlave was hesitant to accept. "I honestly don't know what Kasmiri has in mind for me." Not that she deserved his consideration today, not after her behavior last night. However, as her consort, he might have other duties. He couldn't make a full commitment until he discussed it with her.

"I understand. I have no idea what a consort does. I mean official-duty–wise." Chur flashed him a wink and a grin. "Some of your obligations are rather obvious."

Sterlave knew he referred to the incident in the basin room last night. "Those are the obligations I enjoy." He couldn't keep a wicked grin off his face. "It's what came after that is rather unpleasant."

Chur ended his session, grabbed the two *niclas,* and then drew Sterlave to a corner with some chairs. "We can speak more freely here." He tossed him one of the red-orange fruits.

Sterlave caught it and bit into the top so he could peel the textured outer shell away.

"You know, in Kasmiri's mind, she was only protecting what she considers hers."

Surprised that Chur defended her behavior, Sterlave said, "But Enovese was not—"

"I know, I know." Chur held up his hand, then continued to peel the fruit. "Kasmiri acts first, then thinks later. To call her impulsive is to call this a thick peel—true, but not as informative as it could be."

Sterlave laughed. "Kasmiri is like a *nicla;* tough on the outside, but sweet on the inside. The problem is that getting to the sweet part is a major challenge."

"Give her time. She's young; but if you work with her, I think you will be happy in the end. Like this fruit, she's worth the hassle."

Frowning, Sterlave considered all Chur had said in a different context. "I don't understand what you're getting at here. Do you think I'm going to walk away from her?" The thought couldn't be further from his mind. He would never abandon Kasmiri. Their tiff last night was simply that, a meaningless power play. They would get over it. He didn't think their road together would ever be smooth, but he wouldn't run away at the first sign of trouble.

Shrugging, Chur shook his head. "I'm not getting at anything. I just worry about you." He took a bite of the red-orange flesh. "I consider you one of the few friends I have around here."

"You seem more concerned about Kasmiri." A surge of jealousy infused his spine. What if he, like Kasmiri, wasn't happy with one mate? What if Chur had designs on getting Kasmiri in addition to the stunning Enovese? Sterlave couldn't compete against him before, and now, after his transformation, it was hopeless. "Are you only softening me up for when you take her away from me?"

Chur's brows lowered. "If I wanted Kasmiri, I would have selected her during the Harvest. Believe me, I do not want her for myself."

"Then what is all of this about?" Sterlave had never possessed any skills in interpreting other people's ulterior motives, which was just one of the reasons he found Kasmiri so inexplicable.

Chur took a deep breath. "Changes are already in motion and

more are coming. Kasmiri needs you more than she will admit, and I will need the both of you to see the changes through."

Before Sterlave could ask what Chur was talking about, a murmur of a thousand voices distracted him. As he listened, the voices grew in volume, yet he couldn't make out what they said.

Chur stood. "They are here."

"Who?"

A servant rushed into the room begging Sterlave to follow.

"Go with him. Kasmiri needs you now."

Baffled, Sterlave followed to the Throne of the Empress. In an anteroom, the servant removed his clothing, then dressed him in ancient warrior gear. In quick succession, the servant secured a gleaming breastplate to his body with animal-hide straps, then added a helmet that covered most of his head but left his face exposed. He placed a series of metal plates along his right arm, wrapped a loincloth with metal strips sewn into the fabric around his hips, then added a decorative belt. Dropping to his knees, the servant laced sandals to his feet, then placed the Sword of the Empress on the belt.

No matter how many questions Sterlave asked, the servant refused to answer. He seemed determined to shove him into the clothing as fast as possible. Frustrated, Sterlave grasped the man by the shoulder and shook him. "Is something wrong with Kasmiri?"

Before the terrified servant could answer, Ambo Votny entered, and snarled, "Calm yourself!"

Sterlave let go of the servant and considered shaking the snot out of Ambo. "What's going on?"

"Empress Clathia is dead."

10

Clad in the heavy empress cape, fashioned of red furs and glittering gems, Kasmiri trudged down the crimson carpet toward the massive Onic throne. A vast audience of elite and dignitaries lined either side of her path. She hardly noticed them. Numb with shock, she didn't even feel the threat of tears anymore. Everything went by in a sickening blur of colors, scents, hallowed words, pedantic ceremonies, and endless reminders of her new and crushing duty.

Within her hand, she held a small golden replica of planet Diola to remind her the future of the Onic Empire was hers alone to bear. Glancing down at her gloved hand, it seemed too small for such a mighty burden.

At the end of the red carpet, she ascended the three steps to the elaborately carved black throne. Four servants maneuvered her cape so that she could sit. No weight came off her shoulders. The looming throne behind her only added to the obligations already pressing in on her.

A blare of processional music drew her gaze to the far end of the room. Sterlave walked toward her with even steps perfectly timed to the drumbeat. His brows were low, his eyes hooded, his mouth a compressed slash. Ancient warrior gear glittered while the Sword of the Empress swayed with each movement of his hips. Like a hunter stalking prey, he never let his focus waver from her face. Glorious, magnificent, undeniably male, he ate up the distance between them.

As he drew close, the concern in his gaze spiked fresh tears to blur her vision. Whatever petty argument they'd had was forgotten in the midst of this raw tragedy.

At the top of the steps he stopped before her, dropped to one knee, clasped her hand that held the miniature Diola, and whispered, "My heart is breaking for you, Kasmiri. Before I swear myself to the entire empire, I feel I must first swear myself to you." He lifted and kissed her closed hand. "I will do everything in my power to protect you, to honor you, to defend you. I will die in service to you."

Thick armor around her heart shattered. She had done nothing to deserve his pledge, but he gave it anyway. For the first time, she knew what it was to feel love, real true love, for another. His sincerity touched her so deeply that whatever fear holding her back all these seasons washed away under a tide of empathy.

Uncaring if she broke protocol or not, Kasmiri leaned forward to embrace him. "I apologize for treating you badly last night." It wasn't exactly what she wanted to say, but that's what popped out of her mouth.

Sterlave pulled back to kiss her lightly. "I forgive you." He rose and moved to his throne. He sat with all the dignity and grace of the highest lord and her admiration for him soared.

Her doubts about his fitness as her bondmate dissolved. She could not envision a better man to rule at her side. Any lingering infatuation for Chur evaporated. Looking toward her future, she saw only Sterlave at her side, in her bed, and in her heart.

After each of them swore themselves to the Onic Empire,

Ambo Votny presented Kasmiri with a gem-encrusted cup. She drank of the bitter syrup and then passed it to Sterlave, who could not fight a grimace after he swallowed. She fought down a burst of inappropriate laughter. She now understood why he inspired such instant warmth from others. Sterlave accepted himself completely and by extension, accepted all others for who they were. He asked little and gave greatly in return.

With the ceremony complete, Kasmiri stood. Her servants removed her cumbersome cape, the golden ball of Diola, and then she straightened her shoulders to perform the most painful ritual of her life.

Step by step she moved across the red carpet, leading Sterlave and then everyone else to the Room of Ceremonies.

Rather than the gay affair of last night, this was a most somber occasion. Crimson fabric shrouded the windows, the tables, and the chairs. Rather than a high table with glittering dishes and flatware, her mother lay upon a bed of white furs clothed in her most elegant crimson gown. Someone had taken great care with her makeup and hair because she looked as if she would rise at any moment and proclaim the entire situation a farce. Kasmiri wished so hard for that to happen, but her beautiful mother remained motionless.

Kasmiri removed one white and one crimson flower from the ornate vases beside the table. The rest of the people stood back so that she could have a moment alone with her mother.

Placing the red bloom to her mother's chest, she murmured, "If only I had one more day with you, I would have told you all the things I never said. Like how much I admired you, how envious I was of your beauty, how your faith and your strength of conviction awed and intimidated me."

Wiping away her tears, she placed the white blossom in her mother's hair. "I will miss you more than I can say, but someday we will meet again in *Jarasine.*"

Never had she believed in an afterlife among the gods, but suddenly, she wanted to believe her mother would reside in the misty land of clouds. Somehow, thinking of her mother over her shoulder lending her strength was immensely comforting. Clathia always said believing in the gods was about faith, and it seemed Kasmiri had suddenly discovered hers.

Tenderly, she stroked her mother's cheek. She wanted to say so much more but couldn't talk around the lump in her throat.

When her knees buckled beneath her, Sterlave's strong arms encompassed her, lifting her up.

"I have you."

His strength infused her body.

With one arm around her waist, he placed a white bloom on her mother's chest. "I thank you for entrusting your daughter to me."

Maneuvering her gently, Sterlave placed her in a chair next to her mother, then sat beside her so together they could receive the wishes of the mourners.

Kind words flowed over Kasmiri like rain. She maintained eye contact and nodded in the appropriate places, but her mind was elsewhere. She remembered a day when she was six seasons old and her mother took her to the exotic animal preserve on Chetapye. What she remembered weren't the strange animals from all over the galaxy, but spending the entire day with her mother. Clathia lavished attention on her and listened to everything she said. They shared whipped frozen treats and her mother didn't even scold her when the purple goo oozed onto her dress.

"I never stopped loving you."

The phrase pulled Kasmiri from her reverie. A part of her thought her mother had whispered the words to her, but no, when she looked over she saw a man leaning over and placing a kiss to Clathia's cheek. Oddly constructed with burly arms and shoulders so muscular they swallowed his neck, Kasmiri couldn't place him. When he approached her, Sterlave greeted him by name.

"Helton." Sterlave nodded politely, a strong note of reserve in his normally warm voice.

"Sterlave." Helton turned his sooty gray eyes her way. "My deepest sympathy, Kasmiri. Your mother was a great leader and a beautiful woman."

"Thank you." Kasmiri waited until he moved away, then asked Sterlave, "Who is he?"

"Helton Ook." Sterlave glared at him. "He was a handler until Chur dismissed him."

Kasmiri thought Sterlave's disgust was borne of having this man brutalize him in the training rooms. When she asked, Sterlave dismissed the idea, and said only that Helton proved himself unworthy of his respect. She didn't have time to ponder a sudden strange thought as too many mourners wished to bestow their best wishes upon her.

Drifting in and out of awareness, Kasmiri thought back to her father. His mysterious death over two seasons ago had come as a shock to not only herself, but also her mother, and all in the land. Vital, boisterous, so full of life, he was almost a force of nature. His sudden silence was deafening. Her mother had loved him despite his notorious liaisons with the wives and daughters of the elite. Clathia forgave him every time.

Kasmiri was not so forgiving. As a young girl, she remembered riding high upon her father's shoulders. He would run and jump, making her giggle until her sides hurt. She also remembered his pranks on Ambo and other members of her mother's circle of advisors. He said they were too serious and needed to laugh more. It seemed her father was always laughing even when he hurt her mother so deeply.

Once she was old enough to understand the dynamics of a relationship, Kasmiri pulled away from her father. She didn't understand why he couldn't be happy with one woman. Many considered Clathia the most beautiful empress ever in the history of the Onic Empire, yet her father often set her aside to pursue women far less attractive. Tall, short, thin, fat, young, old—her father's eye never stopped roving. No matter how many women he had, he always wanted more.

A rush of guilt caused her to close her eyes, for she had been almost relieved when he died. Finally, finally, the harsh rumors would end and her mother could find a man worthy of her devotion. However, Clathia had chosen to remain alone. She took no lovers and refused to consider taking a new consort.

When the inquest turned up evidence of treachery but no suspects, Clathia quietly let the matter drop, but Kasmiri had always wondered who was responsible. Her father was a philanderer, but as the consort to the empress, he should have had justice. Perhaps this man, this Helton Ook, who professed to still love her mother, had a hand in her father's death.

Hours passed as she and Sterlave greeted mourners. They took their words and gave back their own. Kasmiri tried to keep her head up, but too much weighed her down. Sensing her distress, Sterlave stood, offered his hand, then quietly led her away from the room.

"I'm supposed to greet all the mourners," she protested.

"You cannot sit there while the entire empire files past. You have done your duty, Kasmiri, and now you will take care of yourself."

His tone permitted for no dispute and she allowed him to take her back to her rooms. At the doors, a guard argued with Sterlave, insisting that Kasmiri would now take up residence in the Empress suite.

"Her bed is not even cold!" Kasmiri had always considered her mother's rooms far superior to hers, but just the thought of sleeping there tonight raised the hair on the nape of her neck.

Before they could argue further, Ambo Votny waddled up, sweat pouring from his florid face. "You are needed in the circle."

"Why are my mother's—my—advisors meeting at this cold hour?" Another chill shivered down her spine. They wouldn't be meeting on this tragic day unless a dire problem presented.

Ambo shot Sterlave a glare, as if asking him to step back so he could speak privately, but he refused.

Kasmiri took Sterlave's hand. "He is my consort and is now a part of the circle whether you like it or not. To show him disrespect is to show disrespect to me."

With a *harrumph,* Ambo offered a slight apologetic bow, then said, "Thousands of villagers surround the palace."

"They have come to mourn my mother," Kasmiri offered.

"They have been arriving since last night and I doubt they are clairvoyant." Ambo appeared truly stricken. His massive eyes were bigger than normal and all his chins quivered with his pulse. "Not only are they destroying the crops around the palace, but they are chanting something about the living gods."

Dumbfounded, Kasmiri shook her head as if that would clear away the confusion. "What living gods?"

"I believe they are speaking of myself and Chur."

Even from far down the hall, Enovese's voice rang clearly, without arrogance or pride.

"What are you doing here?" Ambo's disgust was palpable. He snapped his fingers at the guards, but Kasmiri held them back with a flick of her hand.

Moving so elegantly in a gauzy black dress that she practically floated toward them, Enovese stopped before Kasmiri and bowed with the grace of a servant.

"You call yourself a god, then try to show respect to me?" Kasmiri wanted to take her harsh words back because now she understood the incredible rush of power she felt when she grabbed Enovese's arm last night.

"I am not your enemy." Enovese offered out her hand but Kasmiri refused.

"What do you want?"

Serenely, Enovese folded her hands together. "I want to help you."

On the tip of her tongue rested a vile accusation, but she swallowed the bitter remark. She had vowed to change her ways, and now that she wore the mantle of empress, she must put aside her personal issues and concentrate on what was best for the empire.

"How can you help me?"

The twin suns, *Tandalsul,* slipped behind the Onic Mountains, turning the sky a soft purple. Kasmiri, Sterlave, Chur, and Enovese stood on a sweeping balcony that oversaw the lands around the palace. From this spot, many an empress had read proclamations, but today was unique. Even Undanna, Kasmiri's protocol liaison, had to refer to her massive tome to find the proper sequence of events. Nothing in the book covered how an empress should introduce living gods to her people.

None of her advisors could offer a suggestion as to why the people had come. Visions from their soothsayers or elders was the agreed-upon explanation. Kasmiri decided the why didn't matter. Now that they were here, the only issue that mattered was what to do with them.

If Kasmiri rejected Chur and Enovese, there would be an uprising. If she accepted them, she too would have to show deference. A flash of anger for her mother consumed her. How convenient that Clathia died right before everything fell apart. Had her mother indeed committed suicide rather than deal with what she knew was coming? The Onic Empire would never be the same after this longest day and night.

From where the four of them stood, the audience below could not see them. The people continued to chant softly while they huddled in blankets around massive fires. Most of the crops had been stripped for the harvest and what little remained, they consumed. With no regard, they trampled the fields, laying waste to generations of meticulously maintained gardens.

Kasmiri almost wept at the damage. By their actions, they would anger the gods, for all of this was in homage to them. Apparently, the people were only concerned with these new gods, these living gods; two people who through a forbidden relationship changed the world forever.

From behind a privacy curtain, Ambo had briefed her as she changed out of her mourning clothes and into a grand crimson gown. He explained that somehow, Chur and Enovese's bonding elevated them, transforming them into gods. He had no explanation for how, only that it had happened. Aware of this profound change, Clathia knew she could not exile them, so she set them up in one of the grandest suites for visiting dignitaries. She lavished them with clothing and luxuries, all in the hopes of incurring their favor. Ambo had no idea what they wanted. Kasmiri rounded on him then, for neither he nor any of her advisors had bothered to simply ask!

Chur and Enovese waited outside Kasmiri's dressing room and when she asked, the answer startled her. They wanted nothing for themselves. All they wanted was to change the procedures of the Harvest ritual. Unwilling to accept their lack of avarice, she questioned them in detail. The more she learned, the more she wished she did not know. In her ignorance, she had been blissful.

"Over thousands of seasons, the magistrate and others have perverted the prophecy, taking the empire away from a righteous path and into blasphemy." Chur kept his voice level, but his face glowed with conviction. He believed his words were truth and he would die to defend them.

"Blasphemy?" Sterlave asked before Kasmiri could do so.

"At the end of the Harvest ritual, the elements of the male and female Harvesters are combined to create issue. These children are borne by *tanists,* who are then ritualistically slaughtered to bring forth *paratanists."*

Shocked by the grotesque information, Kasmiri couldn't speak. However, the information explained why Enovese looked like Arianda, because she was her child, created from this ritual. Kasmiri thought that also explained the tension between Arianda and Clathia. Clearly, Arianda had figured out what happened at the end of the Harvest ritual and confronted Clathia. How many other children did Arianda have toiling as servants in the *tanist* house? Kasmiri's gaze flew to Chur. How many children did he have?

"None. Before my transformation I was unable to have children."

An intimate glance passed between him and Enovese. Kasmiri surmised they were either pregnant or trying. Jealousy and fear surged. What if their child came before hers? Would they try to take the throne from her? Danger now surrounded her at every turn and she didn't know whom to trust.

"But how did this happen? Why would they do this?" Sterlave asked.

Appalled that her own people had devised this disgusting procedure, Kasmiri was almost afraid to learn any more.

"In the days of the ancients, the male and female Harvesters would mate after the Harvest. If successful, their offspring, a *paratanist,* was revered and worshiped as a living god. This child had as much power as the empress." Chur flashed Kasmiri a sharp look. "Now you know why many sought to change the ritual. They did not want to share their authority."

"And now you wish for her to do so?" Ambo snarled. "*Paratanists* are servants! They are not worthy to touch the robe of the empress, let alone rule by her side."

Rather than wilting in the face of such vulgar disregard, Enovese tilted her nose, secure in the knowledge that the gods had chosen her, no matter what Ambo said.

"I have warned you before not to denigrate my bondmate, Ambo." Chur stood, towering over the magistrate. His body sparkled and snapped with energy as if his skin could no longer contain his power.

Ambo took two steps back.

Chur's hand shot out, wrapping around his throat.

"Stop!" Kasmiri did not need another round of drama. A throbbing headache threatened to migrate through her entire body.

Chur released him and Ambo gasped for air.

"Leave us, Ambo. I have no further need of your services."

Ambo looked to argue the point, but the fire in her gaze caused him to back away with his hands held up defensively.

Once he left, Kasmiri turned to Chur and Enovese. "I apologize if he offended you in any way." She forced the diplomatic words around the lump in her throat.

Enovese nodded. "You have no control over what that insufferable man says."

"Actually, I do. If he values his position, he'll learn to control himself, or face the blocks." Kasmiri didn't care if she sounded harsh. She had to get a handle on her advisors or they would ruin her empire. "There are many issues facing us, but first, we will handle the villagers who have come to worship you."

Chur chuckled. The low rumbling was so inappropriate Kasmiri wanted to slap him.

Chur held up his hand as if to stop her. "I apologize, Kasmiri, for I do not laugh at your predicament, but at what you said. The people have not come to worship us. They have come to celebrate."

"Celebrate what?" Kasmiri asked.

"The dawn of a new empire."

With that thought weighing on her mind, Kasmiri moved to the edge of the balcony. A hush fell over the crowd.

"My people, I welcome you on this most profound occasion. Today Empress Clathia ascended to *Jarasine*. I would ask a moment of silence for my mother."

All she could hear was the *snap-crackle* of fires and a distant hum of waves upon the shore of the Valry Sea. That they showed respect to her mother put to rest her fears of a violent uprising. Perhaps Chur was correct that they were here only to celebrate the new empire and not to destroy the old one.

"My mother's untimely death has thrust the mantle of responsibility onto my shoulders. I will uphold the laws of our land, perform the rituals to appease the gods, and provide a forum for the people so that I can respond directly to any grievances."

At this last Ambo grumbled, not loud enough for the people below to hear, but loud enough for her and all on the balcony to know his displeasure. Afraid of not only ruling but also facing a multitude of changes, Kasmiri did not need dissension in her ranks. Ambo had been the magistrate since her grandmother's rule. Perhaps the time had come for the seventy-season-old man to step down.

"The Onic Empire follows the ways of the ancients. Their rituals have been handed down to us through thousands of seasons. It has come to my attention that the empire has moved away from the vital essence of those rituals. To remind us of our true path, the gods have sent two heralds."

Kasmiri turned and motioned for Chur and Enovese to join her at the edge of the balcony, one on each side of her. When the audience saw them, they moved en masse to their feet, cheering and shouting until Chur lifted his hand. Immediately, they settled down.

"We thank you for your warm greeting." His rumbling voice carried easily without amplification. Dressed in a pair of loose-fitting black trousers with a sword at his side, his bare chest gleaming in the fading light, he appeared as a benevolent warrior god. "Changes have already begun, but the greatest changes will come from you."

Mumbled confusion greeted his words and a wave of panic stiffened Kasmiri's spine. Was he going back on his word? Would he incite them to riot? She thought of the fastest path to her mother's Golden Bird. If things got out of hand, she would grab Sterlave and fly away.

"Dreams and visions brought you here. You turn to us looking for answers, but those answers lie within you." Chur paused dramatically. "Within each of you lies the truth of the gods. You know what is right, what is wrong, what is just. Return to your villages and spread the word that the gods have heard your prayers."

11

The puny servant was no match for Loban's strength. Easily, he captured the struggling woman, threw her upon the table where she folded her mistress's clothing, yanked up her dress, and ripped away her undergarments.

When she drew a deep breath to scream, he shoved the ripped *mondi* fabric into her mouth. "I don't need a fancy room to perform the ritual. I can accept your sacrifice here in the servant's *tishiary.*"

Loban had discovered the *tishiary* wing of the palace by accident, but once he realized every servant came here to bathe, wash their own or their owner's clothing, get supplies, or exchange gossip, he haunted the place, hiding himself behind fabric-shrouded walls until he learned their rhythms, whom they worked for, and when they were likely to be alone.

The woman below him only came at sunset. He didn't know her name, not that he cared, but he knew she served one of the upper elite for the clothing she washed was sapphire blue. Only the highest of the high wore deep jewel tones. This servant shunned the other servants, not from hubris, but because she was often the subject of their most vicious gossip. They said she obtained her high position by poisoning those before her, not enough to kill them, but just enough to make them ill so she could rise to the occasion and prove herself worthy to serve better in their stead.

Loban cared no more about the truth of that tale than he cared to know her name. All he needed from her was her sacrifice. He didn't even care whether she was a virgin. Chur Zenge ascended through the willing acceptance of virginity, but Loban knew he would find his power by the forceful taking of the spirit.

Rape empowered him.

Loban knew he would rise to dark power by stealing that which none would willingly give: their soul.

With rough, calloused hands, he grasped her trembling knees and forced her thighs apart. When the fabric clung, he shoved the dress up to her hips, exposing her pale and quivering limbs. He would have ripped the dress off, but she had nothing else to wear and he didn't want any evidence of his activities, not that anyone would believe a lowly servant. Loban knew he could Harvest all the servants he wanted without fear of reprisal, for in the Onic Empire, servants were the lowest of the low. Their owners never troubled themselves about their feelings, their needs, or even their health. When one servant died, another of their breed took their place. Loban could conduct his Harvest ritual in private and keep his Harvest secret. The servants wouldn't tell, and even if they did, no one would believe them.

Secrecy would only feed his sinister power.

Hungry eyes examined the thick black curls that covered her sex. With a grunt, he slid her forward, placing her left foot against the hilt of his pathetic stolen dagger. He'd tried to find a sword similar to the Harvester's, but he'd had to settle for this. Before she could wriggle away, he lifted her right foot to his shoulder until her leg was almost straight against his bare chest. When she struggled, he slapped her hard enough to leave a mark but not hard enough to knock her unconscious. He needed her awake.

Loban spoke in her language because he knew she wouldn't understand the ancient tongue. "By might of the blade I claim that which belongs to me."

The woman only gazed at him, her eyes confused and darting about as if seeking help. As a servant, she would have no knowledge of the Harvest ritual.

"I'm going to remove the fabric and you are going to repeat after me. Do you understand?"

Tears leaked from her narrow brown eyes as she stared blankly at him.

He slapped her and asked the question again. This time she nodded vigorously.

Loban removed the wad of fabric from her mouth and told her the words he wanted her to say.

Confused, she stuttered out the words, but when he lifted his hand ready to slap her again, she breathlessly said, "I give myself to you." She'd left out the word "freely" so he slapped her until she gasped out the lie, "I freely give myself to you!"

Sharp, hot spikes of arousal surged down to his prick, swelling the tight flesh until his cock stood rigid against the makeshift codpiece. When he leered down at her, devouring her confusion and fear, she tried to move her head away, but he clutched her chin and ordered her to look at him. Controlling her stimulated him beyond his wildest fantasies. She was his first sacrifice, but he knew she wouldn't be his last.

Loban yanked the codpiece aside. Unlike the Harvester, he didn't prepare himself or her with the soothing *estal* oil. Why cushion his possession when he wanted to feel her stretch to accommodate him? After this, she would belong to him. No matter who took her, or how tenderly they used her, she would always think of him, and this singular moment. Forever after she belonged to him.

Positioning himself to her entrance, he glared down at her, then shoved forward as hard as he could. Narrow eyes went shockingly wide as her body bucked against him and the table. Anticipating her scream, he covered her mouth with his hand, leaned near, and whispered, "Remember, you asked for this, you freely gave yourself to me."

Below his hand, she shook her head. He'd forced her to submit, but he didn't care. He would have taken her had she said the words or not.

"You belong to me." He rammed himself deeply into her, just as the Harvest ritual demanded. She was so tight and dry that her passage scraped painfully along his prick, but he didn't stop until he'd buried himself balls deep. "Only me."

Once he'd pushed fully home, he withdrew, glancing down just long enough to see her blood coating his shaft.

"Take pride, for you are the first of many I will harvest." He let her legs free and helped her from the table. She moved as if to run, but he grasped her shoulder, pulling her against his body, nestling his stiff prick between the tender slit of her bottom. "If you tell anyone, I will kill you and all those you love. Do you understand?"

She nodded, gathered the sapphire blue clothing, and then departed the *tishiary* on wobbly legs.

Loban realized two things: One was that he would have to find some kind of oil to prevent his prick from being rubbed raw because it smarted now after only one sacrifice. Two was that he had no *paratanist* to clean or anoint him. He thought briefly of commandeering a slave to perform those duties, but that could lead to gossip that would expose his plan. In the end, he decided he would have to minister to himself. Let the official Harvester have all the accoutrements and luxuries. He would revert to a pure austerity that would only bring him to the gods faster. They would see that he was far more worthy than spoiled Chur.

Loban snuck back along the billowing curtains to the bathing unit. There, he washed himself and applied a generous amount of oil, the kind the servants used to massage their wealthy owners. He leaned back to wait for his next sacrifice. Within minutes, a lone male servant exited the bath, drying his hair with a towel. The man was small and so delicate of features he almost didn't look masculine but for his flaccid penis.

Anticipation caused Loban's own flesh to grow taut. Before the man knew what hit him, Loban had him flat on his back on the rickety table that held inferior towels for the servant's use.

This harvest was easier than the last because the man was already naked. In addition, he seemed more shocked than terrified, and only babbled questions about what Loban was doing. When he waved a dagger before his eyes and told him not to scream, the servant nodded agreement. In fact, he went utterly limp as if he'd been expecting this treatment.

Loban took a moment to consider his sacrifice. Clear, perfect skin covered his entire body, and few chest or pubic hairs marred the smooth surface. Even his face had only the barest trace of a beard. His hair was dark, but his eyes were deep green, like the gardens in high summer. Two thick lips covered straight and startlingly white teeth.

"Are you *ungati?*"

He nodded with a most becoming mix of pride and shyness.

Loban now understood his passivity. *Ungati* were bred to bestow pleasure on their owners but were forbidden to take any pleasure themselves. Some went so far as to castrate their property to ensure this, and that apparently had happened to this man, given his shriveled genitals and feminine features. Not that it mattered.

Loban told the man what he wanted. After a brief flash of

confusion, where he said he could only perform as his master dictated, and Loban swore his master stood behind the drapes watching, the servant agreed. Such willingness made Loban wonder what other erotic scenarios this man's master had forced him to act out.

Since he did not struggle, Loban was able to perform the ritual more leisurely. He parted the man's thighs, marveling again at how silky his skin felt below his calloused hands. Sliding him forward until his buttocks hit the table edge was almost effortless due to his slight weight. Smoothly, Loban placed his left foot on the hilt of his dagger and lifted the right to his shoulder.

Loban said his words and the *ungati* said his.

When he pushed the codpiece aside and pressed his cock to the man's puckered entrance, his eyes practically glowed with longing. Loban frowned. He didn't want such a willing sacrifice. Shock, fear, and terror had always been his greatest aphrodisiacs. However, he knew he had to do his duty. Shoving forward, Loban found the way much easier thanks to the thick coating of oil. He plunged deep until his balls rested against the table edge, then withdrew.

He swore the man to secrecy and then helped him from the table. Again, he cleaned and anointed himself. Throughout the night, Loban harvested over twenty servants, some male and some female. Again, their sex didn't matter. Most reacted with fear that fed his lust, but some were as passive as the *ungati*, which wasn't as satisfying, but still, he performed his duty. He didn't need *umer* to keep him hard or to prevent him from climaxing. Loban controlled himself by sheer force of will, proving that he was far more worthy than any Harvester.

When night slid toward daylight, he again considered the need for a *paratanist*. By ritual, at the end of the Harvest, a *paratanist* would stroke him to climax. Without one, he would again have to improvise. When an acolyte entered in swirling white robes, Loban was convinced the gods heard his dilemma and sent him this man as a solution. The fact that he had black hair and blue eyes like Chur Zenge was further proof that he should use this man for his ritual.

Chur was the one who kicked him out of the training program so that he could never become the Harvester. Chur was the one who, through what he thought was kindness, didn't place the brand of shame on his forehead and send him back to his village. Chur decided to give him the menial job of cleaning and repairing the recruit's training gear. At first, Loban didn't understand why Chur didn't force him to go home in disgrace, but now he understood that Chur wanted to keep him under his thumb. Every day, Chur watched to ensure Loban did his chores and didn't harass the recruits. Every day, Loban struggled with the overwhelming desire to rape Chur. Only Chur's godlike transformation held him back. Loban knew he could not best him now. That's when he decided to find his own way into the gods' favor.

Acolytes usually came in pairs, but this one often came alone and spent hours in the deep bathing tub. Floating on his back, he would stare up at the ceiling as if studying the figures painted there. Loban had barely given the artwork a glance before turning his gaze away. Art in any form did not interest him. People, power, and perversion interested him.

When the acolyte removed the white robe, revealing a lean body of compact strength with a smattering of thick black body hair, Loban pushed the codpiece aside. While he thought of all the most depraved things he could, using the servant to help him stimulate his imagination, he stroked his cock until he could no longer hold back his climax. His orgasm erupted with such force he lost his breath and his vision for several moments.

Once he regained his equilibrium, Loban cleaned himself carefully, then hid his Harvester gear. He returned to his training room cell to sleep a few hours before his chores began. Once they were over, he would return to the *tishiary* and take more sacrifices. As he lay on his back awaiting sleep, he was dismayed to realize he didn't feel any differently. His lust had been sated, but he didn't feel any special powers. However, he had only harvested for one night. Perhaps he needed several nights or several hundred sacrifices to feel the change begin.

It didn't matter.

Loban would do whatever it took to become the dark champion of the gods.

12

Kasmiri clung to Sterlave's arm, using him to support her as they returned to their rooms. Her exhaustion bled into him. Before she could protest, Sterlave scooped her into his arms and carried her.

"I am capable of walking." She tried to flash him a sharp look, but the dark circles under her eyes ruined the effect.

"Indulge me."

Wearily, she shook her head, then rested her cheek against his shoulder. He wished he could do more to take some of the burden off her. How could one woman carry the weight of her mother's death, and a new and terrifying responsibility as the empress, just as the empire itself stood on the brink of tremendous social change?

Without thinking, he'd gone straight to her rooms. When he discovered the locked door, that's when he remembered they were supposed to sleep in the Empress suite.

"I can't bear to sleep in my mother's rooms," Kasmiri's voice was barely a whisper, and so thick with pain it sliced right into his heart.

"Your wish is my command." Since no guard stood in his way, Sterlave kicked the door, busting the lock and flinging the doors open.

Kasmiri glanced up, her eyes wide with surprise. "Impressive."

He winked and strode inside. Thank the gods the door only appeared to be made of solid Onic timber or he would have broken his foot. That would not have been so impressive. His kick displaced several gems, some of which fell and shattered. He puzzled over the piles of broken glass for a moment because true gems wouldn't break. Were they always counterfeit, or had someone replaced the real gems with shards of colored glass?

Once inside, he set Kasmiri on her feet.

"The lights should have come on automatically when I entered." Annoyed, she fumbled along the wall for the manual switch. When the lighting crystals flared to life, she gasped, pressing her hand to her mouth.

Someone had stripped the room of everything but the most basic furniture. The bed, the table, the couch, and her lighted mirror, with the glass recently replaced from her tantrum, were still there, but the rugs, the tapestries, the linens, her makeup and toiletries—all of that was gone.

"They must have moved your things."

Kasmiri slumped down into the chair before her mirror. She glanced at her reflection, winced, and then looked away. Sterlave wasn't sure if it was the fact someone had stripped her room or the prospect of removing all her finery that was too much for her to bear. He approached behind her and slipped the first jeweled pin from her hair.

"I'll call for Rown."

"I don't mind." Sterlave slipped another pin out, placing it on the table. "I've become rather adept at playing maid." Besides, he was pretty sure they'd moved her servants too.

"My faithful servant." Her gaze caught his through the glass. Her smile was sweet, the sweetest he'd ever seen. In that moment,

Kasmiri looked so impossibly young and so tragically vulnerable she brought out every masculine, protective instinct he had.

"As you please." Bowing, he smiled back at her, then teased his fingers through her hair since he didn't have a brush. She relaxed into his massage with a sigh and closed her eyes.

Bit by bit, he removed her jewelry, her clothing, until she sat before him nude. When he started to remove his clothing, she cracked her eyes open to watch. He stripped slowly, aware of how his body might look to her and hoping to show his form to best advantage. What stopped his performance was the dreaded *echalle.* Unraveling the complicated series of straps that held the swath of fabric to his genitals was a job for at least two people. If he did it alone, he was afraid he would castrate himself.

"Here." Kasmiri leaned forward. "Let me be your faithful servant." She helped him slide the fabric down and off without injury. He thanked her, then followed her gaze to the bed. "Perhaps we should have stayed dressed since we have a bed without blankets."

No way was he redressing her and making her sleep in her mother's room. In fact, when he found out who tried to force her to do so, he would bend them to their knees and make them apologize.

Sterlave glanced around, then discovered the furs he'd used to sleep on the couch were still there. He retrieved them, tossed them on the bed, and then crooked his finger, calling to Kasmiri.

She rose out of the chair in slow motion, drifting toward him as if in a trance. That's when he realized just how drained she really was. Her face was serene and her body becoming, but her eyes, her eyes begged for the singular release of sleep.

Sterlave tucked her under the furs, then joined her, pressing his body against hers. Her buttocks were surprisingly cold when nestled against his hips. So chilly were her cheeks he gave a little gasp of surprise when she curled against him.

She giggled.

When she turned to him, tracing her hand along his chest to cup his semihard penis, he lifted her hand away. "Sleep, Kasmiri. Today has been endless for you."

"I want you," she begged, teasing her other hand along his back to pull him close.

"I want you, too, but you need sleep."

"No, I need to feel you, I want to feel alive."

He didn't have the heart to say no, and he thought he understood. With so much pain and death, she needed the reassurance of life. Tenderly, he cupped her face and placed delicate kisses along her forehead, her cheekbones, her nose, and her lips. Kasmiri melted back into the bed and stretched her limbs out, allowing him to command her utterly. There was something absolutely charming about her ability to relax and receive pleasure.

Rather than seek to arouse her, he tried to soothe her with long, strong strokes up and down the length of her body. Her perfumed skin was sleek, pampered, and after an entire day since her bath, her own scent mixed with the floral fragrance into the most intriguing bouquet. To stop himself from teasing his tongue along her flesh, he carefully rolled her face down and played his hands over her back, buttocks, and down to her feet.

When her toes curled up, she moaned low and deep. He pressed harder along her instep and worked his fingers between her toes. He had to forcefully remind himself he was trying to relax her, not arouse her, or himself, so he left off her feet and worked his fingertips into the muscles of her calves, her thighs, her buttocks, and back.

Her even breathing convinced him she had fallen asleep so he lay down beside her, trying not to disturb her. She took a sudden shuddering breath, and that's when he realized she was crying. When he placed his hand on her back, she curled onto her side, moving away from him.

"I'm fine. I'm fine." She spoke through gritted teeth with a determination to make what she said true.

"I know." Sterlave curled against her back, wrapping his arms around her. He honestly didn't know what to do since he'd never consoled anyone, but he remembered his childhood and how he so desperately wanted someone, anyone, to just hold him. So that's what he did.

At first, Kasmiri struggled from his embrace, hissing, "I'm fine," through her gasping sobs, but he was persistent, following her across the bed until she ran out of room. If she wriggled away again, she'd fall off. Defeated, she rolled over and pushed at his chest.

"I don't need you! I don't need anyone!"

"I know." Still, he sought to put his arms around her, and with a frustrated grumble, she ultimately relented. He tightened his embrace until she rested her head against his chest.

"Why don't you just give up on me? Everyone else does." Her voice was barely a whisper when she added, "My mother killed herself to get away from me."

Sterlave swallowed back his shock. He didn't know her mother committed suicide. He'd assumed she'd died in an accident. Nevertheless, he doubted Clathia killed herself to get away from Kasmiri, and he had a feeling Kasmiri knew that intellectually. However, that was the heart of her pain. Kasmiri felt abandoned by everyone she loved. When they died or walked away from her, she thought it was her fault, that she had done something to drive them away. Sterlave commiserated. For a long time, he thought everything his father did to him, from the silent treatments to the severe beatings, he deserved.

"I will never give up on you, Kasmiri." He pressed his lips to her forehead, but she yanked back.

"You already did," she accused, wiping her tears away with her fist. "You slept on the couch to get away from me."

"That was probably the first of many spats we are likely to

have," he reminded softly. "Bonded couples argue, they disagree, they fume, they play petty power games, but in the end, when they truly care about each other, they always make up." He nuzzled her ear. "Remember what I said before I sat on the consort throne? I swore myself to you. I will do everything in my power to protect you, to honor you, to defend you. I will die in service to you."

Her tears erupted in a great gush. "Why?"

Her suspicion broke his heart. "Because you're my mate." When he tried to wipe away her tears, she curled in, tucking her head to her chest. "I chose you, Kasmiri, because I want to be with you."

"I thought you wanted me for my position."

Using his most salacious tone, he said, "If anything, I wanted you in a multitude of positions. The Harvest pose was just the first of many."

Her laugh was weak but audible.

"Honestly, your position had nothing to do with my decision. I saw you at the Festival of Temptation, so arresting in that crimson dress, and knew I had to have you. I didn't know you were the daughter of the empress until later, long after I'd already decided to make you mine."

"Really?" Plaintive as a wounded child, her voice touched the hurt part of his own heart.

"Really." He hugged her tighter in reassurance. "While I trained to be the Harvester, I always wondered how I would know that a woman was right for me. I would lay awake at night, wondering if it would be a flash in her eyes, a shock along my skin—what, exactly, would tell me she was the one? When I saw you, I knew."

Kasmiri was quiet for a long moment, and he thought he understood why. She had thought Chur was right for her. Doubts still plagued him because he wasn't sure whether she honestly wanted him or only accepted him as second best to her one true choice. Conflicting him further was the fact that Chur was his friend. Sterlave understood why any woman would want Chur—who wouldn't want the tall, dark haired, blue-eyed demigod—but he didn't want to live his life trapped in his friend's shadow.

"I wish I would have told my mother how much I admired her." Kasmiri sniffled indelicately. "I never told her how I tried to live up to her, how I always felt I would never be as beautiful as she, how her athleticism intimidated me. My mother climbed *galbol* trees for sport!" Kasmiri shook her head. "Some were so massive that it took her and her team over twenty days and nights to reach the summit. Once there, they would celebrate with food and drink, then climb right back down. I never understood the point."

"Because it's there." Sterlave had only heard about *galbol* trees, how they could be thicker than a village at the base and taller than a mountain at the tip. He'd never seen one, and doubted he would want to climb one, but he understood the attraction. "Seems to me your mother wanted to do the impossible. Conquering *galbol* trees fulfilled that need in her heart."

Kasmiri nodded, then asked, "Why would she kill herself? Even if the doctors told her she had some terminal disease, she would have fought, just as she did with the *galbol* trees. Why take on one challenge and not another?"

Sterlave teased his fingers along her back in small circles as he considered. "How long had she been fighting the disease?"

"I don't know. She didn't even tell me she was sick."

"She didn't want to worry you." Mothers were like that, or so he thought. His father killed his mother long before Sterlave got a chance to receive much mothering, but he imagined mothers were like that. With one blow, his father scrambled his mother's brains. If only his village had more medical technology, she might have survived.

"She was probably afraid I wouldn't care." Kasmiri's voice had dropped to a whisper. "I did horrible things to my mother."

"I'm sure she forgave—"

"You don't understand. When she tried to force me into bonding, I pretended to be interested in another woman, an older woman, who actually turned out to be Enovese's mother."

His eyes went wide in the dark. He desperately wanted to ask how far the pretending went, but Kasmiri rushed on, "Not that we ever did anything other than kiss, and the woman, she was just using me for her own scheme anyway. No one got hurt, except my mother."

"Kasmiri—"

"When that didn't work, I decided that I would select my own bondmate, not leave it up to her, so I picked Chur. I stole his sword in an effort to force him to select me at the Harvest. When he refused, I placed it on the consort throne. My mother thought he was laying claim to her, but in the end, she did as I knew she would: Clathia ordered Chur to select me or she would kill his chosen."

That explained why Kasmiri was so shocked and angry when Chur didn't select her. She thought her plan was foolproof.

"All I've ever done was cause my mother pain." Kasmiri burst into tears.

Sterlave held her, rocking her gently, letting her cry herself out. "Kasmiri, whatever you did, your mother forgave you, because that's what mothers do. They love their children no matter what." He had heard tales of men who raped, murdered, and stole, and their mothers still loved them. "Someday, our children will do something foolish or even harmful, and you and I will forgive them. We'll love them in spite of what they do."

"What if I don't?" she asked, injecting ice into her tone. "What if I can't love them to begin with?"

"Every mother loves her own children."

"No, they don't. Fathers don't, so who's to say mothers do?"

Sterlave was suddenly very lost. He thought he understood what tormented her, but there was more going on than just the loss of her mother. Had her father rejected her? If that was the basis for part of this, it made sense that she would be afraid of him abandoning her too.

"I don't even like children." She sniffed while wiping her tears away. "They're loud, and all they do is defecate and cry."

"Eventually they stop," he said, trying his best to cajole her. "Then they totter about and get into everything. Then they get old enough to talk back."

"See? Are any of those good things?"

"But then, sometimes they look at you with such love it breaks your heart and makes all of the trauma worth it." He'd only seen this on the outside looking in. He'd envied those kids whose mothers and fathers loved them. Often, he pretended that he had that support, but then, he always had to go home to his father.

She went stiff in his arms. "That's what I mean—my mother didn't love me, she left me without a word of explanation and dumped a world of problems in my lap!"

"I don't know why she didn't tell you. Maybe she was ashamed. Maybe she was afraid you would have stopped her. Maybe it was a spur-of-the-moment decision. Kasmiri, there are a hundred explanations. But even if she did leave an explanation, it wouldn't change what is. She'll still be gone. You'll still be here." He wondered if his words were any comfort at all.

"Of course I'm here, I'm not a coward like her. I wouldn't take the easy way out."

She vacillated between anger and regret, but mixed up in all her emotions loomed her fear of children and her own worries about being a mother. In that moment, he wished he had some kind of manual so he would know the right thing to do, the right thing to say. Maybe Undanna, with her big book of protocol, could help. He doubted it. Every person, every situation, would be different. All he could do was his best.

"So much has changed in a very brief time." He nuzzled her

neck and kissed the curve of her ear. "You became a citizen, bonded, lost your mother, and gained an empire. Give yourself time to let it all sink in."

"Don't forget my duty to breed and work out some kind of deal with the two living gods."

He couldn't see her, but he knew she'd rolled her eyes along with that tiny shake of her head.

"Yes, that too, but take it one day at a time. You don't have to fix everything tonight, or even tomorrow. Don't be afraid to ask for help from people with more knowledge than you. You have advisors, so use them. And most importantly, don't be afraid to lean on me."

She held her breath for a long time, then finally asked, "Will you be there to hold me up?"

He cupped her chin, exerting gentle pressure until she looked up. Her eyes were so wide and hopeful they touched him deep inside. Softly, he swore, "I won't let you down."

Clanging alarms woke Kasmiri out of a sound sleep. Sterlave sat up, taking her with him since she dozed draped across his chest. He told her to stay, then leapt out of bed.

She lay back with an indulgent grin. He was such a man of action. When he kicked the door in last night, his power had aroused her despite her exhaustion. He was a man who wouldn't let anything stand in his way. Even her. She was proud and a little bit afraid all at the same time. Keeping a handle on such a determined man would be difficult, if not impossible.

However, he'd been more than just powerful last night, he'd been there for her emotionally, and she didn't think many men could do that. Sterlave was a lot more than just physically powerful; he had a heart too.

He strode toward the door, determined to find out what was happening, then realized he was nude. He yanked her dress off the floor, wrapped it around his hips, and left.

She pulled the fur up to cover her chest and waited. Only once had she heard alarms wailing throughout the palace and that was when someone had discovered her father's dead body. A cold shiver caused her to clutch the fur tighter. She didn't think she could handle any more death.

Sterlave was gone so long she almost went after him until she realized he had her dress around his hips. She didn't think she could get away with wearing his clothing, but slipping on his shirt did make her feel less vulnerable. As soon as she pulled it over her head, his scent enveloped her—arousing, male, utterly enthralling. After a few deep breaths, she was calm enough to climb back into bed and wait.

Sterlave returned, his face grim, his strides so powerful he ate up the distance between them in seconds. "Has anyone come in here since I left?"

"No."

He nodded and yet proceeded to inspect her rooms anyway.

"Who are you looking for?" Was he jealous? Did he think she somehow managed to sneak a lover in during the short time he was gone?

"I wish I knew." He faced her, one hand holding her crimson dress to his hips. She would have laughed, but his expression was so determined she didn't dare. On the verge of asking him what was going on, he asked, "Who would want to hurt you?"

"Hurt me?" Her mind swirled with confusion. "Why would anyone want to hurt—" she stopped abruptly when she thought of all the powerful houses just wanting for her to fail at providing an heir, or better yet, simply die, so they could ascend to power. Now that she thought about it, many people wanted to hurt her.

"How many houses wait in line behind you?"

Concerned by his sudden questioning, she had to think before she answered, "Eleven."

"Which house commands the best claim?"

"All of them. None of them." She shook her head and shrugged. Her mind was awhirl with possibilities. "They can't lay claim unless I die or I fail to provide an heir."

"I don't think they're going to wait for a bouncing bundle of joy." Sterlave whipped the dress off his hips and tossed it on the bed. "Get dressed."

Crisis or no, she didn't like him ordering her about. "What happened?" she asked, defiantly settling back into the bed.

"Get dressed and then we'll talk." In opposition to last night, he was now all domineering and stubborn.

"I'm not doing anything until—"

Sterlave landed on the bed with his full weight. "Kasmiri, this isn't the time to argue with me." He gripped her shoulders, preventing her from moving away and forcing her to look right at him. "I need you to do what I say so I can keep you safe."

The look in his eyes made her realize he wasn't angry with her, he was afraid *for* her. Her legs wobbled once she rose from the bed. He helped her slip his shirt from her shoulders and then wrap the crimson fabric around her body. Sterlave dressed as well but left off the *echalle.*

"Last night someone started a fire in your mother's rooms."

"A fire?" She rolled her eyes. "It was probably an accident." Irked that he tried to terrify her over something so trivial, especially when she'd once set fire to the fabric along the walls by leaving a candle too close, she yanked her hands from his and strode to the mirror to fix her hair.

Sterlave spun her around.

"How dare you?"

Refusing to back down, he clasped her hands in his. "This was no accident, Kasmiri. The fire was so intense the glass ceiling shattered. If we had been sleeping in there . . ." His gaze drilled into hers. "I doubt someone was after me, which leaves you. Do you get it now? Someone wants you dead."

13

Loban entered the back of the training rooms where a new mound of gear awaited his attention. With the lowered head of one who was truly repentant, he settled himself upon the short stool, picked up the first chest pad, and began to stitch the frayed edges.

Throughout the morning, recruits came in to pick up what he'd repaired only to drop off more items that needed his attention. The parade of gear was endless. For once, Chur did not stop by first thing to fix his freakish eyes upon him.

Always Chur looked to read his mind, but Loban was too crafty. He pictured a shield of black around himself whenever Chur was near. Today would be the ultimate test. If Chur had even a flickering suspicion about what he'd done last night, Loban didn't think Chur would waste time folding him up and shoving him in the *gannett*. He'd just kill him on sight.

A shiver tingled along his back, but he tightened his muscles, forcing the fear away. He had to be strong to prevail. Now was not the time to let panic ruin his plans. The gods only blessed those who were worthy.

Loban was worthy.

He still wondered exactly what Chur had done to earn their favor, for in his eyes, Chur was decidedly unworthy, but he had not been with the man every moment of every day. Clearly, Chur had done something to please the gods.

With a tilt of his head, Loban wondered what Chur would do if he simply asked. Would he answer, or would he laugh, then turn away? Loban didn't think he could stand to witness Chur giving him his back yet again. Dismissal incensed him. No, he was better off keeping his interactions with Chur limited.

Loban lowered his attention to an *avenyet*. A hundred hands had frayed the leather strap wrapped around the center of the double-ended club. Balancing the club between his knees, he removed the damaged leather and wrapped a new strip around the heavy wooden weapon.

Once he'd fastened the band securely, he lifted and twisted the club, testing the grip. Before he could enjoy the sensation of holding a weapon in his hands, a raw recruit came and yanked the *avenyet* away. It took everything he had not to retaliate. Rather than vent his rage on some naive hopeful, he simply picked up the next weapon and set to fixing it.

There was a time when he'd ruled these rooms. When he'd first come from Plete, he quickly realized everyone respected Chur, but they didn't fear him. Within half a cycle, every recruit feared Loban. During the day, they feared his battle prowess, and at night, they submitted to his lustful needs. Even Sterlave, the current consort, had surrendered to him.

That night was one Loban would never forget. Something about the easy-going, soft-spoken recruit from Gant inflamed him. Loban had deliberately sought a confrontation and purposefully injured Sterlave so he'd have a reason to apologize later. When Sterlave invited him into his cell, Loban took what he knew they both wanted. Sterlave tried to resist, but he was scrawny and no match for Loban's mature strength. Besides, he wanted it, just like all the others.

However, that was three seasons ago, when Sterlave was an undernourished recruit. After dedicating himself to training and maintaining his focus despite a thousand distractions, Sterlave flourished. He'd had the guts to officially challenge Chur when Loban had held back. Sterlave lost, and died, but again, the gods found something worthy, something that Loban could not see no matter how deeply he delved. They let Sterlave live and blessed him with the title of official Harvester, while Loban was disgraced and forced to minister to the recruits.

His handler, Helton Ook, assured him that he would soon triumph over Chur and become the next Harvester.

Helton lied.

Shortly after Sterlave became the Harvester, Chur dismissed Helton and demoted Loban. Helton walked away with barely a scratch of shame while Loban was now languishing in servitude to men far beneath his mighty glory. Some nobody became the next Harvester when Sterlave selected Kasmiri.

"It should have been me."

He whipped his head around and blew a sigh of relief that he was alone. Talking aloud to himself would get him noticed and not in a good way. A Harvester had to be both physically and mentally fit. After almost three seasons of languishing in Chur's shadow, his time couldn't come soon enough. Everything Helton had told him to do, he'd done, but then everything went horribly wrong.

Loban reined in his frustration.

Soon, very soon, the gods would recognize his worth, bless him with dark powers, and then, he would rise above them all, forcing them to bow down before him. Once he had gathered the full of his supremacy, he would decimate any and all who did not quiver in dread of him. He alone would be the living vessel for the gods. Chur and Sterlave would kneel or perish. His cock twitched at the thought.

When Loban ruled the Onic Empire, he would have anyone in any way whenever he pleased. He would erect special temples where hundreds of his followers would arrange themselves in various provocative postures. At any time, he could enter and sample his fill. Then, for his amusement, he would couple them off, perhaps more than two, and watch them mate. They would offer themselves up for his pleasure or suffer under the stone.

Loban frowned.

He'd never thought slowly crushing a criminal with progressively heavier stones was a gruesome enough punishment. He thought for a moment about the myriad ways he could punish and kill. Then he decided. Under his rule, those who erred against him would be torn apart by *wroxes*. Since the tiny *wrox* ate by darting and biting, their small, sharp teeth would make the death a long and painful one. If Loban kept the criminal upright, he would be able to enjoy their screams for hours.

A tingle along the short hairs at the back of his neck jerked Loban out of his daydream. He lifted his gaze to Chur. For a split second, he let Chur's gaze penetrate before he remembered to slap up his black shield.

Had he been fast enough? Loban held his gaze for a moment without malice, without joy, then nodded and lowered his attention to his work. Unsure, Loban kept his gaze down. Had Chur read the truth in his eyes? His mind scrambled for a plan, but all he could think of was to run. But where? He had no friends, no allies, no one to offer him sanctuary. In a flash, he realized he couldn't even run outside because the people who'd gathered there worshipped Chur. All Chur would have to do is lift his finger, cast blame upon him, and his followers would rip him apart with their bare hands.

Since he couldn't run, he would have to fight.

There was a time when he couldn't wait to challenge Chur, but Helton had convinced him to hold back. Helton insisted that Chur would choose his mate from the Harvest, and Loban would automatically become the next Harvester.

Three times Loban waited, and three times Chur did not choose. In the end, Helton convinced the recruits to issue multiple challenges, but still insisted Loban hold back. Loban wished he had not listened to Helton. All these seasons he spent biding his time when he could have been harvesting. If he had challenged Chur the first season he came into the Harvester training rooms, he might have obtained the power of the gods.

Moreover, he wouldn't have suffered the revenge rape by one of the recruits, now dead. Loban hated thinking of that day, when Sterlave, scrawny, pathetic Sterlave, had saved him from taking another recruit's cock up his ass while he languished in the *gannett*. Three had already had their turn, but Sterlave stopped Vertase. Loban always wondered why Sterlave had not joined in, but he decided Sterlave was too afraid to seek revenge.

He wanted to look up and see if Chur was still watching him, but that might reveal his trepidation. Instead, Loban focused intently on rewrapping the worn *cirvant* handle. Something deep inside stirred, welcoming the feel of the short curved sword. With two jabs, he could kill Chur. A vision of his golden form jetting crimson stirred his prick anew. Loban actually didn't want to kill Chur. He'd much rather keep him alive, in chains, perhaps as a pet. Just thinking of the things he could make Chur do eased his tension and allowed him to finish his work.

Tonight, he would continue the Harvest.

14

Sterlave didn't want her to see the damage, but she insisted. Where Kasmiri's room was mostly crimson with touches of white and black, the empress suite was mostly white with touches of crimson, black, and silver. Bright sunlight and crisp harvest air streamed into the massive room through the broken ceiling. If not for the soot marks smeared over everything, the whiteness of the walls and ceiling would have been blinding. However, everything was charred, broken, melted, or burned.

When she tried to enter, he held her back. A multitude of servants swarmed through the chaos, cleaning up the mess, but he didn't want Kasmiri to get anywhere near the disaster area.

"But my mother's things," she argued, lifting her hands to his arms. In her state of shock, she didn't push him away so much as she clung to him.

"If they find anything worth saving, they'll set it aside." From the magnitude of the damage, he didn't think they would find much. His heart broke that she might not have any remembrance of her mother other than her memories.

Kasmiri opened her mouth to argue but ceased when one of

the servants held up what once must have been a piece of jewelry. From the shape, he surmised it had been an extremely elaborate necklace, but all that remained was a melted clump of metal with gemstones stuck along the jagged folds.

Kasmiri's dismayed gasp caused several of the servants to glance at her, then quickly away, their eyes downcast with apology. Fearing for her sanity, for how could anyone survive this much turmoil in her life, Sterlave dragged her away. If he thought she would collapse gratefully into his strong arms, he was wrong.

"I'm going to find out who did this, and when I do, I will create a punishment so vile, so painful, so degrading, so, so—no one will dare to cross me again!" She turned on her heel, swirling crimson *astle* in her wake.

Sterlave smiled, pleased that she refused to cower in fear. Whoever did this wasn't going to frighten Kasmiri away. Also, she needed something to focus her anger on rather than her mother or her own fears of becoming a mother. As proud of her as he was, he also didn't want her to use this to protect herself from the pain of grieving. But he would worry about that later. Right now, they needed to find somewhere safe to eat, bathe, and change. He would worry about where they would sleep closer to nightfall.

When he mentioned all of this to Kasmiri, she tossed a smoldering look over her shoulder as she continued down the hall, destination unknown.

"I will be sleeping in the same room I have always slept in." She turned her attention away as she marched on.

"If your mother's room isn't safe, what makes you think your room is safe?" He kept up with her pace, but he had to push harder than usual; she was practically running, in heels no less. "I don't know about you, but I have no desire to be roasted in the night."

"Coward," she spat, rounding a corner.

One place he wouldn't let her take her anger out was on

him. He grasped her arm and spun her around, barely ducking the swing of her other arm. He suddenly realized just how many times he had to grasp her and turn her to get her attention. Clearly, this had to stop.

"You let go or I'll have the guards haul you away!" she threatened.

"Haul me away?" he asked, letting go of her arm and taking a step back.

Lifting her brows and jutting her chin, she snidely asked, "How do I know you didn't have something to do with this?"

His mouth literally fell open. How could she even think such a thing?

With an accusatory finger jabbing his chest, she said, "You forced me to bond to you, tricked me into allowing you into my bed under the pretext of learning to pleasure a man, and then suddenly my mother dies, I'm in charge of the empire, and then someone's out to kill me." When she placed her hands on her hips, she lifted to her full height and leaned into him, as if challenging him.

"Don't be a fool." He resisted the urge to shake her and instead stepped into her, pressing her back against the wall. She maintained her furious look, but her eyes flared with trepidation. "If I wanted to kill you, you would have been dead the night I first came to your room. And why would I set fire to your mother's room when I knew damn good and well where you were sleeping?" He didn't wait for her to answer. Crowding against her until his body pressed the length of hers, he added, "And for your information, I never tricked you into anything. It was *your* idea to use me to learn about sex to please Chur. Besides, you wanted to share a bed with me, so don't try to change facts in your mind now to justify your anger."

"I have a right to be angry." Her breathing was sharp, quick. Her pulse danced wildly, causing the vein in her slender neck to visibly throb.

"You do, but not at me." He lowered his head until his nose brushed against hers. "I'm not the enemy, Kasmiri."

Turning her head away, she whispered, "I don't know whom I can trust."

This he understood. Her mother had a contingent of guards and those men had, in turn, sworn themselves to Kasmiri, but who knew where their allegiances actually lay? Riches could buy a man from his conscience. Promises of women, prosperity, and a life of leisure would be most attractive to a man with little to look forward to in his advanced seasons. Bribing a palace guard wouldn't take much.

"You know you can trust me." Ever so gently, he cupped her chin and brought her face back to his. Her eyes were wide and filled with tears. "I have never hurt you and you know I never would. If you want to stay in your room, then that's where we'll stay. I'll make sure it's fully guarded at all times. Guarded by men we can trust."

A modified pout puffed her lips. "I don't want to live like a prisoner."

"You won't, but I'm also not taking any chances with your safety."

Some of the fear left her gaze then, and she tilted her head up, bringing her lips a fraction from his. "You promise to keep me safe?"

She changed so swiftly at times—from angry woman to frightened girl to playful lover—he found it difficult to keep up. Brushing his lips across hers, he whispered, "I am your faithful servant."

At last, she smiled. He felt every bit of the powerful man he'd been last night when he'd kicked in her door. Never would he confuse Kasmiri for a coward who couldn't take care of herself, but right now, she needed a protector. To do that, he would have to place her in the care of the one man who could actually steal her from him.

"Until the room is secure, you'll have to stay elsewhere."

Kasmiri immediately took off down the hall. "One of the suites for visiting dignitaries should be fine."

"No, somewhere safer."

She rolled her eyes. "Those rooms are carefully guarded. It simply wouldn't do to have one of our guests murdered. Over one hundred guards patrol that wing; it's safer than—"

He knew she was about to say it was safer than her mother's rooms. "There is one place that I know you will be safe."

"Where?"

"Chur's rooms."

When her eyes lit up, he gritted his teeth. Just when he thought she'd given up on Chur, she reminded him that she hadn't, and probably never would. However, if placing her there would keep her safe, he had no other choice. Sterlave trusted Chur more than he trusted Kasmiri.

"The only problem is I don't know where his rooms are."

"I do."

Of course you do.

He followed behind her, watching her primp her hair, smooth her smudged makeup, and adjust her clinging dress, all without missing a step. Suppressing a series of annoyed sighs, he strode through a maze of hallways and up several flights of stairs. Eventually they stood before a pair of massive doors protected by equally massive guards.

Kasmiri announced herself but the guards didn't move.

Curious, Sterlave waited patiently while Kasmiri berated them both for their ineptitude. After a long while, Chur came to the door. His face was sweaty and all that covered him was a black loincloth. Sterlave instantly knew what had delayed Chur. He did his best to suppress a knowing smile, but Chur caught it anyway.

Man to man, they nodded to one another; then Chur graciously moved aside and let them enter. As Sterlave drew next to him, his nose confirmed what his gut already knew. Chur and his lovely mate had been thoroughly enjoying the pleasures of their bed. Once inside the room, another whiff of sex tickled his nose. The scent of pleasure seemed permanently affixed to the place. He wondered just how often the two indulged in the erotic arts.

Sterlave had never had a chance to enjoy the Harvester rooms, but he imagined they would look much like this. Everything had clean lines with no clutter. The furniture was solid, crafted in simple styles with minimal decoration. Almost everything was black or various shades of brown. Masculine but warm, Sterlave felt comfortable the moment he entered.

Most of the room was one large space, with areas for sitting, dining, and sleeping. Only the kitchen and basin were behind walls. When Sterlave looked around, he saw evidence of remodeling, but what really caught his eye was the massive bathing unit that took up the entire north wall. A dozen knobs and gilded jets put Kasmiri's unit to shame. The entire room seemed to focus on the unit, as if this held the greatest importance to them. He puzzled over it for a moment, shrugged, and then turned his attention to Chur.

"We were about to eat. Won't you join us?" Chur motioned to a large wooden table next to the kitchen.

Sterlave and Kasmiri sat down next to each other on the same side, watching as Chur disappeared behind the wall.

"By the gods! Why is the bathing unit in the main room?" Kasmiri asked, glaring at the polished Onic tile as if it had personally affronted her.

"They like to bathe?" Again, he shrugged. "I'll ask Chur about it in the training rooms later."

Kasmiri's eyes rounded and she hissed, "You intend to leave me here alone with that woman?"

A burst of laughter came from the kitchen, followed by the rattling of cooking utensils. Something about that sound caused a surge of envy in Sterlave. He wanted that kind of easy enjoyment with his mate.

Cupping Kasmiri's hand, he said, "I can't very well take you to the training rooms. Besides, you should get to know Enovese."

Silted eyes and a mew of disgust were her only answer.

"Try to be friends with them. Remember, we need their help." But he knew Kasmiri didn't want to be friends with Enovese, not when she thought the woman had stolen the man of her dreams. "You'll be safe here until Chur and I can get your room put to rights."

"And why would he do that?" She pulled her hand from his and made another attempt to fix her sleep tousled hair. Black strands strayed from the knot at her neck.

"Because he's my friend."

Kasmiri paused at that, looking ashamed. She stopped fidgeting and lowered her hand to the table.

Enovese and Chur emerged carrying trays with several platters. They placed them in the center of the table, then returned with plates and utensils.

"Please, enjoy." Enovese, resplendent in a black robe with her hair plaited into a single braid, seated herself to the left of Chur, who took up the head of the table.

Sterlave wasn't shy. He picked up his plate, then helped himself to the food—seared *aket*, fluffy bread, creamed *nicla*, and several items he couldn't identify but tried nonetheless. Everything was wonderful. When he complimented Enovese, she smiled demurely.

Kasmiri kicked him under the table.

He darted her a quick frown when Chur and Enovese were distracted. Kasmiri rolled her eyes, made a face, and then looked away. She didn't even want him complimenting Enovese! Was Kasmiri that insecure, or did she just wish to start trouble to force him to find somewhere else for her to stay?

Spoiled empress or no, she would do what he said. His duty was to protect her, and the empire, so that's exactly what he intended to do, whether she liked it or not. Spending a day with Enovese wouldn't kill her. Perhaps some of Enovese's quiet strength would rub off on Kasmiri.

While they ate, Sterlave conveyed the morning events to Chur and asked for his help. Graciously, he agreed to help him hand-select guards for not only their rooms, but for Kasmiri.

"And what of guards for Sterlave?" she asked, jutting out her proud chin.

"I don't need—" he began, but Chur cut him off.

"They clearly were after you, not him." Chur considered for a moment, discussed something with Enovese, nodded, and then rose from the table. "Come, Sterlave. There is much we must discuss."

Kasmiri looked ready to eat her way up the table, but instead, she plastered a smile to her face, nodded to Enovese, and slid her chair back.

"Are we safe leaving them alone?" Sterlave asked as he followed Chur from the table.

Chur laughed. "Kasmiri will be fine."

"She's not the one I'm worried about." When he looked back, Enovese gracefully removed dishes while Kasmiri stood by and watched. It probably didn't occur to her to help. When he motioned for her to do so, she crossed her arms and glared. He sighed. He wasn't sure if she was being deliberately rude because it was Enovese, or if she genuinely thought such a task was beneath her.

When he turned back, Chur had removed his loincloth, exposing an overwhelming length of glowing bronze flesh. Sterlave gulped but couldn't take his gaze away. Every bit of Chur was chiseled, sculpted, almost unbearably perfect. A dusting of regrowing black hair shaded his muscular body in such a way to make him seem even more powerful. A quick peek over his shoulder confirmed what he already knew; Kasmiri watched Chur with unabashed interest.

"Enovese will be fine as well." Chur pulled on a pair of loose-fitting trousers but not before giving Kasmiri a good look at his cock. That's all Sterlave needed: one more thing he couldn't live up to. Even flaccid Chur was big. The shadow of short black hairs just made him seem even larger, not like he needed help there.

Chur didn't seem to mind that they stared. He was either entirely oblivious or actually enjoyed being on display. Sterlave realized it was the former when Chur slipped a shirt over his head and strode purposefully to the main door. If he was aware of the impact he made, he showed no sign of it.

"Come, we will find the right men to guard the empress."

Kasmiri tried to keep her tongue in her mouth, but with a will of its own, it darted out to the corner of her lips. Chur was magnificent. No woman could look at him and think otherwise.

"While I clean up, you are more than welcome to use the bathing unit." Enovese placed a stack of fresh towels within reach. On top of the stack, she placed a simple black robe. "I will give you privacy." With that, she returned to the kitchen.

Out of all the women Chur could have chosen, why had he chosen her? As Kasmiri undressed, she had to grudgingly concede that Enovese was beautiful, but she was so quiet in comparison to Chur. He was a mighty storm that threatened to engulf the planet, while Enovese was barely the puff from a bird wing. And Sterlave, practically drooling over her with compliments and expecting her, an empress, to clean up like a common servant!

Under the flow of water, she shook her head. Sterlave had a lot to learn. Enovese was a servant, not her. Into her mind crept her thoughts of Enovese from the bonding celebration party.

Enovese, legs splayed, and man after man working to find his pleasure between them. All the while Chur watching, but this time, in her mind's eye, he was not angry but excited by what he saw. His cock pulsed hard and strong, angled up from his body, nodding in time to each man's thrusts. Suddenly, the scene shifted. Kasmiri was on her back with a series of intricate straps and knots holding her down. Sterlave teased his fingers along the lips of her sex until it wept with need. She would have begged him, but a strap kept her mouth closed. Finally, he plunged within. Her whole body wanted to arch up to meet him, but the knotted ropes held her immobile. Again and again, he thrust until she closed her eyes and screamed her climax into the gag.

A small shiver passed through her. To her shock, she realized she'd climaxed without a single touch.

Warily, she opened her eyes, half expecting to find Enovese standing in front of her, but she wasn't. From the kitchen, Kasmiri could hear her humming as she cleaned up. What kind of a woman happily played servant to a man who could afford many?

Kasmiri would never tolerate such a situation.

As she soaped her body, her thoughts turned sultry again, this time Sterlave joined her in the shower, teasing his hands along her flesh, sliding his fingertips across her bottom then to the cleft between. Before she could fully indulge in her wild fantasy, she dropped the soap, snapping herself out of the dream.

Eyeing the elaborate bathing unit, she wondered if it had caused her amorous thoughts. Something about the heated Onic tiles, smooth gilded faucets, and oversized knobs all right out in the open was painfully arousing. She'd smelled sex when she'd entered Chur's rooms, and as soon as she had, she'd grown wet with wanting. Her awareness hadn't been for Chur, but for Sterlave. That's why his attention to Enovese angered her so much. He should only look at her with that lust in his eyes. But, too, there was something more to this than just a scent or the physical aspects of the room itself. Within these rooms lurked a veritable sexual power.

Kasmiri rinsed quickly, dried herself, and slipped on the robe. The rich *astle,* perfectly stitched, was fit for an empress. Again, somewhat grudgingly, she had to admit Enovese had good taste, or Chur did. She frowned. Somehow, she couldn't imagine him selecting something as mundane as a robe. His happy little servant must do that. Kasmiri wondered what other things Enovese did for Chur. With an entire day together, she had a perfect opportunity to find out.

15

Loban entered the *tishiary*, ready to harvest another batch of sacrifices. He'd learned his lessons well last night. This time, he had a small pouch at his hip to hold soothing oil, a cleaning cloth, and if necessary, a gag. Even before he dressed himself for tonight's event, he was aroused.

Painfully aroused.

All day, as he sat and repaired weapon after weapon, his balls throbbed and his cock ached. Every recruit who crossed his vision took center stage in one of his fantasies. Some he simply killed with a few deft strokes, but others he elaborately raped, then killed. He could smell their fear, taste the richness of their blood, and feel the quivering pain in their trembling limbs. Each one helped him prepare for his second night as the secret Harvester.

He paused behind a draped wall, waiting for the larger groups to leave. He would like to try two at once, but he didn't think he could control three without restraints. Moreover, he preferred to hold his conquests down himself.

Chur hadn't spent much time in the training rooms today.

Late in the morning, he strode in and pointed to a few recruits, who leapt to attention, then followed him like love-struck virgins. Loban had no idea where they went or what they did. He didn't care. If they kept Chur and his hateful, knowing gaze away from him, that's all he cared about.

Loban had tried to include Chur in his dark dreams, but he couldn't. Fear held him back. He worried that somehow, just thinking about him might alert Chur, as if he would *know*. He shivered in the warm, moist air. If Chur had any inkling of what he was doing, he wouldn't hesitate. There would be no brand of shame placed upon his forehead as he returned to his village. No, Chur would annihilate him.

"But when power fills me, and we are evenly matched, I will best him once and for all."

Loban turned his attention to a pair of dark haired servants. The two women looked so similar they had to be sisters. Ensuring they were alone, he left his hiding place behind the wall. He was upon them before they could react. He enjoyed the challenge of controlling both of them simultaneously, but he discovered that if he threatened to hurt one, the other would willingly submit. Loban didn't understand why. If someone threatened to hurt another, he would simply run while they did. What would he care if another person were hurt? As he wallowed in their fear, he thought he would never understand people.

When he finished with them, he rinsed the blood from his shaft, applied a thick layer of oil, and then selected his next sacrifice. Twenty times, he repeated his actions. Frustration grew when he did not feel any differently. What was he doing wrong? He mimicked the ritual as closely as he could without having the proper gear. Surely the gods had to understand the limitations he labored under.

Resolute, he knew he had to try a different approach. Determined to feel something, he vowed to make the next one count.

A lone servant, slender, with black hair and blue eyes, entered with an armload of crimson laundry. Loban's skin prickled. Only the empress wore red. He confirmed the servant was the empress's because he wore a crimson sash. Was his mistake in not taking a higher level of servant?

Loban studied the man as he methodically cleaned his mistress's clothing. Mixed in with the crimson items were a few black pieces.

Sterlave's? Loban smiled. There was something unbearably arousing about harvesting Sterlave's servant. Perhaps if he found the right circumstances, he would take his bondmate too. Harvesting the empress would surely empower him. He frowned. Kasmiri had already been harvested, but if he raped her . . .

To his shock, he watched the servant lift a scrap of black fabric to his face and breathe deeply. He sniffed something of Sterlave's, but what? Loban couldn't identify the item. Whatever it was, he clearly enjoyed the scent of it, for under his beige robes his prick stiffened. Loban's eyebrows rose as he considered. In a flash, the answer came to him. He knew what he had to do.

"Does your master know that you sniff his clothing?"

The servant whirled, swirling his robe around his bare feet. His mouth worked as he frantically tried to explain, but nothing came out. As his eyes widened, Loban saw white shards infused in the soft blue, hypnotizing eyes. His skin was smooth, but not feminine like the *ungati* last night. The empress had not castrated this one.

Loban pushed him back onto the mound of crimson fabric.

His gaze darted around the room, looking for someone to help him, but they were alone. He struggled but quickly realized such was futile.

Loban plucked the black *astle* from his hands and held it aloft. "What's this?"

"An *echalle*," he choked out.

Loban ordered him to explain. Once he did, Loban considered the special consort undergarments. Only the elite would have such nonsense.

"Has your master fucked you?"

With a frown at his crudity, the servant shook his head.

"But you want him to."

Refusing to answer, he looked away.

Loban reached under the robe, cupped his balls, and squeezed. "Answer."

"Yes." His eyes watered, but Loban couldn't tell if pain or shame caused his tears. Not that it mattered.

Squeezing harder, he asked, "Yes, what?"

"Yes, I want him to fuck me." As soon as he said the words, he turned his head away. Tears fell, dotting the crimson fabric like rain.

Loban caressed his balls, testing the weight of them, enjoying the feel of twin bundles of heat. His pubic hair was surprisingly soft, encouraging him to explore. The servant's erection was gone, but not for long.

"What's your name?" Not that he cared, but he was curious.

"Rown."

Loban slid his finger between soft cheeks. "Has any man taken you here?"

Unable to answer, Rown shook his head side to side.

A wide smile lifted the edges of Loban's mouth. Now he knew what he'd been missing. It *did* matter that his sacrifices were virgins. Rown would help him find the start of the dark power that would ultimately allow him to triumph.

"Look at me. If you look away again, I will kill you."

Rown did as he commanded. Such terror and shame in Rown's eyes lifted Loban's arousal to a new and dangerous height. He wasn't sure he could control himself.

He must.

This was the way. He could not falter now. With a deep breath, Loban placed the *echalle* over Rown's mouth and nose.

"Breathe. Think of him. Look at me and think of him."

Teasing his fingers along Rown's shaft did not help him to achieve an erection. Aggravated, Loban tried every trick he could. Nothing.

Loban adjusted the *echalle* so it covered Rown's entire face. Still, he gained no reaction.

Pushing the robe up, Loban lowered his head and wrapped his lips about the servant's flaccid flesh. Twirling his tongue around as he sucked caused blood to fill his reluctant shaft.

Loban drew back and whispered, "Think of him. Think of Sterlave doing this to you. Imagine his mouth upon your cock. His finger teasing along the slick, tight need between your legs."

Rown emitted a rumbling groan of reluctant surrender.

Loban continued to tease Rown until he hovered on the verge of climax. At that point, Loban snapped up, slid Rown to the edge of the table, placed his left foot against the hilt of his dagger, and yanked his right leg up along his chest.

Loban spoke in the ancient tongue. "By might of the blade I claim that which belongs to me."

Rown went very still below him and Loban knew he understood exactly what he'd said. Somehow, he'd known that a servant of the empress would know the language of the ancients.

Loban told Rown what he wanted him say.

At first, Rown refused, but a threat to kill his master compelled instant compliance.

"I freely give myself to you," Rown said, his voice reluctant, terrified.

Clearly, Rown thought that if he just said the words, Loban would relent. Not a chance.

Power surged through his cock, swelling him to the point of bursting. He shoved the makeshift codpiece aside. Without preamble, he positioned himself and rammed forward. His teasing Rown with oil-slick fingers helped his prick smooth deep inside.

A rich feeling borne of Rown's tightness and his reluctant pleasure wrapped around Loban's body. This sensation enveloped not just his prick, but also his soul. As he took the servant's virginity as sacrifice, he felt a new and great power infuse his form.

This was his first true harvest.

When Rown tried to scream, Loban shoved the *echalle* into his mouth.

Rown's bucking only allowed him deeper access.

Just as he had with his first sacrifice, Loban leaned near, and said, "Remember, you asked for this. You freely gave yourself to me."

Rown shook his head, trying to spit out the scrap of fabric, but Loban shoved it back in just as he shoved his prick deeper into his ass.

"Forever after, you belong to me." Loban thrust as he wrapped his hand tightly around Rown's cock. Every time he moved forward, he stroked his tight fist down. Rown's strong legs shook against his body as he tried to fight his orgasm; however, Loban had gauged his needs too well.

There was no turning back.

Thrust after thrust matched by stroke after stroke made Rown his willing sacrifice. Quickly, he built a rhythm, driving them both toward the edge.

Loban felt his balls lift and tighten just as Rown's did.

"That's it. Come for me." Loban leaned over his slight, muscular body, riding him toward fulfillment.

"I can't, I'm not allowed!" Panic infused Rown's voice while he struggled in earnest. As *ungati*, Rown could bestow pleasure yet not receive it. Ancient law forbade him from experiencing orgasm by the hand of another. Only alone, and under restrictive ritual, could Rown seek satisfaction. All this, Loban knew. Violating Rown's station would give him the power he sought. He'd not captured this element during his initial harvest. But now, he understood his mistake. He would not make another.

"For me you will come. You will give to me that which you cannot give to any other." Loban continued to thrust deeply into Rown as he grasped his engorged prick. No matter how valiantly Rown tried to resist, Loban's skilled hand and deep penetration forced the servant's surrender.

With an agonized cry, Rown climaxed, jetting his sacred fluid along Loban's fist as Loban spewed his seed deep inside Rown's virginal bottom. So sweet, so complete was his ascension, Loban lost all of his senses.

Plunged into darkness, Loban floated without the anchor of a body, the weight of a conscience, or the tether of emotions.

Here, in the vast nothingness, he was naught.

Never had he been so humbled. If he had knees, he would have fallen to them in supplication, but he was without form. He felt smaller than a speck of dust. So miniscule was he that he was not fit to cling to the bottom of the gods' feet. How dare he think himself worthy of being their vessel?

In a gush of fear, he swore himself to them. However, without a mouth, his words bounced uselessly in the void. With a twitching tingle, he felt something forming from the emptiness. When he found his mouth, he shouted his worthlessness and begged forgiveness. He would do anything, everything they demanded of him.

A voice asked if he would cut his genitals off.

Loban said, "Just give me a knife."

Below him, his body materialized, and in his right fist, he found a *cirvant*. With one deft swing, he sliced his cock and balls off. Blood jetted from his body as he knelt to scoop up his offering. He held his gift high over his head for their approval.

Laughter surrounded him.

Crushed, Loban tossed the rejected offer away. "Tell me what to do!"

A voice cast a light upon a huge phallus, then asked him if he would impale himself upon it.

Without hesitation, Loban squatted over the smooth stone statue. Tears fell as he worked the frigid device deep inside. Excruciating pain doubled him over as he ripped himself, but still he lowered himself until he lodged the entire phallus deep within.

Laughter crushed him, mocking his eagerness.

Everything the gods asked, he did. He willingly performed an endless series of perverse sexual acts. No matter what he did, all that greeted his ears was more laughter. Suddenly, he understood: The gods played with him just as he once toyed with the recruits.

When he refused to do as they bid, the laughter ceased.

Behind him, a beastly breath of fire seared the hairs along his flesh. Flames licked out, charring his skin. Chunks fell off as he screamed in agony, but he did not run or slap frantically at the blaze. He shrieked, but he stood firm.

To his fury, laughter enveloped his battered soul.

Laughter more mocking than what he'd suffered during his childhood made him long to chop off his ears. Once he grew big and strong, he thought he would never hear such taunts again, but even the gods found him pathetic, puny, and pitiful.

Rage burbled from the deepest hurt in his psyche, then erupted, spewing out of his mouth like liquid fire. Jetting wrath replaced the darkness with molten light. Loban vomited his fury until burning rock surrounded him. He spewed until he lifted himself high on an inferno of rage.

"I will not be mocked!" he yelled, thrusting his fist to the sky. "Set me a true challenge and I will prove myself worthy!"

Abruptly, the laughter ended.

He did not trust the silence, for they had mocked him before. When the voice whispered to his ear, he smiled. They asked of him a service he would gladly provide. He would not only meet their test, but he would also surpass their expectations. When he did, they would bestow upon him more power than his mortal body could contain.

Loban would be immortal.

Loban would rule the Onic Empire.

Bit by bit, the real world infiltrated his awareness. He thought he'd been gone for hours but only moments had past. Below him, Rown still quivered with the ravages of his climax while Loban pumped the last of his.

Loban removed his hand from Rown's spent member, then wrapped his fist around Rown's throat. "Look at me."

Wide, terrified eyes met his gaze.

"If you tell anyone what happened—"

"You'll kill me," Rown interjected.

"Oh, no, I won't kill you." Loban paused dramatically. "I'll kill your master." His predatory smile terrified the fragile *ungati*.

Rown shook his head, his eyes beseeching. "I won't tell."

"No?" Such panic gave Loban pause. He devised a new and cruel game on the spot. Never had a moral choice confounded Loban, but he intuitively knew most others were quick to sacrifice themselves. Tender, sweet Rown would have deep moral issues and personal concerns, especially if he was gleefully sniffing Sterlave's undergarments.

"Choose," Loban demanded. "Whom do I kill: you or him?"

Caught in the grip of an untenable dilemma, Rown begged, "I swear I won't tell." Rown squeaked around the force of Loban's grip. "You don't have to hurt anyone."

"I didn't ask you that." Loban pressed close until he was nose to nose, then demanded, "Who will die? You or Sterlave?"

"Please. I won't—"

Loban crushed the air from his throat. "Stop telling me the answer to questions I haven't asked." Loban rammed his softening prick deep into Rown.

His answering wince thrilled him.

"I told you to choose who will die: you or Sterlave?"

Trapped, Rown said, "Me." Casting his gaze down in fear, he whispered, "Don't hurt Sterlave."

Loban laughed as he withdrew. "You'd give yourself in his stead?"

"Yes."

Curious, Loban asked, "Why?"

"He is my master."

"It's more than that." Loban swabbed the cleaning cloth across his cock. "You would give yourself up in place of him. Why? Isn't your life worth as much as his?"

Baffled, Rown shook his head. "Any servant would give his life for his master."

"Only a stupid servant would do so." Once he'd cleaned himself, he helped Rown from the table. Just in case he missed the import of his edict, Loban grasped his shoulder, drew him near, and whispered, "Only a stupid servant would dare to tell what happened to him today." Trailing his tongue up to Rown's tender ear, he whispered, "You are not stupid, are you?"

On a shuddering breath, Rown said, "No."

"Good boy." With a last stroke to his firm buttocks, Loban released him.

With awkward steps, Rown gathered his laundry and departed the *tishiary*. Loban didn't linger. Now that his mission was clear, he wouldn't need to haunt these rooms any longer. When he exited, Helton Ook intersected his path, just as the gods said he would.

"I saw what you did." Helton's arms were too massive to cross over his chest, so he placed his hands on his hips, which only made his squat, muscular body look bigger.

Loban was not intimidated. "And?" His gaze lowered to the prominent bulge in Helton's trousers. "You wanted a private demonstration of my skills?"

Wizened gray eyes narrowed. "I can still take you down."

"Can you?" Loban took a step closer, looming his superior height over the aging warrior. Helton had a lifetime of skills, but Loban now had the blessing of the gods.

Helton leveled his gaze, sizing him up. He showed no fear, only a curious speculation.

"No recruit has ever shown you disrespect, but you're not a handler anymore." Loban trailed his finger along one of Helton's maroon scars. "And I am no longer a recruit."

Helton smacked his hand aside. "You'll always be a recruit because you don't know how to act like a Harvester."

At one time, the insult would have burned his pride, but now, Helton was the one who needed him, not the other way around. The disgraced handler had no one else to turn to. However, Loban should make it clear he was no floor mat for him to push his weight around on.

"If not for you, I would have been the Harvester." Loban's hand strayed to the dagger at his waist.

Flicking his gaze down, then up, Helton cautioned, "You don't want to do that, not when I'm offering you the chance to expand your dark harvest."

Intrigued, Loban left off his weapon. "Speak then, but make sure you say things I wish to hear."

And Helton did.

16

With Chur's help, Kasmiri's rooms had been thoroughly inspected, and over thirty of the strongest recruits guarded her
door and the hallway. Two guards followed her wherever she
went, which she resisted, but Sterlave put his foot down. Her
privacy was important, but her life was more so. After pouting
and trying all of her seductive tricks, she finally relented.

Since all of her possessions were in her mother's room, her
room was mostly bare. Kasmiri didn't seem to care. Once they
entered, she smiled and wrapped her arms around him.

"Thank you." His chest muffled her voice.

"You're welcome."

Her friendly hug changed into a passionate embrace when
she slid her hands down to his buttocks.

"I was thinking . . ." Kasmiri leaned back then flashed him
her most seductive glance. When she wished, she could be the
most alluring woman, all soft curves and luscious promises.

"Don't keep me in suspense." Sterlave was a little leery of
her playful mood. She had no problem using her body to ma-

nipulate him to do as she wished. He had no idea what she had in mind, but hopefully, it was something that involved getting naked and into bed. Too many nights had passed with them fighting or grieving. This night, he wanted to be with her.

"Do you think we would both fit into my bathing unit?" Her gaze darted to the entrance, then back at him.

Simply considering the idea aroused him. Her wet, hot, and sliding against him, how could he refuse? "We'll never know unless we try."

She started to remove her clothing, but he stopped her by cupping her hands. "Why rush?" He had her hold her arms out so he could unwrap her dress. Slowly, he revealed her devastating form—high breasts with dark nipples, a gently curved belly, tight curls protecting her sweet, pink sex, sleek thighs, and her lovely crimson-tipped toes.

Once he had her nude, he lowered to his knees and placed a kiss upon her mound, just as he had during the bonding ceremony.

When he looked up, her eyes were dreamy soft, each pupil so wide it melded with the iris. She teased her fingers across his head, then to his ears, then to his cheeks. With gentle pressure, she urged his face toward her sex.

Ordering him or inviting him? He couldn't tell. Moreover, he didn't care. With a sultry grin, he nudged his head between her thighs and swiped his tongue across her firm, little clit—musky but sweet, like sugar-drenched *nicla*. Her flavor was uniquely wonderful, yet he would never be able to indulge his lust with her standing.

With three graceful yet precise moves, he had her down, on her back, with her legs up and over his shoulders.

Gasping with surprise, she didn't struggle but willingly parted her legs wider for his deft, probing tongue.

Pleased to discover all his brutal training had some practical applications, he lifted his head and whispered, "Be wary of one who kneels to you so eagerly; they probably have an ulterior motive."

She laughed and relaxed. "If your intent is to pleasure me, then I have no objections." Lifting herself up, she peered down at him with a lifted brow. "You learned this technique in the training rooms?"

Smiling up the length of her, he said, "I spent my life learning how to manipulate the bodies of my foes."

Coquettishly, she swore, "I'm not your enemy."

"Of course not, but sex can be a competition. One is always striving to find fulfillment." He paused. "Or give it."

He lowered his lips to hers and drank deeply of her sweet juice. Nothing existed for him but Kasmiri's succulent sex. The more he nibbled and chewed, the wetter she became, and the harder he became. As delicious as he found her flavor, just the sight of her bright pink secrets hidden between ebony flesh sent him over the edge. He wanted to be inside her so desperately he could barely breathe.

Something dark and mysterious pushed at his back. Sterlave struggled to shake it off, but the sensation enveloped his skin, then sunk deep into his body until it wrapped itself firmly around his genitals. Violent need throbbed him to painful arousal. He didn't just want to mate with Kasmiri; he wanted to hurt her. Pleasure would come in subjugating her to his needs.

Shocked by the intense evil of the sensation, knowing in his heart that it wasn't his desire that pushed him, Sterlave gathered all of his strength and shoved the malevolent feeling away. Reluctantly, whatever it was released him. As it departed, he swore he heard a mocking chuckle.

He shook his head, unsure if what had just happened was real, and if it was real, what had caused it? Never had he possessed such sinister feelings toward anyone. The very idea was so alien to him he was convinced it was all just a figment of his exhausted imagination. All he needed was a lustful encounter with his mate and a good night's sleep.

Beneath him, Kasmiri writhed, angling her hips up, begging him to continue his teasing. He lost himself in her essence. Working his fingers and tongue in concert brought her to a fever pitch. When she rose up, her body tightening in release, he plunged his fingers deep inside and worked his thumb across her clit. She gasped out as a series of orgasms twitched her uncontrollably.

Lifting up, he wrenched his pants aside in his rush to mount her. If he hurried, he would be able to feel the last of her contractions.

"Wait, wait," she said breathlessly. "You have to get undressed so we can get in the water." Kasmiri was determined to act out her fantasy.

Disappointed at the delay, he stood, ripped his clothing off, yanked her to her feet, and then hustled them into the bathing unit.

"Why are you in such a hurry?" she asked sweetly. "I thought you were used to denial." She stroked her fingertips along his throbbing cock. "It seems to me you have no self-control at all."

"Easy for you to say when you've been sated." He grasped her hand and pulled her into the unit. They had to squeeze together to fit, not that he minded.

"It's a bit snug." Sterlave turned on a jet of cool water, hoping it would temper his ardor. Much to his dismay, with Kasmiri plastered against him, cold water didn't help at all.

With a wince, she turned the jet to warm, then hot. "It's a bit snug, but"—she hit him with those wild, sexy eyes—"I'm sure you can make this work."

Her gaze offered a challenge he couldn't refuse.

"I know I can make it work." Without preamble, he lifted her against the wall, parted her legs, and slid his cock inside her.

Relief allowed him to release a tense breath. "Does that work for you?"

Purring, she wrapped her legs around him and plastered her mouth to his, kissing him deeply.

He knew Chur's elaborate bathing unit had put this idea in her head, but he didn't care. She was in *his* arms, her strong legs tightened around *his* hips, and her luscious lips were kissing *his* mouth. Chur might have a firm grip on her mind, but only he possessed her body.

Sterlave swore he would do anything to keep his hold on her. As much as he knew Chur would never take her from him, he despaired that Kasmiri would never completely give up on Chur. He didn't think he could continue if Chur would be between them forever. Chur was his friend, a confidant, but he could never live up to a demigod. Moreover, he didn't want to. Why couldn't Kasmiri see that her dreams were beyond her grasp? In the same breath, he didn't want her to settle for him. He wanted her to pick him, to choose him because she *wanted* him, not because he was second best. Frustrated that he'd made little headway with her, he worried that eventually he'd just give up.

Kasmiri noticed his distraction and teased him out of his thoughts with a seductive pout. "Does this really need such thought from you that you must furrow your brow?"

Redoubling his efforts to focus on her, he tried to hold her still and thrust. The floor was a bit slick without much traction, so he slid her down the wall and angled his legs back so his feet touched the sides. With some leverage, he was able to hold her securely while thrusting deeply.

"Is this what you wanted?"

She nodded. "More." She wrapped her arms around his shoulders to hold on.

Sterlave used the slick wall to raise and lower her in opposition to his movements. Every plunge was sweeter than the last as she clung to him, panting in his ear, begging him for more. Wild with need, he tried to pace himself, but the feel of her strong thighs and the tightness of her passage made control impossible. His climax couldn't wait.

He wasn't even sure what caused his frantic lust. It could be his insecurity over Chur, or the fact they hadn't been together in a few days, or her life being in danger, or the strange dark sensation—whatever it was, he'd have to get the cause under control or he'd become her slave. If Kasmiri understood just how much he wanted her, she would be able to crook her finger to command him.

Sterlave sought out her neck, biting her gently at first, then more aggressively as his pace increased. Blinded with need, the world slipped away until all that remained was their entwined bodies. When he felt his climax start, he pinned her to the wall, holding her there while he filled her with his seed. He wanted to impregnate her. He wanted to fill her belly with his child because such would bind her irrevocably to him.

"I can't breathe," Kasmiri gasped.

Pulling back, he took his weight from her, then lowered her feet to the floor. "Did I hurt you?"

"No." She tilted her head to the side, considering him with her enormous dark eyes. "At the end you were so frantic. You've never been like that before."

Reluctant to admit what he'd been thinking of in those moments, he turned away and asked, "Are you certain I didn't hurt you?"

"I'm fine." She teased her hand along his neck. "But were you thinking of me, or her?"

"Who?" He spun his head to face her, genuinely baffled. All he'd thought about was her and keeping her with him forever. If anything, he worried she'd been thinking of Chur. He was fairly certain that's why she wanted to have sex in the bathing unit. He sighed. He'd like to have just one encounter with her that wasn't a threesome.

"You know who." She rolled her eyes and slid past him.

Now he understood. Kasmiri thought he'd been fantasizing about Enovese. Wonderful. Now their encounters had become foursomes. Sterlave shut the water off, dried, and then exited the bathing unit.

Kasmiri stood in front of her elaborate mirror, dripping water all over the floor. "What's wrong with me?"

"Nothing." He grabbed a towel and wrapped it around her shoulders.

"Then what does she have that I don't?" Her voice cracked, breaking his heart.

"Kasmiri," he began, pulling her into his arms, "I have no interest in her. Absolutely none." Catching her gaze in the glass, he kissed the edge of her ear. "You are the only woman I've ever hungered for. My frenzy was because I wanted to get deeper. I felt like I couldn't get deep enough." He still didn't think it was wise to tell her how much he wanted to fill her with his child. She had enough to deal with already.

Kasmiri considered for a moment, looking at him, looking at herself. For the first time he considered them as bondmates. Side by side, they made a striking couple. Her beauty was dark and mysterious with her wide eyes and luscious, full mouth. She literally took his breath away. His bronzed skin contrasted her deep ebony skin, while his light brown eyes complemented her darker shade. Once his hair grew back, they would be even more stunning. Then he realized she was asking why Chur didn't want her. As he moved to pull away, she melted into him, resting her head against his chest.

Now was probably not the best time, but he had to clear the air. "I worried that you were thinking of Chur."

Her shock was genuine. "I wasn't thinking of him." She

turned in his arms and looked directly into his eyes. "I was thinking of you."

He wanted to believe her, but how could he? Every time she heard Chur's name, or was in his presence, she glowed. "Today, when we were going to Chur's rooms, you primped right up until the moment when we went inside." And there was no way she could say she was doing it for him, not when he trailed dutifully behind her the entire way.

Her brow furrowed as she looked down. "I wasn't fixing myself for him." She paused, then whispered, "I was fixing myself up because of her."

"Enovese?" He couldn't have been more surprised.

"I didn't want to look tattered in front of her. I was afraid she'd be all pretty and perfect, which she was, and I'd look disheveled and disastrous, which I did." Kasmiri met his gaze, then quickly looked away. "If you were going to be comparing us, I wanted to look as good as I could."

All of her actions now made perfect sense. He'd worried everything was about her impressing Chur when she'd been desperately trying to impress him. Exerting gentle pressure, he lifted her chin with his hand until she faced him again. "I've never compared you to anyone because you are incomparably beautiful."

Kasmiri rolled her eyes, but then asked, "Am I?"

"Absolutely." A relieved chuckle escaped him. "I fear we have been at cross purposes. I keep thinking you want Chur and you keep thinking I want Enovese." Leaning near until he pressed his forehead to hers, he said, "We must be the two most terribly insecure people ever."

She met his gaze, then lowered it to where her hand cupped against his chest. "I never thought of myself as insecure, and I don't think I ever have been." When she sighed, her puff of breath tickled his chest. With the softest voice, she whispered, "Not until I had someone I was afraid to lose."

All the tension coiled around his body abruptly melted away because she wasn't talking about Chur this time, but him. Kasmiri was afraid of losing him. For the first time in his life, someone actually cared whether he was around or not. Not even his own father troubled himself during Sterlave's extended absences. When he did return, often beaten and bloody, his father never asked how he was or where he'd been; all he cared about was if Sterlave had brought anything with him.

Swallowing hard, Kasmiri pressed herself against his chest, and said, "Not even with Chur did I ever feel this way. I'm afraid the more I want you, the more insecure I become."

Her soft admission sent a reckless pride spinning throughout him, causing him to embrace her tightly. He knew he should not take joy in her insecurity, but finally, finally, she honestly wanted him. Tilting his lips down, he captured hers in a soft kiss, and whispered against her mouth, "You are not going to lose me. How could you think such a thing? I fought for you. I'd die for you." Actually, he did, but Kasmiri didn't know the gods had brought him back. He sighed, rubbing his nose against hers. "Forget Chur, forget Enovese. From now on, it's you and I. Agreed?"

Her lips pursed into a modified pout as she considered. "Only you and me? What about Rown?"

Sterlave lifted his brows. "I wasn't opposed to him teaching you the fine art of oral pleasure, but I didn't realize you wanted him as a regular bed partner." He honestly didn't want to share his lovely woman with anyone. Rown might know a million sexual tricks that he could teach to Kasmiri, but Sterlave would rather educate her himself. Just as she would show him what pleased her most, he would do the same.

Trailing her hand across his two chest scars, she said, "Not a regular one, but how about an occasional visitor?" Her greedy expression clarified that she was more than willing to share him with another. What was it about seeing two men together that gave her such an erotic thrill?

He'd never really thought that much about Rown's position. He liked him but found his obvious fascination a bit disconcerting. Not that he minded, just that he didn't want to encourage feelings he couldn't return. Somehow, it seemed wrong to use a fellow human as a sex toy, whether he wanted to be used that way or not. Sterlave tried to express these thoughts to Kasmiri, but he knew he hadn't explained them well when she immediately set to arguing with him.

"As an *ungati,* his job is to provide pleasure. Moreover, he likes you. I thought that you liked him too." Kasmiri made everything sound so simple, but he knew relationships, especially sexual relationships, were rarely simple.

"I do like him, just not quite as much as he likes me." Sterlave tried again to explain. "I don't want him to be hurt when he realizes that I don't share his feelings."

At this Kasmiri frowned. "Rown knows you cannot return his affections. It is his function to provide pleasure."

"That's what bothers me. Rown has to do it whether he wants to or not."

"But he wants to!" Her eyes flashed with frustrated annoyance.

Sterlave sighed. "I don't know how to explain this to you. I just don't want him to be hurt."

"It's not like what happened to you." As soon as she said the words, she must have realized how harsh they sounded by the way he flinched back and gritted his teeth. "I'm sorry, I didn't mean—"

He cut her off. "Can't we talk about something else?" How did they always manage to find something to fight about? Even when they'd laid out a truce, they couldn't seem to stop bickering about meaningless details. Tonight wasn't a night for arguments. And the last thing he wanted to think about was what Loban had done to him.

17

Loban strode into the Harvest room wearing the official Harvester gear. *Mondi* pants felt cool against his shaved legs, the codpiece nestled tightly to his swollen cock, and the ceremonial sword slapped his thigh. Before him, spread across the endless table, scores of virgins waited, eager to give him their sacrifice.

Helton and Ambo had decided against shaving his head. Such would be an obvious indicator of their plans, but other than that, he was essentially the Harvester. In addition, he found something fitting about a late-night winter Harvest. Out of the cold, he would bring a new fire to the empire.

At the edge of the Harvest room, near the now-quiet fountain, Ambo Votny stood. The little round man darted his gaze everywhere while constantly picking his nose. He winced at even the slightest sound. He practically screamed they were doing something wrong, which irritated Helton to no end. Repeatedly, Helton told the sniveling man to control himself. Ambo scowled back momentarily but quickly his face returned to a frighted scrunch.

Loban's dealings with Ambo had been limited. He'd seen

him at the Harvester functions, such as the Festival of Temptation, but he didn't really know him. Already he couldn't stand his bulging eyes and quivering chins. Raw terror oozed from his very skin, proclaiming Ambo a coward. How had he ever grown into such power as the magistrate with so much weakness in his veins? Loban didn't like him, but he knew he needed his help. Only Ambo could commandeer the Harvest room and keep the palace gossips at bay. However, once Loban completed his plans, Ambo would be the first to die screaming.

Loban smiled. His idea to have those who displeased him torn apart by *wroxes* would work splendidly on this shuddering excuse for a man. Ambo's copious amounts of flesh would entertain the vicious creatures for days, and his thick throat would emit howls that would shake the roof of the palace!

As Loban considered what he would do when the time came, great power rose up in him. For the first time, Loban felt capable of defeating anyone. No more would he be a cowering child, afraid to even breathe lest he draw a bully's attention. Those days were long past. Now he was a man. Clad in the Harvester gear, he knew this garb would be temporary. One day soon, he would wear the mantle of emperor. No more would fragile females rule the Onic Empire. Loban would destroy the house system and revert to a truer form; only his descendents would rule. To ensure there would be no disruption of his family line, he would have many mates. If they did not provide him with a son within two seasons, he would have them executed.

His would be a harsh world.

However, harsh worlds built strong men. If not for the painful childhood he'd endured, he would have grown to be soft and kind, like Sterlave of Gant. Now there was a pathetic excuse for a man. Mated to the empress, but the only one in love with him was his lowly servant Rown.

Loban paused for a moment, for he didn't exactly know if Kasmiri loved Sterlave. But how could she? The man couldn't even fight to protect himself. The night when he'd taken what he wanted from him had been one of the easiest conquests in his life. Sterlave had practically spread his legs and begged for his cock!

Just thinking of that night, that wonderful, almost endless night, where he'd moved from one perversity to the next, inflamed Loban all over again.

Now he was ready to take his sacrifices.

In order to reach the dark gods, they had to change a few basics of the ritual. Neither Loban nor the virgins would have the cushion of *estal* oil. Only slick massage oil would ease his entry. He would not consume *umer* to keep him hard and unable to orgasm because that he could manage on his own, but the greatest change of all came with the sacrifices themselves.

Helton and Ambo had ordered the servants to lie on their backs, nude, so that nothing would get in his way. After prepping them on what to say, they swore them to secrecy on the heads of their masters. They chose only certain servants from the endless hordes that made up most of the palace population. These were special for each of the men and women were virgins. Like his first true sacrifice, Rown, these *ungati* lived to give pleasure, yet never received it. These elite few had owners either too young to use them or disinterested in using them for penetration.

The usual progression was from north to south, so he went the opposite way. From the south end of the table, Loban surveyed his sacrifices. All *ungati* possessed unnatural beauty. Even the strong and virile men were beautiful nonetheless. Each man or woman rested on his or her back, eyes wide, waiting. Only those closest to him could see him. One man and one woman flicked glances at him, then quickly away. When he noticed them holding hands, he hefted the ceremonial sword, but Helton held him back with one strong arm to his wrist.

"You cannot use the sword on the sacrifices," Helton declared. "Such would be an abomination!"

Loban shrugged off his restraint. "That is the old way." He sliced down twice with rapid strokes, cutting the twined hands off. "Welcome to the new way." He pierced their hearts to stop their screaming less they start the others to rebellion.

"Let that be a lesson to the rest of you. Do not defy me. Do not seek comfort from anyone. Only you can help yourself." Raising his voice so it boomed out and filled the room, Loban bellowed, "The only way to help yourselves is to sacrifice yourselves to me!"

Helton shook his head while Ambo looked as if he would die of shock on the spot. Instead, he vomited down the front of his elaborate silver uniform.

Wiping his blade against the black fabric of his pants, Loban returned the sword to the wide leather belt. He approached the next harvest. Tiny, pale, with spun silver hair and deep pink eyes, the woman clearly came from the Ries region. She had been close enough to witness what he'd done to the two holding hands, so she kept hers tightly clenched to her body.

Loban yanked her to the edge of the table. She uttered a high-pitched squeal of fear that shivered pleasure down his spine. He placed her left foot against the hilt of his sword and the right he lifted until it was straight against his chest. He spoke the sacred words with great care, intoning them just so.

She answered in a melodious voice, giving him permission to take from her what he rightly deserved. When he shoved the codpiece aside, his cock sprang forward. Somehow, his prick seemed wider, longer, and heavier. He shoved forward into her, loving the way her entire body tensed, tightening around him. According to the old way, he should penetrate once fully, then withdraw, but that's not what allowed him to tap into the power the gods offered.

Loban knew he had to force each and every one of them to climax. That is what the gods wanted him to do. He had to take their virginity but also their forbidden pleasure into his soul. Corrupting them from their righteous path empowered him along his malevolent path. Yet he knew fear was not the best way to induce orgasm. He'd gotten lucky with Rown, for he'd discovered what he lusted after in his heart. He couldn't do that with each of his chosen. Reluctantly, he'd taken Ambo's advice and would be using *pharas* gel to compel each *ungati's* climax.

Ambo said the gel was similar to the *jaras* gel the empress used during her bonding ceremony. *Yondies* used *pharas* gel to bring their troublesome clients to climax quicker. They used a diluted amount, but tonight, he would use a highly concentrated dose.

Once he'd slammed deep, he touched a drop of pure *pharas* gel to the servant's clit. Within seconds, she clamped around him, spending her sacred juice along his cock. Once she finished wriggling, he withdrew and helped her from the table. He turned to Ambo and snapped his fingers, pointing at the spot next to him.

Stricken, Ambo waddled near.

"Clean me." Into his shaking hands, Loban thrust the cleaning cloth.

Caught between repulsion and terror, Ambo wisely decided to do as he was told, lest Loban separate his head from his neck. Helton kept his position at the heavy doors. His gaze tracked everything Loban did, but his ears were listening for the slightest bit of trouble from outside.

Unlikely, Loban thought, turning to his next sacrifice after Ambo had cleaned him thoroughly. Now that he had the blessing of the gods, nothing would go wrong.

Down the line he went, forcing each sacrifice to give him their virginity and their sacred elixir.

Within, the darkness grew until strength pushed out, turning his skin a deep, dark bronze. Where Chur glowed, Loban absorbed the light. When he looked to the side, he discovered he cast no shadow.

At the last of his chosen, he paused. His hair was silken gold, his eyes the watery green of the Valry Sea. Every turn of his face, from his lips to his nose, was perfectly executed. Such beauty in a man was abnormal. Loban wanted to mar his perfection. If he flayed him but let him live, would his master want him then?

A whisper in his mind cautioned him. Explaining the death of two *ungati* slaves would be difficult enough, but explaining the maiming of another would be impossible. Urging him to use caution surprised him, for the gods should be bold, brash, and do whatever they pleased. Caution was for cowards. Caution would not give him the strength to kill Chur Zenge, for that's what they ultimately prepared him to do.

As he approached the young man, he pictured how he would decimate his face, yet in his vision, he saw himself. Bit by bit, an unseen hand sliced away his nose, his brows, and his lips. Recoiling, Loban removed his hand from his sword. He was the vessel of the gods, not a god himself. If he displeased them, they would destroy him and replace him with another. However, they understood his disappointment and instead offered him a greater perversion.

Loban took the last sacrifice, then turned to Ambo.

"On your knees."

Chins quivering, Ambo complied. His thick body lacked any grace at all, as he more fell to the ground than knelt. Loban didn't care. Once he was on his pudgy knees, Loban stepped forward, slid the codpiece aside, and said, "Suck me."

Ambo shook his head violently, then retched again. The stench of his fear and his last meal filled the air with sour shame.

"You'll do it or I'll kill you." Loban placed his hand upon the hilt of his sword. This time there was no caution from the whispered voice of the gods. This time they offered only greedy encouragement.

Ambo's gaze sought out Helton, who stood soldier-still by the doors. Helton's stolid face betrayed nothing. Not interest or pity. He simply observed.

Tears fell down Ambo's plump cheeks as he sniveled his lips around Loban's cock. Gagging, Ambo almost bit down, but he controlled himself with a quick glance up to Loban's angry face. Biting the prick of a dark demigod was not a good idea, no matter who he was. Ambo controlled his reflex and began to suck at Loban's inflamed member.

For a small man, Ambo had a big mouth. He sucked as if his life depended on it, for it did. Loban peered down through silted eyes, loving Ambo's revulsion, his terror, and oddly his desire to do a good job. Yes, despite his reluctance, Ambo wished to please his terrible master.

Loban rocked his hips, forcing Ambo to work harder to keep up with his needs. Every time he gagged, Loban secretly thrilled inside. Gagging caused his throat to clamp down. Working himself in and out as leisurely as he could only added to his pleasure and Ambo's frustration. Ambo wanted this over quickly, but Loban wanted it to last. And the one thing he was very good at was making his erection last.

Over and over he plunged into his mouth, and again and again Ambo took it. Greed and a desire to maintain power could do amazing things to a man. Such would make him willing to do anything. Ambo knew the truth; Kasmiri wanted him gone. She wanted new blood, young blood, to help her run her empire. Helton had a plan to keep them all in power, but Loban no longer needed either of them. By this degradation, Loban hoped to show them that now they needed him far more than he needed them.

When his climax started, Ambo slumped with relief, then worked his hand and mouth faster. Loban thought he'd probably never worked this hard in his pathetic life, not with his soft hands. So smooth was his grip it was almost womanly. Loban grasped the man's ears, yanked him close, and then came in a great gushing tide. This was nothing like his mortal releases; this was one worthy of the gods. Pulse after pulse jetted from his body, so much so that Ambo couldn't keep up. Cream oozed around his rubbery lips, then escaped in bursts. Ambo swallowed in desperate gulps, but still the climax dribbled down his chin. Once the last had erupted from his body, Loban shoved the man aside.

Panting for air, coughing, Ambo scrambled up and away from Loban as fast as he could, lest he ask for another service. Ambo decided he'd had enough and ran from the room. Roaring with laughter, Loban settled the codpiece over his now soft prick. He swung his gaze toward Helton, then the two dead servants. "Clean up."

Helton offered a barely perceptible nod in response.

Loban decided to let his insolence slide. For now. Soon the time would come for Helton to kneel before him. However, it would be more fun to make him wait, to make him agonize over when it would happen. And how.

Exiting the Harvest room, Loban strode directly to Ambo's lushly appointed suite. There was something wrong with the vessel of the gods living in squalor when a lesser man, a pathetic excuse for a man, lived in luxury. When Loban found the door locked, he pounded with all his might. Reluctantly, Ambo opened up and gave him entrance.

It was the last time Ambo made a decision of his own free will.

18

Kasmiri awoke snuggled up to Sterlave's back. His heat enveloped and comforted her. She blinked against the growing morning light. The last thing she wanted to do was rise and face another day of duty, not with all the current burdens crushing her weary shoulders. Closing her eyes, she burrowed under the covers, pressing herself closer to her bondmate.

With a sigh, he rolled over and nestled down in the covers next to her. In the semidarkness, she saw his eyes were open. He moved his mouth as if to speak, but she cut him off with a kiss before he could. Somehow, whenever they spoke, they ended up fighting. She didn't feel like quarreling this morning.

He responded in kind, kissing her hard, pushing her over into the plush comfort of the bed. Playfully, she wrestled with him, wrapping her strong legs around his waist so she could propel him over. Once on his back, he chuckled, surrendering to her without much fuss.

In that moment she knew she could do whatever she pleased with him. A hundred lusty thoughts filled her mind, each more outrageous than the last. In the end, she crawled astride his supine body, pressing his awakening sex against hers.

His soft moan was one of agreeable surrender. She echoed it, then sought to increase his torment. Why did she feel such a crazy lust whenever he was near? Even when she was furious with him, she couldn't seem to stop longing to touch him or to be touched by him. Everything he said or did fascinated her.

Could it be that what she felt during her coronation was true?

Kasmiri pushed the frightening thought away. For now, she would concentrate on other far more important things, like making him beg for release.

Yesterday he'd forced her to spend the entire day with Enovese and then insisted she allow two enormous men to follow her about. Granted, the young men were unfailingly polite to her, but no matter what she said or did, they would not leave her side. Even when she used the basin, they first examined the room, then refused to let her lock the door.

They subjected anyone who came close to her to intense scrutiny. She pitied anyone who dared to harm her royal self because her two personal guards would tear them limb from limb. From the looks of them, she thought they would immensely enjoy committing such brutality.

Below her, Sterlave lay utterly passive, allowing her to do as she pleased. She began with his face, placing soft, slow kisses to his nose, his forehead, his cheeks, then finally to his mouth. He rose up then, to deepen the kiss, but she pressed his arms back into the bed to remind him to lie still.

With a sigh, he did, but she could tell it took quite an effort. Men by nature were not passive, a Harvester even less so. Why did he have no problem bestowing pleasure to her but was so reluctant to accept pleasure from her?

Determined that he would accept her generosity, she thought

of ways to restrain him. Having him at her ultimate control had been the headiest experience of her life. When he'd been strapped to the bed unable to get away, she'd felt such glorious power. He was hers to command. Hers to tease. Hers to please.

When she whispered to his ear what she would like to do, he grudgingly agreed but made her swear that tonight he could tie her up. She granted his request, then summoned Rown.

Head down, he entered with the fur-lined cuffs on long straps. With deft moves, he slid them under the bed and slipped the manacles around Sterlave's wrists and ankles. When Sterlave tested their strength with a sharp jerk of his wrists, Rown flinched and quickly exited the room.

Puzzled, Kasmiri watched his choppy steps as he left. When she looked down, Sterlave was watching him too. Disappointed that he'd left before she could include him in their play, she turned her attention to her bound mate. Sterlave met her gaze with lowered brows, as if challenging her to use him, if she dared.

With a flourish, she yanked the covers away, exposing him to her hungry eyes. He flexed his body, showing her the strength of his form, the hard sleek power of his muscles. A smattering of deep brown hairs regrew along his legs, his sex, his chest, and his head. His chin had less hair since he'd shaved for her yesterday. She wanted to feel the rough texture of his beard along the tender skin of her inner thighs and then her slick sex. Shaking her head, she turned her thoughts away from her own pleasure and focused on his.

What would she do first?

From the end of the bed, she teased her crimson nail up the center of his foot. He twitched, then moaned. Her guess was correct; he not only enjoyed toying with her feet, he derived pleasure from having his teased as well. Slowly, she worked her fingertips between each of his toes, smoothing the slick side of her nail against the most sensitive spot. Bit by bit, his semihard cock rose.

"I would ask if you enjoy this, but the answer is obvious." She left off tormenting his toes, then gripped his instep as he had done to her.

"I enjoy everything you do to me." He stretched his legs out, settling back into the bed with a groan of pleasure.

His cock became harder and thicker until it bounced slightly with the pulse of his heart. Her mouth watered with a desire to taste him. Working her way up between his forcefully parted legs, she teased her hands along the soft, short hairs, then stroked her nails along his balls. Switching between the slick side of her nail and the rougher touch of her fingertips caused his heart rate to increase.

Suddenly inspired, she settled herself on her bottom between his legs, leaned back balanced on her arms, then lifted her feet to the inside of his thighs. He glanced down at what she was doing, moaned, and then a pearl of moisture escaped the head of his penis.

"Such a reaction and I haven't even touched your throbbing cock with my feet."

He mumbled a swear or a prayer, she wasn't sure which, but he never took his eyes off her. Desperate hunger turned the golden shards in his eyes brighter, which only encouraged her to torment him more. She'd never even heard of a man aroused by feet, but clearly Sterlave could barely contain himself just at the *idea* of having her feet near his genitals. His reaction was so profound she knew she'd never look at her feet the same way again.

Balancing herself on both arms allowed her to lift her foot and arch it above him. Heat shimmered up from him to the pad of her foot. When she held very still, she could almost feel the heat pulsing with the time of his heartbeat. Breathlessly, he waited, his gaze darting between her face and her foot. Ever so slowly, she lowered her leg until her instep curved against his cock. He released a moan that shivered her down to her toes.

His abdomen tightened as he pulled himself up as far as he could, so he could see what she was doing. Once he saw her foot twining next to his sex, he rocked his hips and uttered a guttural growl. If the straps had not held him back, he would have grasped her feet and used them to stroke himself to fulfillment. She knew just by the look in his beautiful eyes.

She was thrilled that she had found a way to delight him so deeply. Moreover, now she had a way to even their erotic games. All he had to do to command her was tease the tip of his tongue to the edge of his mouth. When he did, all she could think of was his talented tongue between her thighs. Now she knew all she had to do was flash him her feet.

Delicately, she added her other foot until she cradled him between them. His skin was slick, hot, and unbelievably sensual. She never knew how sensitive her feet were until he'd played with them. Carefully, she stroked her feet up and down, gripping him with her toes, pressing her heel against the sensitive area below his balls. More pearly drops of moisture escaped. Sterlave continued to hold himself up as he rocked in time to her movements.

"Such sweet torture," she said, pressing her feet together until she gripped him more firmly. Usually by now she'd be worried about her own release, but this time was all about him. Just the thought of spending the entire day with her sex aching aroused her tremendously. Also, she knew that later he would return the favor. Tonight, Sterlave would torture her until she begged for release. He would push her past the point she thought she would break and then, and only then, would he allow her to climax.

Her excitement compelled her to make movements that were more vigorous. He caught his breath on a gasp, then expelled it slowly in a desperate effort to maintain control, but she wanted him out of control. She longed to see him in his primal state. Wanton. Animal.

Deftly she rested her calves against his thighs, then bent at the waist so she could use her hands to guide her feet. The combined pressure caused Sterlave to fall back so he could thrust deeply. He swore in a torrent, tugging at his restraints until he caused the straps to cut across the surface of the bed. Afraid she was hurting him, she started to back away, but he begged her to continue.

"I want to thrust hard between your feet. Press them tightly together, so tight I have to fight to push through."

Aroused and curious, she did as he asked.

Ruthlessly he rocked his hips, forcing his cock between her feet. At first, his violent thrusts tickled, but his intensity stripped her of any mirth. Sterlave strove toward climax. His entire body writhed in need, moving in desperate waves. Drops of moisture oozed from the tip of his cock, slicking her soles. When he slid more easily, she pressed them even closer together.

His panting breath grew deeper, harsher, then with one last mighty thrust he pushed between her tight feet and climaxed, gushing high in the air, then splattering along her toes.

Sterlave collapsed. As he tried to catch his breath, he gasped laughter. "I don't think I've ever had a climax that intense." Wonderment filled his voice. His delighted tone complimented her for her ingenuity and her willingness to experiment.

"No woman has ever used her feet this way on you?" she asked, leaning back to balance on her hands. She didn't want to move her feet just yet.

"Never. And I've thought about it many, many times." He leaned up until he looked right into her eyes. "I'm pleased you are the first and only woman to ever satisfy me this way."

A surge of pride straightened her shoulders while a shiver of possessiveness made her reluctant to release him. In a rush, she wanted to keep him bound. She wanted to ensure only she could tease and please him. Their truce from last night reminded her that he did not think of other women, and she had no reason to doubt his word. Still, she wanted to ensure his fidelity. On the other hand, Sterlave was not her father.

She wondered if all men, deep inside, were the same. Did all men hunger to know a variety of women? Had Sterlave wanted to become the Harvester for just this reason? And honestly, was any man truly happy with one woman? Question after question swirled in her mind until she felt lost in the jumble of words.

"Kasmiri?" Sterlave said her name softly, as if awakening her from sleep.

With a shake of her head, she tossed off her introspection. "I'm fine." A thousand demands already awaited her attention. She leaned forward and freed him with a flick of her finger. Rown had done as she asked and had the clasps redesigned. Before she could move away, Sterlave rose up, wrapped his arms around her torso, and flipped her down on the bed. He swallowed up her protest with a kiss. How she wanted to melt into his embrace and spend the day lost in a haze of pleasure. She couldn't.

"I'm sorry, I have to meet with my advisors." She'd approved the agenda before retiring last night. Today they had multiple issues to attend to, including the repair to her mother's suite. She sighed. It was her suite now.

He growled and nipped her lips playfully. "But I want to please you."

"Tonight." She eased out from under him.

"Is that a promise?"

"I swear that tonight, you can have your wicked way with me." Such was a promise she would have no problem keeping.

With a grin, he flopped back on the bed.

She bathed, then summoned Rown to help set her hair and put on her makeup. Again, his movements were jerky, as if his muscles were wound too tight. He wouldn't meet her eyes and gave only nods to her light banter. When she directly asked him what was wrong, he shook his head and scuttled away.

Her concerned gaze met Sterlave's. His nod indicated he'd noticed Rown's odd behavior as well.

"Go to your meeting. I'll find out what's going on."

Once Kasmiri swept out of the room, Sterlave slid out of bed. After the nonstop activity yesterday, he didn't think he'd be able to sleep. One good release with Kasmiri was all he needed. To wake this morning to another was a dream come true. Just thinking about her delicate feet, crimson-tipped toes and all, wrapped around his cock aroused him all over again.

Only once before had he shared with a woman how much feet excited him. She'd mocked him. Between gales of laughter, she'd denigrated him with vile names and tossed him out of her bed. Of course, she'd done so *after* he'd pleasured her. Since then, he'd kept his unique interest to himself. Somehow, with Kasmiri, he felt safe. She wasn't opposed to trying something different. He'd been building up the courage to ask for what she'd done this morning. Lucky was he that his bondmate could read his mind.

While Sterlave bathed, he repeatedly replayed the moment her foot touched his shaft. He turned the water to cold because if he didn't, he wouldn't be able to focus all day. When he exited the bathing unit, Rown was setting a platter on the table. Before he could shuffle away, Sterlave called him over.

Rown came near but kept his head down. Rown responded to his questions but refused to meet his gaze. Puzzled, Sterlave asked him to help him dress, something that Rown usually enjoyed. Today he practically threw his clothing on him with no lingering sighs or stolen touches.

"What's wrong?"

Rown shook his head and moved to go.

Sterlave grasped his shoulder. Rown flinched and then shuddered deep into his bones. Instantly, Sterlave removed his hand. Never had Rown reacted to his touch with terror. His greatest fear was hurting this young man and apparently, he had.

Regret filled him with tremendous shame. "I'm sorry if I hurt you."

At that, Rown looked up, shaking his head. "You didn't hurt me." Bloodshot eyes only intensified the soft blue of his irises and caused the white shards to seem impossibly bright.

It was clear he'd been crying. His pale cheeks were chapped, and his lips looked chewed. Even the tip of his nose was red from wiping away the tears. Whatever tormented him was not something minor. Someone had traumatized the normally bubbly, effusive servant into a cowering young man filled with fear.

Sterlave's gut plummeted when he put it all together.

"Who hurt you?" There was no other explanation. Someone raped Rown. Sterlave was positive. The flinching from even the gentlest touch, the tears, the slumped shoulders, and the shame-lowered face—Sterlave had done all of those things after Loban's attack.

Rown's eyes went wide, terrified. "No one, it's nothing. Please, I have chores to attend to."

He spun away, but Sterlave grasped his hand. This time he didn't flinch but clung to him desperately.

"Tell me, Rown. I can help you." Sterlave would not let Rown do this alone. If he'd had someone to lean on, perhaps the pain and shame wouldn't have lingered for quite so long. Chur had tried, but Sterlave's pride wouldn't allow him to accept his help. He'd be damned to the nothingness before he'd let Rown suffer alone.

"I can't," Rown whispered. "He said if I told anyone he'd kill you."

A bitter taste of fury burned at the back of Sterlave's throat. Whoever attacked Rown knew how much he cared for Sterlave.

To use that against the young man infuriated him. When he caught the bastard who'd hurt Rown, he was going to destroy him.

"Look at me." Sterlave encouraged him with a touch to his chin. "No one is going to hurt me."

"He will." Rown glanced away. "He's crazy."

Sterlave considered the information. "What does he look like?"

Rown shook his head but didn't let go of his hand. Rown's hand was so small compared to his. Fragile, even. How could anyone take pleasure in hurting such an innocent?

Sterlave drew him to the couch so they could sit side by side. Rown sniffed deeply, then rested his head against Sterlave's shoulder. Carefully, Sterlave wrapped his arm around Rown's waist. They sat together for a long time in silence until Rown calmed. Sterlave waited, knowing he would talk when he was ready.

"He was hideous. How could the gods create one so perfectly formed yet still so repulsive?"

Something about the description jarred a memory. "Was he very pale?"

"Yes, with tiny bronze blotches. His lips were red, as if smeared with fresh blood."

"And the blackest eyes you've ever seen." Sterlave shivered as that horrible night rushed back. Forced into position after position, taking Loban's verbal and physical abuse as he prayed desperately for him to climax and leave him alone. Endlessly, Loban violated him, and then when he was done, he simply laughed and walked away.

"How did you know?" Rown lifted his head.

For a brief moment, Sterlave considered lying. What happened to him was shameful and not something he wished to discuss. However, it wasn't his fault any more than it was Rown's fault. All the blame lay squarely on Loban.

"I know because he raped me too."

Rown shook his head in disbelief. "But you're a Harvester, one of the strongest men in all the empire."

"I wasn't always a Harvester. Three seasons ago, I was simply another raw recruit. Back then I was skinny, undernourished, barely a young man when I arrived in the training rooms. Something about me set Loban off. His predatory eyes followed me everywhere. Whenever it was time to spar, he inevitably chose me as his partner, and then he would pummel me until I begged for surcease. After one such beating, he came to my cell under the pretext of apologizing, and that's when he raped me."

Rown slipped his arm around his waist in comfort. "Why didn't you tell someone?"

If he'd known Loban would continue, he would have, just to save someone else from the trauma. "I was afraid he'd do it to me again. Afraid of people looking at me differently, like I was weak, or I deserved it, or worse, that I asked for it." Sterlave tilted his head down until he caught Rown's gaze. "I'm telling you because I don't want you to feel that way too."

Rown shook his head. "I won't, not now."

Some of Sterlave's guilt eased. "Someone found out and I told him the truth, but I begged him not to tell anyone else." Chur Zenge hadn't wanted to keep the secret, but he did because he respected Sterlave's decision. "Thank you for trusting me enough to tell me."

Rown nodded, rubbing his chapped cheek against his shoulder. "You won't tell anyone?"

"No." He knew Kasmiri was going to ask about Rown's behavior. He'd have to tell her something. "How badly are you hurt? Are you bleeding?"

"He used some kind of oil. I'm sore but not torn." Rown ducked his head and lowered his voice. "I always thought my first time would be special, with someone who wanted me."

Sterlave wished he could undo the damage. Servant or no,

Rown's initial encounter should have been with someone who truly desired him. Sterlave didn't think he was that man, but if he were his first, he never would have hurt him.

"He violated everything I am as an *ungati*."

"I don't understand." Sterlave's knowledge of the *ungati* was limited to what he'd learned in the last few days.

"By my station I'm not allowed to climax by the hand of another. Only alone and by strict ritual may I seek fulfillment."

Sterlave's brows rose. He had wondered why Rown would willingly participate in his and Kasmiri's games but always leave before he climaxed. Now he understood. So not only had Loban raped him, but also he'd forced him to go against his code. The idea of forcing him to enjoy the act turned his stomach. At least Loban had not done that to him. But why Rown? There had to be hundreds of *ungati* servants in the palace. Was it a coincidence that Loban had selected the only one connected to him?

"Did he follow you from here?" Sterlave asked, thinking it was personal, that Loban had deliberately sought out someone from his house.

"I don't know. He came upon me in the *tishiary*." At Sterlave's blank look, he explained, "Where the servants gather to clean their master's clothing, bathe, and gossip."

"Did he know who you were?"

Rown shook his head. "He would know I was of the empress due to the crimson sash on my robe." Delicately, Rown trailed his fingertips over the elaborately embroidered sash. "All who see me know my mistress."

They'd also know your master, Sterlave thought. But why after all this time would Loban seek revenge on him? Not once had Sterlave sought him out for payback. Only one ugly incident, where Chur had challenged Loban in a misguided attempt to honor Sterlave, had ever occurred. Even that was not at Sterlave's behest. Chur acted out of his own indignity at Loban's rude words that denigrated the role of Harvester. When the two fought and Loban cheated, the recruits hauled him away, placing him kneel bound in the *gannett*. When Sterlave discovered those same recruits raping Loban, he stopped them and released Loban. At that moment, Sterlave considered the entire mess ended. Apparently, he'd been wrong. But why after he'd saved him would Loban desire revenge?

"I don't want you to go there anymore. I'll send—" He cut himself off. He couldn't send anyone until he knew if Loban would continue to attack those who worked for him. With a shock, he bolted straight up, dislodging Rown from his shoulder.

Rown recovered himself, and asked, "What?"

"Kasmiri."

19

Kasmiri faced her advisors. Around an open pit, what everyone called the *circle,* seating went from high to low depending on that person's station. She sat in the highest and most luxurious chair. Her two personal guards loomed behind her.

At face height before each person floated a blue screen that flashed data, diagrams, and charts—information to explain whatever topic of discussion they'd reached. Half a day into the meeting, after they'd discussed how to repair the damage left by the horde of peasants, and a multitude of minor issues, the bulk of the advisors left. They would see to the resolutions by passing on her edicts to the workers. A handful of her closest people turned their attention to the repair of the empress suite.

Helton Ook, someone her mother installed as the head of the palace guard right before she died, sat several levels down from her. His sooty gray eyes calmly assessed everything and everyone. Distressed by his bulky appearance, Kasmiri tried not to look at him, but she couldn't seem to stop. He was so oddly formed that her gaze continually tried to understand how he could move without pain. His shock of white hair made him seem old, but he possessed the grace of a much younger man. Bulky muscles crossed his shoulders, swallowing up his neck, so he had to move his entire upper body to turn his head. His arms were too short, his legs too long, but there was something so familiar about him. When he caught her staring, she turned her attention elsewhere.

Her gaze fell on Ambo.

Ambo had stumbled in late, then collapsed gratefully into his seat. All throughout the meeting, Ambo continued to shift uneasily in his chair, as if he couldn't sit still but didn't want to leave. Back and forth he rocked, with his hands cupped around his distended belly, almost as if he were comforting himself. For once, he wasn't picking his nose. In fact, every time his hand crept up, he would wince and forcefully lower it, as if someone were hitting him. He'd paid no attention to the problems under discussion and barely glanced at his information screen. Lost in his own little world, Ambo did not respond to Kasmiri's question until she shouted his name.

Ambo startled. "What?" He hit her with huge, terrified eyes. For several moments, he forgot to blink, then did so in rapid succession.

"I asked for an account of the royal treasury." Her mother, her grandmother, and all the women back for generations had contributed to the royal account. With a multitude of galactic investments over several thousand seasons, the total must be more than she could comprehend.

With shaking hands, he reached for his touch screen. Page after page whisked by, but no information was forthcoming.

"I can't seem to locate the file." Ambo stopped his half-hearted effort. He darted a glace to Helton, then clutched his hands together, dropping them into his lap.

Kasmiri blew out a tense breath. She was exhausted and her day wasn't even close to being done. The last thing she was willing to tolerate today, or any day, was insubordination, especially from someone she intended to dismiss. Ambo had been able to find and share the palace treasury account for the repair projects, so he should be able to locate her personal funds.

Calmly, she asked him to try again. He made a great show of searching, even tossing out several frustrated sighs, but turned up empty. With a shrug, he waved the screen away and stood.

"I haven't dismissed you."

Ambo wavered, his back to her.

"I want to see the royal account." In the future, she would make sure she could retrieve the information herself. A spark of fear started in the pit of her belly, working up and out across her limbs. There had to be a reason he didn't want to show her. Had her mother squandered all their funds? How could she? There was reputed to be enough money for several decadent lifetimes, but such could all be talk. Kasmiri honestly had no idea how much funding her mother had left for her. "If you cannot find the information, I will have you replaced."

At that, Ambo spun, his eyes narrowed to slits. "Replace me? You can't replace me." Before he could take a step toward her, the two guards leapt into his path, effectively blocking his access. Ambo stumbled back. He would have fallen if not for Helton's stabilizing grip.

Helton leaned near and whispered something in Ambo's ear.

Ambo looked to argue the point but forcefully swallowed. With a tense smile, he returned to his seat, flicked a button on the base of the chair to reactivate the screen, thrust his finger three times, and then sat back with a smirk.

Kasmiri turned her attention to her display. It took all her might not to let her jaw drop. Wordlessly she dismissed all her advisors. Ambo and Helton refused to go.

"Go, or I'll dismiss you permanently!"

Helton wisely kept his distance, but said, "You won't dismiss either one of us, not now, not ever."

Her guards sensed his threat and tensed.

204 / *Anitra Lynn McLeod*

With a deft hand gesture at Ambo's screen, Helton caused a new set of information to flash before her. At this, her jaw did drop.

"Lies! It's all lies!" But something in his sooty gray gaze told her this was no falsehood. Everything she'd learned in the last few moments was not only true but also explained why her mother didn't even try to fight her disease.

Why bother when she had nothing to live for?

Sterlave spent most of the day trying to find Loban. When he asked around, he found out where his cell was located, but his room was mostly bare, his bed untouched. No one had seen him since last night. Sterlave went to the training rooms to see if Loban had shown up for work. He hadn't. Frustrated, he asked Chur.

"Why this urgency?" Chur asked, turning his attention away from sparring recruits.

Sterlave opened his mouth to speak, then abruptly closed it. He'd promised Rown he wouldn't speak of his rape to anyone.

"You don't have to; I can read the truth on your face. He hurt someone." With a shake of his head, Chur sighed. "Some-one close to you?"

Sterlave nodded.

"You don't have to tell me who." Chur called forth one of the more skilled recruits to oversee the sparring students. He issued his final instructions, then left.

Sterlave followed behind as Chur led him out of the training rooms.

"Where are we going?" Sterlave examined the narrowing hallways with interest. He didn't think he'd ever been this way.

"Somewhere private." Chur continued his long-legged strides, eating up the distance with forceful intent. His entire backside rippled with muscles as he moved. Sterlave found it difficult not to stare when all Chur wore was a loincloth. No wonder

Kasmiri's nipples stood at attention whenever she saw Chur—
his practically did. The man couldn't help but ooze sex appeal.
At the end of the long, straight hallway, Chur pushed open a
door and stepped out onto a circular balcony.

Once Sterlave joined him, he pushed the door closed.

"We won't be disturbed here." Chur gripped the metal railing. "Last night, something strange happened to me. I was with
Enovese and she was . . ." Chur trailed off. "It doesn't matter
what she was doing. Anyway, I felt something, a feeling, a force—
whatever it was, it tried to possess me."

Chur's description was similar to what Sterlave had felt last
night. Hesitantly, Sterlave asked, "When it left, did you hear it
laugh?"

Chur caught him with his intense gaze. "How did you
know?"

"It tried to get me too. While I was with Kasmiri." Sterlave
held his gaze, afraid if he looked away Chur would know that
he'd come between him and Kasmiri last night.

When Chur turned his attention to the decimated lands,
Sterlave released a tense breath.

"Something's brewing, something dark, something evil,"
Chur said. "It couldn't find a home with me, or you, and who
knows how many others, but it did find a home last night. I can
feel it building."

Below, the destruction was a perfect backdrop to their discussion. As winter came with its icy grip, a cruel, heartless force
came with it.

"But what does it want? It tried to get me to hurt Kasmiri,
nothing more. As far as evil plans go, it doesn't seem to be
much." As soon as he said it, he wondered if that was the point
of the force—to hurt people sexually. Both he and Chur had
been with their mates when it attempted to possess them. Had
it found its way into a more welcoming body?

When he suggested this to Chur, he nodded speculatively.

"Perhaps Loban proved to be the perfect host." Chur's knuckles turned white as he gripped the railing. "I made a foolish decision to keep him here."

A breeze washed over them, salty and fresh, from the Valry Sea. Calmly, Sterlave asked, "Why *did* you keep him here?" He'd never understood Chur's reasons for wanting such a dangerous individual around. "Why not brand him and send him home in shame?" A part of him stung that Chur hadn't made Loban pay for what he'd done.

"You once told me not to fight your battles for you." Chur considered him with a sidelong glance. "Now you're angry that I haven't."

Sterlave bristled at the subtle reprimand. "This wasn't my battle. Sending Loban home would have saved others from his brutality." Rown's broken posture and his tormented face filled his thoughts, spurring his rage. "If you're looking for me to make you feel better for a bad decision, you best look elsewhere."

Rather than reacting with anger, Chur fixed his gaze on the broken land around them. "I thought I could help him. I thought if I showed him that he could be a better man, he would be. I had no idea he harbored such resentment toward you."

Surprised by Chur's composed admission, Sterlave said, "I don't think this is only about me. I'm sure he's just as angry with you."

"But he didn't hurt someone I care about."

Chur had to know Loban didn't attack Kasmiri. Her two hand-selected guards would have ripped him apart. Which meant Chur knew it had to be one of their servants, for Sterlave had no other friends. He'd never gotten close to anyone in the training rooms, other than Chur himself. Even his handler, Helton, kept himself distant. Friends were a luxury Sterlave could never afford in his village. Things hadn't changed when he'd come to the palace for training.

When Rown related the details of his attack, Sterlave had worried about Kasmiri. He'd rushed to her advisor's room but stopped short of pounding on the door when he remembered her guards. Neither man would let Loban anywhere near her. Besides, Loban had a penchant for young men, not women.

"What if there are others he's attacked?" A great wall of dishonor rose up, encasing him. What if Loban had hurt many young men all because Sterlave was too ashamed to confront what he'd done? If Sterlave would have stepped forward, he might have prevented a lifetime of pain for others. Had his cowardice allowed a monster to flourish?

"I know it's private, but can you tell me where the attack occurred?"

"In the *tishiary,* where the servants—"

"I know where it is. It's the perfect hunting ground for someone to prey upon defenseless individuals."

For the first time since Chur's miraculous transformation, Sterlave saw worry settle across his noble brow. When Chur turned his attention to the Onic Mountains, his shoulders lifted with his deep breath. Every muscle in his body tensed, as if preparing for a fight. A great blast of freezing wind rose up and enveloped them, chilling Sterlave to the bone.

"I fear that with everything I've done, everything the gods have done for me," Chur said, "I am still too late to save the Onic Empire."

Loban relaxed, draped across a silky, padded couch while two young men performed for his amusement. One day soon, he would have thousands of servants ready to please him in any way he saw fit. For now, he would have to settle for a handful. Ambo's suite was large, but it would hold only so many people.

Ambo preferred young women, but Loban quickly grew bored with their simpering need to please. The men fought back. Eventually they did submit but never willingly, which only fueled his excitement. He demanded only those trained to perform with women, then forced them together with men.

Sniveling, Ambo huddled in a chair next to him, his watery eyes darting everywhere but at Loban himself or the lusty display. When his pudgy finger crept up to his nose, Loban smacked him, hard, in the fleshy part of his upper arm. With a yelp, Ambo lowered his hand to his lap. Even if he had to break his arm, Loban would break Ambo of that disgusting habit. When he'd first come into Ambo's rooms, dried snot wipes covered the furniture and even some of the walls. It took Ambo most of the night and a staff of ten to clean up the mess.

Loban had made other changes too. He ordered that heavy wall fabrics, in black, be hung across the brightly painted murals. Servants reupholstered all the silver furniture in black and crimson. When Ambo argued about the danger and difficulty in obtaining those particular colors, Loban waved him off.

"Let them know that I am here. When they come to fight, I will be ready."

Only the Harvester could wear or decorate with black, and only the empress could use crimson. Since Loban considered himself the ultimate Harvester and the soon-to-be emperor, he was entitled to use the proper colors. None could deny him. Even after only one harvest, his power rose, darkening his flesh, increasing his powers. Above him, he felt Chur Zenge. His goodness pushed a foul taste into the back of Loban's throat. Worse yet was the power emanating from Sterlave. How could one untouched by the gods have such terrible influence? When Loban had sought guidance, the gods were strangely silent.

Ambo insisted he only had so much funding to carry out changes to his rooms. If they did too much too soon there were those who would ask pointed questions. Loban ordered him to find more funds and to stop worrying about anyone finding out. As of today, Chur and Sterlave already knew the gods had selected him. They just didn't know where to find him. Besides, with the secret they held about the empress, funding shouldn't be a problem. If he so desired it, he could have Kasmiri willingly on her knees before him, begging him to keep silent.

Loban had no true interest in Kasmiri. He wanted to torment her only because she belonged to Sterlave. Always he'd felt something was different about him, even as a raw recruit Sterlave projected a quiet, pure confidence. Loban wanted to destroy his poise. How dare Sterlave naturally possess something that eluded Loban?

A niggling doubt invaded his mind. What if, by raping him, he'd actually made Sterlave stronger? No. Loban shook his head. Brutality crippled. Taking from others destroyed their confidence, their peace of mind. Rape stole the soul. That's what empowered him. All those battered and broken souls piled up at his feet allowed him to stand tall among men. So tall did he stand he now touched the heights of godhood.

A knock at the door drew his attention from his inner thoughts. Ambo shot to his feet, stumbled, then waddled to the door. Panting, he opened it a bare crack and peered out. Helton almost knocked him off his feet when he swept the door open.

Helton registered the changes to the room with a frown. His displeasure increased when he saw the two young men writhing before Loban's couch. With a shove of his massive hands, Helton dislodged the two.

Loban simply laughed as he waved them away.

"You lack discipline." Helton refused to sit. Instead, he loomed above him, glaring down, injecting his stare with a simultaneous dose of fire and ice.

"I don't need discipline." Loban uncoiled from the couch, then stood a breath away from Helton. "I'm a god." With a flex of his body, he faked a punch to Helton's face. To his credit, Helton didn't flinch. He didn't even look concerned. Helton held his place and continued to glower.

"You're not a god yet." Helton turned his head and spat. "You still need us just as much as we need you."

"Perhaps," Loban said silkily. "But someday the time will come when I don't need you at all. What then, Helton?" He snapped his fingers at his glass. A serving girl refilled it, then departed. "Will you and Ambo band together to fight me?" Casually, he sipped. They had to know that he felt no allegiance to them. He understood why Helton helped him, as he would do anything to humble Chur Zenge, but in Loban's empire, there would be only one ruler: Loban.

Helton narrowed his eyes. "Unlike you, I have discipline."

He refused to say any more, so Loban said, "Tell me what you intend to do."

Helton laughed. It was the first time Loban had ever heard the man laugh. Unpleasant, his laughter sounded like two rocks rubbing together. When Helton shrugged, the spicy scent of his armpits wafted up. Not a distasteful smell but surprising when Helton needed no longer exert himself. He wasn't a handler anymore. What was he doing with himself all day? His bronzed face was oily, his white hair plastered to his skull as if he hadn't rested for hours.

Deciding he didn't care, Loban turned away. "Would you like something?" Loban lifted his hand to the multitude of servants. "We have a little bit of everything. What's your pleasure?" He'd always wondered what aroused Helton. Did he crave the smooth touch of a young woman, like Ambo, or the hard muscles of a young man? Or, he stifled a chuckle, perhaps he craved the illicit. Did Helton mate with animals or perhaps the diminutive *serbreds*? Did he find his pleasure alone, or did he own a servant with whom he shared his bed? The only thing Loban knew for certain was that Helton did not have a mate. He'd had one, for he'd selected her when he was the Harvester, but she'd died shortly after. Helton could have had any woman in the land after that, but he'd remained alone. The only reason

Loban knew this tidbit of information was that Ambo babbled incessantly when threatened.

With a snort, Helton dismissed the offer. "Again, I have discipline." He turned to Ambo. "We need to talk."

Ambo nodded so vigorously his chins slapped into each other. He took two steps before Loban clasped his hand to his shoulder. Ambo squealed, jumped, and quivered simultaneously.

"You'll discuss whatever it is in front of me."

"This doesn't concern you." Helton tried to drag him away, but Loban refused to release his grip.

Ambo made a keening sound at the back of his throat.

Once, when he was very young, Loban's mount had become stuck in a vast mud pit. As he sat on the edge, watching the beast sink, the creature made a similar sound. Poor Ambo. He'd gotten himself into something thick and bottomless. As the sludge swallowed his head, he didn't know what to do. Loban would have felt sorry for him, but he didn't. Ambo was stuck in a trap of his own making.

With a soft voice that belied his true intent, Loban asked, "Is it about your daughter?"

The very word caused Helton to stiffen. Unable to turn his neck, he turned his entire body.

"As far as discipline goes, Ambo has none at all." Loban flashed a rapacious smile. "He told me everything."

Ambo's whine deepened.

Helton's grip on Ambo's wrist clamped down until his bleating increased in pitch. When Loban did the same to his shoulder, Ambo vibrated the tone until he collapsed from a lack of breath.

Furious at his betrayal, Helton kicked his unconscious body.

"You can kick him all night; it won't take back what he said."

"What do you want?"

Now that he had Helton's undivided attention, Loban paused to take a sip of his wine. Smooth as *astle,* the crimson liquid flowed down the back of his throat to warm his belly. Ambo might be a glutton, but he was a glutton with excellent taste.

"I want what I deserve. You are going to help me obtain my rightful place, or I will kill your daughter. Well," he paused, considering his glass, "I'll kill her after I defile her."

A gritted jaw displayed Helton's fury. With an expert eye, he weighed and measured the threat before him. Loban knew how drastically his appearance had changed. His pale skin had turned burnished copper, so deep it drew in the light, refusing to reflect it. His lips, always blood red against his white teeth, were now even more predatory. Fathomless and cruel Onic black eyes now glittered with the lust of a thousand vicious torments. Helton weighted, measured, and realized he could not subdue the monster he'd created.

"Leave my daughter be and I'll do whatever you want."

20

Kasmiri marched back to her room with her head held high. She had to bite her lips to keep her tears at bay. Normally, she would have let them fall, but her guards paced her. She doubted they saw the information Helton and Ambo had sent to her screen, but she still would not appear weak before her subjects.

Once she left them at the door, her tears flowed along with great sobbing gasps. In that moment, she prayed for Sterlave to be there, waiting for her, but he wasn't. Just once in her life, she wanted someone to be there when she needed them. She thought of sending Rown to look for him but didn't want to face Rown, not when she couldn't get herself under control. It was bad enough she'd taken her anger out on the poor boy; the last thing he needed to see was her falling apart.

Sharp spikes of dread stabbed into her belly. Doubling over, she fell to her knees. Her entire life flashed before her eyes and all of it was a lie. Her mother's face, so beautiful, was a mask for a woman with shameful secrets. All of her permissiveness with her consort was to present the image of a long-suffering, devoted bondmate who was subtly misdirecting attention from her own foibles. How long had her mother lived in fear? When Clathia found out she was dying, had she smiled? When she let go of the *galbol* tree branch, had she breathed a sigh of relief rather than a scream of terror?

Casting her gaze to the glass ceiling, Kasmiri saw only cloud-shrouded darkness. Tonight, the first snow would turn the land crystal white. Beautiful, spiritual, sterile, but the snow was also oh so cold and utterly heartless. Everything caught in its grip died. Fleetingly, Kasmiri wondered how long she'd last outside. If she went out now, dressed as she was, she would never see the sun rise.

Galvanized by the thought, she removed her jewelry, her clothing, and then strode to a room just on the other side of her servant's quarters. Ages had passed since she'd been here, but no dust marred the intricately patterned wood floor. She'd trained her servants well. At the wall, she selected a slow tempo dance, wrapped a flowing *sarye* around her body, and then took the center of the floor.

With her eyes closed, she simply let the music envelop her until the tempo moved her body. Leaping high into the air, she landed delicately on the ball of her foot and then crumpled down, as if falling, but it was a controlled collapse. Once her body completely touched the floor, she popped up. Repeatedly she performed the motions of "the death fall" until she felt perfection in her form. When she did, she moved on to a different set of steps.

Kasmiri had no idea how long she danced. Sweat poured off her skin, her limbs trembled, but still she spun across the floor, desperate to find peace. Faultlessness would grant her tranquility. Mistakes caused pandemonium. Faster and faster she spun until the world around her blurred. This time when she collapsed, it wasn't controlled. The back of her head hit the floor with a sickening smack and everything faded away.

*   *   *

Kasmiri woke to the sound of her name. Fluttering her eyelids, she expected to see Sterlave, but she gazed up into fathomless black eyes. She blinked rapidly to correct the obvious delusion, but he was still there, smiling at her with blood red lips. When he parted them to speak, his light pink tongue danced between glowing white teeth, pointed white teeth. Before she could scream, he cupped his hand over her mouth.

"Listen to me very carefully, little empress."

His strangely burnished skin exuded a sour smell of rotting leaves. His flesh felt hot and dry against her mouth. She wanted to bite him but gagged at the thought of having his taste upon her tongue. Trapped and terrified, she nodded below his massive hand.

"You belong to me."

Unable to keep her face composed, her eyes bulged with shock and then repulsion. Before she'd submit herself to him, she would throw herself out into the deepest drift of snow. Desperately, she darted her gaze about for Sterlave. Again, never in her life when she needed help was someone there for her. She should be used to abandonment by now.

The monster laughed. "Oh, calm yourself, Kasmiri. I am not interested in you in *that* way." He rolled his eyes in mimic of her; then he trailed his hand from her face to the space between her breasts.

When she'd fallen, her gown parted, exposing part of her breast. Gauging her reaction, he teased one long nail across her nipple. When she hissed in shock and pain, he laughed and removed his hand.

"When I wish it, my touch is quite painful." Leaning over her, so close she could smell his putrid breath, he leered and said, "Can you imagine how excruciating the thrust of my cock would be?"

She swallowed a sharp retort; angering him would not be a wise strategy. Neither would asking pointless questions he wouldn't answer, like how he'd thwarted an entire contingent of guards to get into her rooms. "What do you want?"

He settled back on his overdeveloped haunches. "My kind of woman. One who wants to get right to the point." When he smiled, she gritted her teeth to fight the urge to vomit. "You belong to me because from now on, you're going to do what I tell you to do. No questions, no second guesses, you will simply obey."

Maintaining a level of dignity, even while on her back on the floor, she asked, "Why would I do that?"

Her small show of defiance seemed to please him. "Because I know something that you don't want others to know." He tilted his head unnaturally to the right. In a singsong voice he said, "I know your secret."

Calling his bluff, she coolly considered him with one lifted brow. "You don't know anything."

Coyly, he pressed his finger to his lips, then lifted it up. "One: I know what your mother did with the royal account. Two: I know why your mother killed herself. Three: I know who killed your mother's consort. Four: I know who—"

"Stop!" Kasmiri turned away from his gleeful expression.

She heard his nails click on the floor when he lay down beside her.

He whispered directly to her ear, "You didn't let me tell you the best one of all."

She held her breath, hoping he wouldn't continue.

Ever so softly, he cooed, "I know who your father is."

Her heart lurched as she closed her eyes.

"There's no running away from the truth, Kasmiri." He stroked his fingers through her hair, heating the strands until they smoldered. The stench was unbearable, but she couldn't move away, no matter how much she tried. "Don't worry, I won't tell anyone, especially not your pretty little mate."

How anyone could call Sterlave pretty or little she didn't

know, but she wasn't about to correct his assessment. Not when all he had to do to destroy her was to whisper one of those damning secrets into the right ear. If he did, her entire life would end. Moreover, it would create a power vacuum in the Onic Empire that would make an already unstable structure more unbalanced.

"Do you think Sterlave would stand by you if he knew?"

In her mind, Kasmiri let the question dance across her emotions, softly at first, but then the steps became stomps. Would he? Sterlave swore he wanted her, not her position, or her power, but if all of that was suddenly gone, would he still find her irresistible? Speculation was one thing, but reality would be an entirely different matter.

"Let me tell you another secret, my pretty pet, one that you might find difficult to believe." He stretched his neck until his face loomed over hers. "You see, I don't want to tell anyone, not unless you make me." Lowering his face until he was a bare breath from kissing her, he added, "I'm going to be very quiet about your secret shame. Not because I care, because of course I don't, but because silence suits *my* agenda."

Terror held her enthralled. If she moved, if she spoke, she would touch his face. Heat rolled off him, singeing her eyebrows. Even breathing caused her to pull his hot, rancid scent into her lungs. Each breath burned. Just when she thought she would die from a lack of air, he pulled away. When she gasped, he laughed a mighty, booming laugh that chilled her despite the heat.

"You interest me, Kasmiri. How could one so delicate be so strong?" What little light there was in the room shied away from his form, as if even the smallest particle of brightness couldn't bear to touch him. "Remember, though, you will never be stronger than me."

Against her will, she nodded. As he gave her his orders, she committed them to memory because she knew he would ask her to repeat them. When he did, she reeled them off exactly as he bid. Pleased, he patted her head without burning her, as if she were a pet who performed well.

He uncoiled from the floor. His once-human form melted and oozed below something evil, as if the two battled for supremacy. With a shock, she realized he was the opposite of Chur. Where Chur glowed with benevolence, evil burnished this creature. For a fleeting moment, she thought the gods had chosen these two mortals to fight their battle for them. If such were true, what part would she play in their game?

She couldn't do what he ordered and keep her relationship with Sterlave. If she didn't do as he demanded, he'd tell everyone who her father was. Once they realized she was not the product of an empress and a consort, they would strip her of her title and exile her to Rhemna. Kasmiri couldn't let anyone find out that Helton Ook was her real father.

The fire in her mother's room had nothing to do with a failed assassination attempt. Setting the fire was misdirection from their real intent of terrifying her so they could use her for their own ends. Clathia had kept her secrets well, but this one could topple the empire. Holding this over Kasmiri's head made her their pawn because she couldn't accuse them without damning herself.

The monster was only keeping her in charge because he didn't want chaos to rip the empire apart. Divulging her secret too soon would spiral everything into pandemonium. She would be his puppet until he was ready to take over. As she watched him walk away, she wondered how long that would be.

Moreover, what would he do with her when he no longer needed her?

By the time Sterlave entered, she'd bathed away her visitor's stench, perfumed and powdered her body, placed her most provocative shoes upon her feet, then arranged herself across the bed. When he glanced in her direction, she twirled one of the manacles, then presented it to him.

Worry creased his brow so deeply he was almost glowering.

At first, she was afraid he wasn't going to accept her offer, and she was going to look like a fool climbing out of bed with her pointed heels on. He must have remembered his promise this morning that he would tie her up, because suddenly, his brows lifted, his eyes glowed, and he strode toward her with a sexy half smile. Her relief was so profound she actually slumped back on the bed.

Apparently he decided that whatever was on his mind could wait until afterward. If she played this right, he'd be too tired to talk tonight. All she needed was some time. A night or two would give her a chance to decide how she would tell him. She knew she would tell him eventually. Her greatest fear was that he would want to fight that hideous creature. Sterlave was strong, but he'd be no match for a monster who sucked the light out of a room and could heat his skin at will. Just the thought of Sterlave in his evil clutches broke her heart. She'd battle the monster herself before she'd let that happen.

As Sterlave climbed onto their bed, she realized she loved him. The truth didn't hit her in subtle waves but in one immense blast. The understanding stunned her. When he'd dropped to one knee and sworn himself to her during her coronation, she had felt it then but refused to acknowledge the truth, but now she had no choice. She didn't want him to fight with that horrendous fiend because he could be hurt, or worse, killed. Even if her life were in utter disarray, she couldn't picture living without him. Oh gods, if she told Sterlave the truth, would he walk away?

"Don't look so terrified," he murmured, slipping the first cuff to her wrist. "I'm not going to hurt you." He paused and grinned down at her. "Not unless you want me to."

She laughed to cover the real reason why she panicked. "No

pain, please, but a lot of satisfying teasing would be wonderful."

"As you please." He said it with his willing servant tone, but the sparkle in his eyes told her the truth: pleasing her pleased him. He wasn't playing master and servant but mate to mate. Perhaps it was only wishful thinking, but it seemed to say that he loved her back. How unfair that when she'd finally found love, she might lose it through no act of her own. She considered. If she didn't tell him the truth, it would be her fault.

"Sterlave, there's something—"

"Shhh. There will be time to talk later, Kasmiri, I promise." Beseeching eyes met hers, and that's when she realized he needed tonight as much as she did.

With a soft nod, she laid back, surrendering herself completely to him. Once he had both manacles on her wrists, she relaxed utterly. For now, she did not have to agonize over her position, the empire, or anything to do with the future. Her entire focus was purely in this moment, with Sterlave in charge.

She trusted him implicitly.

Once he had her arms bound, he moved to the foot of the bed and inspected her feet. "Did you wear these for me?"

She nodded. She'd correctly guessed that seeing her naked clad only in a pair of sexy shoes would thoroughly distract him. Manipulative, she knew, but she needed time to think, to decide what to do.

Kneeling, he examined her crimson shoes closely, teasing his fingertips between the cleavages made by her toes. She found the sensation unbelievably arousing. It was as if he touched between her breasts by stroking between her toes. Slowly, he traced around the cup of the heel that sloped down to her instep. Once there, he kneaded his fingers between the shoe and her foot.

When she glanced down, she noticed he was fully erect. His cock pressed tightly against his loose-fitting trousers. It was then that she realized he wasn't dressed as her consort but to help Chur in the training rooms. Baggy black *mondi* fabric allowed him to fully extend his body while training. At the moment, the thin weave gave her tantalizing glimpses of his hard muscles, peaked nipples, and painfully aroused sex.

Lifting her leg up, he forced her knee to bend so her foot rested against his hip, nestled next to his cock.

He groaned.

Watching his reaction caused her sex to wet and her nipples to harden. Knowing that she was the cause of his excitement empowered her greatly.

"I thought this was about me," she asked coyly.

"You shouldn't have worn these shoes." He shrugged, as if truly disappointed. "By doing so, you've made it impossible for me to focus on anything else."

"So it's all my fault?" Her pout slid slowly into a sultry frown. "Sounds like I need to be punished."

His wicked grin caused a shiver from her toes to her nipples. Punishment by his hands would be sublime.

In a flash, he lifted both her legs by the ankles. Ever so slowly, he parted them as wide as the reach of his arms.

Forcefully, he kept her gaze.

Her breath caught as she waited for him to examine her vulnerable, exposed sex.

He didn't.

Sterlave kept his eyes riveted to hers. "I don't have to look. I know you're wet." He closed his eyes and drew in a deep breath through his nose. "Gods, you smell good. Never have I ever smelled anything as sweet, as wonderful, as compelling as you." When he opened his striking brown eyes, they focused again on hers. "I don't have to look to know how beautiful your luscious pink secrets look hidden between ebony folds. How wisps of curly black hairs only add to the delicious mystery." Again, he took a deep breath without looking. "Do you have any idea how difficult it is for me not to fall between your thighs and lose myself in your ambrosia?"

Unable to speak, she shook her head. He wasn't pretending. He wasn't being dramatic as part of their play. Sterlave confessed the truth because he trusted her not to use the information to manipulate him, just as he'd trusted her with his erotic compulsion toward her feet. Suddenly, she felt very guilty about using her sexy shoes to misdirect his attention this night. She'd met his honesty with nothing but exploitation.

"Every moment I'm around you I struggle not to touch you, to feel you, to have some type of contact with you. I've never been a man consumed by drink or chemicals. But somehow, in a very short time, I've become completely addicted to you."

"I didn't want—"

"You didn't make this happen," he said, cutting her off, holding her legs apart while maintaining eye contact. "Somehow, everything came together and I found exactly what I'd been missing my whole life." With a dramatic pause, he lowered himself while keeping her gaze and pushing her legs farther apart. "I found not only my bondmate, but my soulmate."

Stunned by his confession, she couldn't even breathe.

He held her gaze as he lowered his face to her sex while keeping her long legs parted wide.

"I can't imagine myself with anyone but you," he whispered. At the last moment, he broke eye contact and plunged his tongue into her sex.

Involuntarily her body arched up toward him, greedy and grasping for pleasure. His wriggling tongue teased every nerve along her sensitive flesh, but moreover his hunger captivated her heart. He spoke the truth. Sterlave's appetite craved her, and only her. No other woman would satisfy his longing. For the first and only time, Kasmiri felt desired, not for riches, position, or possessions, but for who and what she was.

Sterlave craved *her.*

Another woman might soothe his needs but only she eased his erotic desires.

"Sterlave." His name was a whispered prayer upon her lips.

His answer was a hungry nibbling of her sex. Teasing swirls of his tongue assaulted her clit, catapulting her into the air. Only the manacles around her wrists and his grip upon her ankles kept her from floating away. Over and over he plunged then twirled his magical tongue. Breathless, she could no longer speak his name; all she could do was coo subtle sounds of encouragement and submission. As her climax built, he pulled back, keeping her just on the edge, so close to tumbling over she thought she would die. When the urge faded too much, he used the rough hair along his chin and above his lip to push her back toward the edge.

"When, when will you—" She couldn't even finish gasping the question.

"When will I stop tormenting you?" He punctuated each word with a flick of his tongue to her clit, causing her to bounce in response. "When you want me as much as I want you."

"I do! I do!" She struggled against the bonds in earnest, thinking if she could just touch him, she could show him how much she wanted him.

"Do you?" Her inner thigh muffled his voice.

"Yes!" Lowering her voice to remove the strident edge, she begged, "Please, Sterlave, I can't take any more."

He lifted up until he was on his knees between her splayed legs. Slowly, he pulled his shirt over his head, exposing his sleekly muscled chest. She wanted to lick her way up from his belly button to his nipples, then back down to his hips. Once there, she would wrap her lips around his cock and tease until he screamed between begging gasps. Who was she kidding? If she had half the chance, she'd toss him on his back and ride him until she squealed with release.

After he tossed the shirt away, he slid his hands to the waistband of his trousers. Gradually, he eased them down, until the head of his cock slipped out. The tip was taut, dusky red, and when he flicked his thumb over it, moisture sparkled.

Involuntarily, she licked her lips.

"Did you want a taste?"

Rather than nodding, she deliberately stroked her tongue across her upper lip.

Pushing his pants down farther, he grasped the base firmly and stroked his hand up and down while staring at her mouth. She didn't think it was possible, but he got bigger. When she pursed her lips, more drops of moisture pearled from the tip. Gracefully, he removed his pants. He crawled up her body until he straddled her chest. Heat filled his eyes as he gazed down at her. He seemed so enormous looming above her, which only excited her more.

"You only move when I tell you."

She nodded her understanding.

Bending down, he teased the tip of his cock around her lips, slicking them with his lust. Desperately she fought her desire to snake her tongue out and taste him. Waiting only increased the tightening in her sex and nipples, spiraling rigid waves of desire throughout her body. When she looked up, he'd lowered his lids, sweeping his long lashes across his powerful gaze, softening the intensity to a dreamy quality.

"Taste me."

Obediently, she parted her lips and he slipped the tip inside her mouth. Salty and slippery, his taste smoothed over her tongue. His flavor was the sea, the sky, the very breath of the air. When she closed her lips to draw him in deeper, he inched back, flashing her a most wicked, playful smile.

Repeatedly, he teased himself around her lips, giving her tiny tastes. Just when she thought she could draw him into her, he pulled back until she was mad to taste all of him. Ever so slowly, he slipped more of his shaft between her willing lips.

His chest hitched with a deep breath and his cock twitched inside the hot hollow of her mouth. With a groan, he tore himself away.

Behind his back, she smiled. Apparently, she gave as good as she got. He could no more resist her than she could resist him. Before she knew it, he was back between her legs, lifting them high against his chest until her ankles rested on his shoulders. He took a moment to stroke her feet and her crimson shoes, then angled his body above hers. As the weight pressed onto his arms, the muscles and veins stood out, prompting her to reach out to touch him. Her hands were bound.

"Set me free."

He shook his head in refusal as he stroked his cock between her slick nether lips. "I want you held while I ride you." Turning his head, he licked her shoe and her foot, causing a stab of desire to surge another creamy jolt to her sex. "I want you to lie there and take everything I have to give."

Her sex was so tight with longing she was afraid it would simply collapse upon itself. His heated words only increased her tension. If she thought it would speed him up, she would beg him, but that would only slow him down. Torment was a leisurely process. Always, when they started, she thought she could stand prolonging the moment when he entered her, but when her body rose up in need, she cursed every delay.

Pushing himself up with his arms and legs, he rocked his hips, stroking his cock lightly along her clit. Zinging bolts shot across her skin, focusing all her cravings into that one tiny bit of flesh. If only he would go faster or press harder, she could find release. But no, he grinned down at her, enjoying the way she tried to reach out to him, the way her body writhed in denied ecstasy. His untamed eyes drilled into hers, pinning her.

"Please." The word tumbled from her lips before she could stop it.

"Please what?" he teasingly asked. He pressed more firmly

against her, then rolled his hips in a circle, sliding his shaft along and around her throbbing clit.

He wanted her to say it. Of course he did. Proving himself superior in denial excited him just as much as her lusty words.

Meeting his gaze directly, she said, "I want you to fuck me."

With a satisfied groan, he pressed harder. "Say it again."

She did as he asked, saying those hard, sexy words repeatedly until they became a chant.

He slid down until the head of his cock pressed firmly against her passage.

They uttered a simultaneous groan.

She waited breathlessly, loving the feel of his impeding possession. The moment just before he entered was pure lust. If he denied her, she didn't know what she would do to soothe herself. Nothing would match the feeling of him, her bondmate, the man she loved filling her completely.

Just when she thought she could stand no more, he thrust forward, stretching her passage to accommodate his girth. Releasing a shocked gasp of pleasure caused him to sink deeper, pushing her legs back until her thighs touched her breasts. Bliss. Even though he was on top, she felt that she'd captured him. Exerting all her strength, she clamped her inner muscles around him, ensnaring him between her legs.

Mumbling swears, he glanced down and realized he had her bent in two.

When he pulled his weight off, she blurted, "It doesn't hurt." Plaintively, she whispered, "Please don't stop now. Ride me like you said you would."

Her ankles cradled his face while he stared down at her.

"Like this?" He thrust so hard her head snapped back.

"Yes, just like that." He plunged so deeply it almost verged on pain, but it was a good ache, a necessary hurt, because she needed to feel entwined with him.

As he rode her, sweat beaded across his forehead, then gathered, spilling down to his temples. Small beads bloomed across his chest, then rained down on her in hot, salty drops. Her legs became slick, allowing him to slide deeper with each thrust, so deep did he go she felt he might split her in two. Each rock of his hips scraped his body along her clit, lifting her closer to ecstasy.

Snarling, he pulled his lips back, exposing his teeth as he continued to slam into her. Brutal, ferocious, he was no longer a man but an animal in heat, an animal driven to mate. In that moment, he was everything she'd ever longed to have in her bed. He was no pretty boy with poetry on his mind. Sterlave was a beast compelled to find satisfaction.

Below him, she felt tiny, helpless, trapped by his power, drugged by his intensity. Parting her lips, she had to breathe in when he moved back and out when he rammed forward. His movements were so fast she was panting. His breathing matched hers, as if they breathed together. Energy gathered along her nerves, then into her clit. One great thrust lifted her body up and then pleasure shattered her. For a long moment, she was blind, deaf, and dumb.

As reality intruded, she heard and felt Sterlave climax. His mighty roar caused another rush of contractions to ripple her passage around him, which only deepened his bellow. When the last of their mutual release faded away, he collapsed on her for a brief moment.

Carefully, he moved her ankle from his shoulder, then rolled beside her. Now that the moment was over, would he want to talk? And if he did, what was she going to tell him?

21

Sterlave had the weight of the empire on his shoulders until he saw Kasmiri clad only in a pair of crimson high-heeled shoes. Everything he'd planned to discuss went right out of his head. All the blood in his brain rushed to his penis. With a shrug, he decided one night of delay wouldn't hurt. As he teased and tormented her, he could barely maintain a show of cool aplomb, for it was a masquerade. He wanted to be inside her so badly he had to hold back snarls of frustration.

Burying himself inside her silky heat made everything in the world disappear. Here, with her, all was as it should be. Alone with his beautiful woman, he didn't have to worry about finding Loban, soothing Rown's pain, or even protecting Kasmiri's life. If anyone dared to enter this room with a mind to hurt her, he would have killed them with his bare hands. None could touch his mate but him. In a very short span of time, she inspired a primal heat that made him want to pound his chest, flex his muscles, and engage in vicious battles to prove his supremacy.

Something in her eyes was different tonight, though. Genuine panic lurked just below the surface of her wild, wicked gaze. At first, he thought she was worried about him binding her to the bed, but that wasn't it. In that, she trusted him. Something else terrified her.

"Kasmiri, did something happen today?"

She caught her breath, then turned her head to him. "What do you mean?"

Suspicious that she'd answered a question with a question, he straddled her hips, levering himself above her. His searching gaze caused her to struggle to make her face appear innocent or seductive, he wasn't quite certain which.

"You're upset. I want to know why."

"I'm fine." She held his gaze just a little too forcefully. "Today was very busy, but all I could think about was you."

Lowering her proud chin, she kept her eyes wide and innocent. He had his answer when she pursed her lips. Clearly, she was going for seduction. For a moment, he considered letting things slide and taking her up on another round of passion. Her hot, sexy scent and taut nipples caused his erection to gradually return. She stretched in the restraints, clicking her shoes together, which drew his attention to her feet. When he glanced over his shoulder, he spied her curvy legs capped with slinky red shoes. Blood thrummed hot and fast to his cock. Visions formed of her on her knees, him behind her, plunging hard while slapping her rounded bottom and gripping her shoe-clad feet . . . He shook his head. She was very, very good at distracting him.

"Stop it."

Guiltily, she lowered her gaze. "Unbind me."

"Not until you tell me what happened today."

Kasmiri shook her head. "Everything's fine. I'm just tired." However, she would not meet his eyes. Normally she'd erupt in fury that he didn't do as she bid. Whatever plagued her had to be serious for her to take such a passive approach.

Determined to get an answer, he stroked his hands up her belly to cup her breasts. Gasping, she now met his gaze. Her smile proved that she thought she'd won. Pinching her nipples between his fingers and thumbs, he let her believe that she'd distracted him. Sultry eyes lowered as she arched her breasts firmly into his hands. Ripe, round globes made him forget his motive. When she licked her upper lip, his cock twitched. All he could think of was how beautiful she'd looked with her luscious lips wrapped around his shaft. He'd lost his mind when she wantonly sucked him like the sweetest candy she'd ever tasted. Kasmiri was a woman accustomed to the most decadent treats, but she found his cock the ultimate gourmet delicacy. With a wince of painful reality, he wondered if she wanted to do that to him, or if she had done so only to control him.

Demurely, she lowered her gaze, as if she willingly submitted to him. As far as keeping up a cool facade went, Kasmiri was his master. She gauged his reactions, then mirrored hers to increase his passion. Such manipulation didn't anger him exactly, because her motives intrigued him. He wondered just how far she would go to keep him from talking things out. Kasmiri was hiding something, but what, and more so, why?

Lifting up, he knelt over her so he could drop his hand between her legs. Trailing his fingertips between the dark curls that guarded her secrets caused her breathing to hitch and catch. Kasmiri was good, but she could keep up an excellent show for only so long.

"You're going to tell me."

Her gaze jumped to his. "I don't have anything—"

He cut her off by plunging two fingers into her channel.

Shock caused her to gasp, then clamp her lips together.

As he pumped his fingers in and out with a slow beat, she writhed. Her sweet cunny sucked at his digits just as her lovely mouth had done to his prick. Shoving another finger into her caused her to buck uncontrollably against his hand as she rubbed her clit against his palm.

When she caught his rhythm, he stopped.

Her furious gaze snapped to his. Nothing angered her more than denial of her release. He knew she was hiding something big because she held her tongue. Never had Kasmiri censored herself. His deliberate smile caused her to drop her gaze.

"Tell me."

Turning away, she refused to even acknowledge he'd spoken.

He thrust his fingers furiously into her tight, hot channel.

Her gaze swung back to his, her teeth bared against tense lips.

"Tell me, Kasmiri. I have no problem keeping you bound until you do."

At first, she tried to ignore him, but his words and his lusting hand were impossible to dismiss.

"Stop!"

"I won't stop until you speak."

"Please," she begged, dropping any tone of command from her voice.

He felt sorry for her then and almost relented, but a subtle little lift of her brows told him she was trying to manipulate him.

Plunging his fingers while teasing his thumb across her clit kept her on the edge of release. Just when she started to tumble over, he stopped. Her breathing became erratic and her gasps became frustrated snarls.

"Tell me, Kasmiri, and I'll let you have your pleasure."

She shook her head, defying him despite her tortured body's needs. Such strength of will she possessed, but his was just as strong, and he wasn't the one bound to the bed. Again, he stroked her to the edge, and again, he pulled her back. Trashing wildly, she now lifted her legs in an effort to distract him from her slick sex. Sterlave slid off her so he could enjoy looking at her legs while touching her. Sleek, strong muscles from her tummy to her hips flexed as she rubbed her legs together. She also tried to prevent him from continuing his strokes between her legs by pressing them together, but she wasn't strong enough to block his access.

Eventually she stopped struggling with a strangled cry of submission. "I'll tell you," she said, her voice weak and defeated.

He stopped teasing her but kept his hand on her thigh, ready to continue if she tried to trick him.

Kasmiri met his gaze with her big, wild, sexy eyes and softly said, "I love you." A lone tear tumbled down her cheek. "That's what happened to me today. I discovered that I love you." She turned her head away. "Are you happy now that you've forced the truth out of me?"

Hearing those words should have filled him with joy, but instead, he felt awful. No wonder she'd looked panicked. Everyone she'd ever loved left her or died. In her mind, giving him her heart would likely lead to heartbreak.

"I'm sorry, I thought it was something . . . else." Gods, he was going to make this worse if he didn't shut up. With quick movements, he unbound her. She rubbed her wrists, then rolled away from him. Lowering his body next to hers, he breathed out against the sensitive skin of her neck. "Please forgive me."

When she burst into tears, he had to bite his bottom lip not to follow suit. He swore he would never hurt her, but there was no denying what he'd done. Never in his life had he felt like such a beast. What kind of a man tormented a woman until he forced her to confess? He'd taken a happy, wonderful moment and turned it into a trauma that she would never forget. Likely, she would never forgive him for it either.

He opened his mouth to speak, then slowly shut it. What

could he say? Everything that came to mind sounded stupid or hurtful. Instead of talking, he stroked his hand along her back in small circles, hoping he could convey his regret without words.

Her tears continued for a time, but at least she didn't flinch away from his touch. After a while, she stopped crying. He left her for a moment to retrieve a small, moist towel. When he placed it into her hand, she thanked him, wiped her face, between her legs, and then tossed if off the side of the bed along with her shoes. He wondered if she would now toss him away so easily. Not that he could blame her. Once, he'd asked her if she loved him, when she didn't answer, he'd let it go, thinking she hadn't been ready. When she had, he ruined the moment.

He lowered the lights, climbed back into bed, settled on his back, and pulled the covers up. Tension filled his body to the point he couldn't relax. Sleep would never come to him like this and he needed rest so he could meet the challenges of tomorrow. Facing Loban would take all his strength. Sterlave didn't know what he would say when he confronted him. Thoughts of beating him to a pulp only fueled his tension. Fighting would not solve the problem, but talking things out would have no impact either, not on a man like Loban. Chur wanted him brought before an Esslean tribunal, where all the recruits in the training rooms would decide his fate. Sterlave didn't think that would be harsh enough punishment.

With a sigh, he rolled over to his side. He heard Kasmiri sigh, too, and roll toward him, pressing into his body. Her warmth soothed his ragged nerves. He didn't dare speak for somehow ruining her tender show of forgiveness.

"I'm sorry," she whispered, her face resting just below his.

Her apology shocked him. What did she have to be sorry for? "I'm the one who—"

"I didn't want to tell you that I loved you, not like that. I wanted to wait, but you wouldn't stop, and I didn't know what to do." She rubbed her cheek against his biceps.

He pulled her into his embrace. "I promise I will never do that again." He kissed her forehead affectionately. "Bondage games should never be about anything but pleasure. I overstepped and turned it ugly. For that, I am truly sorry."

She held very still for a moment, then asked, "Don't you have something else to say to me?"

His mind went blank. He'd already said he was sorry and he swore not to do it again. What more did she need from him?

She drew a sharp breath, then let it out slowly. "You don't have to say it back." Fresh tears slid down her face to splatter his chest.

What an idiot he was. "Oh, Kasmiri, I—"

"Please don't say it, not now. Not when it's like I made you." She wiped her tears away, then nestled a little closer against him, tucking her head down so the top of her head touched the center of his chest. "Tell me when you're ready."

That stung. If only he'd left her alone, she would have told him when she was ready, not when he'd forced it out of her.

As she fell asleep, he thought about loving her. Did he truly love her, or was he going to say it because she had? In his village, he'd told many women he loved them as part of the moment. It was meaningless, an automatic response to their words. Only once, when he was very young, had he thought he was in love. Sex with Valse, the baker's wife, was different from sex with the other women in his village.

Sterlave never told Valse he loved her because she hadn't said it first, but he'd felt it, and he trusted her enough to tell her his longing to have her wear her shoes while they were in bed. To this day, memories of her mocking laughter still caused his testicles to retract into his body. How viciously would she have mocked him if he had said he loved her?

Love was dangerous. His mother died for love. His father

abused him out of love. What if he gave his heart to Kasmiri and she only stomped on it and kicked it back at him? Wincing, he wondered how he could even question her reaction after what he'd done when she gave her heart to him. His mind worried at the questions like a poor man worried at a bone.

Sleep was a long time in coming.

Sterlave woke on his back with Kasmiri straddled across his chest. In her hand, she held a small bowl. He didn't have to look to know she'd bound his arms and legs, because the weight of the fur-lined cuffs pressed into his wrists and ankles.

Revenge?

He peered up at her serene face. All traces of her tears were gone. This morning her eyes were bright, her smile gentle.

Playfully, she pulled something out of the bowl, then held it close to his mouth. One breath told him it was sugar-drenched *nicla.* When he parted his lips, she popped the treat inside. Sweet and tangy, the smooth-skinned fruit slid against his tongue. Chewing slowly, he let his gaze slide down to where her sweet and tangy cunny pressed against his chest.

"The treat was nice, but you taste better."

With a pert smile, she offered him another piece, which he ate. Several times she repeated the motions. He started to wonder if she was planning to feed him his entire meal this way. Above them, the glass ceiling revealed only the barest blush of morning light.

Kasmiri placed a piece between her lips, then leaned over, offering the *nicla* to him. After he swallowed it, she slipped her tongue into his mouth, tasting him, the fruit. She fell into the kiss, so much so that she set the bowl aside. Cupping his face, she deepened the contact. Using her lips, teeth, and tongue, she made love to his mouth. Never had anyone kissed him so thoroughly. When she pulled back, he lifted up, trying to follow her, but his bonds held him securely.

Her expression was one of soft arousal. Her nipples peaked, her body thrummed, and he could feel how slick her sex was since she created a wet spot against his chest.

Leery of her magnanimous behavior, he settled back, waiting for the moment when she extended her claws.

He didn't have to wait long.

Tossing her midnight hair over her shoulder, she climbed gracefully to her feet. Standing over him, she glared down into his face.

"Did you enjoy your treat?"

He tried to keep his attention on her face, but his gaze slid down to the sweet secrets between her thighs. With her legs spread, he had a pretty good view.

"I asked you a question." She placed her foot on his chest and her hands on her hips. Now she was all commanding female. Fire blazed in her eyes; her body glowed with power. Oil slicked along her flesh, showing off her sleek, yet powerful form. Against his will, blood surged his cock to painfully hard.

"I enjoyed my treat," he confirmed, holding her gaze. He had no idea Kasmiri harbored a dominating edge to her sexual appetite. It made a kind of sense, in that she was so authoritarian in her personal life, but to discover she wanted to dominate him sexually was as shocking as it was arousing. Perhaps her anger prompted her attitude, but that wasn't what drove her to control him. She enjoyed bossing him about, but this was another layer to the act of tying him up. This wasn't about controlling him physically; this was about controlling him mentally.

Most men would have rebelled instantly. Never would they allow a woman that much power. Sterlave trusted her. She might be hurt at what he'd done, she might be sad he didn't return her words of love, but all that allowed her to express her deepest, darkest, most dangerous desire. Kasmiri longed to dominate him.

Pressing her foot down into his chest, she commanded his attention back to her face. "You're going to do whatever I want."

Nodding didn't satisfy her. She demanded he answer "yes, my lady" or "no, my lady" to her questions. He swore he would do whatever she wanted. The question was, what did she want?

With a lift of her brows, she left the bed. Sterlave propped his head up, but he couldn't see what she was doing. His heart started to race, causing his cock to bounce ever so slightly. One thing he knew for certain, Kasmiri would never bore him.

She returned with a scrap of black fabric in her hands. As she climbed up the bed, he realized what it was.

"Kasmiri, I'm not—"

"Did I ask you a question?"

"No, my lady." He drew a deep breath and let it out slowly while she covered his eyes with the makeshift blindfold. Plunged into sudden darkness, he tried to relax with the deep breathing of *kintana,* but he could not center himself. He'd never been blindfolded. Losing his ability to see frightened him because he relied so heavily on his vision.

When Kasmiri placed her hand on his chest, he flinched.

Her laughter only added to his discomfort. He almost told her he didn't want to do this, but he also didn't want to ruin the moment. After what he'd done to her, he owed her something.

Relying on his sense of sound and touch, he heard and felt her shift on the bed. He couldn't use his sense of smell since all he could smell was the strong aroma of *nicla.* She climbed off and padded away. Waiting breathlessly, he forced air into and out of his lungs in an effort to calm himself. Just when he found a measure of peace, she returned. Her weight pulled the surface of the bed as she climbed between his widely spread legs.

A series of clicks increased his anxiety. What was she doing? Sudden visions of her tormenting his cock and balls caused him to strain against the manacles. Was she really so angry that she would hurt him? Gods, what had he gotten himself into? When he heard humming, he had to still his breath to identify the source. At first, he thought Kasmiri was humming happily to herself, but then he realized whatever it was maintained a steady tone. Through the panic emerged a great arousing curiosity. Just what *was* she going to do to him?

Suddenly, the humming stopped. Kasmiri left the bed again. He heard a door open and close. Sharply, Kasmiri shushed someone.

Now his heart beat so fast he could feel it in his neck. She'd invited someone into the room! Who was with her, and what did they make of his bound form? Was it Rown? He shook his head. He couldn't let her bring Rown into this, not after what he'd recently suffered.

"Get on the bed between his legs," Kasmiri said.

Sterlave felt the bed dip below someone's weight.

"Put this on."

He wasn't sure whom she was ordering, but then he felt the other person moving about.

Lowering his voice to a bare whisper, Sterlave asked, "Rown?"

"Did I tell you to speak?" Kasmiri's voice boomed off the walls, coming at his ears from every direction.

He flinched. From listening, he couldn't tell exactly where she was. "No, my lady, but—"

"You want to know who waits so patiently between your thighs." Her voice seemed to be almost directly above him. "I don't have to tell you, but I will tell you it isn't Rown."

Right after he released a sigh of relief, he drew in another tense breath. If not Rown, then who? Curiosity was eating him up. He wanted to know not only who was there but also what they intended to do.

"Lift your knees, Sterlave." Kasmiri's voice now came from the foot of the bed, as if she were directing him and the person kneeling.

On the verge of refusing, he ultimately did as she bid. Resistance would only prolong the agony. Kasmiri would do as she pleased and he couldn't resist. As he drew his knees up, the straps tightened, pulling his ankles out, spreading him wider.

"Lift up."

When he did, someone slid a firm pillow under his ass. As he settled his weight upon it, he had a sneaking suspicion of what she was doing. She'd said she wanted to see him with another man. Sterlave was convinced that if he opened his eyes, he'd find one kneeling expectantly between his widely spaced thighs. But what man would take a part in kinky games with the empress and her consort? Perhaps another *ungati*? Kasmiri wouldn't dare force someone to do this to him. Or would she?

Gods, the suspense was killing him. As much as he just wanted to get this over with, he also wanted to extend the moment indefinitely. He wasn't sure he was ready. It wasn't rape, as he was willing, but was the other man willing too? That mattered a great deal to him. Sex should always bring pleasure to those involved. Moreover, he wanted to see Kasmiri's reaction. What would she do while she watched another man work his prick into him? Would she touch herself until she climaxed? Would she straddle his face and make him tongue her to orgasm? His cock twitched with the thought.

"Seems my captive is more than ready to begin." Her lowered voice dripped sex and power. But still, he couldn't tell where she was.

Two hands settled on his feet, making him jump. Blindness amplified the contact. He thought he could feel each tiny ridge of his fingertips as he teased them between his toes. Short nails scratched up his calf, toying with his regrowing hair. Settling his grip behind his knee, he felt the man pull him forward, as if to put him into a better position for penetration. Sterlave tensed, pulling away from the direction he was being led into.

"Don't fight him." Kasmiri warned.

"Yes, my lady." Sterlave deliberately relaxed and gave himself over to direction. Fighting would only make this uncomfortable. Since he had no choice in the matter, he decided to wring all the pleasure he could from this encounter. Would this feel as good as the wand Kasmiri used on him? That had blown his mind. The intensity of that orgasm left him damn near blind. Of course, that wouldn't matter now, not with the black fabric over his eyes.

Once the man had pulled him down a bit and adjusted the pillow, he slid his hands along the inside of Sterlave's thighs. Pressing just enough to show he was in charge caused a strange thrill to coil tension in Sterlave's gut. The man's hands felt small but strong. When he reached close to his balls, Sterlave held his breath, waiting for the first contact, but it never came. Instead, the man teased his hands across his upper thighs, then around his hips. Soothing circles drew close to his throbbing penis but did not actually touch. So sensitive was his flesh he felt the heat of his hands when they drew near. Every time the man moved them away, he groaned with disappointment. Waiting for the moment when he would touch him there was excruciating. Picturing his hands upon his aching member caused another involuntary twitch.

Kasmiri uttered a pleased moan.

As the man worked his hands up his chest, Sterlave struggled to hold still. He wanted to lean into his caress. On the tip of his tongue danced the need to ask for harder touches, but he didn't want to defy Kasmiri again. In truth, he was afraid if he did, she might stop this crazy, erotic, maddening game. He didn't want this to end. Deep inside came a need to feel another man thrust into him, not for dominance as Loban had done, but to provide pleasure, as Rown and Kasmiri had done with the wand. Craving the adventure of doing something utterly different, something he would likely never do on his own, aroused him to a fever pitch. He literally felt blood flush across his skin.

"I can tell that you want something," Kasmiri whispered very close to his right ear. "You may speak this one time."

In a tumbling rush, he said, "Touch me harder, press more firmly, hard enough to hurt. Twist my nipples and bite—"

"That's enough," she cut him off, then chuckled. "Didn't you once call me a greedy *yondie?*" The question lingered for a moment, ratcheting up his tension. "Seems to me you're the one with a long list of wants and needs."

One of them twisted his nipple, zinging a bolt of pleasure straight down to his cock. Must be the man since the nails were short. When he did it again, he thrust his hips and almost made contact with his body.

"Hold still," Kasmiri admonished, apparently not allowing the other man to speak at all.

If he heard his voice, would he recognize it? What if he wasn't a servant but one of the recruits? Or even one of her guards? What would she have promised him in exchange for this? Perhaps that's why she blindfolded him; he couldn't act oddly around this man if he didn't know who he was. For some reason, he found that unbelievably freeing. No repercussions, no hurt feelings, no awkward exchanges. They would have this moment and then never have to worry about it again. The man would know he pleasured Sterlave, but he didn't have to openly admit his part in this adventure. Would he forever after smile privately to himself when Sterlave passed him? Would Sterlave know who it was one day when he saw a certain flash in another man's eye or the barest twist of a smile? What if Kasmiri blindfolded the man as well? Just the thought spurred another round of lusty thoughts and curious questions.

Settling back on the pillow, Sterlave waited for the next teasing movement. After tweaking his nipples until he groaned low and deep in his chest, the man moved on to hard strokes along his ribs, his sides, and his shoulders. Pressing firmly caused friction, which, in turn, sent more heat to his genitals. Right now, his balls felt so hot and heavy he feared they would explode.

The man settled his hands on either side of his hips, pressing him down into the pillow. He released and pressed him several times in quick succession, as if he were already pumping into him. His cock bounced, so taut with arousal it hurt with each quiver. In that moment, he wanted his shaft buried inside Kasmiri. How would it feel to have her snuggled around him while the man slammed deep into his ass? Imagining the scenario caused more surges of pleasure to ripple across his body. Everything gathered strength as it wrapped around his hips. Now he helped the man bounce him by adding his own thrusts.

"That's it. Rock your hips. Try desperately to find something to plunge your aching cock into."

Kasmiri's breathless voice only added to his torment.

Frantically, he humped the air but found no relief. When the man stopped bouncing him, he couldn't help but growl. Now he didn't even have the jiggling to offer some stimulation to his prick. He would have begged, but Kasmiri would only prolong his distress.

He felt the bed give way under his feet and he imagined the man took a wide stance between his forcefully spread legs. Was this the moment? Would he finally feel the man's cock sliding slowly up his ass, or would he plunge deep and fast?

Anticipation caused him to pant in dire need. When he felt a silken touch to his cock he practically jumped out of his skin. One lone fingertip traced along the throbbing vein that ran from the base to just under the head. Unbelievably, he got even harder. So taut was his cock it truly ached. Deep down into his body he hurt. His balls, his prick, the whole region of his hips felt swollen with blood.

The lone finger continued to trace along his shaft, then around the head, teasing around in smaller circles until it pressed against the weeping slit. Unable to hold back, he let loose a body-shaking moan and thrust his hips, forcing the finger to rub hard and fast down his length. Such a quick touch stimulated him strongly but wasn't enough to soothe him.

"I told you to hold still!" Kasmiri's voice was directionless again.

"Yes, my lady," he responded between panting breaths. Pressure mounted as he waited for another touch. Something, anything would be better than nothing at all. Cool air wafted across his overheated body but failed to pacify him in any way. When he drew breath through his nose, all he could smell was the *nicla* Kasmiri fed him, which, in turn, made him think of her sweet sex over his mouth. If she were there right now, he'd tongue-fuck her every nook and cranny until she creamed all over his face. Such raunchy thoughts only made things worse.

Turning his attention outward, he tried to slow his breath so he could hear them, but he couldn't catch it for longer than a second. Time moved at an endless pace. How many hours did he lay still, straining, praying, and begging in his mind for Kasmiri to order the man to do what she'd brought him here to do?

"Are you ready?"

"Yes, my lady." He practically screamed the words.

Her laughter was gentle, a soothing caress to his ears before she whispered, "Trust me, this is worth waiting for."

Gods, did she mean to prolong this further? If she did, he wouldn't last. A tentative touch between his cheeks caused him to inadvertently clench them tightly together.

"Relax, I don't want him to hurt you."

Gently, the oil-slick fingers worked their way around his ass, then pressed into his channel. He tried not to wiggle, but he did anyway. Probing fingers were a prefect prelude to what would follow. The pillow held him up but also tilted his hips slightly back, so the man had unfettered access to every sensitive spot, and he seemed to know just where to touch.

Once he'd slathered him with oil, Sterlave heard another

blast of oil against something, but he didn't touch him. After a moment of confusion, Sterlave realized the man was covering his cock with oil to further ease the way.

Now Sterlave's thoughts turned another direction; how big was this man? He pictured a hair-dusted hand wrapped around a cock as hard as his, stroking up and down, distributing oil until the length gleamed. Gripping it hard would cause the head to swell and darken. Sterlave tried to picture the man more clearly, but he had nothing to go on. For some crazy reason, Chur popped into his head. Sterlave tried to remove the image, but it was too late. On his knees between Sterlave's spread legs, he pictured Chur in all his glowing magnificence. Now, the hand around the cock was bigger, stronger, and his massive glossy cock shined like a magical device designed to deliver endless orgasms.

The weight on the bed changed and Sterlave felt the man's knees slide under his raised thighs. Before he could marvel over the sensation, he felt the tip of the man's cock press against his anus. Behind the blindfold, Sterlave closed his eyes tightly, not in anticipation of pain, but in a sublime surrender. Ever so slowly, the man pushed forward until just the head of his cock plugged him. Holding the position, the man placed his hand around Sterlave's cock.

A moan of longing erupted from his throat and bounced off the walls. His grip was loose, but even the slight contact was magnified in his deprived state. Sterlave craved more and he tightened around the man's cock, pulling it deeper. He thought he would hear the man moan, but he was remarkably well restrained. All Sterlave could hear was Kasmiri's breath catching, then releasing on plush sighs. An image of her sultry eyes lowered as she fingered herself popped into his mind and caused him to twitch in the man's grip.

In response, the man held him more firmly, then slid his hand down at the same pace as he slid up Sterlave's ass. Dual sensations almost pushed him over the edge, but he held on, wanting to wait until his orgasm built to a shattering new height. Hot, thick, and pliable, the man's cock plunged fully into Sterlave. No pain possessed him, only a tingling pleasure that zipped along his sensitized nerves. He understood that's why Kasmiri teased him for so long; anticipation amplified each sensation.

The man rocked his hips, moving in and out, as he performed the same motions on his cock. Sterlave shook in confusion; he didn't know whether to thrust up into his hand or down onto his prick. Such a maddening dilemma left him unable to move at all. He simply lay back and let this mysterious man do as he wished.

Increasing his pace, the man pushed harder into Sterlave. When he angled up, he rubbed the smooth, hot tip of his cock right against that small magical spot buried in his bottom. He'd never known the spot existed until Rown showed him with the wand.

This man knew exactly where that spot was and deliberately altered his strokes to press firmly against it. Faster and harder he went until Sterlave thought he would lose his mind. Never had he longed for release so profoundly. If he could see, he imagined the man's hand would be a blur on his cock. So quickly did he stroke, and in such perfect rhythm to his plunging prick, that for a crazy moment Sterlave thought he was fucking his own ass. When he laughed at the thought, he tightened around the man's cock.

Kasmiri moaned as if she'd felt what he'd done.

"I'm going to make you come so hard you'll never forget it."

Her voice puffed hot and sultry against his sweaty chest. Clearly, his mind was playing tricks on him because she couldn't be above him, not unless she sat upon the man's shoulders.

With each pulse-pounding, bed-shaking stroke, Kasmiri whispered, "Come for me. Come for me."

How could he refuse? Past the point of no return, Sterlave

let her voice usher on his climax. He felt his orgasm start deep in his balls, then erupt from the tip of his cock. Jetting spurt after spurt onto his chest caused his entire body to contract. At the same time, he felt the man's contractions follow as he pumped into his ass. At that precise moment, Kasmiri whisked away the blindfold.

Aftershocks of the orgasm convinced him his eyes weren't working because what he saw couldn't be true. There was no man between his legs. Blinking several times didn't change what was.

Kasmiri knelt there, resting one hand on his rapidly deflating cock while the other cupped her own breast to tweak her nipple as she continued to thrust her hips during her orgasm. When she finally finished, she slumped forward onto his chest. As her cock deflated within the tight channel of his ass, he was convinced he was losing his mind. He'd been up, down, and all around his mate's body, and he was certain that she didn't have a penis.

Slowly, she opened her wicked, wild eyes. When she caught his stunned gaze, she smiled, and said, "Surprise."

22

Kasmiri didn't want to move. She'd used every bit of her strength thrusting into him. Watching his head roll back, his mouth working as he moaned out his pleasure—she wouldn't soon forget that moment. Sterlave's stunned expression caused a tremor of apprehension to stir in her belly.

"Just tell me how you grew a penis on such short notice."

His wry comment caused her to laugh, which pulled her temporary cock out of him. He winced, and so did she as she eased her weight off him. Removing the pillow, she sat cross-legged on the bed below him.

Between her legs, the smooth phallic device released from her body now that her orgasm was complete. She gingerly removed the toy from where it anchored around her hips and in her sex, and tossed it off the bed.

"Remember how I told you that many of the elite gave us sexual gifts after our bonding ceremony?"

Frowning, he nodded. "I thought they were destroyed in the fire."

"They were, but dignitaries from all over the universe have

been sending gifts too. Apparently, someone captured our moment and distributed copies."

His chuckle eased her trepidation. "So a collection of voyeuristic *barsitas* are enjoying themselves while watching us?" He tilted his head to the side. "I'm strangely flattered."

"You take pleasure in being on display?" Fury consumed her when she first heard that off-planet inhabitants, *barsitas,* viewed her most intimate and private moment for their own titillation.

Shrugging caused the manacles to pull on his wrists. "Let them look. They'll never have me or you."

Possession turned his tone sharp, pleasing her feminine pride. He hadn't been able to say he loved her, but he clearly wasn't going to share her with anyone. Hopefully, he saw her daring sexual encounter this morning as evidence that she honestly did love him and would do anything to please him, sexually or otherwise.

With four flicks, she released him from his bonds.

He stretched his arms over his head and straightened his legs out on either side of her. "Tell me more about this most amazing transformation device."

She described how the device oozed around her hips and up inside her, taking her arousal as a woman and translating those impulses into a man's reactions. "Every time you clenched around the phallus, I felt it inside my sex. Each thrust stimulated my walls." Mere words couldn't describe how amazing the experience had been. It was as close to being a man as she was ever going to get. "Watching you struggle with longing and fear, but trusting me to not hurt you, aroused me in ways I can't explain. Your trust was the most empowering of all."

Pumping her cock into him caused her to grit her teeth and understand how the act of penetrating someone, fucking another being, was so brutally exciting. In that moment, she possessed him utterly. Every move he made, she felt. The subtlest reaction of him amplified around her cock, then surged into her sex. She glanced away when she worried that such a powerful feeling could be addictive. Would he ever let her do that to him again? She certainly hoped so.

"What was the clicking and humming about?"

She held up her hands so he could see her shortened nails. "I clipped them, then smoothed the edges. I didn't want to hurt you."

"And it truly added to the illusion you'd let a man in here." He glanced at the door. "You just opened and closed it."

She nodded. "I thought the shushing was a perfect touch."

His laugh pleased her. "I actually thought . . ."

"Are you disappointed?"

"No, I'm impressed with your lusty, creative mind." He kissed her shoulder. "Is there such a device for me?"

She considered his question. "I honestly didn't notice." A hot blush rose up her cheeks. "Once I saw that one I didn't look at anything else."

Lifting his head to gaze at her, he smiled, and said, "You lusty *yondie.*" He fell back. "Tell me where I might find this cache of gifts so that I can find something to use on you."

She told him she'd had them sent to a storage room off the servants' quarters. Anticipation tingled along her fully satisfied body. What else was in that room full of presents? Reluctantly, she rose from the bed to prepare herself for another day of meetings.

"Wait a moment." Sterlave captured her between his legs. "It's proper etiquette that after you fuck a man silly you should at least kiss him."

She kissed him hungrily, then slid off the bed. In the bathing unit, dread stiffened her spine. In her haze of lust, she'd forgotten all about her visitor last night. She didn't want to face him today. Sterlave thought her strange mood had been about holding back the truth of her love, and she felt terrible for lying to him, but she didn't know what else to do. He wouldn't stop tormenting her until she confessed to something. Love was less dangerous than that monster.

Hurt that Sterlave hadn't said he loved her back, she also didn't want to force the confession out of him. Such a compelled declaration would be meaningless. When and if he said that he loved her, she wanted him to mean it. He'd called her his soulmate, and that touched her deeply. For now, it would have to be enough.

Even the hottest water couldn't stop her from shivering. Today she would have to do as the monster asked. If she didn't, he wouldn't hurt her, he swore he would destroy Sterlave. Kasmiri shook her head, terrified to do or not to do as he demanded. Her own people would rebel. She'd lose whatever allies she had. What did it matter if she stayed in power if she had no one to rule over?

After drying herself off, she moved to her mirror and summoned Rown. Whatever bothered him seemed to have passed. Today he met her gaze with his soft blue eyes. Rown dressed her, applied her makeup, and fashioned her hair with his usual grace and efficiency.

She thanked him, settled herself at the table to review her plans for the day, and then dismissed him with a nod.

Sterlave rose, stretched, his muscles distracting her from her floating blue agenda. How could fragile skin contain so much masculine power and grace? She did not know another man who would be secure enough to let her do what she did. Tearing her gaze away, she turned her attention to her advisors' meeting. Sighing, she tapped out her changes, requesting a block of time to address some emergency concerns. She had no idea how she would present the idea, only that she had to give the monster something today to buy more time.

As she considered his demands, she chose the least of all the evils. Giving him the Harvester rooms wouldn't hurt anyone.

The current Harvester could find accommodations in the training rooms. If he complained, Kasmiri would tell him to be grateful he'd left with his life. She was certain that if he protested, the monster would simply hunt him down and kill him. As to the second part of the monster's request, she didn't know how she could do as he asked. Naming him the official Harvester was a power she did not have. He would have to fight and kill the current Harvester to take his place. From her understanding, one could only challenge the current Harvester right before the Harvest. Closing her eyes, she feared that's exactly what he intended. The monster knew he'd asked for something she couldn't provide. She thought it was a way to either expose her or force the current Harvester into a battle, one the monster would certainly win.

Rown settled several platters on the table, but she couldn't eat. Her stomach roiled at the thought of what would happen at the next Harvest. How would the virgins react to seeing the creature between their tender thighs? His skin could burn on contact when he chose. Would he burn them with his cock, relishing their screams of horror and pain? How could she do this to her own people?

She slapped her hand on the table. They were not even her people! When her mother hadn't been able to resist Helton Ook, she'd taken him as her secret lover. Why she didn't just make him an official consort, Kasmiri would likely never know, but the fact remained that she hadn't, which made Kasmiri a nothing. Worse than a nothing, because she was a *pharadean,* the product of an elite house and a Harvester. Such had happened over the seasons but not to the royal house. Parentage was strict for the reining empress's children. For the other elite, it didn't matter, because they were not in power. Once they came into power, their children must be the product of an empress and an official consort. If Kasmiri's house had another legitimate daughter, Kasmiri could simply step down, but she was the last of her line. This meant that no matter what she did, she had no right to rule. Being the daughter of the empress didn't count, not unless she had a consort for a father. And given that she was *pharadean* and last of her line, they would want her exiled to Rhemna so that she couldn't attempt to gain power for her house again.

She swallowed back a defeated little laugh. All her life she'd wanted to abandon her duty of being the empress. It seemed the gods had granted her request in the cruelest fashion. They had waited until she had a reason for wanting to be the empress, then promptly took the role away.

If her mother hadn't drained the royal accounts paying bribes to silence Ambo, Kasmiri would have had the funds needed to run away, but even that her mother couldn't leave her. Clathia left her in a deep hole. Kasmiri had thought of selling her jewels, but Ambo pointed out that all the plush decorations around her rooms were fakes. The real items had been sold long ago to pay off the ever-increasing bribes. Kasmiri didn't have enough to even fuel her mother's Golden Bird to the nearest planet.

Mockingly, Ambo said the only real riches left were slung around her consort's hips. At first, she thought he'd been referring to Sterlave's penis, but he'd actually meant the Sword of the Empress. How ironic that the one valuable item she possessed belonged to the one man she truly loved? If she gave everything up, would he come with her to face the unknown? What would they do to earn funds? Kasmiri had no skills but dancing. Sterlave was a fighter. In what world could they find a place?

"Everything all right?" Sterlave asked, joining her at the table.

His nudity distracted her and she fumbled for an answer. "Meetings and official duties will consume my entire day when I'd rather be here with you." That was no lie. She'd give anything to spend the day with him, lost in pleasure, sleeping, talking; anything would be better than what her day held.

Since he had yet to bathe, she could smell the enticing aroma of sex on him when he leaned over to kiss her hand.

"Don't work too hard." He stood, rooted around under the platters, found a tidbit he liked, popped it into his mouth, and then strolled off to the bathing unit.

Gathering her courage, she was gone before he came out.

Today the advisor's room was packed with many faces Kasmiri didn't recognize for they came to meetings so rarely. They'd come today because she'd insisted on a full gathering of all the advisors and the house representatives. The seating venue expanded to accommodate the influx, and Kasmiri let her gaze slide past her soon-to-be rivals. From her elevated perch, she had an excellent view.

Each house was notable for its unique color. In all, there were twelve houses, including her crimson house. Yellow house probably had the best claim in that the current family had four daughters and all were strong enough to withstand the rigors of competing for the empress throne. Violet house had three daughters of the right age, but they were spoiled and soft. Green house had no hope at all, for they had no daughters old enough to compete. Blue house had the opposite problem in that their daughters were too old. Blue-green house had the sorry curse of creating only male children for the longest time. Red-orange house, the one closest to Kasmiri's, had many daughters, but they were physically and mentally slow from too much inbreeding.

Discouraged, she stopped considering their claims. Whether she left voluntarily or they exiled her, crimson house would cease to exist. Grandmother had told her how once there had been hundreds of houses, each a subtle blend of many colors. As the houses merged or fought, they'd finally fallen into six distinct colors with six blended colors. Intense rivalries at the times of a power shift decimated the houses even more. Season after season of war left the land battered and the populace destroyed. To prevent further destruction, Empress Vrisha, who had no children and didn't want bloodshed at her death, had determined the system for how a new empress would come to power. No more would wars be fought. Instead, everything rested on the woman herself.

Kasmiri did not envy the women of those houses. Empress competition was fierce. They had to prove themselves beautiful, strong, artistic, intelligent, and fertile. She shivered at the last one. Nothing could compel her to place herself in the breeding cage.

When she glanced out again, she caught Helton's gaze. She wanted to spit in his direction, but she calmly held her poise. He offered her a tentative smile that she rejected with a toss of her head. How dare he? Grinning at her like a fool when he'd ruined her life and her entire family line.

A few seats over, Ambo fidgeted worse today than he had yesterday. His eyes were sunken into his head and he seemed slimmer. His gaze met hers with a terrible sadness, almost a begging for forgiveness that she recoiled from. Now that he'd ruined her life, he wanted her forgiveness? Was he mad? He started all this. Given half a chance, she'd destroy him.

Hours passed as many brought forth their business. Most items she quickly shuffled off to the particular advisor who oversaw that function. When the time came for her to make her announcement, she ensured her guards were behind her. Rather than two, she'd selected twenty. What she had to say might erupt into a dispute. If it did, she wanted protection. Not that anyone had ever attacked an empress, but she thought it wise to be prudent.

"My esteemed advisors, I now ask for your indulgence. A visiting dignitary has made an unusual request that I am compelled to grant." She took a breath to steady her pounding heart. If she phrased this just right, all would be well for another day. "He has heard great things about our Harvest." Several people nodded approval for they thought their ways were best. "To this end, he wishes to learn of our rituals, perhaps to take them to his own planet." Murmurs of approval washed over her. "In order to gain a full appreciation for our unique ceremony, he would like to spend his visit in the Harvester suite."

Her heart stopped at the dead silence, then pounded harder than ever. Tossing up a quick prayer to all the gods in *Jarasine*, she kept her gaze steady but was ready to dash for the exit.

"Where will Kerrick of Cheon stay?"

The woman spoke too quickly for Kasmiri to pinpoint who or where she was. Kasmiri assumed Kerrick was the name of the Harvester who'd taken over when Sterlave selected her. "He will stay with the recruits in the training rooms." Some grumbling prompted her to come up with an alternative on the spot. "Or, if he chooses, he can stay in one of the suites reserved for visiting dignitaries."

"Why don't the visitor stay there like he's supposed to?"

The lower-class syntax told her the speaker would be far in the back and on one of the lowest seats.

Kasmiri lifted her hand. "Please, he asks little and we could gain greatly from this cultural exchange." Actually, they would avoid a tremendous amount of violence. She waited a moment, then settled at her screen. "Please vote in favor of this small gift to a great power." She added the last in case the monster lurked, for she hoped such would appease his ego.

Below her fluttering heart her empty stomach clenched. A sudden need to rush to the basin to vomit possessed her, but she fought it down. There was nothing in there to come up. Time moved slowly as the votes were imputed, counted, recounted, and then finally she had her answer.

*   *   *

Loban filed his teeth while watching three slaves pound away at another's upturned bottom. When they finished, he thought he might take a turn too. Silky blond hair fell into the eyes of the one on the receiving end as he lowered his head to take their thrusts. Loban would like to pull his head back while he rode him so he could see his pain in the mirror across the room. And there would be pain. His penis, large when he was human, was more so now. Bulbous, the tip swelled over the shaft and turned angry purple-black with his arousal. When he climaxed, his seed jetted forth with shocking strength and in copious amounts. Along the underside, he discovered several bumps. If they were like the ones on his back, barbs would eventually rise from the centers.

Loban had just placed himself behind the young man when Ambo waddled in, fresh from the advisor's meeting. Rather than stop, Loban tormented the blonde by fingering his ass while he spoke to Ambo. Let him wonder if he'd actually have to take the enormous cock he saw in the mirror.

"Did she do as I demanded?" he asked, teasing his fingertip around the now-slick ring.

Ambo blanched, trying not to look at the dark hand buried between pale cheeks or the thick purple prick jutting up from Loban's hips.

"She gave you the Harvester suite," Ambo said hopefully. When one of his serving girls brought him a glass of wine, he gulped it gratefully and immediately asked for a refill. Ambo found life easier to cope with when he was inebriated. Food no longer brought him the pleasure it once had. Within days, his rotund frame had wilted.

"Did she name me the Harvester?" Loban rammed his finger into the slave's bottom. His grunt of shock danced a smile upon Loban's lips. He wasn't hurt when Ambo shuddered and turned away. Pointed teeth made his smile beyond chilling. No word was dark enough to convey the horror of his appearance.

Loban despaired at first, for he'd always thought himself a handsome man, but this was the image the gods had chosen for him. Tall, but curled over with bones that could bend and mold to his needs, his blackened skin was hot and smooth. Over-developed muscles in his haunches and his arms gave him tremendous strength. Day by day, he looked more gruesome and terrifying. Perhaps the gods thought this form was the best for keeping the populace in line.

Ambo guzzled another drink, then answered, "She cannot name you the Harvester."

"She is the empress!" Fury caused him to ram another finger inside his slave. His answering whimper soothed him slightly.

Quivering, Ambo lifted his hand for another drink. "You know you must wait and issue a challenge to the current Harvester right before the next Harvest."

Confusion caused him to shake his head. His human mind knew that. How had he forgotten? For a moment, Loban couldn't remember why he wanted to be the Harvester. Such a position was beneath him. He wanted to be the emperor. That was worthy of his exalted self. Refusing to appear weak before one of his minions, he acted as if he'd known what Ambo reminded him of by nodding. Then he immediately turned his attention elsewhere. "Did she remove Chur as the premier handler?" Bored with tormenting his blond slave, he yanked his fingers out and sent him back to his mat in the corner.

Ambo's hesitation was answer enough.

Loban grabbed the edge of Ambo's billowing shirt and wiped his fingers off. Apparently, his call on the little empress did not motivate her sufficiently. Another visit loaded with terror might change her mind. Loban couldn't take over the training of the recruits with Chur in residence. Once Kasmiri removed him, Loban would turn the recruits into his personal army and Chur into his personal slave. His men would enforce his edicts and scour the lands for the most compelling slaves. Of course,

Loban would have to dispatch Helton, for Helton entered into all of this for the express purpose of running the recruits himself. When Chur dismissed him, Helton swore he would see Chur humbled. In his drive to obtain his goal, Helton had unleashed a monster on the world. Loban smiled at the thought.

Turning his full attention onto Ambo, he gave detailed orders for what should await him in the Harvester suite. When Ambo hesitated on reciting his orders, Loban made him write them out. He wanted his first night there to be perfect.

Ambo hurried off to do his bidding, relieved, no doubt, that he didn't have to look at him anymore. Sick of his appearance himself, he turned away from the mirror.

Loban settled on the couch, determined to remember everything he knew before he changed. He wanted to be the Harvester because . . . He couldn't remember why it had once been so important to him. Had he gotten all he could from that ritual? Harvesting the *ungati*, forcing them to pleasure, that opened him up to the gods. Perhaps harvesting them was all he needed. When he closed his eyes, looking within for the answer, he was soothed by a quick series of their faces as he took their virginity. Before he could become lost in the rich memories, he forced himself to stand. Whenever he tried to remember his human thoughts, the inner voice always used those memories to lull him into submission. Who was in charge of his mind, he wondered, him or the gods?

Pacing now in great strides across Ambo's rooms, he tried to remember the other things he demanded of Kasmiri. None of them seemed as important as one thing, and it wasn't Chur's removal from the training rooms. There was something he was supposed to have asked her for, but he'd refused because . . . one of the bound servants howled then, breaking his concentration.

Loban stomped over to him and ripped his head off with one twist from his mighty fist. Tossing the head away, he stood riveted by his hand. He remembered his human hands. They were a bit too large, which gave him excellent control with weapons, but now, his hands were claws. Massive, five-jointed fingers extended from his enormous oblong palm.

"What have I become?"

"I didn't want it to be like this."

The voice followed Kasmiri down the hall. When she turned, she found Helton standing there. Her guards went on alert, but she asked them to step back. Getting as close to Helton as she could without causing her guards to overreact, she hissed, "Haven't you done enough?"

"This wasn't what was supposed to happen." Helton reached for her hand but stopped after glancing at the two burly men. He was a big man, but they were bigger, and there were two of them. "All I wanted was Chur removed so I could be a handler again."

He'd unleashed a monster on her over a position as a handler? Kasmiri shook her head in frustration. "What more do you want from me?" She didn't know why she asked when she didn't intend to give him anything else. He might be her father, but she owed him nothing.

When he didn't answer, she glanced back at her guards, made certain they were out of earshot, and then asked, "Why didn't you just become my mother's official consort?" Doing so would have saved her the ruination of her entire world.

Straightening, he snarled, "I would not be second to a man who had no discipline."

His answer infuriated her, and in that moment, she knew that Helton killed the man she thought was her father. Helton killed him, not to be with her mother, but to stop him from cheating on her. Her mother's refusal to seek out the killer was because she knew exactly who the killer was. Clathia hadn't turned listless for mourning her consort; she'd become depressed because even then, Helton refused to become her official consort.

"For your stupid pride you destroyed my life."

He had the grace to look ashamed. "No one was supposed to know."

"Then how did Ambo find out?" She knew it had to have been him or her mother.

"Your mother's consort told him." There was no escaping the disgusted tone in Helton's voice. "He thought it would shame her into not seeing me anymore when all it did was drain her funds to bribe Ambo into silence. That was the kind of man he was. He wouldn't stop philandering, but he wouldn't let her—" Helton cut himself off for his voice started to rise. Lowering his booming tone, he finished, "I never touched another woman but Clathia. I loved her more—"

"Don't speak to me of love!" Kasmiri didn't care if her guards heard her or not. "If you loved my mother, you would have sacrificed your pride to be with her!"

His eyes blazed. "You ungrateful child. You made her life miserable with your mischief. Just like him, you have no discipline."

At that, she slapped Helton hard enough to leave a palm print. "Go back to Ambo and your monster. Tell them I won't be your puppet." Once she said the words, she knew confession was the right choice. She felt nothing but filthy after the lies she'd told to Sterlave and her true advisors; however, the subterfuge ended now. "I will announce the truth myself."

23

Heavy snow turned the world into an icy wonderland of sparkling drifts. Sterlave gazed out at the endless expanse of white. Usually the big storms didn't hit for another cycle, but nothing about this season was normal. As the sun set, slanting rays turned the land glorious mixed colors of pink, purple, and orange. At his side, Chur squinted into the distance.

"Why would she do this?" Chur asked.

"I don't know." Sterlave tried to keep the cold from filling his heart. Kasmiri had betrayed him. He felt like a fool for agonizing over whether he loved her, when her confession of love had been a lie. What a fool he'd been to feel bad about tormenting the supposed truth out of her. He'd barely been able to sleep last night from his horrible guilt. As he gazed into the heart of bitter cold, he wondered if she'd fallen asleep with a secretive little grin on her face. Laughing at him, mocking him, as the villagers used to do.

"Is it possible she is in league with him?" Chur asked the question quietly so as not to disturb Enovese, who sat at the table reading. Sterlave figured the loose pages she considered must be old from the musty smell and the way they curled at the edges. Her concentration was so deep that Sterlave thought he and Chur could engage in a screaming argument and she'd barely notice. Never had he seen anyone sit so perfectly still and so fully engaged.

"You're the one with the connection to the gods, why don't you tell me." Sterlave hated the bitter tone in his voice, but frustration turned outward struck the closest target.

Without anger, Chur answered, "That's not how they operate. I felt something evil brewing, I thought it might be Loban, and it clearly is, but Kasmiri has never struck me as evil. Determined and manipulative yes, but malicious or vindictive? No." He paused, then asked, "Do you think she is capable of something like this?"

Sterlave considered the idea of Kasmiri and Loban working together. How could such a thing be true? "I thought I knew her, but now . . ." He watched his reflection in the glass shrug and turned away. He couldn't stand the shocked pain on his face anymore. Trust had never come easily to him, but he'd trusted Kasmiri with all his heart.

When he turned, his gaze fell on Chur and Enovese's neatly made bed. What Kasmiri had done to him this morning was just more manipulation. Sterlave stilled his thoughts for a moment, running back over not only this morning, but also all the times he and Kasmiri had been together. She couldn't have faked all of it. The moment in the basin room during their bonding celebration wasn't phony, nor was the bonding itself. Every time they'd come together, she'd been anxious for release and more than willing to please him in return. A truly selfish woman would have taken her pleasure and not given a thought to his. Kasmiri had tried almost desperately to project that attitude, but he'd seen the truth.

Sterlave turned back to the window.

"Don't condemn her just yet," Chur cautioned. "We don't know why she gave over the Harvester suite to Loban."

"What innocent reason could there be?" Sterlave had been searching for Loban from one end of the palace to the other when the current Harvester, Kerrick, informed Chur that he'd been forced to give up his rooms for some visiting dignitary. Kerrick gave Chur a copy of the edict, which he, in turn, shared with Sterlave. Chur hadn't heard about anyone coming to observe the rituals, neither had Sterlave, but Enovese was the one who actually put everything together. Enovese said it only made sense that Loban would want to stay there if he'd felt cheated out of his position as the Harvester. Kasmiri couldn't tell the advisors who she really wanted to give the room to, so she made up the tale of a visiting dignitary. How Loban compelled Kasmiri to do this was another matter.

"I don't know what to think." Sterlave wanted to leave the safe haven of Chur and Enovese's room, but he didn't know where to go. He didn't want to go back to Kasmiri's room to confront her. He also didn't want to confront Loban, not when he'd gone there earlier and saw what Loban had become.

"And you're certain the creature was Loban?" Chur offered him another glass of *soony*.

Sterlave passed on a second drink. "There's no mistaking that smile of his. Of course, he's shaved his teeth into points, but those blood red lips are exactly the same. So are his glittering Onic eyes." Sterlave couldn't stop a quick shiver of revulsion. "Underneath that *fauben* shell, it's all Loban."

"I believe that is what he is."

Sterlave gave a little jump and turned. Enovese stood between him and Chur. She moved so swiftly and silently he found her a bit disconcerting.

Tilting her face up, she smiled at him, as if acknowledging she'd inadvertently startled him. "I think Loban welcomed in one of the fallen ones."

Her voice was lilting, musical, and had a tendency to go right to his groin, a feeling he consciously ignored. The last thing he wanted was Chur to throttle him for having impure thoughts about his gorgeous bondmate. Worse, Sterlave didn't want Chur to realize he'd had lusty thoughts about him too. How could he be in the middle of the most dangerous situation of his life and still be thinking random sexual thoughts? Determined, he focused his attention outward.

When he'd seen Loban, Sterlave thought Loban had threatened Kasmiri into giving him what he wanted. But how could he have gotten near her with her guards? Even if he had threatened her, why hadn't she come to him, her bondmate, and the supposed protector of the empire, for help?

"Why would anyone want to share their form with a fallen one?" Sterlave had heard tales about the evil creatures, but he'd always thought they were myths, much like the gods themselves. Of course, Chur's transformation changed all of that. If Chur could become a demigod, then why couldn't Loban became a *fauben*?

Softly, Enovese said, "The rejects of *Jarasine*, the fallen ones, drift in nothingness. They can see us, hear us, but cannot connect to us unless we invite them in. Once the invitation has been made, the person must perform a sufficiently wicked act to grant them entrance. An offering of sorts."

"What would be considered a sufficiently wicked act?" Chur asked, wrapping his arm around Enovese and pulling her to his side.

Understanding hit Sterlave. "Raping an *ungati* and forcing him to climax."

Chur asked what an *ungati* was and Enovese explained. Sterlave was relieved he wasn't the only one who'd never heard of them before he'd met Rown. They must be strictly for the elite.

Within the circle of her bondmate's arm, Enovese said, "Vi-

olating an *ungati's* strict code would grant a fallen one entrance."
At Chur's confused look, she added, "They are allowed to pleasure others, but they can only experience orgasm alone as part of a complex ritual."

When she launched into a description of this masturbation ritual, Chur blushed and cut her off with a soft, "I don't need to know that much."

Sterlave tried desperately to ignore the signals between them, but sex itself hung in the air, saturating everyone it touched, until lust ensnared them all—raw, naked, brutal lust. Something in what Enovese had said reminded Chur of something they'd done. Something he'd clearly enjoyed, for his cock awakened, pressing against his loincloth.

"Why would anyone want to let a fallen one in?" Sterlave asked, returning his gaze to the frozen land. He hoped the vision of ice would help cool the heat that suddenly rose within.

"*Faubens* possess great powers," Enovese said.

That didn't sound good to Sterlave. "What kind of powers?"

"There are many tales and myths." Enovese's reflection in the glass shrugged delicately, causing her robe to slide over her pointed nipples. "However, the powers seem to depend on a combination of the *fauben* and the host."

"They enhance what you naturally have?" Sterlave asked the question from somewhere because he was lost in the thought of what her naked breasts looked like.

"Yes and no, they take what the host naturally possesses and turn it to their own use. *Faubens* do not share with their host. Once they have control, they will push the human out, sending him to drift in the nothingness."

"Then why would anyone invite them in?" Chur and Sterlave asked the question simultaneously. Glancing at each other, they both realized the other was aroused. Sterlave expected Chur to dart his glance away, but he didn't. He held Sterlave's gaze, penetrating into him, conveying not only acknowledgment, but also encouragement. Convinced he'd read the signal wrong, Sterlave quickly looked away.

"Arrogance," Enovese said, teasing her hand along Chur's back. "There are always those who think they can control the fallen one."

Arrogant described Loban perfectly. Sterlave had never met a more conceited, overconfident man in his life. There had to be an explanation. One didn't become self-important for no reason. What happened to Loban to craft him that way? He considered the question while trying not to notice that Enovese was now teasing her hand along Chur's ass. Not to be outdone, Chur lowered his hand from her shoulder to her breast. Repeatedly, he twisted her nipple between his thumb and forefinger. Each time he did, Sterlave felt the motion along his own body.

Mesmerized, Sterlave watched them fondle each other through the glass and with his peripheral vision. The darker it became outside, the more clearly he saw their reflections.

Sterlave stood and observed, not certain if he should leave. Chur answered the question for him when he turned, facing his back to the glass, and cupped his hand around Sterlave's straining bulge.

Shock froze him to the spot. Chur's hand wasn't just warm, but hot and massive. He knew just how hard to hold and press his stroking fingers through the fabric. The weave was thin enough that Sterlave could feel the moist heat of his touch, but too thick to let him feel his amazing caress directly.

Enovese watched him for a moment, then stood on her toes to whisper something in Chur's ear.

Chur's touch became more aggressive, apparently at Enovese's suggestion. Sterlave throbbed with sudden painful need. He wanted to feel more than just Chur's hand; he wanted to feel his mouth. Lust clamped around his hips, demanding release, screaming for more than contact through clothing. Sterlave wanted to make Chur feel and taste his flesh.

Enovese deftly removed Chur's loincloth, exposing his golden cock. Sterlave gulped at the sheer commanding size of him. He couldn't help but watch how expertly Enovese teased her fingertips under the most sensitive skin where the shaft met the head. Each brush of her fingertips swelled him harder and turned him deeper gold. Without missing a beat, she turned and slid Sterlave's loose-fitting trousers down. Now, Chur mimicked in perfect synchronicity Enovese's strokes on his cock to Sterlave's. It felt as if Enovese stroked him through Chur.

On a deep breath, Sterlave thought of stepping back. They shouldn't be doing this. They were his friends. And Kasmiri would be devastated. Every time he tried to leave, he discovered he couldn't. His legs simply wouldn't move him toward the door.

Sterlave didn't know what to do with his hands, but as Enovese pressed herself into Chur, her hair sparkled over the length of her back, falling to her calves. Beautiful harvest-colored tresses compelled him to reach out and bury his fingers in the strands. Soft as *astle,* he lifted a hank to his nose to breathe deeply of her scent. Feminine musk assaulted his senses, compelling him to move closer into the circle of their bodies.

With a better angle, Chur was able to pull his prick with firmer strokes, working him more skillfully than Sterlave had ever handled himself. How could Chur know what he liked? He had to be using his god-given powers because his touch was utterly divine.

When Enovese removed Sterlave's hand from her hair and wrapped his fist around Chur's cock, it was as if she'd closed a circuit. Fire erupted within his body, consuming all his attention as he marveled at the smooth, heavy weight of Chur's golden shaft.

Encouraging them both to continue, Enovese stepped back, melding into the shadows of the room as if she had never even been there. Chur dropped to his knees and looked up. Beautiful blue eyes, the exact color of an intense summer sky, peered up the length of Sterlave's heaving chest. Black hair, still short from his recent shave for the Harvest, dusted his head.

"This is what you want, isn't it."

It wasn't a question, which was obvious when a single drop of moisture pearled at the tip of Sterlave's cock. He wanted this. Nothing could compel him to step away now. He wanted Chur's firm lips wrapped around his aching prick. Deep into his throat, he wanted to push and then to hear Chur choke while he sucked down every last drop.

Sterlave shook his head at the violence of his need. He didn't want to hurt Chur. Something within pushed at his mind, forcing him to turn his attention back to Chur waiting so patiently on his knees. All he had to do was grasp the back of his head and pull him forward. Resisting caused a throbbing pain behind Sterlave's eyes.

"Worship me and he's yours."

When Sterlave looked into the glass, seeking the owner of the voice, he saw Loban's face as he'd looked before his transformation.

"Kneel to me and I'll make him kneel to you."

Repulsed by the very idea, Sterlave took a great step back while screaming, "No!"

Chur lifted his brows and retracted his hand, which held a small glass. All he'd been doing was offering him another drink. Chur wasn't on his knees. He wasn't naked and hard. Chur was standing at the window looking at him as if he'd lost his mind.

"What happened to you? You drifted off into your own thoughts for a moment." Chur handed the cup to Enovese, who placed it on the table near her scattered pages.

"He's trying to get to me. He's sending visions into my mind." Sterlave shook his head, desperate to drive the last of the wicked thoughts away.

"Lusty visions," Enovese said, nodding to his bulge.

When he looked down, a large wet spot darkened the front of his trousers. Embarrassed beyond words, Sterlave turned away.

"It's not your fault," she said softly. "And now we know what kind of *fauben* Loban has welcomed into our world."

Holding his breath, Sterlave entered Kasmiri's rooms. When he discovered she wasn't there, he exhaled. Now was not the time for a confrontation with her. In order to banish the creature Loban had unleashed, Sterlave needed a unique weapon.

Only Rown could help him fashion it.

He'd argued against the idea from the start, but Enovese showed him proof in her pages. "Loban is what you felt in your vision: Lust. Lust without conscience, lust without honor, lust without tenderness. To fight him, you must use the opposite."

Unable to think clearly with his erection still pressing against his pants, Sterlave asked, "What's the opposite of lust?"

"Passion." Her gentle smile radiated a purity that entranced him.

Frowning, Sterlave said, "I thought passion and lust were the same thing."

"Lust is mindless in its need. Passion is mindful in its longings." At his baffled expression, she continued, "Lust causes one to take by force, passion causes one to persuade." After a moment, she tried again. "Lust cares not who is hurt as long as wants are met. Passion dies if hurt is involved." She paused for a moment, considering Sterlave with her speculative gaze. "The vision he forced on you involved forcing another, yes?"

Gritting his teeth, he nodded. Sterlave didn't want to think of that hallucination again. He felt doubly guilty because the scenario was one he'd thought of all by himself, with no help from a perverted creature. Of course, in his version, Chur was acting of his own free will.

"You stopped because you would never force another to give you pleasure."

"Of course I wouldn't." His tone was rather defensive.

"That is how you are different from him. You are filled with passion, and it knows no bounds, but you would never give yourself over to your lust, because that would involve hurting another."

Sterlave understood what Enovese was trying to say but still didn't see the true difference. "I lust after Kasmiri. The things she does . . ."

"You feel lust but temper it with your passion. Lust isn't a good or bad thing. Lust simply is. How one twists their lust is what turns it good or bad."

That made more sense to Sterlave. "I feel lust, but I control the extent of it."

Enovese nodded rather wisely, as if pleased he'd finally understood what she'd been trying to teach him. In that moment, he remembered that she was a *paratanist,* one destined to die a virgin and live her life hidden behind the cowl of her robe. However, they also taught the Harvesters all they needed to know. She was a living, breathing book. How brave must she have been to show herself to Chur? Lust must have compelled her, but passion gave her strength. Once he understood that, her lesson became clear.

After he called out for Rown, Sterlave took another deep breath. He would need strength to prepare for battle, and he would need passion to win. He fought for the empire he'd sworn to protect, but also, even after what she'd done, he fought for Kasmiri. He didn't know why she'd done Loban's bidding, but he didn't think she'd been willing. As he waited, he only hoped that Rown would understand.

Rown entered, his face breaking into a wide smile when he saw Sterlave standing there alone. When his gaze dropped to his moist trousers, he offered a modified pout. "I will fetch you fresh clothing—"

"Wait."

Rown turned, his uplifted brows awaiting instructions.

Sterlave didn't even know where to start. "I need your help."

Darting his gaze around with some trepidation, Rown whispered, "Is Kasmiri here?"

"No." Sterlave hesitated. "Does it matter?"

With a shrug, Rown said, "I don't think she wants me *helping* you that way when she isn't here."

On any other day, Sterlave would have laughed. Today, he flashed only the barest of smiles, and asked, "What if I helped you that way?"

Immediate excitement brightened his features, but then Rown's face fell. Not the reaction Sterlave was hoping for.

"You know I can't." Black hair tumbled down, covering his soft blue eyes, shielding his gaze. Slumped shoulders conveyed his disappointment.

Four long strides brought him near. Rown flipped his head back, his eyes wide with longing and fear. "I'm not going to hurt you, but again, I need your help. I need you to trust me."

Rown's frown turned down the edges of his quivering lips. When a lone tear tumbled from his eyes, Sterlave took a step back with his hands lifted.

"No, not that, not what he did. That's not—" he cut himself off. Determined to find another way, he dismissed Rown.

However, Rown didn't leave. "I do trust you. I just don't understand what you're asking of me."

Sterlave explained as completely as he could. "The man who hurt you, Loban, when he hurt you, he allowed a fallen one, a *fauben*, entrance to our world."

"I was his offering?" Rown shuddered at the thought.

Sterlave nodded, grateful that he seemed to know some of

the mythology. "The only way to stop him now is to . . ." he trailed off, unsure how to explain. "We need to reverse your offering."

Fondling the edge of his crimson sash, Rown peered up at him. "How would we do that?"

Sterlave offered out his hand. When Rown accepted, he drew him over to the couch where they'd talked earlier. Once they settled in, with Rown's knee tentatively resting against his, Sterlave explained what he wanted to do and why he thought Rown's sacrifice would work. Rown listened with an open mind, which was all Sterlave could really hope for, since he asked for an incredible gift. When he finished, they sat there silently for a long time.

Rown stood with the dignity of a warrior. "I will do as you ask." In that moment, Rown matured. He was not a servant forced to act, but a man deciding for himself. "What Loban stole from me, I will grant to you."

After bathing, then anointing himself in scented oils, Rown knelt before a statue of the *ungati* god. Sterlave didn't know the god's name, but his thin face was serene as he knelt, gazing upward with one hand over his heart and the other over his crotch.

Nude, Sterlave sat behind Rown, placing the *cirvant* beside them. When the time came, Rown would lift the short sword into position. At the moment, Rown professed.

Using a low, repentant voice, Rown admitted to every lusty thought he'd had since the last time he'd professed. Sterlave blushed. Most of Rown's wayward thoughts were about his mistress's consort. In an effort not to embarrass him, Rown called him that, rather than using his name, even though they both knew whom he was talking about. Dressing him, cleaning his clothing, watching him eat—everything Sterlave did prompted a sexual thought in Rown. Flattered as he was, Sterlave also remembered when he was Rown's age and *everything* gave him sexual thoughts, even such mundane things as the baker shaping dough caused odd flickers in his nether region.

Sitting cross-legged, Sterlave waited patiently behind Rown. Once Rown finished listing his transgressions, he began the laborious process of *strocating*, or ritualistically touching his genitals to bring forth his release. Rown explained the act took quite some time, which Sterlave thought he was ready for; however, he grew bored as Rown brought himself to arousal with only two fingers from his right hand and three from his left.

Peering over his shoulder, Sterlave watched how intricately his touches worked the entire genital area. Actually, Rown was hard before he started, but he still had to perform the strokes in order. Sterlave was certain he was responsible for Rown's arousal even before he heard his profession. When he'd undressed, Rown didn't try to hide his probing gaze. When Sterlave glanced at him, he smiled shyly but continued looking. At least Loban had not ruined his bashful sensuality.

Rown was slight but strong. Underneath his plain brown robe lurked a surprisingly well-formed, mature body—narrow hips, broad shoulders, long legs, and a short but thick cock nestled in curly black hair. Sterlave wondered if he shaved or if the rest of his body was naturally devoid of hair. Unlike Sterlave himself, Rown wasn't awkward in his nudity. He moved about with easy grace.

For a servant, he had a spacious but mostly bare room decorated entirely in beige. Thick rugs softened the wooden floors, and clear lighting crystals lined the ceiling—luxurious modesty. Rown was a servant, but he served the empress. A narrow bed took up one wall, a small bathing unit another, shelves with various devices took up the wall with the door, and the fourth was a shrine to his god.

"I am close," Rown said, leaning back into Sterlave's waiting arms. Rown's voice did not hold the frantic tone that Sterlave expected. If Rown was on the verge of climax, he controlled it well, which Sterlave thought was rather the point.

Wrapping his arms around him, Sterlave pulled Rown into the hollow created by his crossed legs. Rown's body was slick from the oil and cool from the air. He felt small against Sterlave's bulky frame. Once settled, Sterlave leaned back so that Rown could lay flat as the ritual required.

"Let his hands be my hands." Rown cupped Sterlave's fingers around his cock. Shockingly hot, Sterlave marveled at how soft the skin of Rown's shaft was, and how sensitive. The barest brush of touch pulsed blood deep, twitching him. To Sterlave, this made sense since Rown was not allowed to touch himself except for this ritual. His body must be starved for contact. True to his station, Rown did not buck or groan. This wasn't tawdry pleasure; this was an offering to a god. Sterlave took it just as seriously as Rown. He didn't think of lust or pleasure, he thought of the passionate devotion Rown had for his god. With Rown's hands upon Sterlave's, he moved him through the last of the *strocation*.

"Accept my sacrifice, Behdera. Accept my seed in service to you." Rown lifted his hands and placed the curved sword against his belly. Placing his hands over Sterlave's again, he stroked all five fingers from base to tip three times, then wrapped his entire right fist around his shaft while cupping his balls with the left.

Contractions jetted Rown's climax across the blade of the *cirvant*. Sterlave simply held on, keeping the pressure in his fist tight, but not too tight. Apparently, he'd gone too loose because Rown wrapped his hand around his fist, squeezing firmly. When Sterlave tightened his grip, Rown nodded. Unlike Sterlave's orgasms, Rown's went on and on. Every pulse jetted more fluid, but his balls seemed to have an unlimited supply. Even in his youth, Sterlave had not ejaculated such copious amounts. He thought at best they could coat the edge of the blade, but when he looked down, there was enough to make the entire sword wet.

When the last of the contractions faded away, Rown gently released his hands from Sterlave's. Careful not to jostle him in his sensitive state, Sterlave lifted his hands away, then removed the weapon from his belly. Together they sat up, returning Rown to his knees.

"Please, Behdera, let my offering anoint this blade so that Sterlave can banish the one who forced me to betray you."

The statue's little face didn't give any sign of acceptance or refusal, but Rown seemed pleased. He lifted the sword and coated the entire surface with his milky offering. When he finished, he placed it at the feet of the statue to dry.

With his magical blade, everything was now up to Sterlave.

24

After her confrontation with Helton, Kasmiri strode with purpose to the advisors' room. From there, she called for an exceptional assembly. Once the bulk of her advisors arrived, she would tell them the truth. She didn't care if they placed her under the stone or immediately exiled her to Rhemna. Only the truth would set her free from the clutches of the creature. He said he didn't want to reveal her secret because it served *his* purpose. If she told, he'd have no power over her.

What her life would become after that moment, she didn't know, but she knew Sterlave would be there by her side. At least she hoped he would be. He swore her station didn't matter, that he wanted her for her, that she was more than his bondmate, that she was his soulmate. In that, she had to trust. For once, when she needed someone, she believed with all her heart she could count on Sterlave.

She wanted to tell Sterlave of her decision first, but she couldn't find him anywhere. All she could do was include him in her demand for an audience. After she'd sent her message, her two guards watched her pace. So engrossed in watching her, they never saw him coming.

The creature swooped in behind them, placing his hands upon each of their heads. Before Kasmiri could scream, he twisted. A wet, snapping sound echoed off the walls. Placing her hand over her mouth didn't stop her from retching.

"You were going to tell," the creature spoke in a singsong voice.

Terrified beyond words, she backed away, already knowing there was nowhere to go.

"You were going to ruin my plans." Gangly, with his long limbs and awkward gait, he strode toward her, swinging the disembodied heads in his hideous hands. Her trusted guards' faces were slack, their mouths open in mute screams.

Shocked, she still registered that he'd changed since their last encounter. He was taller, more hunched over, with spiked fingers shooting out from massive palms, and his horrible, horrible teeth. She wanted to scream, but she couldn't gather sufficient breath.

"You are going to help me get exactly what I want."

Her mind ran through his list of demands, but all of it was lost now. She gave him the Harvester suite but couldn't name him as the Harvester, nor would she willingly remove Chur or put this monster in charge of the recruits. There was nothing else she could do for him.

When the door opened, the creature tossed the heads, then sped toward her. Without stopping, he grasped her waist, tossed her over his shoulder, and sped off. His shoulder was bony and dug painfully into her belly. Hot, slick skin was hard as tanned leather and smelled of rotting meat. Barbs emerged from conical bumps along his back. She didn't even want to think about what lurked between his thighs.

He moved so swiftly down the hallways, and up and down

the stairways that she had no idea where they were. Once the advisors gathered for the meeting, they would see the two dead guards and sound the alarm. Everyone in the entire palace would be searching for her. She hoped by the time they found her she was still alive.

Without missing a step, the monster kicked his way into a room. Kasmiri had never seen the Harvester suite, but she knew this wasn't it. This room was barely big enough for the two of them. A low ceiling caused him to hunch over until she almost slid off his shoulder. Grunting, he tossed her back up. He took two deliberate steps and her world turned sideways.

Lights swirled around her eyes along with whistling winds screaming into her ears. She yelled, but the vortex ripped the sound away while flinging her hair into her mouth. Unable to lift her hand to pull it away, she tried to spit the strands out, but the wind crammed them back in. Tucking her head down into his back only gave her a full blast of his horrendous smell. No amount of wind could scrub the noxious odor away.

When the chaos stopped, she found herself in an enormous room carved out of what appeared to be one solid piece of rock. Their entrance echoed a popping noise off the shining floors and walls. The creature dumped her off his shoulder and she slumped gratefully to the floor.

"Where are we?" Smoothing her hand over the stone, she peered at the strangely colored polished rock laden with silver sparkles. She was unable to even describe the unworldly color. She shook her head, afraid the vortex had ruined her eyes. Tears blurred her vision for a moment; then she became aware of the heat. Sweat popped up all over her body, trickling between her breasts, her legs, and behind the cup of her knee.

Rather than answer, he laughed. His mirth sounded like screeching metal and screaming children. The massive empty room only echoed the sound back at her from all directions until she covered her ears and shrieked.

His gangly arms were so long he didn't even have to bend over when he flicked out his index fingers and stabbed them into her shoulders. Her scream became a screech of searing pain. Gripping the rest of his claws around her upper arms, he then slowly lifted her off the floor.

Dangling in his grasp, she screamed louder until he shook her. His fingers slid in and out of her flesh, blinding her with pain, causing her breath to turn into gasping pants of shock and terror.

"You will remain silent until I tell you to speak. I did not bring you here to suffer your pathetic fright." A slow smile spread his crimson lips against pointed teeth. "I brought you here because you will help me obtain my rightful due."

Dizzy from pain and the sweltering heat, she blinked listlessly at him.

"Call for your consort."

At first his words made no sense; then she realized he wasn't after her, he was after Sterlave. "No." Let him mutilate her. She wasn't going to be responsible for bringing Sterlave into the mess she created. Maybe, just this once, rather than needing someone to be there for her, she would be there for herself.

The monster shook her until blood oozed around his plunged fingers, but still, she refused.

"I'd rather die than bring him to you."

His distorted face became a mask of fury; then he forced a hideous smile. "As you please, empress."

He said the words in mocking jest of Sterlave, but all he did was harden her heart. No matter how he tortured her, she would not cry out. All the hurt she'd suffered became an impenetrable wall around her as she closed her eyes, imagining herself in the center of her dance room, alone. Twirling in circles with her arms and head thrown back, she smiled up at the sky, oblivious to the pain in her body.

From her back, he pressed his nails into her until they broke through her gown, her skin, and deep into her flesh. Curling wisps of smoke rose up, choking her with the stench of her own burning flesh, but still she danced. The last thing she remembered before the blessed darkness came was the creature bellowing his rage as he tossed her aside.

25

Sterlave stood still while Rown attached the anointed sword to the belt around his waist. Sadly, it didn't feel magical. When he'd first placed the Sword of the Empress onto his hip, he'd felt something. Perhaps not anything magical, but certainly something tingled along his nerves. Now, he didn't feel anything at all.

What if all he had was a semen-stained blade that Loban would crush between the fingers of his freakish hands? Sterlave was placing a lot of faith in Enovese's plan. Letting her sway him was easy because she spoke so passionately about her idea. Enovese claimed if Loban took Rown's seed to grant the fallen one entrance, Sterlave should be able to banish him with a weapon blessed by Rown's seed. Sterlave thought it sounded good in theory. Like two hands at opposite ends clapping together to crush Loban between. He just hoped it would work in actual practice. Somehow, Sterlave was certain that he would have only one shot at killing the creature Loban had become. Luckily for Enovese, if he failed, he wouldn't be around to point the finger at anyone.

When he laughed, Rown glanced up, and asked, "Are you prepared?"

"As much as I'll ever be." Sterlave straightened his belt and allowed Rown to slip on his boots. Nerves caused him to tremble slightly, which upset him because he hadn't ever been this nervous, not even before challenging Chur for the right of Harvester. That night all he could think of was Kasmiri, and that he would die to possess her. When he failed that fight, the gods brought him back; however, he was certain they weren't going to do that magic trick twice. If he died now, death would be permanent. Rather than dwell on what might happen, Sterlave focused his attention on what he wanted to happen. He refused to let doubt undermine his determination.

"I still think you should wear your consort clothing." Rown frowned at his loose training pants with the stain on the front. Sterlave didn't want a clean pair; he wanted a reminder of how sneaky Loban could be. To win, he would have to fight with his body and his brain. "You *are* defending the empire," Rown said, smoothing the hopeless wrinkles in the fabric.

"I can't move in that stuff." And the last thing Sterlave wanted to do was show off his genitals to Loban. Parading around as Kasmiri's sex toy had been fun, but the fun was over. As worried as he was about his own life, he worried more about Kasmiri. Another death would crush her. If he failed, he feared that she might never recover. Although, as soon as he thought that, he reminded himself that Kasmiri was strong. She would find a way to survive. Or so he hoped.

"At least wear a shirt."

"No." Clothing gave an opponent something to grab and use as an advantage. Sterlave would prefer to fight in the nude, since that's how he'd challenged Chur, but he didn't want to stomp around the palace naked, waving a sword and looking for a mythical creature. Sterlave enjoyed being on display, but he didn't need that kind of attention right now.

Sighing, Rown stood. A barest tremble to his lip conveyed to Sterlave just how worried the young man was. In a gesture of friendship, Sterlave clasped his hand. Rown threw himself into Sterlave's arms.

"You're not boosting my confidence with this show," Sterlave teased, squeezing Rown with a hug, then setting him free. "You do have faith in me, don't you?"

Pealing bells caused them both to jump. Sterlave had heard those alarms only once, when the empress suite was set on fire. His heart plunged straight through the floor. Where was Kasmiri? Before Rown could answer, Sterlave brushed a kiss to his forehead and ran toward the advisors' meeting room.

"I do have faith in you!" Rown yelled to his retreating back.

It wasn't much, but it lifted Sterlave's spirits. Now if only he could find Kasmiri and hear her say the same. Unfortunately, the closer he came to the meeting room, the more cluttered the hallway became. Dozen of confused people milled about. Excited voices babbling about carnage and the empress cut his nerves to razor edge, compelling him to force his way through the throng.

At the door, he saw two headless bodies and blood streaking across the floor toward the open pit seating. Darting his gaze frantically for any sign of her, he found the missing heads of her guards. Two good men who had clearly died protecting her. A part of him wanted to turn away at that moment, because he couldn't bear the thought of finding her broken and bloody, but he had to know. Sterlave stepped into the room and stood above the sunken seats. Huddled beside her chair was Ambo, clutching something in his fist.

"Where is she?" Sterlave asked. Ambo ignored him and continued to rock himself. Jumping down into the pit, Sterlave grasped his shoulder, wrenching him around. "Where is Kasmiri?" Ambo's normally pudgy face was sunken, pale, his eyes wide, and his lips slack. He was in shock. In his hand, he clutched a half-full container. Sterlave knelt down and grasped Ambo's face in his hands, forcing him to focus on him. "Where is she?"

A flicker of life flowed into his gaze. "He . . . he took her." Wine saturated his breath.

Sterlave didn't waste time asking who. "Where did he take her?"

"Helton's world."

On the verge of slapping some sense into the wine-addled buffoon, Sterlave lifted his hand. Kasmiri screamed right above him. He dropped and rolled onto his back but saw nothing. Ambo must have heard it, too, because he covered his ears and moaned low in his throat.

"Silence!" Sterlave couldn't hear where it had come from with his whimpering.

Again, Kasmiri cried, her voice high and gasping, clearly in terrible pain. Oh gods, Loban was torturing her. Whatever doubt still clung to him Sterlave shook off in that moment. When Sterlave found Loban, he was going to kill him.

"Kasmiri? I'm coming!" He yelled up at the ceiling for lack of anyplace better to focus his voice.

"You don't even know where she is." Loban's singsong voice came at him directionless.

"Stop shouting." Ambo fumbled at the base of Kasmiri's chair. "Here, it's coming from here on all the chairs." He pointed to a small, flat disk mounted under her chair. When Sterlave looked, he noticed every chair had one.

"Tell me where you are." Sterlave lowered his voice but still projected power in his tone.

"Why would I do that? Maybe I want her for myself. She is quite soft in all the best places. Something I'm sure you know." There was no true passion in the voice, only cruel mockery.

Sterlave had always known that someday he would have to face Loban. Letting his brutality go unacknowledged was irresponsible, but letting his crime go unpunished was reprehensible. Sterlave had a part in allowing Loban to turn into the monster he'd become. He had to make his mistake right, and Kasmiri had nothing to do with his cowardice.

"You don't want her, you want me." Sterlave stood, waiting for Loban's response. After a moment, he heard his voice waft over the room.

"Come to me, Sterlave. Have Ambo show you the way."

Every time Ambo slowed down, Sterlave shoved him forward. Kasmiri's life was on the line and nothing was going to stop him from rescuing her. Ambo stumbled and dropped his wine. When he bent to retrieve the container, Sterlave kicked his rear. Hastily, he grabbed the bottle and stood, clutching the glass to his chest like a shield. Tears of frustration rolled down his face, but Sterlave had no time for kindness. Also, he knew Ambo was mixed up in this mess. He knew it as surely as he knew Helton was too. Those two had been hand-in-glove over getting every recruit to issue a challenge to Chur, and Sterlave knew they were the same here. Perhaps they both saw Loban as the rightful champion. Not that it mattered. Once he disposed of Loban, Sterlave would take care of Ambo and Helton. There would be no forgiveness this time. They would have a choice of exile to Rhemna or suffer under the stone. Mercy would not sway him to make the same mistake Chur had.

"How does Helton have his own world? Moreover, how does it fit in his room?" In the last few days, Sterlave had had to change his perception about many things. Someone having a world in their room wasn't very much stranger than fallen ones possessing people or his friend becoming a demigod.

Sniffling, Ambo wiped his hand across his nose. "Empress Clathia received the world as a gift after her bonding ceremony. She didn't know what to do with it. Her consort discovered there were no alluring conquests there, so as a token of her esteem, she presented the gift to Helton." Ambo wiped his hand down his trousers, then took another swallow of his wine. "The world isn't in his room, but the portal is."

Only the elite would give worlds as gifts. "Aren't there inhabitants on this world? What do they think of being passed around?"

Drunken eyes assessed him coldly. "They are inferior. Hardly in a position to make demands."

Sterlave shoved him again. Not that he needed to, but he was certain Ambo thought *he* was inferior. What arrogance the elite possessed. No wonder Kasmiri had sneered when he'd claimed her. Ingrained into their collective conscience was a misguided belief that they were better simply because they possessed wealth. As he continued stomping along the hallways, listening to his boots echo, he wondered if he had changed Kasmiri's mind. Did she see him as an equal, or was she only biding her time with him until she selected another more appropriate consort?

As soon as the doubt crept in, he knew they were getting close. Loban was flinging uncertainty at him just as he'd flung lust. Sterlave did his best to shake the suspicions off. He and Kasmiri agreed to just the two of them, and he would trust her word. But another thought occurred to him: What lurked in the room full of gifts Kasmiri received? Had a *barsitas* been so moved by her bonding ceremony that he sent along an entire world?

"We can simply close the portal." Ambo stopped and turned, wavering a bit from side to side. "He can't come back if the door is shut."

"Sounds like a great idea except he has Kasmiri."

Rolling his eyes, Ambo said, "She is an ungrateful *pharadean*. If she does return, she'll be put to the stone anyway." Clearly, he'd forgotten whom he was talking to. A smidgen of sobriety entered Ambo's eyes as he looked up into Sterlave's angry face.

"Explain that word to me."

"It's nothing."

One fist around his throat changed Ambo's mind.

"She is not the rightful empress." Fear caused Ambo not to mince words. "Helton Ook is her father."

Stunned, Sterlave released his hold. He thought her father was the one who cheated on her mother, but apparently, her mother cheated too. He thought only the mother mattered as the line of power went from mother to daughter; however, he wasn't about to ask Ambo and reveal his ignorance.

"I don't care." And he found he didn't. She could be the daughter of a servant and he would still save her. Kasmiri was his bondmate. Even if she weren't, he wouldn't leave anyone stranded on a strange world with Loban. Sterlave spun Ambo around and forced him down the hall.

Growing weary at the delay and cursing the shear size of the palace, Sterlave wondered, if he saved Kasmiri, did Ambo intend to have her killed? To that end, he asked, "How many know this about Kasmiri's birth?"

"Myself, Helton"—he swallowed hard before continuing—"Loban."

"Does Kasmiri?"

Snickering, he said, "Of course, that's how Loban forced her to give him the Harvester suite."

Sterlave released a tense breath at Ambo's snide comment. She wasn't working with Loban, he'd threatened her into doing what he wanted, or he'd reveal her secret. As relieved as he was, he couldn't help but feel hurt. Why hadn't she come to him for help? Did she honestly think he wouldn't stand by her? But then, he could understand her reluctance, given her past, and the fact they hadn't been together very long. For now, he pushed the problems away. He knew they would work out the details later.

Sterlave marched Ambo along. He realized they were in the right place when he saw the shattered door.

"In there." Ambo pointed, then tried to back away.

"Oh, no, you're coming with me." He wasn't about to let Ambo close the portal behind him.

Ambo struggled, but even sober he was no match for Sterlave. Lifting him by his collar, Sterlave forced him into the room on his tippy toes. Helton had the room of a servant. Cramped of size and lacking any luxuries, the room contained a bed, a small washbasin, and a cloth hung across the room to act as a closet. Within, Sterlave found the portal. Sparkling in roughly a man-shaped oval, the doorway to the other world hovered about a foot off the floor.

No way was Sterlave going to leap blindly into the un-known. Loban could be waiting on the other side ready to strike. After a moment's consideration, Sterlave didn't think he was because Loban *wanted* him to come. If all he wanted was to kill him, he could have snuck up on him a hundred times in the last few days. Loban wanted something specific. To talk? To make him beg? To make him watch Kasmiri die? Sterlave knew it could be any or all of those things. Straightening his shoul-ders, he readied himself to confront Loban.

However, there was no reason to take undue chances. "Say hello to your friend for me." Sterlave placed Ambo in front of the portal and kicked. Before disappearing, Ambo bellowed and clutched his wine. After a second, Sterlave gripped his weapon and leaped in after him.

Wind whipped around him in a squeezing circle, causing him to clench his sword tightly to his chest. His pants offered little protection from the cold, but the sudden plunge into chaos was so shocking he barely felt the temperature change. As if spit out of the mouth of an angry beast, Sterlave stumbled out of the maelstrom, then fell to his knees on a smooth stone floor.

Immediately, he leapt to his feet, assessing the situation. Ambo was huddled not far from him, mindlessly swaying and holding his wine. Crumpled on the floor, Kasmiri lay unmoving. Black hair tangled across her makeup-smeared face, her once-beautiful dress was tattered, and her feet were bare, bruised, and bloody. Fearing he was too late, his gut twisted. He suppressed his first instinct, which was to rush to her side. He needed to find Loban first. He glanced about the rest of the room.

On the opposite side, Loban lolled in what looked like a throne carved into the very wall. Either the throne was small or Loban had grown; it was difficult to tell from this distance. Loban smiled and picked his pointed teeth with his slender, multijointed finger. Light avoided his burnished skin, which wasn't really skin anymore but a hardened shell.

Mesmerized by the gangly strangeness of him, Sterlave hardly registered the otherworldly colors of the room. With a start, he turned his gaze to Kasmiri. Had he raped her? Upon closer examination, he realized her dress was frayed but intact. When he saw her chest rise and fall with her breath, he almost sagged from relief.

"Return to your knees."

Even though Loban's misshapen mouth struggled to form the words, Sterlave still had no problem understanding him.

Squaring his shoulders, Sterlave said, "I told you once, and I'll tell you a thousand times, I will not kneel to you, no matter what you offer."

Loban laughed a sickening chortle that made Sterlave's short-shorn hair stand on end. "Didn't you take pleasure in your interlude with Chur? Judging by the stain on your pants, I'd say you thoroughly enjoyed my vision."

Sterlave refused to dignify his statement with a comment.

"You were so easy."

Sterlave's gut tightened. He knew to what Loban referred. If he thought such talk would unsettle him, he was correct, but it wasn't going to stop him. Perhaps he didn't confront Loban before because he was too frightened. He wasn't now. Moreover, he didn't care if Ambo, Kasmiri, or the entire population heard. Loban committed the wrong. Sterlave's only mistake had been in not speaking up sooner.

Realizing Loban wished to talk first, Sterlave lowered his sword. "After all this time you're finally going to admit what you did to me."

"I did what you wanted me to do." Without any clothing to cover him, Sterlave couldn't help but notice Loban's erection, especially when he casually stroked his hand along the length. Spikes protruded from conical bumps along the underside, lying flat as he stroked his hand down. The barbs prevented him from stroking upward, so he teased his fist to the base, lifted it away, and started down from the top. Rhythmically, he stroked while he talked. Loban's transformation managed to outwardly express all the ugly that once lay hidden deep within.

"I didn't want you to rape me." Sterlave's words echoed in the hot air. So shocking was his accusation that Ambo lifted his head and considered the tableau before him. Drunken eyes finally swung toward Kasmiri. Tentatively, he crawled over to her.

"You invited me in." Loban's fingertips clicked musically as he continued to stroke his prick.

"To apologize."

Glittering Onic eyes narrowed. "To fuck."

Sterlave shook his head. Young and foolish, he'd actually believed the swaggering bully wanted to say he was sorry in private so the other recruits wouldn't know his shame.

"You didn't even fight." Loban gave himself one long, hard stroke while lifting his hips.

"I was afraid." Confronting the truth empowered him rather than shamed him. "You'd already beaten the sense out of me earlier that day. I thought if I fought, you'd kill me." Even during the worst of the bullying in his village, Sterlave had never feared for his life, not like he did that night. As Loban used him in every way a man could, Sterlave alternately prayed for death and for Loban to climax, then go. Either way, he'd have peace.

"You wanted me." Loban flashed a wide, creepy smile. "I never heard any complaints."

"All I ever wanted was to be accepted. I thought when I came to the training rooms, I would find friendship, but all you showed me was brutality. I almost gave up, but one man showed me camaraderie. He reminded me that I was worthy of not only being the Harvester, but of being loved." Sterlave owed Chur a debt of gratitude for what he'd done. Without him, he wouldn't be standing here now. He would have given up, retreated into a shell, and ultimately failed. In the end, they would have sent him home with a mark of shame on his forehead, confirming what the villagers had always said about him. Without Chur, Sterlave would have become like Loban—a miserable creature so consumed by lust and a need for power that he would do anything to achieve his goals, even allowing himself to be possessed by a *fauben.*

"Worthy of being loved?" After a burst of laughter, Loban mocked, "I thought you considered yourself a man, but obviously you have more in common with a woman. No wonder I slid into you without a struggle." Loban spared Kasmiri a glance. "You certainly didn't have any problems offering your willing ass up to her."

Sterlave didn't question how Loban knew such a thing. If he were able to insert lust-driven fantasies into his mind, he could certainly steal information out of it. Again, Loban probed a spot that was not tender. Sterlave had no shame over what he'd done with Kasmiri. Given half a chance, he would do it again. They might have conflicts everywhere else in their life, but in bed, he and Kasmiri were of the same mind. Pleasure without

292 / *Anitra Lynn McLeod*

pain and a fearless openness about their desires was the only way they would ever be. Sex wasn't about who penetrated whom, but about providing pleasure. Together, they tempered their lust with great passion.

In that moment, Sterlave grasped what Loban didn't or couldn't understand: the give and take of a loving relationship. To Loban, it was about power and dominance, taking and never giving. To Sterlave, it was about trust and sharing, taking *and* giving. What he'd always missed in his other relationships was the sense of safety he felt with Kasmiri. He could tell her anything, and she would not mock him. That Loban chose to do so spoke greatly about his own twisted mentality.

Again, Sterlave wondered what would shape a man to be so brutal. Loban did not come into the world formed this way. Experiences crafted him into a bully who used sex to dominate those weaker than himself. With a start, Sterlave understood why Loban was the way he was.

"Did you cry when they raped you?" Sterlave let his arm hang lax. His words cut deeper than any blade.

Jolted out of his stroking rhythm, Loban turned on his throne. "I never let them see me—" Cutting himself off, he calmed his voice and said, "I'm not weak like you."

With his response, Loban confirmed what had only been Sterlave's suspicion. Probing further into the tender spot, he said, "They used you for their own vicious pleasure. You hated yourself for being weak. That's why you are the way you are." Deep in his heart, Sterlave knew the truth: Loban had suffered greatly at the hands of his villagers. He became one of them to protect his own fragile psyche.

Unfurling himself like a great banner, Loban stood, placing his hands along what used to be his hips. His bulky haunches looked awkward but strong, looming his superior height over the entire room. Waves of heat billowed off Loban, giving his anger a palpable presence.

Refusing to be intimidated, Sterlave asked, "How old were you the first time?"

"I am not weak!" Loban snarled, exposing a mouthful of pointed teeth.

Without raising his arm, Sterlave readied himself for battle by clutching his *cirvant* tightly. Dry heat enveloped him, sweating his hand against the hilt, but a fresh leather wrapping provided an excellent grip.

"The gods have chosen *me* to embody their power! They would not select a weakling who let himself be used."

"You think your form is godlike?" Sterlave realized that Loban hadn't meant to let the fallen one in; he'd been trying to attract the attention of the gods. Chur's stunning transformation must have inspired him to take this dangerous path. "You lured in a *fauben*, not a god."

Onic eyes went wide as Loban's body roiled. His arms and legs jerked frantically, as if something within fought desperately to break free. Sterlave took an involuntary step back. He flicked a glance to Ambo and Kasmiri, but Ambo had already pulled her away from the center of the room.

"I am a god!" he shrieked. "I let you live so that you would kneel to me!" Leaping across the distance between them in two bounds, Loban stretched to his full height, and bellowed, "Go down on your knees before your master!"

Fearless, Sterlave stood his ground. "I forgive you."

As if the words splashed cold water against his rage, Loban struck him so hard and fast he had no time to react. Sterlave flew sideways as Loban ripped four great slashes across his arm and chest. Blood streaked across the floor.

Climbing slowly to his feet, Sterlave said, "That's why you were so angry with me, because I forgave you. When I stopped the recruits from raping you and chose not to rape you myself, you were furious. Because you knew the truth; that I forgave you for what you did to me."

Panting breaths blew fire across Sterlave's bloody flesh when Loban asked, "Why didn't you seek revenge?"

"Because if I did, I would become like you." Sterlave couldn't help but recoil at Loban's form. "And I'd rather die than be like you."

Fire glittered in Loban's eyes. "Then die!" Lifting his hand, he brought it down, swiping the razor tips across Sterlave's chest.

Thrusting his *cirvant* up, Sterlave fell back and stabbed the blade at Loban's belly but missed.

Lumbering over him, Loban smiled and lowered his face as if to bite. Sterlave shoved the sword as hard as he could at Loban's belly, but the blade barely penetrated the thick hide of his skin, but then, the point slid inside his gut with sickening ease.

Squealing, Loban lunged back as sparks of power glittered across the surface of the wound, forcing the gap wider.

Sterlave scrambled to his feet and backed away. Searing pain burned along his wounds, but it was nothing compared to what Loban must feel.

Loban's feral cry was endless as he grasped uselessly at his ever-opening belly. His inhuman eyes sought out mercy, but Sterlave could offer him no comfort other than his forgiveness. As the shell pealed away, folding into the shimmering hole, Loban retook his human form. Huddled in blood, he clutched at the blade in his stomach. To Sterlave's shock, Loban considered the hilt and laughed.

"This is one of the weapons I repaired."

Sinking to his knees, Sterlave leaned over him.

Blood oozed from Loban's mouth when he laughed. "*Now* you kneel." Sobering, he caught Sterlave's gaze. Knowing the end was near, he whispered, "They raped me every day. My tears only prompted more brutality, as did my silence. When I summoned the courage to tell my father, he turned me out, repulsed by me. He called me ugly, worthless, and weak. I wanted to run, but there was nowhere I could run to."

Sterlave knew the Plete region spent most cycles shrouded in chilling mists. Little grew, which meant there was even less to hunt. The inhabitants survived by trading in goods and mining minerals. They prided themselves on the strength of their men and the beauty of their women.

"I thought I was destined to be a *dran'greth,* a man who earns his keep by providing pleasure to other men. But one day I realized I was not a boy. A recruiter came, looking for those who would enter the Harvester training. When I stood to compete, they laughed." Bitterness ate up his face. "When I beat them all down, they stopped laughing."

Despite everything he'd done, Sterlave understood that he and Loban had a common childhood. They both were unwanted, rejected, and traumatized. The male villagers hadn't raped Sterlave, but once he matured, the women used him just as surely as the men used Loban. He'd never felt human, only an object worth what he could provide. The comparison was uncomfortable but no less true. By the grace of the gods, Sterlave had not become like Loban.

"I guess I never stopped trying to beat them down." Loban's eyes watered with self-pity. "Do you really forgive me?"

"For what you did to me." Sterlave nodded. "I cannot offer forgiveness for the others you hurt."

Wincing, Loban's eyes misted over. "I thought the voice, the power, was of the gods. I had no idea it was a *fauben.*" He laughed without mirth. "I guess the gods found me as unworthy as my father."

The spark in his eyes sputtered, then died.

Sterlave stood. He took no pride in killing; he'd done only what was necessary. When he turned, he found Kasmiri struggling to lift herself. Pointing, she muttered something, then collapsed. Whipping his head around, Sterlave saw Ambo just before he slipped into the portal and disappeared. By the time Sterlave ran across the room, he was too late.

Ambo had closed the doorway.

26

Kasmiri simply couldn't understand why her arms wouldn't do what she wanted them to do. After a moment, she couldn't even remember why she was trying to get up. Exhausted, she fell onto her back, looking up at the perfectly smooth ceiling. It hadn't been that long ago that she'd been on her back waiting for the Harvester. As if summoned, Sterlave's face came into focus.

Joy greater than any she'd ever known filled her heart. He was here, by her side, when she needed him most. She tried to speak, but tears welled up, and her throat was raw from screaming. In a panic, she tried to sit, to see where the creature was, but Sterlave held her back. She relaxed because she knew he wouldn't let anything hurt her, not her powerful bondmate, her champion, her one true love.

He had come to save her.

He cupped her face tenderly and kissed her lips. She tasted blood, sweat, and tears. When he pulled back, he lifted her into his arms.

"I've got to get you somewhere cooler."

Holding her close to his bare chest, she became aware of his scent. Masculine with sweat, she startled when she smelled blood. So much blood. Turning her head, she saw huge gashes along his chest. She would have struggled to be let down but didn't want to cause him any more pain. Her lies had done enough of that.

Sterlave stood still for a moment, looking about the strange carved room. "There's no door."

Kasmiri wondered why he didn't just return through the opening. Then she remembered why she'd been trying to get up; stealthily, Ambo was making his way toward the portal. If he wasn't planning to do something wrong, he wouldn't be sneaking. She knew he would close the doorway once he was on the other side, leaving her and Sterlave trapped with the creature.

When she looked about, she saw the naked body of a well-formed man with pale skin and copper hair. A short sword protruded from his belly.

Sterlave saw her looking, and said, "His name was Loban."

The name meant nothing to her.

"He was the monster that tormented you."

Again, she looked, baffled as to how one who appeared so normal could become something so vile. Slowly and succinctly, Sterlave explained about the sacrifice, the *fauben,* the anointed weapon, and his painful and tangled history with the man on the floor. Listening intently, Kasmiri was glad that he was dead, because she would have killed him herself for what he'd done to Sterlave. Her mate's strength truly impressed her. A lesser man would have let the rape destroy him, but not Sterlave. He rose above it and continued to welcome the world with open arms. If only she could learn that most valuable skill.

She wanted to tell him everything but still could not find her voice. Soon, she would confess all her secrets. If he was the man she knew he was, none of it would matter. He'd come with her to Rhemna. Together, they would fashion a life for themselves out of the frozen wasteland.

After a time, Sterlave strode toward the wall opposite the carved throne. The doorway shimmered as they passed through. On the other side, they found a passageway, not much taller than Sterlave's height. Following along, she could tell he became weaker by the step, but he wouldn't put her down. Frustrated, she reached out her arm. A doorway shimmered. Ducking within, they found neatly ordered stacks of cloth, bottles, and wooden containers. Sterlave didn't hesitate to kick the softest cloth into the center of the room. Once he'd padded the stone floor, he laid her down.

Turning away, he checked through the items. Hefting a large glass container, he worked the covering off, sniffed, blinked rapidly, and then set it aside. From her position on the floor, she caught a whiff of something pungent with alcohol. He repeated this with several of the containers. Finally, he found one that passed his test. Using the lid, he poured pale pink liquid into it, sipped, and then helped her hold her head up so she could drink.

"It's some kind of wine. It will have to do until I can find water."

She drank greedily The taste was sweet, not unlike the wild berries that grew along the shores of the Valry Sea.

"Not too much." He pulled the makeshift cup back.

She would have argued, but she was exhausted.

Dipping some cloth into the container with the pungent smell, he dabbed it gently to the wounds on either side of her chest. The creature had penetrated straight through from her front to her back, right below her shoulders. Possibly the only reason she didn't bleed to death was he'd heated his flesh, burning the inside and the outer edges of the wounds. Still, the liquid burned and she did her best not to flinch.

When Sterlave wavered, trying to hold his balance above

her, she pulled on every bit of remaining strength she had to sit upright. "Lie down." A push was all it took. She gathered the clean cloth, dipped it in the strong-smelling drink, and then dabbed it to his gruesome wounds. From shoulder to waist, the creature tore gashes along his chest that were knuckle deep. Part of it was burnt, but part of it was still raw and bleeding. How had he been able to not only pick her up but also carry her?

"I thought he was going to kill you." Sterlave reached up, cupping her chin.

She kissed his hand and placed it back by his side. "He would have if not for you." Discreetly, she left out the part where Loban had tried to get her to call for Sterlave by flicking his nasty fingers against the soles of her feet. "Rest now."

"How will we get home?"

"I don't know." The portal would only open with the device, and that was on Diola. Once Ambo closed the doorway, they had no way to return, not along that path anyway. She glanced again at the contents of the room. She wondered if these goods were in storage for use or for trade. "First of all, we must find out where we are."

When she rose, he grasped the skirt of her dress, and demanded, "Where do you think you're going?"

Even injured and sprawled on the floor, he still commanded a certain level of authority. Taking pity on him, she knelt down. "We have to find out where we are if we are to escape."

He frowned. "I know where we are. We're on Helton's planet. The one your mother gave him." Kasmiri felt her eyebrows climb. Before she could say anything, he continued, "I know Helton is your father. I don't care. Maybe, rather than going back, we can stay here."

Touched by his easy acceptance, and the fact that he would willingly give up everything he knew to be with her, she brushed a kiss to his forehead. "I would like nothing better than to stay here with you, but I have to go back. I have to face the consequences of my mother's actions." Always she'd wanted to run from her duty, but now she knew she had one last obligation to perform.

"You are very brave."

His praise meant the world to her. "I was a coward to lie, to try to run away from the truth." She sighed. "I think I can even understand what my mother did and why she turned to another man." With duty hanging over her head, her mother turned to strong arms for solace, arms that embraced only her. Kasmiri believed Helton had been faithful to her mother. Enraptured by her beauty and ensnared by her charm, he still could not overcome his pride and submit himself to her as second-best consort. Kasmiri could even understand that now too. She wouldn't want to be second best either.

"Why didn't you tell me?" Hurt shown deep in his eyes.

"I was afraid you wouldn't want me." She touched his cheek as if to memorize every feature of his face. "I have to go back, but you don't. When I confess the truth of my birth, they will offer me but two choices—the stone or exile. If you are with me, my choice will become your choice."

A frown crinkled the skin of his brow. "Those are not the only choices, Kasmiri."

"I am a *pharadean,* worthless as a leader to my people. The other houses will not abide my rule, not when they have their own legitimate daughters to thrust onto the throne."

His hand gripped hers tightly. "Don't call yourself worthless again. I won't tolerate such nonsense from others, and certainly not from you."

Then she understood Ambo had told him, probably in an effort to get him to turn away from rescuing her. That Ambo's denigrating comments hadn't swayed Sterlave said more to her than words ever could. And Ambo, that coward, when she did return to Diola, she would have to do something about the meddling drunkard before she was stripped of her power.

"Lie with me for a while. The world will not disappear on us." Sterlave pulled her down to snuggle in his arms. His wound had stopped bleeding, and for now, they were safe. What did it matter if they rested for a moment? She felt as if she hadn't slept in days and the fabrics were so soft, and Sterlave so solid and warm . . .

When she woke, she had no idea how much time had passed. The world hadn't disappeared, but it certainly had changed.

"Sterlave." She nudged him gently. "You must wake up now, we have guests." Honestly, she didn't know what to make of the tall, thin, and extremely pale people surrounding them. Clad in odd fabrics that shimmered strange colors, Kasmiri looked for some sign as to which was the leader. Having dealt with numerous *barsitas,* she used her learned skills in ferreting out their chief. They were all roughly the same height, with similar loose and flowing hairstyles. All of them had the same beautiful silver-white hair. The garments they wore hid their sexes, as did their androgynous faces. Silver eyes blinked slowly, revealing vertical-shaped pupils that widened to the sides. No jewelry, weapons, or decorations offered any show of distinction. How could she find the leader when they all looked the same?

Sterlave dreamily cupped her breast. "Later we'll rise, I want to touch you first."

Aroused and embarrassed, Kasmiri took his hand from her breast and gave it a little pinch. "You shouldn't be so familiar before our new friends."

He growled and rolled over, blinking rapidly when he saw the strange people surrounding them. Automatically, he reached for his belt, but he'd left his sword buried in Loban. Besides, she didn't think they needed protection because the people seemed harmless.

When she rose up, they took a small step back on their bare little feet. Smoothing down her hopelessly ruined dress and tucking back her disheveled hair, she bowed to them, and said, "I am Kasmiri, Empress of Diola, daughter of the Crimson House."

Unimpressed by her title, they simply continued to stare at her with their slow-blinking eyes.

"Who commands you?"

More blank stares.

"I don't think they understand you." Sterlave rose, and this time they moved forward with a collective indrawn breath.

Out the side of her mouth, she said, "They seem to like you."

"Let's hope it's like and not hunger." Her frown prompted him to add, "For all we know that's how they look at food. And they do seem fascinated by the wounds on my chest."

One pointed to the gash, turned to another, who also pointed, then they both lowered their arms. They exchanged no words, but Kasmiri was certain they'd spoken.

Long ago, when she was very young, she remembered a culture of people who did not speak. They thought their words to one another. Kasmiri considered their mouths. Knife slits in their faces with hardly any lips at all probably meant her assessment was correct.

"I don't think they speak, not as we do."

When the group of them turned to the doorway, Kasmiri and Sterlave followed behind. Her feet throbbed painfully with each step from Loban's brutal treatment, but she gritted her teeth and ignored the feeling of walking on shards of glass.

Sterlave noticed anyway. "Let me carry you."

"I'm fine."

"No, you're not, you're hurt. Let me help you."

Their argument caused the group to stop and turn.

Reluctantly, she allowed Sterlave to scoop her up into his arms. Despite his wounds, he lifted her easily. When the pale people saw her feet, they again stepped forward with great interest, except this time they didn't point. After a moment, they turned and walked off without a word.

As they continued down the hall, Kasmiri wondered what interested them so. Was it the sight of raw flesh or the color of their blood? Who knew what intrigued an alien culture. From the back, she noticed some had much longer hair, though all had locks to at least their shoulders. One had hair down to the back of his or her knees. As she watched, the strands swayed back and forth, lulling her.

After a time, they came upon another shimmering doorway. When Sterlave stepped through, Kasmiri almost screamed in shock. Down to the very last detail, someone had reproduced her mother's rooms. Almost everything was blinding white with only touches of crimson, black, and silver. Kasmiri expected her mother to emerge from the bathing unit, whole, unhurt, ready to forgive her for everything. When nothing of the sort happened, Kasmiri felt her mother's loss all over again.

Sterlave placed her on the bed, where she sank into plush comfort. When he tried to move away, one of the pale people pointed and he fell onto his back. The creature hadn't struck him physically, but Sterlave fell nonetheless.

One of them climbed onto the bed and straddled Sterlave's hips.

Kindly, he lifted his hands, and said, "I'm really not certain where this is going, but I'm bonded to her." He pointed at Kasmiri. "I don't think she'd like—" He stopped talking suddenly and his arms fell back, palms up, as if he surrendered.

When the person lifted slender arms, Kasmiri realized she was female. Tiny breasts appeared as the fabric pressed against her body. Jealousy surged along Kasmiri like fire. She wasn't about to lie here and watch some lusty *barsitas* take advantage of her bondmate!

As if she heard the thought, the woman turned her head in Kasmiri's direction. No expression showed on her smooth face, but her eyes widened, probing into Kasmiri with subtle intent. Tendrils brushed along Kasmiri's mind, examining her thoughts, prying into her most private memories. Satisfied, the woman nodded, then turned back to Sterlave.

Pressing her hands into his chest, she sat perfectly still atop his hips with her eyes closed. Sterlave blinked rapidly, his hands jerking spasmodically as the woman touched her hands from one end of his wounds to the other. Ever so slowly, the skin knitted together until his chest was smooth.

Silver eyes swung her direction and Kasmiri fought the urge to back away. The woman didn't have any harmful intent, but she was so peculiar. Without moving off her perch, she cupped Kasmiri's feet. Alternate flashes of hot and cold prickled her skin, tickling her. Kasmiri tried desperately not to laugh, but she did anyway. When she finished with her feet, the woman slid off Sterlave and worked her way up to sit upon Kasmiri's hips. Placing her hands on either side of her damaged shoulders, she healed her with the same soothing sensation.

Unable to thank her conventionally, Kasmiri simply clasped her hand and squeezed, thinking hard about gratitude. Expressionless eyes considered their joined hands; then she moved away. Another stepped forward with a tray laden with food native to Diola. She and Sterlave ate without comment while the group stood and watched. When they finished, they removed the tray and stood patiently.

"What are they waiting for?" Sterlave asked.

Kasmiri shrugged.

Without a sound, they turned and quickly filed out of the room. Before they could discuss the matter, a contingent of palace guards burst in. Too stunned to struggle, they quickly bound them both. Kasmiri hoped the silver-haired people wouldn't get in trouble for helping them.

Smugly, Ambo strode forward, glared right into her eyes, and said, "Your reign is over."

27

Sterlave stood at one end of the advisors' room. Hundreds of people surrounded him, but he felt alone. Unnaturally quiet, they watched and waited for Ambo to begin the inquisition. Once he realized that Sterlave had killed Loban, Ambo returned to his previous lifestyle. Whatever weight he'd lost he rapidly gained back, and then some, all within the few days he'd let Sterlave languish in holding.

Sterlave hadn't minded the austere conditions as the cold stone floor, exposed basin, and raw food were similar to his training room cell, but he worried about Kasmiri. She was not used to such harsh surroundings. If he could, he would give her what little he had, but even suggesting it caused the guards to laugh. He wanted to rail at them, that they couldn't hold him when he'd committed no crime, but he held his tongue. Soon, the time would come for him to speak. When that time came, he would be ready. The only thing he'd clung to was the fact they hadn't exiled or killed Kasmiri. He knew this from eavesdropping on the guards. As he stood, unshackled, but with eight guards at his back, waiting for the show to begin, all he could think of was Kasmiri.

When four guards ushered her in, his eyes ate her up. She'd never appeared more stunning. Head high, proud chin thrust forward, she'd turned the destroyed dress into a gown fit for an empress. Apparently, nothing they did could break her spirit. No tears of self-pity marred her beautiful face. A determined brightness sparkled there, warming him clear through to his bones. No matter what happened today, she would not be cowed.

Kasmiri caught his gaze and winked.

His pride soared higher than he thought possible. She hadn't lost her saucy authority, her lush imagination, or her utter disregard for those who sought to bring her low. In that moment, he knew that he loved her. She fascinated him anew and probably would do so for the rest of their life together. And he would do anything to ensure they would have a very long time together.

Ambo must have seen her display, for he clapped his hands, calling the gathering to order. As he pontificated about her misdeeds, many of which she hadn't committed, Kasmiri appeared to be listening politely. When Ambo reached the point where he revealed she was not the product of an official consort, gasps of outrage rose from the crowd.

Kasmiri yawned.

Sterlave laughed.

Ambo swiveled his head, sparing him a blistering glare before he continued. Repeatedly, Ambo invoked the prophecy, denigrating Kasmiri for violating the rites and rituals as set forth by the ancients. At the appropriate moment, Ambo dramatically pointed his finger at Helton.

Proudly, Helton rose, gaining Sterlave's respect. Helton had made horrible mistakes, but he attempted to atone for them by standing up for his daughter. Finally, she'd found someone else who would not abandon her at the first sign of trouble. Sterlave surmised she was touched as well, for she flashed Helton an accepting smile and a brief nod. Sterlave doubted he'd ever be able to fully forgive Helton, but if Kasmiri could, he would find a way to make peace with him.

Ambo's diatribe went on endlessly. Even the crowd, which had been so vested in hearing each wicked crime, now grew bored with his outrageous claims. Sterlave sensed they were impatient for punishment.

"I relinquish my crown." Kasmiri's voice rang clearly in the crowded room. All eyes turned her way. "I renounce my title." When she lifted her hand to the fastener of her dress, murmurs rippled through the group.

Without seduction or modesty, Kasmiri peeled her clothing away until she stood before the entire assembly nude. The pale creatures from Helton's world had repaired all the damage inflicted by Loban, so none of the people knew what she had suffered to protect them. Men and women examined her perfection with critical eyes. When the women couldn't find a flaw, they grimaced. When the men couldn't, they smiled. Keeping her gaze fixed to Sterlave's, she walked toward him with smooth, rolling grace. So shocked were her guards that they made no effort to stop her. Cool air peaked her nipples and washed small bumps along her flesh.

Mesmerized, Sterlave had to remind himself to breathe. Never had he seen her looking so exquisite. In response, his cock stirred, pressing against the front of his filthy trousers. A sharp sudden longing hardened his body and watered his mouth.

Once she reached him, she said, "I come to you with nothing."

When she tried to kneel before him, he grasped her upper arms, pulling her against his chest. "You will not kneel before me. As my bondmate, you will stand beside me." The last thing he'd ever wanted was her kneeling before him. At first, he didn't understand why she had stripped down, but then he did. She gave up everything from her previous life, from her crown to her clothing. By doing so, she showed him that she would willingly give up anything to be with him. Like in the bonding ceremony where he had to kneel naked before her, she now tried to do the same for him. Still, he didn't need such a show of submission.

Peering down, her wild, wicked eyes captured his attention, ensnaring him. She didn't need anything extraneous to possess his mind, body, and soul.

"I take you with only that you have now." When he tilted her head back, she parted her lips in anticipation. "I love you, Kasmiri."

Her smile lit up every dark corner of his heart. No more would they be alone, not when they had each other.

Lowering his head, he pressed his lips to hers. In a timeless show of passion, tenderness, love, and even lust, he kissed his beautiful bondmate.

Enraged, Ambo sputtered, "This won't save you from the stone!"

Reluctantly, he pulled back from her plush, passionate lips. "It does," Sterlave said, wrapping his arm around her shoulders and pulling her into his embrace. He swore this would be the last time either of them was exposed in public. "She renounced the throne."

"That doesn't change—"

"She surrendered her power before you had a chance to strip her of it and render punishment." Ambo had taken too much pleasure in decrying her. He could have swiftly listed her crimes and pronounced her penalty, but he had to prattle on endlessly, enjoying the attention. "Since I was the Harvester and I selected her as my bondmate, I've decided that we will live here, without reprisal, for as long as we wish."

Red suffused Ambo's face. Through his blathering self-aggrandizement, he'd lost his chance to castigate Kasmiri. When he opened his mouth to argue, Sterlave softly reminded him of the rites and rituals.

"You wouldn't wish to invoke the displeasure of the gods, would you?" Sterlave asked pointedly.

Ambo shivered, probably at the memory of Loban, but the cruel slash of his lips told Sterlave Ambo would never stop seeking a way to banish them both. But for now, he could do nothing. Regretfully, Ambo dismissed the guards.

Helton smiled and settled in his seat. Ambo could not punish him without revealing his own place in unleashing the monster, and there was no crime in bedding the empress. Unless Ambo could prove corruption, Helton would remain head of the palace guard.

Stunned by the sudden turn of events, most of the crowd erupted in spontaneous gasps that turned to whispered speculations. Some were in support of Sterlave, but most were violently opposed. They feared Kasmiri would try to claim the throne in the future with her children. What they thought didn't matter. He was a Harvester. He had a right to select any sacrifice as his bondmate, and he had the right to live in the palace if he chose to do so.

Through gritted teeth, Ambo calmed the masses. He had no choice but to uphold Sterlave's claim. Sterlave realized he couldn't punish Ambo directly for what he'd done, but watching him squirm as he was forced to uphold the law was quite pleasant. In an effort to inflict some type of reprimand, Ambo gave them a room far on the east side of the palace, but Sterlave insisted on a room closer to Chur's because he would be training the recruits.

A flicker of emotion crossed Helton's face, but it quickly vanished. Perhaps he realized that he would never again be a handler. Sterlave had to content himself that it was punishment enough. Since he could do little against Ambo, he had to throw his trust in the hands of the gods. Surely they would craft a better punishment than he ever could.

Scooping Kasmiri into his arms, he knew there were two more details he had to take care of before he could lose himself in her embrace.

28

Kasmiri considered their new living quarters with a grateful smile. It was nothing compared to her old room, but it was so much better than what they would have had in Rhemna. She would willingly exchange luxury for freedom. For the first time, duty did not hang about her neck and she felt lighter. There were things she would miss, such as her room devoted exclusively to dance, but the palace was large with innumerable places where she could practice without interruption. She would also miss her enormous bed. This bed seemed so small in comparison, barely big enough to hold Sterlave, let alone her. However, the posts at each corner would certainly come in handy.

Now if only Sterlave would return.

Fiddling with the tie of the robe that Enovese had graciously allowed her to borrow, Kasmiri wondered again where Sterlave had gone off to in such a hurry. For a while, she'd played host to Chur and Enovese but realized her skills were woefully inadequate. She had no food to offer them, and even if she did, she wouldn't know how to prepare anything. Kindly, Chur and Enovese explained how to order weekly provisions from the majordomo, and Enovese agreed to teach her how to cook. In the meantime, Enovese and Chur shared what they had, so when Sterlave did return she had a meal waiting.

At first, it was difficult to accept Enovese's help, but rather than being pompous with her knowledge, Enovese was very humble, with a clear desire to share. The first few threads of a tentative friendship formed, almost without Kasmiri being aware. After a while, she wondered how she could have ever hated the woman. Enovese was so solicitous and generous. She now understood why Chur had chosen her. Together, they were an amazing couple, and she was proud to call them friends. With her heart securely granted to Sterlave, she could now gaze upon Chur with appreciation for his handsome form, but no lustful designs on obtaining him.

Restless, she lifted a cover and picked at the meal. She was starving, but she was determined to wait for Sterlave. When he finally entered, she wanted to throw herself into his arms but held back when she realized someone followed behind.

"Rown?" she asked, fighting back an impulse to hug him. She knew it was inappropriate to treat servants like family, but then she decided she didn't care. When she wrapped her arms around him, he tensed for a moment, then hugged her back.

"You are no longer the empress?" he asked, straightening his robe.

"No," she answered, smiling.

"And you are glad of this?" He seemed perplexed, probably because he had rarely seen her smile.

"I couldn't be happier." When Sterlave placed his arm around her, she turned and kissed him deeply. Rown would have to get used to her smile because she intended to show it often.

"Then I am too." Rown removed his crimson sash.

She would have to find him a black sash at some point, but he didn't seem to mind having a billowing robe for now.

Sterlave showed him his room. The space was smaller than

the one he'd had off Kasmiri's old room, but again, he didn't seem to mind. He was honestly happy just to be with them. As Rown went off to move his possessions, Kasmiri leaned into her mate, and asked, "How did you manage this?"

"I can be . . . persuasive." Playfully, he nipped the tip of her nose.

He turned to several recruits who stood waiting in the hallway. Each had an armload of items. Sterlave pointed out a storage room, then turned back for another kiss.

"What is all that?"

"Our bonding gifts." He lifted his eyebrows suggestively. "I found the most interesting item."

His wicked smile flushed heat all the way to her toes.

Battling her lashes, she asked, "Now that I have no power and you do, you won't lord it over me, will you?"

"Only in bed," he whispered, kissing her temple.

Teasingly, she said, "I feel in need of a soft bed."

He scooped her into his arms. "As you please, my lady, as you please."